# POTOMAC TURNING

# POTOMAC TURNING

Adwit Pundit

PARTRIDGE

**To order additional copies of this book, contact**
Partridge India
000 800 10062 62
orders.india@partridgepublishing.com

www.partridgepublishing.com/india

# CONTENTS

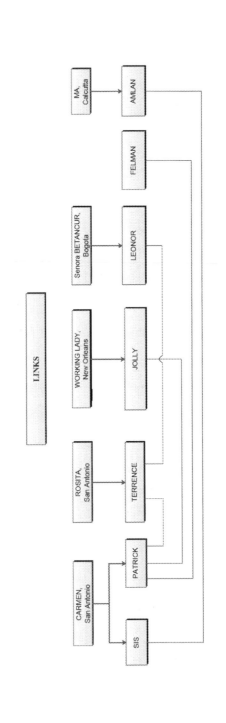

LINKS

MA, Calcutta → AMLAN

FELMAN

Senora BETANCUR, Bogota → LEONOR

WORKING LADY, New Orleans → JOLLY

ROSITA, San Antonio → TERRENCE

CARMEN, San Antonio → PATRICK

SIS

# Book I

# Escape From San Antonio

Patrick Gould, eighteen, was heading towards Washington, District of Columbia. He had become convinced that, if he was to escape the ultimate persecution, he had better flee and take refuge in the stony lap of Abraham Lincoln, about whose legacy he had recently been illuminated at school. Despite a tone of casualness in Brother Rinaldi's voice and a slight indication of doubtfulness in his expression as the priest recounted the events of the war between the North and the South that reflected his inevitable empathy for the latter, Patrick had been impressed with the narration of his history teacher. Back home that night, after dinner, he stared at the cover of the book, which announced in bold letters, 'American History, by C.P. Hill'. He had flipped open the chapter on Lincoln again and again, especially the section where the president had been shot in the lonely recesses of a dark theatre, and a feeling of deep remorse had enveloped him as he read and re-read that bit.

Not only did Patrick feel sympathy for the slain northern president, but, simultaneously, he felt a certain elation envelop him at the thought of a million freed muscular black men, walking out of the cotton fields, their sweat glistening in the afternoon sun, or leaving ornate drawing rooms, throwing away their starched white aprons, and flinging away their tight white gloves to free their pressed fingers. Patrick did not ponder what had happened to their families, since he was confident in the belief that they were never allowed to marry, the children their women bore being habitually sold as stock to the highest bidder on market day, imbuing the muscular, dark males with an enviable freedom that the institution of church had made sure other men would never enjoy.

Patrick was carrying his prized volume with him in the backpack that his mother had hurriedly packed for him. He had thrown in the book—an afterthought that it might serve as a reference and guidebook in his future life. Since he enjoyed perusing history, it should offer him welcome reading during the unknown future he had resolved to embrace. It had already provided him encouragement, inspiration, awe and disgust. So he thought he would carry the book to Lincoln's city, that repository from where the commander-in-chief had once conducted a fratricidal war to safeguard equality and decency for posterity, and where his fellow man had struck him down in hatred. Nevertheless, Patrick could not escape a nagging doubt about walking across the line to the *other* side, the north-south divide having been carved into the family psyche in more ways than one.

The book had always offered him enjoyable bouts of reading, but not always with agreeable consequences. True, despite Patrick's playful nature that often tended to confound, confront and contradict any steady, median approach to assigned projects, Brother Rinaldi already perceived in him the makings of a scholar because of Patrick's questioning nature and an innate ability to interpret history intelligently. Brother Rinaldi harboured hopes that, one day, Patrick would be able to appreciate the details of his own unfinished

symphony, an intricately researched thesis on the account
books of twelfth-century Hungarian monks from which he
had not only been able to track their mundane daily life and
the practice of inflexible ethical standards, but had also begun
to obtain telling insights into their less stern human habits and
their closely held secrets of both asexual and sexual nature.
However, Brother Rinaldi had to abandon his endeavour and
return to America because of lack of funds when his father
fell ill and his father's legal practice shrank to zero. Brother
Rinaldi narrated this account to his students often enough so
that this fact or excuse had come to take hold as the tested and
verified truth in all their minds.

Even Brother Rinaldi recognised that sometimes
Patrick went too far, but would never cut him short for his
argumentative tendency. For example, during a lesson on
Benjamin Franklin, it was mentioned that Mr. Franklin was
known to boil his milk before drinking it. When queried
unnecessarily about this by a ne'er-do-good student whose
only motive was to somehow see to it that the conclusion of
the lesson was delayed and nothing else, Brother Rinaldi fell
upon a rather fanciful explanation, admittedly without much,
if any, historical support attributing it, rather vaguely, to: "I
seem to recall that Mr. Franklin suffered from a stomach
ailment, requiring him to boil his milk before drinking it."

Patrick had no qualms in confidently shooting back,
rather matter-of-factly, in front of the entire class, and much
to Brother Rinaldi's embarrassment and irritation, "Brother,
everyone would have drunk boiled milk during those times
because Monsieur Pasteur had not been around yet."

Patrick then proceeded to slowly turn his smiling head
around, basking in the obvious approval expressed through
the inadequately suppressed bursts of laughter, emanating
inadvertently – like spouting backyard water taps gushing
water and air alternatively when first opened on a dry, hot,
Texan summer afternoon – from his classmates who had been

paying rapt attention to his attempted correction of Brother Rinaldi's narration of a fact of history.

Brother Rinaldi had put up too long with Patrick's persistence in pursuing a point. Still, he never struck him physically or slapped his face as some other teachers were prone to do as retaliation for his impudence, even though he felt Patrick deserved it sometimes. For Patrick was clearly his favourite student and, despite his knowledge that quite a few sticks had already been broken on Patrick's back by other purveyors of knowledge, he never used one. Instead, as on other similar occasions, he merely delivered a stern, but meaningless, rebuke for the impertinent behaviour, ostensibly ignoring Patrick for the rest of the class.

For a moment, the episode flashed across Patrick's mind, but his state of mind and mood would not allow him to smile at those fond memories of Brother Rinaldi, his favourite teacher. He faced, without anticipation or preparation, a possibly dire and uncertain future. His cheeks were caked with a thick residue from a mix of streaming tears and fine powder dust blowing in every direction through the open windows of his pick-up truck. It left, in its wake, a grimy compound as thick as droppings of a flock of crows on his face below his eyes that meandered towards his finely defined jaws. He sobbed and, in trying to control it, his chest and shoulders heaved, but he could not stop. He wiped his face and cleared his eyes from time to time with the back of his elbow to be able to see as he drove on.

Patrick had become convinced that he would be drafted into the armed forces and sent to Vietnam, a distant corner in South-East Asia that he had become curious about as protests against the war there had mounted in the nation's capital. He had learnt that the war had spread like a prairie fire across the frontiers of Vietnam to the small, peaceful, neighbouring Buddhist nations of Laos and Cambodia, and many a time had he spun his globe around in dread to see and memorize the position of these countries that were embroiled in a war that did not mean anything to him, but about which he had a premonition that, somehow, it might engulf him. He was certain that even his father did not approve of the war, since he had revealed no enthusiasm for it. Indeed, he had criticized it often enough at the dinner table, though Patrick could not help but notice that he concealed his opinion in the presence of his business colleagues, neighbourhood acquaintances, or the clergy. However, Patrick was confident about his father's true feelings and convinced that the conspiracy to draft him was nothing more than punishment meted out by a vengeful headmaster. Without any doubt in his mind, though fearful of his aloneness, he drove on.

*    *    *

The realization that the army could take him in had come upon Patrick at the very moment that he saw, through the classroom window, the headmaster talking to a bunch of agents in army fatigues in the sun-drenched schoolyard, occasionally pointing a stealthy thumb – or was it just one of his fat, bulbous fingers – towards the window against which Patrick would always sit, and was currently seated. Patrick moved back reflexively, away from the protruding landing, in order to be able to see the men without being seen himself.

Patrick stalked the headmaster's glances while precariously avoiding the algebra teacher's attention. He had to remain mindful of the teacher's droning, as he dished out formula after formula in a humming, atonal voice. The teacher's head swayed from side to side as he spoke, his squinted eyes moving briskly across the glaring, sunlit classroom, hunting for prey with a sadistic smirk on his face, waiting in anticipation to strike out with a veined, cane-like right hand, firmly holding a sharpened stick that he had chopped himself in the schoolyard from a mango tree long used to vicious amputations of the kind by overeager educators employed by the academy.

Visitors, mainly comprising parents and inspectors, often marvelled at the unique mango tree in the school yard. Yet, Texas grew various types of mangoes within its perimeter. Haden was most common, about one and a quarter pounds and matured in June. Irwin was smaller at one pound and Tommy Adkins the same size as Haden, and both matured in June as well. And there were more. Kent and Keitt were largest, one and a half pounds each, and maturing in July and August respectively. Thus a mango tree in the yard should not have drawn much attention but it did since it was none of the above-mentioned varieties. It was a Langda from India which was famed for its extraordinary aroma and veinless flesh. It thus drew everyone's attention in particular when, in season, the ripening young mangoes filled the yard with their mesmerising scent. The sapling had come from India years back with Brother Jesudas who had brought along quite a few seeds and saplings of which this one was the only one that seemed to have survived and had grown into a gigantic, fruit bearing tree. Langda means lame, the legend being that the owner of the orchard from where the mango originally hailed had been lame.

The headmaster wore a cassock with a deep green sash tied above a Laughing Buddha belly, with the sash flopping up and down across his tummy. His cassock was black, indicating the unique position of a headmaster, the Father. However, that colour transformed him convincingly and irreparably in Patrick's mind into a raven. No, an entire unkindness of ravens, as he stood there with evil eyes, erratically pointing his arthritic, knobbed finger in Patrick's direction, quite oblivious of Patrick's awareness of his inaudible soliloquy and theatrical finger pointing.

Patrick was well aware of the priest's shameless ability to ignore his own follies, for he never divulged any sign of remorse, for example, after forgetting to say Hail Mary whenever he over-napped well beyond the dong of the school bell at the appointed moment, or after picking up the cane and inflicting unflinching, deliberate strikes on the boys' palms or behinds for the slightest infraction on their part. Patrick was perennially aghast at the headmaster's ingenuity in finding ever-new forms of persecution and felt helpless, indeed, alarmed by the mere presence of the man. Patrick peered carefully, for his eyesight was never that good, to discern the expression on the headmaster's face. He could see the drops of sweat on the man's forehead, as they were made gigantic by the sun's refracted rays, dangling like unstrung glass beads breaking out towards the ground. He could view the intensity and vehemence in the man's expression, just as when he was ready to mete out a bout of caning, an experience Patrick had been subjected to many a time over his school years.

Patrick's misdeeds that resulted in corporal punishment included phenomena such as a whispered joke that he had heard the previous night from a visiting nomadic uncle, bawdily and loudly rendered at the dinner table, or an escaped grunt at some joke scribbled into an exercise book and making the rounds surreptitiously through the various rows of lacklustre pupils. There was no escape once he was spotted whispering or smiling. The obese man would gargle out a demand, "Gould, do share your secret with the rest of the class! I too await illumination by your sharp intellect and erudite rendition!"

Patrick would, of course, remain silent, face down with eyes steady on the floor. After a moment of anticipation, the headmaster would turn back to the class, letting his catch marinate, so to speak, through a long, tortuous wait till the end of the class when, like a ram prepared for slaughter, Patrick would be marched to the office of the headmaster, where he would bark, "Hands on the table! Bend over! Pull them down!"

A moment later, Patrick's buttocks would smart from the sudden, sharp, incessant contact with the strip of thin, hard leather, flaying through the air, yet unfailing in its strike. The repeated attack would cease only when the indefensible wrath of the headmaster had been spent, his whim satiated. The job successfully completed, Patrick would be allowed to pull his shorts up, over his perfectly round, young, beautiful, wounded, hot, red buttocks, a sight that, without fail, would give the rotund man momentary pleasure, but the nature of which he never did comprehend or ponder because of his overarching, crass nature.

Another time, the sin that brought on punishment was a harmless prank, merely the dropping of a pencil. Though intentional, Patrick had only a limited objective, that of testing the command, "Pin-drop silence!" thundered aloud by the headmaster every morning before beginning Catechism class. Upon hearing the pencil drop, the master had instantaneously halted mid-sentence, picked Patrick out in a second, as though he held powers of the Omniscient or, equally, Patrick was convinced, of the Devil.

This time, the persecutor did not wait. He hauled Patrick, without the slightest remorse, off to sharpen his whip on Patrick's butt. As the young prisoner suffered the jailer's wrath, he wondered about the incongruence and inconsistency of *moral science* lessons, that students had to undergo every morning for half an hour, being interrupted by violence perpetrated by the powerful on the powerless. Though these inner reflections did not help him, in any manner, to be saved from his predicament, he remained convinced that he had done no wrong and, instead, he had been seriously violated.

Yet again, once, Patrick had lost track of time in a spree of playing to win marbles. As he sauntered into class with soiled hands just moments after the rest of the school had seated itself and fallen silent, the headmaster, as he paced the corridors on his military watch, spotted him from a distance just as he crossed the threshold of the classroom door. The visage in the cassock glided like an avatar through the corridor, appearing right in front of Patrick. It was easy to accuse him of wandering aimlessly. He screamed, "I can smell your marbles."

Patrick could not but wonder, *how* does he know?

The bully lied, of course; it was just that there was a shuffling, jingling sound caused by the shifting marbles in Patrick's bulging side pockets as he skipped along, not any smell. The marbles were immediately confiscated and thrown into the large drawer of the man's secretariat table, the repository of an assortment of confiscated objects and articles. They included fountain pens, picture postcards, marbles, polished belt buckles, pen knives, and one Omega pocket watch with a long silver chain into the bargain that, in happier times, had all belonged to various schoolboys but, sometime in the distant or recent past, had been impounded, under one pretext or another.

This time around, Patrick was thoroughly clobbered with the aid of a foot-long ruler, which the improbable instructor used more often as an instrument for disciplinary action than for its intended use in geometry class.

Every time Patrick received punishment that he deemed unjust and irrational, he felt victorious in a subterranean, subliminal way. Now was no exception. He repeated to himself, *the powerless shall rise one day*. Without his own conscious knowledge, perhaps, he was speaking to himself about himself.

Only once had Patrick felt that there was some rationale to the caning, that it was inevitable. That was when, in English literature class, after sucking out the flesh and juice from an aromatic Langda that he had picked from the mango tree in the schoolyard, he had chucked, without checking, its large, shapeless stone out of the window next to his seat. Patrick had been habituated during the school year to carrying out a well-rounded operation of consuming mango and freeing himself of the seed. He always did it in Brother Aberystwyth's class. This teacher was prone to allow every freedom to his students. Rather, he was obliged to suffer such lawlessness for, alas, he had fatally lost control of his class over time.

Being an import from Wales in Great Britain, Brother Aberystwyth's accent was beyond the comprehension of the ears of the San Antonio lads familiar to the flat, nasal Texan twang, but totally unfamiliar with the lilting, musical, sing-song, yet peculiarly atonal, Welsh accent. They quickly learnt to ignore his implorations to maintain order by simply pretending not to understand him. Eventually, they realised that they could have a field day within the confines of Brother Aberystwyth's classroom, a fact he was too ashamed to admit for fear of being rebuked by the headmaster. Thus, the Brother would simply bolt the heavy wooden door as he entered class, seat himself in front of his insolent students, shut his eyes firmly, and initiate long, arduous quotations, more often than not, from Shakespeare:

> "Wherre shall we thrrreeeee meet again?
> In thunderrrr, lightnning, o-o-o-o-rrrr in rrain?
> When the hurrrrly burrrrrrrly's done;
> When the battle's l-o-o-o-o-st and won;
> That'll be erre the ssett of sun."

Some boys would throw back their heads and laugh openly, while the less bold would laugh under their breath, as they all mistook Brother Aberystwyth's rolling 'r's and his staccato 'o's for unending, convoluted stammers, expressed through his contorted face, appearing to be funnier by the moment. Others would swish around the classroom in tall, pointed paper caps like giant inverted ice cream cones, preferably with long, narrow broomsticks between their legs that they had stolen from home just for the day of the literature class, in replication of Macbeth's witches.

Still others would merely chit chat while, on occasion, Patrick and his group would suck, in rotation, on a mango or two, stealthily plucked from the schoolyard tree. At the end of the communal endeavour, only he, seated at a vantage point next to the window, would have the honour of aiming the wet, voluminous stone at a chosen mark outside, be it a bird perched on the tree or the ice cream box of the Negro vendor who stood under the tree all day for the boys to emerge from the school building during breaks and make intermittent purchases on credit from the vendor. This time, uncharacteristically, and for an unbeknownst reason, Patrick's concentration wavered for an instant and, instead of taking aim, he merely dropped it by extending his arm outside the window.

Though Patrick did not consider it his fault that the headmaster had chosen to walk there at that very moment, oblivious of the stone's trajectory, fate had it that it landed with a loud thud on the headmaster's head. Patrick, with his companions, would have remained in blissful ignorance of this confluence of occurrences, except for its obvious impact and the headmaster's loud, penetrating groan.

"Aaaahhhh!"

They knew the worst was yet, or just about, to come!

Unfortunately, there was nothing to cushion the contact, for the man was not only round like a genuine Pickwick, but irretrievably bald. The stony, sharply edged seed had plonked hard on the shiny, reflecting globe – there were no two ways about it. Patrick was convinced that it had the Devil's hand in it, for how, otherwise, would the two events coincide at one moment and at that particular spot below the window? He was also realistic enough to prepare himself for the unearthly onslaught that was to follow.

The beast thundered to the classroom and, even as good Brother Aberystwyth began to open his eyes, Fatty started to bang on the bolted wooden door, not only in shock because of the event that had just transpired, but also in a mounting hysteria from the disbelief that the classroom had been cordoned off from his right of access. Echoes of his passionate banging reverberated through the school. By the time the bolt was unhinged in a hurry, Patrick was already at the door like an anointed sacrificial lamb for the gods, making sure to spare his classmates the vengeful wrath of the spiteful invader.

The rest of the school had emerged from the confines of their classrooms in response to the howling and the banging. Teacher and student alike were now positioned behind the demon, donning expressions alternating between shock and awe, and in gleeful anticipation of the eventful scene that was sure to follow and the punishment that was to befall the already designated instigator.

Strangely, the headmaster, exposed to all his subjects and verily at the same moment, suddenly appeared calm, thereby robbing the school of any possibility of further excitement. He seemed to form a sentence for his large audience, but did not utter it. Instead, he stared at Patrick and said, his voice low and quivering, "Off to my office!"

Patrick was seen to march in that direction, stepping in time to a chorus of sighs and moans from the depth of the dispersing, despairing crowd. Once in the safety of his office, the headmaster meted out to Patrick the usual punishment and not much worse, using only slightly greater force, inadvertently at that and only for the initial couple of strikes. Then he let Patrick go, still unable to believe what he took to be audacity beyond compare of the boy, and quite convinced that his bald head had been the intentional bull's eye for the fellow's shot-put attempt with the mango stone. Having received the blows, Patrick marched out of the office defiantly as usual, and without batting an eyelash.

That was the only time when Patrick had felt that somehow the caning had been inevitable, not so much as just punishment for some sin he had committed, but for his inexcusable loss of guard, momentary though it was. As a fallout from that episode, needless to say, the classroom door was never bolted again, for the headmaster took up the practice of dropping in on the class regularly and, of course, unannounced. He made sure to find Brother Aberystwyth, his face bathed in a newfound, perennial smile, narrating verse after verse, not from Shakespeare any longer, since that phase was over, but from his favorite Romantic poets, Browning, Hardy, Keats, Shelley and Wordsworth.

However, he refrained from quoting Lord Byron, since he felt certain that the headmaster, if he had been aware of it, would thoroughly disapprove of that poet, with his questionable sexual impetuosity. Certainly the conservative headmaster would not like Byron to be mentioned before impressionable boys, easy customers for unsavoury waywardness and doubtful practices. He himself was not concerned or apprehensive that Byron would cut a sorry figure for boys in their formative years, or would pose any great danger to their natural naivety. Rather, Byron might do them some good, to assess for themselves what was good and what bad in chalking out their own personal trajectories. Nevertheless, he took pains not to mention Byron or his life or to quote from him to safeguard against any angry interference from the headmaster.

With the censured, disciplined and regularly monitored routine, the boys made rapid progress in their comprehension of the Welsh accent, as well as in rote learning Shakespearean verse and Romantic poetry. They recited passages in a particularly mannered fashion, marked by overemphasised vowel and selected consonant sounds, much to Brother Aberystwyth's delight and the headmaster's obvious approval. The latter even made them stand three deep according to weight and height on the temporary stage erected for the next annual Parents' Day and prize distribution festivities, and repeat selected stanzas in a sing-song chorus as a part of the Variety Programme, much to their embarrassment and helpless disgust and to the parents' amazement and pride.

*     *     *

Scholar that he was, an uncomfortable realisation of himself that Patrick had to slowly accept was his imperfect eyesight, apparently inherited from a line claimed to be of scholarly, introverted Catholics, the majority of whom had joined the priesthood, forever imbuing the family with a sense of pious complacency and enabling it to bask in the, by now well-established, adage that their ancestors had fled to America from religious persecution in reformist Northern Europe. However, no one had ever verified this. As the family had become absorbed in the Roman Catholic hierarchy and embroiled in the municipal politics of San Antonio, Texas, such verification seemed pointless even when a member of the family's breakaway Rochester, New York, branch claimed that their flight to America had more to do with the pangs of poverty than piety or religiosity.

The extent to which any reliable information was available on the wider family tree was limited to information based on its branching out from New York City in two directions. The first group was adventurous, and wanted to experience America fully, and what it had to offer. They went southwards as far as San Antonio. The other more cautious and risk-averse branch went only a short distance northwards to Rochester. At least this had come to be the Southerners' interpretation. The Northerners' interpretation remained a matter of dispute that their smaller branch had moved north towards Canada at the time of the nation's independence, as part of a small minority that had been vehemently opposed to slavery and had interpreted the Declaration of Independence as a mere whitewash for the permanent establishment of the reprehensible practice of slavery. However, that branch had had to stop at Rochester with the onslaught of a Great Lakes winter, replete with snowstorms and blizzards, and never managed to cross the border into Canada. It was, therefore, explicable that, over the generations, even limited exchange of information between the two branches had faded, and then ceased.

In the early era, a modicum of formal, congenial connection was, indeed, maintained. Eventually, what cut the cord for good was the blatant, though possibly unavoidable, lack of interest expressed by the high-nosed Northern branch to ever pay a return visit to their Southern cousins. This became a matter of derision for the more numerous Southern branch, for one May eons back they had taken the long route north to attend the famous lilac festival of Rochester, mainly as an expression of their inclusive Southern ways; but they had also expected that there would be a return visit to the south by their Northern cousins. Instead, as one and all were making their way through the elegantly sculptured Highland Park of Rochester with appropriately located trees weighed down by dangling, aromatic lilac clusters of various shades of cream and beige to indigo and magenta, the Southerners were startled by the extremely rude comment by a Northern cousin that the imperatives behind the parent family's flight from Europe were practical and based on the pangs of hunger. Worse, it was uttered coldly, without grace or composure, as if the Southerners were mere poor cousins whose feelings did not need to be considered.

That night, the Southern cousins murmured to one another their resolve to cut short their vacation, despite the unenviable prospect of having to saunter southwards through the unforgiving, approaching summer and the occasional rabble rousing still possible from the American Red Indians, despite their dwindling numbers and emasculated state. They left the following day without any explanation, their deep religious sentiments resurgent and, much to the astonishment of their usually stiff upper-lipped Northern cousins, forever nipping the possibility of any sustained future contact.

That was more than a century ago, tucked in the annals of this Catholic family of solid Germanic descent, the Gouldsteins, and, if asked today, few in the Southern branch would be likely to recall the exact year of that break, though Patrick had heard accounts of those events from his grandmother when she had put him to sleep on an occasional night and he had insisted not to be told fairytales, but *real* stories. In any event, soon after the family's fracture, civil war between the North and South had intervened, and the separation then became irrevocable and final. By now, the family had been gobbled up somewhat in San Antonio's Hispanic cultural environment. It was, nevertheless, protected at an elevated social level by virtue of what was still construed to be its pure, strictly Aryan descent.

Whatever the original cause of poor eyesight in the family, however, it continued to afflict especially the male members. That was reason enough for them to avoid or be rejected from actively participating in the Alamo, the US Civil War, or the Spanish-American War, for that matter. However, with the appearance of spectacles, there was no longer sufficient cause or excuse to preclude being conscripted in subsequent wars. As a result, several male members of the family had died predictable and horrible deaths and, by the end of the Second World War, Patrick's father, a pragmatic, intrinsically intellectual man who subsequently managed to escape conscription during the Korean War, was the only living male, apart from a few priests hindered by celibacy, to carry the seed forward, at least with legitimate progeny, for the Southern Goulds. Would the Vietnam War now abort the Southern Gould line forever?

Patrick had to narrow his eyes to focus on the headmaster's vengeful face, dotted with dangling beads of sweat, magnified and glowing in multiple tiny rainbows as the sun shone through them. He told himself that there could not be a more tell-tale signal for him to scoot if he was to escape a strike of ferocious finality carried out assuredly and with impunity by the ruler on the ruled. He knew he would be conscripted by the armed forces if he remained in San Antonio. He knew it was time to run.

*     *     *

Patrick had heard of the futility of war being discussed incessantly by his father. He would talk in a derisive tone of voice, disrespectful of those who had dragged the nation into one protracted episode after another. In his inimitable monotone, he complained that the papers never fully explained the genesis of any war. In his vocal reflections, he usually began with the First World War that he considered the harbinger of the war-infested century. Was it the assassination of an Austrian archduke in Sarajevo, or the sheer ruthlessness, ambition, blind conviction and egotistic pride of a German *kaiser*? Or was it just a family squabble among hateful English and German cousins? Or did it have deeper roots? Could it have been the barbarity of revolting, bearded Serbs, supported by the crumbling and increasingly impotent Czarist Russia? All were gone now. The Czarists were deposed by the Communists and these Reds had already spread their tentacles to the far eastern reaches of hitherto-unknown mongoloid, Moslem societies, bringing them to their knees and out of their *chaddars*- shawls - and *burqas* - gowns worn over the head and body - in their cold climates to cover their odorous bodies unfamiliar with water, reining in their nomadic ways, and herding them into bounded, yet unsettling, communes and cooperatives. Did the Reds then have designs on the more genteel Western Europe as well, using, as their instruments, their less civilised relatives, the Slavs and Transylvanians, who were more attuned and easily prone to cutthroat thuggery?

Patrick's father would move quickly on to the Second World War and, like Hitler and other anti-Semites, and perhaps reflecting the family's own ethnicity to some extent, say that the war was caused by German unemployment and hyperinflation, which were the result of the terms of the Treaty of Versailles and the alleged control of wealth by European Jews, who not only controlled all wealth in Europe but, simultaneously and paradoxically, were all Communists. Like Pius XII, the leader of his church, he felt the Nazis were engaged in a crusade against the atheistic communists and the Shylockian Jews. He did not consider that there had been sufficient enough reason for America to jump into the theatre of war, in particular on the side of the British, who had been perpetrating famine and disease in their colonies on a sustained basis. He had unmistakably noted the news of the millions who had perished in India's Bengal famine of the early 1940s, in which an artificial curb in supply had been created so that grains and cereals could be diverted from the granaries of Bengal to the Allied troops and their British masters ensconced in the drawing rooms of London and Bath. He also remembered how such news items had suddenly disappeared from radio bulletins once the United States joined the Allied cause. Patrick was mesmerised by the distant horizon of Bengal, looking into the atlas and his globe, and admiring how his father could be aware of such a far-off corner of the Earth, forgotten by the civilized world, at least as he knew it. Little did Patrick know that his father's contrarian arguments and ability to read and interpret between the lines of history were having a deep influence on him, or that the peripatetic mention of the Bengal Famine—Churchill's Secret War—would be etched in his memory and take him some day to that far corner of the world.

Patrick's father would quietly let slip his considered view that Japan's bombing of Pearl Harbour had been an effect, not a cause, comprising Japanese reaction to excessive bombing by the Allies across the areas held by the Axis. To prove his point, he would cite the subsequent nuclear bombing by the US of Hiroshima and Nagasaki in Japan, the first and last use of such a devastating device in the history of humankind. He would fail to comprehensively justify his view to Patrick for, at this point during his narrative, he would become emotional. The family, he would simply relate, had forsaken their German inheritances and acquisitions to escape the tight reins of European conformity and to become assimilated into American society. So why, he would ask, should the United States get dragged into the same confusion of Europe once again, propelled by the cruelty perpetrated by one set of Europeans on another? He was especially critical of the outcome of the 1939-45 War that seemed to sow the seeds of future dissension in Central Europe, to forever sink a big chunk of West and East Asia into perpetual conflict, to lead to anomalous demarcations that resulted in new countries carved out of swathes of colonial territory in East Asia and Africa as well as East Europe, and to result in the consolidation of Communism in the larger parts of continental expanses. Nevertheless, perhaps because of his pro-German feelings and the fact that Germany and Japan were allies, he expressed even less understanding of why the fear of the yellow race should now cause even more deaths and destroy even more families of ordinary Americans.

*     *     *

Vietnam! Listening to his father's presentation of arguments, though neither terribly clear nor flawlessly reasoned, Patrick's young mind was convinced that war must invariably be fallacious and, therefore, wrong for the family in all circumstances. Moreover, his intuition told him that it had to be disastrous for not only Vietnam, but also for the United States. Yet the Devil was offering Patrick to the gods of this latest war, not for any valiant cause, but as an act of punishment, impervious to its mindlessness. Patrick had to get away or perish. He knew that, despite his lack of respect for the Vietnam War, his father was ever respectful of clergy, especially the ones donning the phantom black cassock. He would not be able to stand up to the headmaster if he came to their home one Sunday afternoon and told his father, over his mother's delicious biscuits and rich Colombian coffee, that the young fellow should best advance in his education by serving his country on the battlefront. If the Devil did not come himself but, rather, sent his emissary in the guise of an army drafter, the result would be even more precipitous, for there would remain no avenue for his father to deny the demand for Patrick. His mind was made up. He was certain as to the course he should take.

In an act of firm resolve to flee San Antonio, Patrick got off the rickety, wooden chair next to the window that had become so central to his participation in school life. He had exerted his claim on that chair with determination at the beginning of the school year itself, for, being imbued with a certain quickness of mind, he had immediately observed the advantage of its location. The chair's position enabled the occupant to glance sideways without moving his head, to get a clear, though slightly obtuse, view of the schoolyard and all its goings-on, and rendered him free from the slightest awareness and, therefore, anger of the teacher sitting or standing at the head of the class.

Patrick had established property rights over that chair not without some pain, and only after some significant skirmishes in its vicinity. He would scramble towards the seat as half a dozen others fell on it simultaneously, like a heap of rugby players. His dexterity in games, his lithe smallish shape rippling with ever-changing, newly forming, emanating muscles, and his quick mind capable of a jestful ferocity that manifested itself on demand, but otherwise remained dormant, combined to enable him to dive into the heap like an indigenous youth hunting for fish in the nether waters of a deep waterfall. He would rise under it while pushing the heap up and away from him, and making just enough room to adjust to a hunched, yet stable, position on the chair, pushing and pushing further up until he acquired an erect seated position. He would then laugh a low laugh, the laugh of a victor, proud, but not boastful, the laugh of a leader elected for his bravery, but not feared for his cruelty.

Patrick's classmates would nod in amazement and in approval, and compete to pat him on his shoulder, some hard and some softly, mindful of his relatively slight build compared with many. They would dash back to other available chairs, just in time for the next teacher to walk into the classroom. The same rites of passage would be repeated for the first several mornings of the school year, till the occupancy rights to the chair were established, more through repetition than by treaty.

Yet, every morning, Patrick had to make a show while heading for his chair and do it with aplomb, as a king might when approaching his throne to the bowed heads in his court. True, his classmates did not bow to him, but many of them looked on in admiration, cheering and smiling, while a few baulked. Those were the probable usurpers ready on the sidelines to break a gentlemen's agreement at the slightest opportunity, and of whom Patrick was never oblivious. However, those menials did not have the nerve to challenge his position, being fearful of the thought of his gallant knights, ready to come to their king's defence at the slightest instigation, ever-ready to initiate another boisterous brawl, another delightful, sweaty encounter.

Thus, Patrick had gained the confidence of his peers and superiority over his competitors for the best spot to survey his realm inside and outside of class. Now, without a thought or doubt, for he had not a moment to ponder, he forsook his chair and, together with it, his cherished friends and the hard-won vista it had afforded him.

He crawled out of the classroom, attracting the attention of the rest of the class even as they switched to pin-drop silence in an instantaneous conspiracy in which they willingly and happily partook without the slightest preoccupation or curiosity as to its genesis or content. They only knew that their king was on the move again, for a new exploit perhaps and for which they might be summoned momentarily. They smiled and gestured as Patrick slid out the door and disappeared from their sight even as Brother Jesudas shot into Latin.

Jesudas's usual teaching subject was algebra, being the proverbial Sub-continental mathematician of Brahmin stock. It was happenstance that, figuratively speaking, he had been bussed from India some years back in an ephemeral attempt at amalgamation in this particular Catholic order. His great-great-grandfather had converted to Catholicism in a trying personal moment after enrolling in a mass conversion event conducted by a beautiful, young Portuguese priest with a combed, black beard. He had conducted the ceremony under a peaceful, wildly hued sunset sky on a southern beach strewn with conch shells and winkles, pregnant with mass hysteria and overcome by fresh jasmine smells brought unabashedly by receding sea breezes towards the unfurling waters of the humming sea. Though Jesudas's ancestor had been subsequently repentant, repentance was useless since ex-fellow Brahmins would not allow re-conversion as per Hindu practice. So the family remained Catholic, but did not shed their caste superiority which they carefully nurtured and maintained.

Among available methods of Christian proselytization of heathens, this was benign, full of promise, and guaranteed of a certain success. Thus, the young pacifist European priests preferred it, until they became older and hard, having had enough of the Eastern undisciplined and stampeding masses. However, the method continued to be used on unsuspecting Indians, many of whom would give anything for an alternate religion that brought them out into the open from the insides of the temple dungeons where they would have to herd themselves for evening *arati* - ablutions - not knowing then that next, in their new incarnation, they would have to go into church and sit silently through the cacophonous chants in unknown languages and be stared at by the lifeless faces of pale foreign gods and goddesses, in newer versions of cruelty beginning with outstretched bloodied limbs, nailed to wood boards and scooped-out hearts held in palms drooping blood, and dressed in crowns of thorns that dug into their scalps, while their faces managed not to reveal any physical pain but, rather, to exude a piety that verged on a masochistic reverie.

Upon realisation that their new religion was an ogre of even greater cruelties, it would be too late to get out. Nevertheless, unlike in the Hindu temples, their Christian temples did have long wooden benches on which they could sit in reasonable comfort through an entire religious ceremony. Also, they were no longer asked to remove their sandals, the loss or theft of which had posed a perennial threat so that such loss had come to take on the mark of an inevitable sacrifice to appease their earlier, Hindu gods. The fact that low caste converts had to sit in the wings of a church, away from direct view of their high caste counterparts, did not diminish the benefit, such was the acceptance, inevitability and continuance of caste differences even within the Church. Of course, the vicissitudes of conversion faded with time and later generations produced venerable priests, knowledgeable in the history of the Indian church, and interested and active in its preservation and spread. Brother Jesudas, a scion of such a family, had been considered to hold great promise to carry the Church forward, except that, in an accident of events, he was put on a ship to the Americas by his uncle, the Bishop of Chennaipet, as a signature of his earnest belief in the efficacy of world integration of the Catholic Church. Brother Jesudas could easily have ended up in Brazil, Bolivia, or Buenos Aires but, as luck would have it, he ended up in southern Texas, thus slightly protected from being entirely lost to the netherworld of South America. However, having been thrown into the arms of the senior priesthood of San Antonio, and being perceived as rare if not exotic, Jesudas was spoilt to the core and treated as being above reproach, a condition he had comfortably eased into.

That morning, however, Brother Jesudas had been asked to stand in for the Latin teacher, the actual instructor being absent, having fallen prey to an occasional attack of gastritis as a result of his compulsive attraction to jalapeno peppers from Mexico. Now, with his eyes closed, Brother Jesudas was babbling an unfathomable verse in an itinerant, journeyman style, "*Latinum Platinum Cerebrum Cerebellum Medula Oblongata Anno Domini* before *Christo.*"

The last portion was in an undertone, for he had forgotten its Latin counterpart. Among the few meaningful phrases he knew was '*Virtus in Arduis*', which he articulated time and again but, for fear of being ridiculed for repetition, he mixed the correct phrases with conjured ones that he felt the cunning students would have greater difficulty deciphering. Unlike a quack alchemist whose incompetence was bound to be discovered once the ramifications of his randomly prescribed potions became obvious, this impostor anticipated a comfortable escape with the dong of the bell that would terminate the Latin period and, therefore, had no qualms regarding the breadth and reach of the yarns he was spinning.

Nevertheless, in order to ensure that Latin-sounding words kept flowing without interruption, he had to keep his eyes shut and his mind focussed. Patrick was in luck, as though unseen guardians of his ilk were ushering him away, for this was in sharp contrast to Brother Jesudas's usual practice of keeping his eyes wide open, with his orange-red eyeballs rolling, his pupils focussed on the search for prey with the same steadfastness as that of a hound on a hunt. Now, one could still see his eyeballs rolling beneath his fallen eyelids, devoid of lashes, a curtain with an ashen hue, transforming the spot where a glowing red had been to a pale, spotted grey, for ugly freckles had not spared the lighter skin above his eyes, showing like pock marks with his eyes shut. He did not dare open his eyes, lest he should have to succumb to any unwelcome discontinuity in his monologue, delivered through assiduous plucking of random Latin words.

Latin was a language Brother Jesudas had always considered better dead and buried and, as a result, had bunked all training during his student years, preferring to work, instead, on polynomials and complex numbers or, during more mischievous, curious or perky moods, to read forbidden novels by D.H. Lawrence or Tolstoy. Indeed, he had been caned, even at the advanced age of twenty-one, for getting caught with selected torn pages from the former's *Lady Chatterley's Lover* under his pillow, after having been excused once before for having been found with a copy of *Anna Karenina*. He could never forget that episode, for it had reduced him in the estimation of his junior classmates who had, until that moment, revered him as a genius but, from then on, began to consider him a bit stupid, if not an imbecile, to have been caught red-faced, not once but twice.

The unfading, nightmarish, recurring memories of that episode had possibly contributed in no uncertain terms to young Jesudas's subsequent abandonment of doctoral studies at the seminary in Yercaud, that idyllic southern Indian village sitting on the rolling blue Nilgiri Hills, dotted with coffee plantations, and his being transported by his aforementioned uncle to a schoolmaster's job in a faraway, unfamiliar, foreign land, as different in terrain and culture as one could possibly imagine. The severe change of scene slowly reduced him from an absent minded, likely genius to a culture-shocked, suspicious, starved of curry and, therefore, ill-humoured, instructor. Now, an epoch later, Latin and his disdain for it had come to haunt him once again in this foreign land. As his eyeballs rolled behind shut eyelids, Patrick bolted without impediment or obstacle, and darted towards home.

\*     \*     \*

As he fled, Patrick bemoaned his inability to say goodbye to his friends or the Brothers. In his perception, the mere Brothers, who taught class, gave physical training, conducted drill and sports, or carried out various administrative chores, were unfairly relegated to wearing only white cassocks, with not even a sash, making them look like whirling dervishes as they circled the school compound playing soccer with the boys.

They were Patrick's doves, his swans, and one, in particular, his majestic bald eagle even though, or perhaps because, he had sometimes fondled Patrick while playing soccer, brushing him on the side and elsewhere, making it seem sudden and accidental, nevertheless arousing a strange fearful sensation inside Patrick as it happened. A strong stirring and swelling made him lose a breath or two, yet made him abhor it immediately thereafter, despite inexplicably making him crave for it to happen again, if even just once, till it happened the next time and the same contradictory, confusing cycle repeated itself.

Patrick had sometimes seen Brother Abraham, strongly built and robust, as almost a fatherly figure, as a ravishing predator, and himself as the prey, but could not hold himself back from following him from a distance on some afternoons at the break of class, craving to view him from different angles before he eventually headed home. This compulsive stalking tended to occur especially on those days when the physical training period turned out to exclude soccer, a decision that was never announced until the very last moment, and by the black-cloaked Devil himself. Now, as he ran, Patrick was overcome with thoughts of the playful scrambles and the multitudes of conspiracies with his peers and the exciting field games with the Brothers. Ironically, it relieved him temporarily from his fear of the dark-cassocked Devil and the wretched plans of delivery into the arms of the military that he harboured for Patrick.

Faces of his school friends flashed across Patrick's mind until he groaned in confusion and pain at the thought of never seeing them again. He thought of his classmates and the fun times they had had together. However, most of all, it was Jolly's face that flashed ceaselessly in front of him. She was a rather plump girl, two years his junior, attending Holy Angels School next door and doting on him for the past six months, taking care not to ignite the nuns' curiosity regarding her newfound interest. She would run up the slope to catch up with him when he walked home, perennially attempting to strike up conversations that she hoped would be of interest to him.

Intuitively, he had found her appearance attractive, perhaps because she was ebullient or perhaps simply because she had paid him attention, over and above all the other boys who were taller and better built than he was. He had also been fascinated by the sound of her name, the way her mother called after her when they would reach her home and would stop to exchange a word or two, he, uncomfortable, squirming to hurry away, yet, in some undefined way, warming to the encounter, and she doing her best to prolong her banter with him.

"Jolie!" her mother would cry from inside, trailing away softly. "Sholeee!" The 'sh' beginning with only a slight tinge of 'J'.

To Patrick's ears, it sounded… well, European, perhaps?

What a strange way to say the name, Patrick would think, especially as he had heard others, such as the nickel store owner in town, pronounce it with the usual Texan drawl: 'Jaali', when he, from time to time, would steal into the store with her for a moment, no more, to buy her a lozenge or Cadbury chocolate bar, all the while looking over his shoulder to see if any of his school friends were around for, if so, he would have to immediately duck in order to obviate any encounter with them. He knew that, if he was discovered by his classmates consorting in any manner with this girl, younger than them, as though having appeared from an unknown infantile resource bank, when they themselves were after more voluptuous, provocative female peers, he might lose his place of primacy or, in the least, would be put to stern physical or psychological challenges that he could not quite imagine, but could only apprehend.

Patrick remained cautious about calling her Sholee, since it sounded foreign, if not effeminate; indeed, he avoided using her name at all when talking to her. This changed when, entirely by chance, he heard Brother Aberystwyth, the English teacher of Welsh extraction, pronounce the word in a loud rendition of *He is a Jolly Good Fellow*, which he commandeered the senior school boys to sing for the wretched headmaster's birthday that year. The audio effort was a 'thank you' gift for the success the brother had had in consolidating control over the various classes he taught, almost as a miraculous ramification of the whipping the headmaster had perpetrated on Patrick after he dropped the mango seed on the bald man's head.

The English teacher pronounced 'Jolly' with a breathtaking emphasis on the 'o', an almost operatic touch. It reminded Patrick of the type of sound that he heard on the His Master's Voice brand gramophone with the well-known dog and loudspeaker logo. It had stood on the sideboard for as long as he could remember and, as his Dad played the *Barber of Seville, Marriage of Figaro, Andrea Chénier, Madama Butterfly*, or *Le Coq d'Or* on it, they had slowly crept into his soul, moving him, softening him, somewhere from within. They had all become more than familiar—his favorite—sounds. After the English teacher's vociferous 'o', his double 'l' faded away quickly under the breath. Patrick knew that must be the right way to say Jolly since, after all, the teacher came from Great Britain, the origin and repository of the English language and, since then, with a bit of toning down, he could confidently pronounce the name of the person whose friendship he did not want to recognise in public but, in whose prolonged absence, he suffered a peculiar emptiness.

Once he had the pronunciation right in his own mind, confident that he was saying it like an upper-class Englishman with the correct intonation, Patrick wondered why Jolly's mother pronounced her daughter's name in such a sensual way. Indeed, without his own knowing, it almost sent him into a delirium when he heard the name called out by her. That, in turn, had raised his curiosity about the mother. However, he had never seen her from the outside yard though, a couple of times, he had a flicker of a view of flaming red hair, curling upwards like a volcanic eruption, pass by the bay window in front of the little wood frame house in which the mother and daughter lived by themselves.

\* \* \*

What Patrick or, for that matter, Jolly herself, did not know was that her mother had joined Jolly's father in Texas after she had come there from New Orleans, her city, the city of culture and life as she had known it and defined it. She could never have imagined that, one day, she would have to emigrate to San Antonio, an almost border town with Mexico in the depths of the unknown, treacherous expanse of Texas. She did not even really get to know her daughter's birth father. True, both had felt an uncontrollable physical compulsion for each other when they perchance met in the Preservation Hall late one night where they had both gone to listen to the Negroes play the mesmerising beginnings of jazz.

Not that she went into the miniscule square hall often, and he was only an itinerant Northern traveller, a robust man in his mid-thirties, in search of a pair of full adult breasts to knead on a nippy night. Hearing waves of unusually plaintive melody, occasionally accompanied by thunderous voices, he had strolled in from the pavement. She could never figure why they happened to come together that night, but she conceded that the attraction was immediate and unquenchable. They left together early, at a moment when all five musicians were strumming and blowing, huffing and puffing, their large bodies humped over their equally large violas and wind instruments. They tiptoed out amidst the din of the vocals. The night that followed was bliss.

She had had a terrible time the previous night with a Frenchman whose actions had been obviously inspired by the autobiography of Marquis de Sade. Tonight, this man with his butterfly moustache and his strong arms and legs was oh so gentle with her, fondling and kissing her breasts, then her neck, then downward till her navel, where he lingered by thrusting his tongue in circular slurps and, finally, continuing his tongue onto her clitoris until she came in shrieks of satisfaction. He then moved his hand on himself and softly directed her mouth to it. He moaned to a steady, repetitive sound of relaxed breathing and, eventually, emptying her mouth, came on her still-aroused, hardened breasts for her to see. The smell of ripe semen mingled with the scent of magnolia floating in with the warm night breeze and permeated the darkness, transporting her into a momentary, and too quickly truncated, ecstasy.

It was so different from the previous night when she had to endure being turned over and then buggered from behind. Though she had been rewarded at the end of the ordeal with more cash than her usual charge, it had left her sore, but not because of the act itself for, as a result of practice, her rectum always remained dilated enough for a penis, even a large one, to be inserted from behind. However, it was because of the speed and force with which the man had humped her with the obvious intention of hurting her as much and as rapidly as he could, for it had appeared to her that he might even be afraid of losing firmness before ejaculation. So she had to move her buttocks about, to manage the pain and to cajole the ramrod to ejaculate.

Tonight was different. She refused to be paid when the moustached man who, looking big and hunky once again, had washed in the large tub of water in the corner of her meagre quarters, a small room in a bordello for which she paid by the week. The next morning, she re-dyed her hair, breaking the usual longer cycle, in a flaming red. He stayed on in New Orleans for another week. They spent the days taking the streetcar to different parts of town, and once they hired a little boat that was rowed by a Negro man whose fixed grin failed to make them comfortable in his presence, despite his general affability, annulling any possibility of a second boat ride on the river. For all excursions, he always paid. They discovered that they liked to frequent the funeral grounds with coffins standing on top, rather than buried underground, enclosed in beautiful, sometimes erotic, marble sculptures for all to see. These provided them inspiration for the long, wakeful nights of sweet ignominy and abominable ecstasy for, apart from the act of common consummation, they did to each other things that possibly may have faded with the ancient Greeks and Romans, or so one might presume. She never thought of being paid for the nights and it did not occur to him to pay, either.

The week eventually came to an end. He was travelling on to Texas, which was where he was going to seek his fortune in oil. She could not imagine not accompanying him, yet was doubtful and hesitant about leaving New Orleans, the only home she had ever known – from infancy when she had been brought up in the same surroundings by her mother and her sometimes affable and sometimes squabbling friends. She had beautiful memories of most of them, having long forgotten the few nightmares of the rapacity of visiting clients who wanted only youngsters in their bed. She felt comfortable – protected and familiar – in her bordello.

He picked her up, face front, very high, as though she was a child, and brought her down halfway so that their lips met at the same level. It was a long kiss.

"Goodbye, sweetheart."

He had hardly called her name this past week. Did she know his name? As they parted, there were smiles and sadness. He turned away. There was a thud in his heart that he had never felt before when he had parted from a hundred other girls at every which port of call. He would not ask her to come with him, he told himself quickly, for he knew what the answer would be. He could not snatch her from her life. He had no right. He had no idea about his next day. He only knew he had an uncle in San Antonio who had not promised him any financial support other than to get him a job on the rigs, but even that letter was a year old, if not older. Was his uncle alive? He had forgotten how old he was, but only that when, years ago, he had met him last, he was a boy and the uncle had seemed like a man who was moving on in years.

However, he turned back, nevertheless, and asked for a pencil. She ran to her dingy room upstairs, and then returned to him with a writing tool. He got the dog-eared oblong envelope out of his pocket and slowly copied the uncle's address down on the flap of the envelope, which the letter presumably occupied.

He tore the flap out and, in an unconvincing sort of way, said, "Honey, if you ever need me, maybe this will help."

As an afterthought, he added rhetorically, "We met, didn't we?"

Then he turned and just walked away.

He walked a long distance on Prince Street, and she saw him become smaller and smaller. Far, far, away, he turned the corner at a grilled garden wall. She went back up, kept the envelope flap in the drawer of her dressing table, looked at herself in its cracked mirror and shut her eyes, for she could see the pain on her ashen face more than she could feel it in her suddenly numbed heart.

She went back to her routine. Sometimes she fantasised about him when in bed with a client who was ugly though, in general, she avoided those to whom she was not physically attracted. She nonetheless hated the fantasy because she felt small and that she was belittling the memory of their having been together. So she stopped thinking about him, and he receded quickly to a mere memory. Sometimes she asked herself whether they had really met, or was it a dream encounter amidst all her nightly professional experiences. Ultimately, she told herself that she would keep her dream safely fixed at a spot from where she could draw it out for reminiscing during those low moods that engulfed her sometimes. However, nothing more.

A month later, things changed when she missed her periods. She knew at once she was carrying his child. She was ecstatic to be blessed with his indelible signature but, as her pregnancy began to become obvious, the madame of the building told her in no uncertain terms that she would have to get rid of it or leave, for she did not want any children growing up in the wrong environment! However, she was good enough to give a month's notice for any arrangement that might need to be made.

The soon-to-be mother, barely twenty, wrote, but did not receive any reply from the Texas address she had been given. In desperation and convinced by her Catholicism of the eternal damnation that would ensue from an abortion, she set out for the San Antonio location jotted on the inner side of an envelope flap. She carried her leather suitcase, filled with almost all her belongings – her bordello dresses, torn and dirty from prolonged dragging behind her on dusty ground, a faded Bible that she kept as a fetish or amulet against any curse or evil eye rather than for her reading pleasure or religious fervour, several bottles of hair colour, and a few other things of meagre and mundane consequence that otherwise served well to fill up the space.

When she reached his uncle's home, having spent her last penny on the arduous journey, she got the news. He had been blown off the rig into the Gulf of Mexico in a tornado the likes of which were commonplace in that part of the world. The uncle was mourning the sudden loss of his nephew who had recently appeared at his doorstep unannounced and unanticipated, whom he had thus recently discovered in a divine stroke of serendipity. His ephemeral hope that he would have someone to leave behind his small fortune, the one who would take care of him in his old age, had been dashed. All this he narrated in one breath, with the continuing lament that his unfulfilled life, spent in the endless task of survival without time or opportunity to settle down or beget progeny would, forever, remain thus.

She was listening to him in a daze, her mind switching from uncle to nephew to uncle. Where was she? Why did she come here, to nowhere? What would she do now with her bulging tummy? As she looked downwards, so did he focus his eyes on it, and they gleamed. In an instant, he offered to marry her to legitimise his nephew's child and she acquiesced by not answering in the negative. He immediately had the priest come over to the house to solemnize the marriage and, with that blessed act, to earn a handful of high-valued coins.

They spent the night together. She let him hug her and pinch her breasts, but he remained soft. Nevertheless, the next morning, he seemed happy at having at last established a home, hearth and family for himself. They had breakfast together at the bay window of his little wood-frame house. She withdrew into herself, lurking in a speechless world, for a while trying to putter around in the kitchen, hardly ever having boiled an egg or even water, for she had always been served a grotesque-looking stew of pigs' feet and okra in her room in the bordello by a Negress, who was like a slave of the madame in the whorehouse. Her husband ignored her inabilities in his newfound felicity, often overlooking mealtimes and, instead, looking forward to the moment of sliding in next to her under the sheet at night. In any event, he was happy enough with the culinary efforts of his own Negress, who came every day to put together a meal. Over the years, he had become quite used to her endeavours that placed heavy, greasy concoctions on his square table that sufficed for both study and dining.

As far as the mother-to-be was concerned, she got into the habit of spending much of her time in front of her new, un-cracked mirror and using one of her dyes to touch up her hair, sometimes without the break of even a day. She walked about the house in a halo of flaming red, or orange, or violet, like a queen from an extraterrestrial colony, and Uncle obliged by gazing at her with soaring admiration. Every night, he tried his best to arouse himself by pinching her tits or her buttocks, or by shoving his forefinger into her arsehole, which made her groan in a diabolical fulfilment. Or he would manually excite her clitoris, which she allowed in a barter with her manipulation of him, especially when he did get hard for a split second or two. However, he always got worked up, panting and huffing next to her until, one night, he simply collapsed in ecstasy and, with a smile on his face, breathed his last.

Jolly was delivered the next month by the Negress. The mother did not bother to hold her baby and, as soon as she could get out of bed, within the week, resumed floating about the house in the flaming strands atop her head and her dragging, muslin or satin gowns. Jolly, instead, got used to tugging at a phantom nipple, her little eyes ogling at the stark contrast of lime white milk drops that she missed sucking off, strolling down the bulbous black breasts of the Negress as she clutched onto them in her desperate thirst. She never learnt to call anyone 'Mama'.

The priest arranged the estate duty and court papers, taking ten percent of the inheritance for his religious order without announcing it or asking permission, for he considered it unnecessary. With the ninety percent, the three females settled into a make believe world. The mother, a generally wordless recluse, repeated, 'Sholie! Sholie' from time to time, more to herself than to her daughter as she moved listlessly from room to room. The dark nanny became a loving mother to the little white girl, and the girl never had to say 'Mummy' or 'Mama'. Instead, reflecting the devotion and care received from the black surrogate mother, she was soon on the way to blossoming into a precocious, talkative girl as though in compensation for her mother's aloofness.

The only man around the house was a large black man, Jesse, the gardener, who kept the garden tended during the day, but, at night, filled the nanny with his white stuff in the back utility room where they copulated routinely. On moonlit nights, when red flame tossed and turned in a restless stupor, he stole in to fuck her too, making her sweat and pant in the summer heat. Her receded and confused state of mind did not allow her, or she did not choose, to remember the intercourse the next morning. In a temporary stay until the next full moon approached, she simply continued her prancing about the house, indulging in her hair dyeing ventures.

If anyone in the neighbourhood suspected the household arrangement to be rather strange, it was never discussed in the open. The priest reminded his Sunday congregation time and again not to throw stones at others when one was living in a glass house, perhaps because he knew, or perhaps that was his favourite proverb that could stand in for an Eleventh Commandment. Members of the congregation stole secret accusatory glances at one another across the aisle and up and down the pews, but were cautious or intelligent enough to keep their mouths shut. The three adults with the little pet kid, the jewel of their eyes, thus carried on their daily lives with unbroken stability in the midst, perhaps, of many similar arrangements along the road, equally concealed and possibly even stranger but they did not arouse their curiosity one iota.

In the women's view, the only distortion to their model was when Jesse trotted off on occasional nights to get into

Rosita's bed down the road on the backside of the Goulds' hacienda. The two women knew about this to be sure for, the following morning, it was obvious that neither of them had had Jesse, but they knew that he could not be stopped from his triangular routine. Jesse liked the tapestry of white, black and brown and, with that, he remained happy and seemingly fulfilled. They were sure that he would never take on a fourth woman and they were satisfied with that. A silent envy appeared only when Jesse was made to marry Rosita by the priest.

*      *      *

No one could disagree that, as she approached puberty, Jolly was growing up to be a friendly young lady, always inquiring after the welfare of the elders and their pets – cats, dogs, birds, and iguana – without seeming unduly curious, while being able to amicably avoid answering intrusive questions regarding her own elders. Indeed, everyone in the neighbourhood appreciated her outgoing manner, often expressing perplexity at her openness, despite hailing from an obviously mysterious household that, they assumed, must disguise and hide strange, obscurantist practices. It was, of course, beyond their imagination that their admiration for Jolly reflected the free spirit of a communal child, who was shared by two mothers, loving, yet inimitable in their own practices, their own foibles, and with little time or interest to cling to her or impart to her any deep-seated self-concern or fleeting sign of selfishness, that essential marrow of adulthood, though she was certainly not immune to or fool enough not to develop a sense of self-protection or cover.

Patrick, too, had become a secret admirer. Though her mother's immaculate appearances aroused his curiosity and invariably intrigued him, he knew that his primary attraction was Jolly, and her shape and body, even though he was embarrassed about her being younger than he, since, as is the law of nature, he saw the difference in their ages in proportion to his own age. Occasionally, he longed to hold her and realised that such feelings enveloped him more and more whenever he met her. However, he never did.

Now, as Patrick fled, his mind was transported to Jolly, her face, her posture, and her developing curves. He deeply regretted the moment when he had accidentally discovered her sobbing behind a tree when hurriedly returning home a little after suppertime, for he had lost track of the flow of time while sharing a stolen cigarette butt with a group of classmates. He had been impressed by Jolly's staying behind for him even after he had ignored her, as she had tried to keep up with his pace, in his excitement to catch up with his chums and participate in the clandestine, punishable act of inhaling tobacco. They had to be especially cautious since, if the headmaster smelt cigarette smoke on anyone within the school compound, he took it as sufficient license to fetch his cane without further ado. Any chance for a smoke outside of school was, therefore, especially cherished, and Patrick was not about to miss out on this rare opportunity. He had no alternative but to ignore Jolly, leave her behind and run along. Indeed, he had taken a slight sadistic pleasure in doing so, for he could not help himself sometimes in feeling a whiff of irritation pass through when she dogged him, and this time was one such occasion.

Patrick had not imagined, however, that he had hurt Jolly so deeply that she would lose sense of time herself. On his way back, he saw her still weeping silently, hidden behind the banyan tree whose trunk was so broad and whose vintage so ancient that it had exposed a large cave-like opening that served as an impromptu clubhouse for various groups of lower-grade boys who would tend to stop at the spot to commiserate for a few moments before heading home. Indeed, it had become such a Mecca for so many that there had emerged an unwritten acceptance that the spot was for all, and not for anyone in particular. Even as the practice had emerged, no single group encroached into another. If there was one group loitering at the club hole, the other would linger respectfully at a distance for its departure or, if there was little sign of that occurring, leave to return at a more convenient time. It was a pristine, orderly world concocted by the Lilliputians, where rules had developed and were respected naturally, free of the incomprehensible strictures formulated by any neighbourhood association comprising adults.

Returning towards home after participating in the rite of smoking a second-hand cigarette butt, Patrick was briskly passing the club hole. He felt a shame envelop himself to discover Jolly, looking tiny and wilted against the huge solid trunk, with her head bent and face hidden in an arm folded back, her body shaking slightly. As she heard someone approach, she exposed part of her face, barely, to see that it was Patrick, but enough for Patrick to see that she had been shedding a cascade of tears. She quickly hid her face again.

It did not occur to Patrick that Jolly's budding feminine ability for manipulation, childlike and harmless though it still was, would lead her to position herself at a spot assuredly on Patrick's route home. Her sad, tearful face rushed an irresistible wish in him to embrace and cuddle her, but a natural respect, verging almost on reticence, of the male for the female body imbibed somewhere along the way as he crossed puberty, restrained him. The obvious shape of Jolly's forming breasts as they protested against the dark blue denim of her school tunic spun his head with a sweet giddiness, but he did not stretch out his arms towards them. Instead, he laughed nervously, and stretched one hand to pull her up with a start, seemingly unconcerned, yet afraid to be discovered by any of his peers in a moment of weakness or in an act of pure compassion.

"Come o-o-n," he merely uttered tersely.

Patrick dragged Jolly along and bade her goodbye in front of her house, and then ran home as fast as he could, with his heart pounding hard and loud, and almost breaking out of his chest, unsure of the source of the sudden excitement, and drowning in an uncontrollable longing that he had hitherto not experienced in such intensity. The sensation, almost a pain, stayed with him even in bed. He tossed and turned until he fell into a fitful sleep. The next morning, he found that he had inexplicably wet his bed with a gooey substance and had to rush to the shower, a necessity he was more habituated to postponing every morning until the moment of calling when his mother bawled at him from downstairs with repeated ultimata.

That evening, after he returned home, Patrick went quietly up to his room and lay in his bed, with his hand under the back of his head, dwelling on what had come to pass the previous night. He once again felt the rush. It made him bolt to the toilet and, naturally, yet astonishingly to himself, made him touch his penis, an act from which he had been forbidden by his mother when he was a little boy and which, over all these years, he had unquestioningly obeyed, except for the allowable, indeed, required, act of holding it up to urinate and then to shake it well before inserting it back into his fly.

Incredibly, as Patrick touched himself, he focussed on himself for the first time ever, and a narcissistic abstraction for himself gripped him at the sight of a solid white fluid spurting out of his erect manhood. It engulfed his body, mind and soul. He died for a moment, but was jolted back from his ecstasy almost instantly, having passed out for but a few infinitesimal seconds. After that, the sweet, cajoling, whimpering face of Jolly appeared in his mind's eye many a time and many times did he repeat the delicious act, suddenly oblivious of his mother's early admonitions not to touch himself in wrong places.

The effect of this adolescent event and its occurrence in the form of a solo consummation on Patrick was, however, that of a dark foreboding. Looking at Jolly in public would bring on the sweet, yet dreaded, sensation, which he anticipated with desperation when he was by himself. However, in public, he feared that, if discovered, it would embarrass or compromise him among his friends or bring shame, opprobrium, if not punishment, from elders. He began to avoid Jolly with great deliberation. Expectably, this brought on even sadder looks from her, for she quickly learnt not to attempt to skip along his side on the way home to avoid possible rejection and, instead, opted for tearful glances from optimal distances. Patrick played it safe, fearful of forging a bond that would expose his weakness, despite his intuition propelling him towards it, with every bone in his body craving the actual physical embrace that he had evaded successfully so far, but which he contemplated often.

Instead, Patrick kept himself busy with his cohorts in their joint activities, often playing soccer in the school yard or, on other occasions, venturing into escapades such as skipping class and rushing to the river, smoking cigarette butts, carving provocative, romantic-sounding names such as Lolita and Soozie on tree trunks with his Sheffield pen knife, a gift from a priest uncle, holding it firmly by its mother-of-pearl handle, or simply killing time.

*     *     *

Now, as he darted towards home, Patrick deeply regretted his stance of ignoring Jolly these past two years and, for an instant, turned as though to run back to say his last goodbye to her. However, his practical side made him turn full circle. Once again, he ran homewards, trying desperately to hold back tears, but he could not control them. They blurred his vision and he tripped and fell more than once over sharp, shapeless stones and broken brick bits that lay in his path. Each time he got up quickly, steadied himself, attempted to brush off the dust from the scratch or wound acquired from the most recent fall, and resumed his rapid journey. When he reached home, he leapt into his mother's arms.

Patrick could freely transform back into his mother's baby whenever the situation demanded, harbouring no qualms in rushing to her in any emergency. As he dove into his mother's bosom, he wept uncontrollably, and his mother folded him into her arms. Though Agnes could not help but love her son blindly, she feared that his sixth sense had led to his being somewhat self-absorptive and overprotective of himself. She had seen how he sometimes tended to overreact to situations, simple or grave. If he felt he was coming down with fever as a result of a slight cold, he would skip swimming even though that was his second love after soccer, for days, if not weeks. Or, when his baby sister, his heart and soul, caught the mumps, he refused to go into her room, though he would read to her from Grimm's Fairy Tales for hours, continuing even after she had fallen fast asleep, in a raised voice from outside her room.

Agnes could not hold herself back and began to weep involuntarily with her son, for she could not recall his ever drenching her apron with tears. She cupped his face in her palms and pulled it slowly, yet firmly, upwards towards herself. As she reached down to kiss his fresh smelling, but sweaty, forehead, she looked at his tearful face closely. Yes, he had an attractive face, though it had been exposed to the elements. Agnes had given up protesting against his pursuit of outdoor activities with his armada of frolicsome friends, daring the ferocity of the Texan sun or braving thunderstorms brought inland from the Gulf and unleashed from jet black skies. When he returned home after his jaunts, all sweat or drenched to the skin, she would make sure that he had a warm bath, changed, and parted his smooth black hair in the middle and combed it straight back with gel.

Focussing carefully, Agnes noted his dark, perfectly shaped eyebrows that almost joined in mid-temple. A deep hollow separated eyebrow from eye, each shaped like a peeled almond. She wished for a moment that her second-born, a daughter, had such beautiful eyes, but it was only a passing thought. She noticed that Patrick had grown into an attractive youth, with high cheekbones, the deep hollows below giving his face a sharp contour, like that of a ballet dancer who might acquire it after bouts of planned and arduous dieting. His lips were full and raised and, in their wetness, appeared to be deep pink. Cigarette smoking, his newly acquired habit that she was completely unaware of, had not yet had any lasting, ravaging effect on their colour.

Agnes gasped at her realization that this young man, just eighteen, was, indeed, beautiful, and tilted her head back to look at his face from a slight distance. His long, thin neck fell back over her arms as she brought her face forward to reach down to land a peck on his lips, faltering on them for an instant, and pulling back almost with a start. She composed herself quickly, wiped her tears with her palm, and gave Patrick a quizzical look, imploring him without words. Her eyebrows waved and her pained eyes filled with tears again, as she sought an indication as to the cause of his consternation.

Patrick looked lost in the misery that engulfed him, and did not respond immediately. For a moment, he put aside his practical nature and his sixth sense, as he took refuge in his mother. Without any guidance from Patrick, Agnes fell back into a sort of stupor. She looked at the son, her first born, as the one on whom she doted, despite the arrival and constant presence of her next born, the daughter whom she thought of as her little baby. After all, he had been born as she had touched eighteen, conceived as a result of an arranged union with a much older man.

*   *   *

Fifteen years her elder, a promising young lawyer who defended cross-border interests with Mexico through depositions, as well as in court, and who was known for being fulsome and decently healthy, her husband had a caring disposition towards Agnes, but the difference in their ages created a silent, unbridgeable gap right from the start. They would never have been put together had it not been for a deal whereby the heavy debt of Agnes' father was forgiven in exchange for her hand in marriage. Nevertheless, they had developed a liking for each other, carrying out their respective conjugal duties with responsibility, attention and, perhaps, even a conservative sort of love for each other that grew with time. However, they had never been *in* love.

Agnes' memory floated to the vivid, unbearable pain of giving birth to her first child, followed by a trance-like relief as she saw a little head appearing from her vagina. Her water had unmistakably broken to accommodate the emergence. As she exulted, the crushed, creased little body connected to the glistening placenta shook its tiny, dirty arms and more of it emerged, bringing into full view a speck of a penis with matching testicles, remarkably noticeable for a just-born. Gasping, she almost shrieked, "It's a boy, darling! It's a boy! Thank you, St. Patrick!" Momentarily, she thought, *he will be called Patrick* despite cautioning herself against naming her son after a saint, lest he should also abandon the everyday world for one of religion, repose and renunciation. "He is Patrick! Patrick!" she cried.

The best or, at least, the most costly, obstetrician in town, who had looked after her during her entire pregnancy and was delivering the baby, gave a final strong pull and two little, perfectly formed legs emerged. He pulled Patrick up with the umbilical cord attached, turned him upside down on the large, open palm of his right hand, and applied a sharp smack with the left on the baby's shrunken, creased buttocks. The newborn's face cringed and a loud cry emanated from his vocal chords. Father, mother, doctor and nurse all laughed.

That would, of course, be the first of many smacks that Patrick would receive as he advanced rumbustiously through school, unscathed and unaffected by such lashings. Now the new eighteen-year-old mother attempted to raise herself on one elbow as the baby screamed, declaring his presence on Earth as the century moved into its second half. It was 1950. She saw the umbilical cord being snapped, but her emotions remained caught in the body of the ugly little being whom she desperately wanted to hold. For a moment, her eyes floated outside the sun-drenched window to the clear azure sky. She breathed in the freshness of the crisp fall morning. She closed her eyes, capturing the external brightness of the day into a brilliant glow inside her eyes, and she transferred it to her mind. Slowly, she was surrounded and engulfed in a light in which she said her usual prayer. She simply thanked Him.

The baby was handed to her. As she held him, their bodies touched while the doctor and nurse on either side of the bed congratulated her as the souls of mother and son mingled and played, unnoticed and unobserved by others. Momentarily, she fell back, exhausted and fatigued, into a fitful sleep and with an unmistakable smile on her face. The nurse then removed Patrick from his mother's arms and planted a kiss on his plum-like cheeks.

The father smiled on, proud and unable to think further. He quickly retreated to the corridor where he had been pacing for the last several hours before he dashed into the delivery room when Agnes' shrieks had grown unbearable. He was just in time to behold his emergent son, whose head had just appeared and looked like a shrunken skull. He had had to stop himself from vomiting when his eyes beheld, for the first time, his own grotesque creation. Nonetheless, he had uttered a hearty laugh in unison with the others present. Then, he dashed out to announce the happy news as best he could, with toasts of sherry with the clergy and close relatives – again, mainly priests – and, later that night, in more comfortable surroundings at the local bar with his neighbourhood buddies, where they all got sloshed over free-flowing beer and booze, oblivious and unconcerned about the condition of wife or son lying in the inner depths of the one-storey adobe hospital.

It was not surprising that, soon, Agnes' husband would become anxious, and even somewhat envious, of Agnes' turning her attention from him, though he never stopped noticing the son's qualities as he blossomed, admitting to himself that they mostly reflected his wife's nature and attributes, which he never ceased to admire. Once, when Patrick was five and asked his dad, who was nodding behind an open newspaper, to read him a story from Grimm's Fairy Tales, he woke with a start and had to, as it were, think on his feet. He shook the newspaper, making it shiver and crackle, dove into the sports columns for a moment, looked indirectly towards his son, and proclaimed, "Dad can only read these b-i-i-g pages. Ma can read the small pages of your small little book. I am sure she will be happy to do so for my b-i-i-g sonny boy. Ggo-ggo to her!" Then he ushered him towards the settee on which she was seated.

He smiled more to himself than at Patrick, engrossed in his own cleverness at diverting the bothersome intruder away. It was only much later, as Patrick grew into an intellectually oriented young man, that his father would reveal the secrets of knowledge, delving into his interpretations of history and religion that would so mesmerize Patrick.

Baby Patrick, in the interim, was nonetheless big enough to realize that his dad's prescription to run to his mother was not possible to follow, for Ma was busy with her routine chores. He also did not feel that 'b-i-i-g' himself. A surge of tears filled his eyes and almost choked his breath, but he fought back. He looked from a distance at his mother, sitting cross-legged on a backless divan, breast feeding his little sister. She, too, looked up at Patrick, unable to reduce the physical distance between them. They smiled at each other, she with an intensely longing look, while his look emanated pure love. He glanced at the rather heavy volume that he was holding, snapped it open, stared at the words that appeared in front of him, and then succumbed to flipping the pages to view the many dainty pictures that filled the book. She heaved a soft sigh, but, as she turned back towards the new little creature and replaced her enlarged nipple into the baby's mouth, an expression of contentment covered her face.

The steady drone of Dad's snoring had infiltrated the wood-panelled family room by now. The room was made doubly comfortable by a low-burning fire on that mild, though slightly biting, winter night. Rosita, Patrick's Mexican nanny, who had looked after him from just after he was born, and who was always aware of every situation that affected him and of his every move, rushed from the kitchen and ran her fingers through his hair to pacify him. Patrick tried to ignore her, but succumbed by grazing her side a bit. Then, he reverted to looking at the coloured pictures in his book.

By eighteen, Patrick had become somewhat resentful of Agnes' vicissitudes of daily life. He had witnessed her labour physically with the weight of her progeny and, despite Rosita's invariable presence, the volume of her own housework, robbing her over the years of her beauty, though not her zest for life and her ready acceptance of her experience of married life and motherhood. However, he missed her picture-book features, her glow, the way he remembered her from infancy when he alone had been his mother's sole preoccupation.

Patrick had never stopped having flashbacks of warm dreamy nights when he would lie on her lap in the inner courtyard of their square hacienda, under an open night sky, fresh with myriad twinkling stars that illuminated the silhouette of her finely defined face. She would hum a sweet tune, then she would form the words, drawn out and slow, as though she was drunk with the sweet smell of jasmine, growing like wildflowers everywhere in the wide courtyard,

"Cherry ripe, cherry ripe, ripe I cry.
Full and fair ones come and buy."

Though cherries had never been a common fruit found in her vicinity in the depths of Texas. Perhaps she had picked up the lyrics in some bygone era at her own primary school or later. It did not matter.

*    *    *

Patrick suddenly snapped out of his misery and looked at Agnes' drawn, tense face drowned in worry. He began to explain his predicament to her. Agnes was slow in recovering from her own stupor to pay attention to her son, who seemed to be agonising over something terribly grave and monstrously forbidding. Yes, she had great expectations of him and knew that he would have to be ready to brave the world in the not too distant future. But, after all, he was and always would be her baby. She had become used to his tossing and turning in her bosom, sobbing or sleeping fitfully, after losing a soccer match in an interschool tournament, or receiving a thrashing from the headmaster, or a cut or two in a neighbourhood brawl. She would cajole him and caress him, knowing full well that, when he was up and awake, she would have to acquiesce to his every whim or fancy, whether it be baking his favorite tangerine cookies, or letting him sneak out with his friends late in the night aimlessly wandering the by-lanes and alleys of San Antonio only to return in the wee hours of the morning just before his father was up at sunrise for his daily constitutional.

Finally, Agnes straightened herself and, in what sounded like a stern voice, asked, "Son, what is it?"

Her prior use of 'Son' in addressing Patrick had not exceeded more than a handful of times, if that, and only on the odd occasion of dire emergencies or deep dilemma. She knew something was wrong, but she was not prepared for what she would just hear. As he began to speak, a strange fear engulfed her that something most unanticipated, unimagined and precipitous was about to occur. Just as a sparrow closes its wings around its wounded chick, so did Agnes close her arms and pull Patrick in towards herself.

"M-a-a, they are about to take me away," Patrick dragged out in a tone he had used since infancy without any discouragement from her, and despite Dad's occasional expression of irritation at the way he invariably dragged the word out whenever he transformed himself into her baby. He continued without pause, "I do not want to go to war! I *shall* not go to war! I must run. You have to help me pack, M-a-a. Pack whatever you think I would need. Oh! How shall I escape? Should I run to the Amtrack station? Or take the Peter Pan bus to Washington? M-a-a, please say something. Why are you silent? Sa-ay something! M-aa-aa!"

Agnes tried to clear her head, invaded by confusion and dread.

"What are you talking about, Son? What *are* you talking about? What happened?

"What has Washington got to do with all this anyway? Oh! St. Patrick, help me, help me! Help me! For I believe and depend on you always, forever and ever and ever!" She recited her prayer, memorised years back from her long-dead red-haired grandmother of pure Irish stock, God rest her soul. She hoped for immediate guidance and, as always, the solution flashed in her mind instantaneously as soon as she comprehended Patrick's predicament as he narrated it. She didn't ask more, though Patrick continued to pour himself out.

Not only was the transmission of his fear of the headmaster to his mother successful, but the headmaster's diabolical plans for Patrick were also immediately presumed to be true by a doting mother's unswerving faith in her son's convictions, aided by her cardinal fear of his stubborn views. She understood Patrick's fear and told him so. She had never liked the obese clergyman anyway. For one thing, he had no control over his eating habits, unable to hold himself from lapping up all her tangerine cookies and all the herbal tea in her teapot whenever he stopped by. A man with such little control in public was bound to possibly hide a shuddering cruelty behind a typically sociable and friendly façade, she had figured. Despite her suspicions, she had never confided her view to her husband, for she felt certain his affability would stand in the way of his understanding, let alone acceptance, of her opinion.

Agnes also knew that, once Patrick had made up his mind, no one could change it. Of course, not his father, his soft-natured, fun loving, intellectual and ineffectual dad, who was only able to spoil and hand out pocket money and celebrate with his son at fun times, but equally distant and recoiling at moments of much needed interaction; nor she. She was aware of, but disliked, this blasted sixth sense, something from within Patrick that would push him to a corner in a crisis. Yet, some part of her had even come to envy the rearing of this inner strength of Patrick over which her will or persuasion could never hold sway. She had eventually come to interpret it as an extension of her own intuitive skills, only in a more masculine and formidable version that was taking shape in this still-developing lad.

Her son. Agnes glanced at him ruefully, then looked away and began to move about briskly to prepare a bag for his certain, inevitable departure. She wondered, *will he go away forever? St. Patrick! Don't desert me! Show me the way! Guide me for the sake of my first born!*

Her limbs moved with lightning speed to fill a denim backpack that she had bought for Patrick at the country fair earlier that year, and which, so far, he had hardly used, preferring to keep using his dirtier, torn knapsack, which, too, she had bought in the distant past from a Chinaman's shop in San Antonio, set up by an early immigrant from San Francisco, a failed cook from a Chinatown restaurant there. The older one had been Patrick's skin, while the new had remained new. Now, Agnes decided, a change could be introduced, for Patrick, perhaps, would not care to object. This, indeed, turned out to be the case and Patrick got a new knapsack.

In an instant Agnes became Patrick's co-conspirator as soon as she was convinced that he was clear in his mind that going to Washington was what he wanted to do. She volunteered his dad's truck to Patrick. She did not insist on knowing why Patrick had selected Washington, DC, for how could she have been aware that it was based solely on his recent fixation with government in general and with Abraham Lincoln in particular? She only feared that he might be too young to undertake that long, arduous, if not impossible, journey. However, she knew him only too well. She knew his mind was made up. There was little point in reflecting any longer. She did not let the Gould family's century-old North-South divide impede her approval, despite Washington's being carved out of Maryland, a northern state, a matter of contention in the south from the very moment of–even before–its conception. If she accepted this moment, she had to embrace its truth, for Patrick had chosen to cross the line and go north.

Patrick wavered at the mention of the truck. He knew that his dad depended on it to go weekends to the country home that reigned over his far-flung arable lands, cultivated by tenant families who had lived there for many generations, some descended from slaves, freed generations ago when Texas was in Mexico, and who harboured no grudge from the distant past against his father, but rather held him in awe and respect, for he generally found no reason to mistreat nor take undue advantage of them. Or so he had heard many a time at the dinner table from his father. He had believed him, for some of them regularly came over to the hacienda during their free day, or helped his mother on important family occasions. Some even had the temerity to invite the Goulds to their own, generally tumultuous celebrations.

Agnes could not always make it to such events, but her husband made it a point to respect such invitations and to attend, though mainly as an excuse for participation in yet another, usually happy, exuberant social event. He did not shy away from the occasional funeral either, whether they were for the old and infirm or for a newborn who could not survive the inadequate medical care that poverty made inevitable. Patrick wondered how his father managed to keep up with the variety of his social commitments, despite the heavy demands on his time from his legal firm, and Patrick came up with an explanation: Dad did not care to allocate much time for his children although, in the case of his daughter, he did accompany her for her first day in school, as well as to her communion. He always remembered her birthday, which was just before Christmas, and told Agnes to prepare a good feast that would be an occasion for wide celebration.

By contrast, Patrick's birthday usually passed with little, if any, fanfare. Possibly that was because it fell in autumn, the nights filled with a gloom bearing the heaviness of the impending winter. To compensate for such gloom, his father was sure to have spent the previous evening in hearty revelry at the local bar. Consequently, this left the family bereft of much energy for preparing for a big social gathering the next day. It did make an indelible impression on Patrick's mind from the very first occasion when his sister's birthday was celebrated with a house full of guests while his had just passed with a mediocre home-made cake with a sugar-filled icing that was baked by Rosita. Yet, he had always thoroughly enjoyed the occasions of Sis' birthday and never bore any grudge over a matter relating to his younger sister. At this moment, going through childhood memories, he was, nevertheless, uncertain over robbing Dad of his truck, upon which the man so relied.

\*  \*  \*

Agnes did not consider it an issue. She had made up her mind that Patrick would need to take the truck for his long journey ahead. She knew there was no time to waste. She continued to move around the house with great speed until she had filled the new backpack with Patrick's favourite clothes, not the formal ones that he detested and was required to wear to church every Sunday, but the normal ones: his two blue jeans, one pair of black trousers tailored more like jeans, but having a slightly formal look solely because of its colour, which she considered might serve the dual purposes of informal and formal wear as and when required, three collared shirts, five white T-shirts that Patrick usually wore solo, but could be worn as undershirts, five matching underwear, five pairs of white socks, a pair of sneakers, a belt, a pair of black leather boots, the type Johnny Cash wore, which had to be folded over at the top to fit into the remaining space in the seemingly bottomless bag, and an heirloom heavy woollen sweater after she got rid of the mothballs in which she had preserved it, since no one in the family ever had occasion to use it in the southern Texan climate, but which she knew would be needed for the harsh Washington winter. Still, there was space left over, which she allowed Patrick to fill with a few unnecessary, but intimate, items that had little utility value.

Agnes grabbed a cloth bag, loosened the draw string and threw in selected basic toilet items such as a wooden comb imported from Japan that she had saved all new for years, a talcum powder tin, her husband's short shaving knife, since Patrick had not begun to shave regularly, but she knew he would soon need to use it to get rid of the pronounced stubble that had begun to appear on his face on a daily basis, which the barber came to shave off once a week. She complemented these items with her husband's shaving brush, a block of soap that could be used for the body and the face, and bay rum. She did not overlook a wad of cotton wool, a short roll of gauze and bandage, a soft toothbrush, a large toothpaste that she took out of the locked walk-in closet, which she had had redesigned for storing household goods that accumulated at the beginning of every month, usually the outcome of a major grocery shopping trip, which she invariably undertook with the help of Rosita and her son.

Ordinarily, Patrick would never have allowed his mother to go into such excesses for him. When he went camping, for example, he only let her pack as few clothes as possible to keep the weight down, even though he knew that would mean wearing the same sweaty, smelly attire for days on end. He did not care, because his friends did the same. However, now, he let his mother do as she pleased, not only because he was feeling weak from all the exertion he had just undergone, coupled with a hollow feeling that he was about to be going into deep oblivion, but also because, this once, he did not have the heart to hurt his mother's feelings. So he let her do as she pleased. Further, his practical side told him that Agnes would know better than he what he might need to wear in the immediate future.

Breathing heavily, Agnes ran into the kitchen, straight to the long, rectangular, wooden icebox. She picked up the straw picnic basket that sat on top, but, reflecting for a moment, quickly put it back exactly where it had been. She knew Patrick would be irritated about having to carry a picnic bag for himself, and did not want to worsen his state of mind in any way. She whizzed past Patrick to her bedroom and ran to her teak wardrobe crowned with a floral design carved on a mahogany and ebony panel.

Agnes snatched the bunch of keys that she kept tucked into her skirt waist pocket, ignored the long mirror that comprised the left door of the majestic armoire, without looking at the bunch, fitted the right key into the keyhole, turned it, and opened the door on the right. Agnes took a large, black satin silk scarf that Rosita had brought back for her from one of her visits to Mexico to her rarely mentioned family. She relocked the gigantic period furniture with the satisfaction of knowing that Rosita would like Patrick to carry a memento from her.

Agnes had no idea that Patrick was about to be carrying away with him not only Rosita's scarf, but also her jewel, her heart. Perhaps even Patrick had not contemplated it at that point. Or perhaps he already had. Being practical, it was possible. Perhaps his was an attachment that he could not abandon, even though, or because, he did not have the wherewithal to comprehend its nature. So he would choose to rob Rosita's dearest possession within the next hour and, possibly, this most precious possession of Rosita's was himself waiting to be usurped by Patrick.

An atmosphere throbbing with uncertainty and anticipation, from which neither Agnes nor Patrick was free, pervaded the living area of the hacienda. Running back to the kitchen with the black scarf, Agnes opened it across the square kitchen table, its corners falling over the table's four edges in cascading waves. She went first for the fruit, putting together all the apples from the kitchen, parsimoniously purchased as they were, informed by their invariably high price in hot Texan towns, as well as the more abundantly available and cheaper tangerines and, on second thought, Patrick's favourite fruit, a couple of mangoes, throwing him a look that indicated that he had better consume them quickly for, otherwise, they would spoil.

Agnes took out a giant loaf of homemade bread from the icebox and the rough-edged bread knife that had had its place in the cutlery drawer for at least three generations, now requiring occasional sharpening from the silversmith who came by every quarter. She cut several thick slices of bread and, using the same knife, scooped as much butter as she could from the butter dish, and slapped it on the bread generously. She then sliced, as many and as thinly as she could, slices from salami. She grabbed some American cheese out of the cheese basket and clumps of lettuce and a couple of tomatoes from a mound of vegetables that occupied the base of a triangular table standing, otherwise unobtrusively, in the corner. She threw all her components together in the form of six large sandwiches.

They all crowded together into the scarf, nestling with the variegated fruits that were already there and, against its black background with the three-dimensional table on which it lay, she stole a moment to appreciate her hurried creation. It could have been a Flemish still-life, except for the absence of some pearl necklaces, overturned colourful, dead pheasants, bleeding dead rabbits and human skulls used as decorative garnishes. Clinging to herself, she gave a soft, almost motionless shudder, her body craving to embrace her son in a hug. However, she resisted this urge, for she knew they had no time to lose. The younger child would return soon from school, and she had to get Patrick on his way and out of the trap of the army before that. Agnes jerked her head towards Patrick and then at the icebox, so Patrick could fetch water in two plastic jugs as she folded the scarf and tied the two sets of edges into a crossed knot. When done, it looked like a monster dumpling, and Patrick could not but smile at its giant, dim sum-like appearance, wondering when he would actually consume its inhabitants, and how long it would take to finish it all.

Still smiling, Patrick turned to his mother and moved towards her. They spread out their arms, smiled and furrowed their brows to control their deep mutual pain. They embraced each other tightly and firmly. They knew they were parting for a long time, though neither could venture that it could be for always. They were mother and son. He, an adorable, perfect youth; she, a still-young mother, inextricably linked to every aspect of her son's life until this moment. Without their knowing, their pain-filled embrace became an embrace of two adults, as though they were mother and son no longer.

Then, silently, like two strangers, Agnes reverted instantly to her world of husband and daughter just as Patrick separated from her, his sight towards his future. Their umbilical cord had finally snapped. In a split instant, there was a parting of their universes. They could never recreate their plaited past and would only move along separate trajectories from now on. Their consciousness could never again allow the just-experienced intensity of feeling, of belonging, except for the care and concern of a proverbial mother for a son, or a devoted son for a mother. Even that limited relationship might not pass the test of time but fade like the evening glory of a moving sky.

\*       \*       \*

Both ran across the hacienda's inner courtyard, skirting at its centre the huge terracotta pot shaped like a tall Roman jug showing its own antiquity with the requisite broken edges and chipped white limestone interior. An expansive mint plant, dwarfed like a bonsai because of over-plucking to maintain a steady supply of leaves for many a soup that Rosita concocted for the family in the winter months, stood on the pot. As Patrick ran past, the familiar scent of the mint weakened him for a moment. A whiff from the stale jasmine that had blossomed the previous night, but had succumbed to the heat of the day, added to his nostalgia, but he did not look back.

Outside the main gate, the red truck stood in all its old glory, completely unaware of the immediacy of its new task or of its new master. Agnes flicked her key ring out from her skirt waist and rolled out its spare key, separating it from the others. The keys made a cantankerous jingle jangle as Agnes tucked them back and handed over their separated sibling to Patrick in a simultaneous gesture. Their parting was instantaneous, yet deeply painful, since they did not have the luxury of anticipation of this moment. Now solitary, the spare key sparkled in a metallic shine. Patrick would have it for quite a few years until, finally, it would be separated from him when he would give the van over as a gift to a museum for vintage vehicles at Luray, Virginia. There, it would go with the key inserted forever into the keyhole on the driver's panel, residing partly visible, half-buried in perpetual retirement.

Mother and son hugged once more, this time in a hurry, just a movement that had to be completed, for the real parting had already taken place and their minds, if not hearts, were already separated. As Patrick turned away a last time, Agnes gasped as though she had forgotten something, covering her suddenly opened mouth with her left palm while picking out with her right hand a man's wallet from her skirt pocket. She snapped it open and took out a wad of folded ten and hundred dollar bills. She counted several and separated them from the rest, which she refolded and put back into her wallet. Abruptly, she took them out again and counted them once more. She took out several more. She put all of them together, two thousand dollars in all, and handed them over to Patrick. She would worry later about household and repair expenses for the rest of the semester.

Patrick looked uncertain, but did not protest. He jumped into the driver's seat, shut the door, inserted the key in its hole and started the engine, as he had done many times before, at the beginning, in jest, and increasingly, in recent months, for moving around. It did not start. From the floor of the car, Patrick lent his mother the steel bar that worked as a starter and with the use of which Agnes had been fully familiar. She inserted it behind the license plate in front of the car and cranked it while Patrick turned the ignition key. A thunderous sound erupted in Agnes' ears, she turned, handed Patrick the steel bar, and ran back into the house. Without looking out or backwards as the truck went forward with a start, Patrick set the gear, pressed the accelerator, and let the wheels move forward. He adjusted himself in his seat and, at the end of the hacienda grounds, turned the corner to the right, for a few moments more lingering along the side of the only home he had ever known. The next moment, he was finally on his way.

Patrick began to feel the blowing wind as he pressed harder on the accelerator, and the dancing dust clung to his face, now freshly wet from new tears that streamed down as a thousand conflicting thoughts of school, teachers, friends, Jolly and family confounded and confused him. He felt alone, terribly alone. He doubted whether he could survive the ensuing loneliness for too long.

At this moment, the face of Terrence appeared and loomed before Patrick. Terrence had been at the back of Patrick's mind. Now he clarified his thoughts and decided to act on them. Patrick's decision became their combined destiny. His journey with Terrence was about to begin.

The parting of Agnes and Patrick, as well as his escape, had been completed with not more than a mouthful of words between them. That was unusual for Patrick. Although Patrick was no chatterbox, he was certainly looked up to as leader, guide and, sometimes, counsellor and confidant by his classmates. He often had to use his gift of the gab and talent for oratory to maintain his standing in their midst. Nevertheless, his extrovertedness concealed a very personal, private side when it came to home and all it represented. The first was his intrinsic bond with his mother that had flowered over the years in an imperceptible, unspoken, yet deliberate way. Second, in the space between home and school, he had a secret life ruled by a silent, invisible companion and consort.

Patrick's affinity to Terrence had been based on few words. Rather, it was determined mostly by the senses. Perhaps Terrence, its object, might not have been fully aware of its nature. To Patrick, Terrence was not concrete evidence, but a flight of fancy, a compulsion, ethereal and undefined, to be experienced ephemerally but repeatedly, someone who lurked perennially, without doubt or needing proof. Despite knowing that Terrence could not go to his school, Patrick missed him in school every day, wondering why Lincoln had been unable to ensure that all children had access to the same schools regardless of how they looked, especially the tone of their skin over which they had little say.

When Patrick was much younger, he had been all the more confused, for he had found Terrence gallant and brave, beautiful and strong. He could not fathom why he would not be let into his school. As he grew older, the realization and recognition, though not acceptance, of unwritten boundaries dawned on him slowly, till the moment when he was seven and went to the railway station one Saturday to greet Uncle Sam, a younger brother of his father returning from the Korean War. He felt thirsty and ran to a water tap. Standing in front of it, a notice pronouncing in bold letters 'For Whites Only' attracted his attention in passing. He bent forward to gargle in the fresh, cascading water, till a belch announced that his thirst had been quenched.

Terrence, who had tagged along with Patrick, in order not to interrupt their ongoing game of catch-a-thief, also felt parched, the outcome of their running to catch each other all the way to the station. It was he who had been relegated by Patrick to undertake much of the catching, at which he had had significant difficulty since, at seven years of age, he was a head shorter than Patrick. Seeing Patrick drink, he ran after him and, when Patrick had finished, went straight for the water. The stationmaster, surveying this development from a distance, galloped up and shoved him aside, albeit trying his best to do so gently, possibly cognizant of his tender age, and ushered him in the direction of the men's room that had a Negroid silhouette made clear by its telltale swollen lips, stuck on a dirty, greying door, slapped on with the word 'Negroes', written boldly under the diagram.

The man in uniform said, "There is a tap in there, boy."

Slightly shaking his head as though in wonder at children's improbable follies, he turned and hurried away in search of the next error in progress that he perceived himself as being paid to rectify. Terrence stood paralysed in his tracks, unprepared for the strength of the older man's hold on his arm. Without looking up at Patrick, he headed in the indicated direction. They did not exchange words, but Patrick felt himself miss a heartbeat, and, unbeknownst to him, a resolute stubbornness made its home in his guts at that moment, a doggedness that he would have little control over, but the signs of which his mother had already observed, and others who would know him later would notice with time. With that nascent resolve, an infinite bond was established that would skip life periods, but still remain strong, which might falter, but not diminish, which might sometimes eat into itself, but also deepen - a bond between the two boys of similar age, but of different skin, hair and accent. Yes, Jolly was Patrick's adolescence, but Terrence comprised his soul.

*　　*　　*

Patrick was struck by two matters. Terrence did not know how to read; so how could he have known not to drink from that tap just from the embossed silhouette? What could motivate elders to separate them by decree and with a mere stamp on the wall, and for no apparent reason, when they obviously were and, therefore, preferred to be, together? Neither had yet the capacity to comprehend their difference. Both already felt inseparable in a predestined sort of way. Patrick realised for the first time that, to nurture this friendship, he would have to work for it in a special way, much different from his myriad friendships at school. He interpreted this as a need to caress his closeness in private, relegating, from that moment, his wish to play or merely to squander time with Terrence to a separate, clandestine world.

Simple childish desires grew, without Patrick's own realisation, into an intense longing, until they were sated. He found himself quite willing, if necessary, to concoct yarns to leave the hacienda in anticipation of meeting up with Terrence, who would be walking along, kicking up dust or sitting hunched on the ground with a stick poking an earthworm. Patrick knew well the sight and sound of Terrence, who could easily be identified at long distances by his grin that revealed his sixteen pairs of shiny white, slightly protruding teeth. Shorter than Patrick, he would hop and skip along with him, unconsciously joining hands, unaware of Patrick's initial embarrassment, and drag him along until Patrick, too, fell in step with this elemental phantom of a boy anointed with a purity oblivious of colour.

The world around the corner, so desperate and legalistic to separate the whites, reds, yellows, browns and blacks, did not witness the boys walking hand in hand into the sunset over a Texan sky, resplendent with an intermingling of the most brilliant colours in their gaudy oranges, shocking pinks and deep purples. It was as though Clotho, Lachesis and Atropos, the three sisters believed to be the controllers of destiny by the ancient Greeks, had brought the boys together. The Fates kept them safe from all the differences humans had created and protected them from the separation they had been prescribed and against which they had little power other than to discreetly avoid by retreating to a subterranean, free world of their own. It was as if Hadrian, the philosopher-warrior emperor of Rome, had met Antinous of Turkish descent, except that their ages were contiguous, rather than being far apart.

Years later, when reading the introductory chapter of his history book, Patrick would wonder aloud in class about the term 'leader of the free world', as he had heard his country being referred to. He cited a fake, made-up instance of an experience of the likes of Terrence and, on that basis, questioned the meaning of leadership for, to him, a leader should have to be impartial to all he leads. Brother Rinaldi had readily agreed with his view and had inspired Patrick to improve the world in the new post-war era, but some tattletale must have filled the ear of the headmaster for, without any apparent reason, Patrick had been summoned for a caning by the headmaster. The admonition subsequently meted out to Brother Rinaldi by that bulbous wimp remained forever unknown, except for the poor man's giveaway evasive responses to Patrick's subsequent comments and questions about some historic episode or other, which had earlier comprised intellectual fodder for the teacher.

Now Brother Rinaldi seemed subdued and devoid of all inspiration. Luckily, it was only a temporary phase, lasting but a week, after which the man bubbled with his usual enthusiasm at every opportunity to pass on a new slant or question in the nation's history to Patrick, seated amidst a mass of usually disinterested, taciturn students. However, the incident had a lasting effect on Patrick, since in no small way did it impact on his choice of Washington as the location of his transfer which, he figured, should represent the best spot from where he could change the world. Needless to say, it also cemented his distrust and loathing for the headmaster as much as it clinched his reverence and respect for Brother Rinaldi.

\*    \*    \*

Terrence was a special breed, a cross between black and brown, a result of the gardener's third-nightly visits and insertions into Rosita. However, Terrence, though exquisitely handsome since childhood, was dark enough and his hair a bit too curly so that the wider world placed him at the bottom of the heap, the third rung. He was decidedly below the first rung, the pure white, and the second rung, the exasperating, but more acceptable, yellow, red and brown, who were acknowledged to be somewhat more valuable for the conduct of daily life. He was irretrievably categorised with the third rung, the uncleansed who, according to no other than Thomas Jefferson himself, the revered genius and author of the United

States' *Declaration of Independence,* were somewhat sweaty, smelly, and dark.

Rosita's Mexican egg had been impregnated by the strong, solid Negro strain, the result of many generations of careful matching of hybrid slave stock until Lincoln won his war and lost his life in the bargain. Rosita's X chromosome combined with the gardener's Y, and her orthodox Catholic heritage played its part in bringing Terrence into the world rather than being packed off to oblivion in the early stages of his conception. In reality, Rosita's Catholicism prodded her only to look for support in her decision to deliver the baby, and not for any other support. She had inherited a fear of the Devil and of copulation for any reason other than for begetting from sermons bellowed out by the celibate Jesuit priest in the little pueblo church where she had been dragged by her grandmother every Sunday morning since she was an adolescent growing up in Mexico. The relative silence of evening mass or holy communion in the waxed-in darkness of the church, which the few lighted candles could never penetrate, did not allay the fear; rather, it only served to heighten it.

Much to the gardener's delight, he was always allowed to ejaculate inside her in contrast to the French-speaking mistress or the ever-wet Negress of his own race, who would contract conveniently as his penis demonstrated signs of its final bloating prior to the burst, making it slip out in a quick painful slide, suddenly bare and devoid of its warm, slithery cup. Though he was clever enough never to interrupt the rotational routine lest he should raise the ire of any one of them and lose the benefit they showered on him, especially since he had an unfailing, well-confirmed admiration for variety, there was no doubt that his favorite bed continued to be Rosita's, the only one in which he was allowed full consummation. Because of this, she had become pregnant quite early, well before the arrival of the other two in his life. Yet their appearance into his life did not bother Rosita too much for it did give her some respite from the colossal manhood that she had begun to prefer to accommodate only intermittently. He knew that Rosita was aware of the special arrangement, not that it bothered him either, since most of his ancestors were forced to be conceived out of wedlock and, for that matter, it had become acceptable in his present community.

As the three women became aware of one another's existence, Rosita had attempted friendship. She had approached her red-haired co-sister. She poured out her story of pregnancy out of wedlock, though the name of the man was never raised. She had hoped for empathy and commiseration. Instead, the answer she got was stony silence for, after all, she had solved her own similar predicament by suffering matrimony with a much older man. So why should Rosita too not solve it in some similar fashion?

Rosita failed to comprehend why her co-sister could not understand what she had gone through and, briefly, she had even contemplated suicide. She had quickly abandoned the thought of course, because of the certainty of eternal damnation as its only possible outcome. In fact, even though she had never brought it up, Rosita had always wondered how, within a few days after her arrival in the neighbourhood, the red haired flame managed to carry the seed of an old man who died soon thereafter. At this point, all she had expected was a bit of sympathy for her story of unexpected pregnancy. But that was not to be.

In reality, Rosita's experience had been even worse. She had gone to Agnes when she found herself with child. Agnes had been helpful. She herself had offered to be the midwife to abort, as an exception, the foetus to save Rosita the shame of having to face the world in her condition. Rosita realised that Agnes' offer revealed a preference for a conservative stability in the conduct of everyday life, and not having to accommodate an illegitimate child within its parameters.

Rosita had left silently. For her own self respect, she never mentioned this to anyone again.

Taking a deep breath, Rosita walked with her head high into the church and asked its Irish friar if he would enter the rickety confession box to hear her confession. He did. Once in the confessional, Rosita saw the priest's eyes shine through the cobwebs on the wood filigree, like the glistening eyeballs of a vulture before it swooped down on a sitting prey. Under his breath, he muttered by rote the words of forgiveness in God's name, rose from his chair and dashed out without losing a further second, as though afraid that she might escape from his clutches. As a priest in a sea of despicable, immoral humanity, he was neither godly nor human enough to forgive her. As she still knelt, he boxed her right ear and pulled her up. He looked down at her from his tall, lean West European frame, his hooked nose almost touching her upraised face, her tearful eyes shut, ready to receive a slap that materialised after the anticipated swish of air that preceded it. Now, she was able to open her eyes into what seemed an eternity.

Realising that he had the plebeian native vanquished and bowed in front of him, paternal feelings suddenly gripped this intermediary between man and God.

"My child, rise!" he declared in a tone imitating his imagination of Saint Paul, completely forgetting that she was already on her feet. It was just that he was a couple of hands taller than her. He admonished, with absolute authority and full conviction, "You have s-sin-n-n-ed. Yes, you have." Then, nodding in slow motion, narrowing his eyes and lowering his voice, he whispered, "Who is the father?"

Rosita immediately realised that the priest had already annulled the possibility of abortion and thanked God for it. For a moment, she shut her eyes and rolled her pupils heavenwards.

Seeing that she was hesitating to respond to his question, the priest boxed her ears again, harder this time. Rosita blabbered out the Negroid name, at whose pronouncement the priest withdrew his clutching fingers from her ear as though he had been touching the Negro himself. He had long found comfort in racial difference and the notion of untouchability for the dark colour soon after his landing in America and heading for the South under the prescription of his religious order when he was barely seventeen. Later, when he failed to show promise in either administration or conversions, or even education, he had to be eventually transferred to officiate in Latin-American churches crowded primarily by illiterates, where he drew succour from the superiority of his white colour. He took it upon himself to remain ever vigilant to maintain order and separation among, and from, the lower colours.

As he grew older, however, and as the younger, more dynamic priests had to be transferred to the rapidly colonising areas of the West, where the prostitute culture had to be subdued and the remaining red natives had to be proselytised, this priest had to be allowed, slowly but steadily, to re-enter the churches and homes of the upper classes. Eventually, he became a fixture in Agnes' household and quite a few others like hers. His position and authority in society that mattered were reinstated, but he also had to carefully nurture every policy and action needed to protect their safety. He did so by not only catering to the needs of such families, but also by monitoring their servants, keeping them in check, within bounds and beneath the threshold, ensuring that they did not give cause for any unnecessary preoccupation or irritation within the circle of his benefactors.

He was accordingly stunned at Rosita's pronouncement. At his wit's end and unable to perceive an easy solution, it dawned on him that imitating a Virgin birth could turn out to be a soothing, equilibrating solution for the community. However, he knew he needed the Virgin's sanction. Turning away from Rosita, he knelt towards the altar still at a distance from him, and called upon the Virgin Mary to corroborate his proposal. He was not ready for the rebuke he was about to receive.

The Virgin appeared instantly. She was floating lightly atop the altar as the sun's rays streamed in through the tall, plain glass panels that fit into unmatched wood panels along the far wall of the church on the two sides of a colourful Jesus in crucifixion, brightly painted in a plethora of oils. She admonished him in scathing, unutterable language through her laced veil – Belgian, it looked like – the same one, he realised, that his mother had given him as an heirloom to take along on his long-forgotten journey from Limerick on the west coast of Ireland to the *New World*, and that he had placed on every Mary in every church that he had ever visited, its current place being to adorn the altar in front of him. From up there, Mary castigated him for his ludicrous proposal, not overlooking to remind him of his utter failure to improve himself in 'administration, conversions, or even education', and adding with a tone of finality that there was, and would forever be, only one Virgin birth in the history of all *revealed* religions.

Lest one should forget, those were the religions that had emerged from accounts of events repeated, for every denizen and throughout the ages, by men endowed with an unusual cardinal sense, whether inclined towards pecuniary benefit, power, and control of others, or blessed with exceptional sexual orientation subject to the possibility of societal censure. Even though she admitted their earthly shortcomings, they had, nevertheless, been the perfect media for divine revelation, whether in stone tablets, animal skin or papyrus, lists of dictats for everyday living that were never to be questioned by science or conscience, or countered by doubt or evidence. The only acceptable evidence, she enjoined in no uncertain terms, were miracles in which she, or her emissaries, appeared, irrespective of whether or not that vitiated at least half of the church's carefully selected sainthoods.

Finally, the shrouded Virgin cautioned that, among all revealed religions, the only true one was hers, the unique talisman and protection from eternal damnation and from the fires of Hell, and that all breakaway fragments were equally blasphemous, beginning with the one that catapulted out of a syphilitic king's penchant for sex with newly captured wives and for their subsequent beheading once he had had enough of their tantrums or failure to produce sons. The Virgin also said that a new disease, worse than syphilis, would appear on Earth. This disease would be called 'acquired immune deficiency syndrome (AIDS)' and there was nothing the Roman Catholic or any other Church could do, despite its wishes to the contrary, to stop AIDS. It could only be controlled with direct divine intervention.

Then, with one teardrop falling from her eye that she condescendingly, if not scornfully, offered him as a token of her appearance and which he narrowly missed catching even as he jumped forward, and with a little heart with arteries in full exposure and still throbbing on her outstretched, open, bleeding right palm, she quickly vanished. However, before that, she did console him with a short, yet erudite, recitation of the importance of avoiding scandal, including sexual abuse by priests, assuring him that she might put it on her agenda if rumours of its prevalence continued to leak and simmer, but not until some further decades had passed, since she already had a full diary of unattended social corporate items to attend to.

Snapping out of his reverie, he stole a glance at the altar. He noticed that the veil had gone; Mary had absconded with it. Then he looked down at his dry, outstretched palm, moaned slightly, came to his senses and looked backwards at Rosita to see her reaction to what had just transpired. Her obliviousness of the Virgin's appearance or disappearance confirmed his suspicion that the miracle was meant only for him, and a profound change came upon him. From then on, he saw himself as specially ordained for solving mankind's problems, even if confined to his own little flock. Soon, without going into any detail, he would recount the Virgin's appearance to his audience and, with simple repetition, the story took hold with appropriate modifications and embellishments, and his views regarding naming, schooling, selection of profession, choice of life partner, and time of death when the last rites would be read, were all taken with the utmost seriousness in every household that competed to reach for his involvement in its daily life.

With his newfound conviction and confidence, his first post-miracle act was to inform Rosita that she would be saved, that he knew the solution, and that she would be married. Telling her to return later that evening, he entered his small room on the left of the altar, took out his diary, opened the frayed black leather folder, flipped to the current page identified by a string pulled across its length, and wrote, 'The Virgin appeared today. She showed me the way to get Rosita married to the Negro gardener'.

He looked around to see if any ghost was privy to this ghastly decision. Seeing none, he put ink to paper again. '*She* obviously sanctions the mixing of races. However, it will take great courage on my part to officiate. From now on, I *know* that I shall have to do many brave things, for I have been *chosen*. Oh, yes, she also said that some ancient king has bequeathed a disease, *AIDS*, upon the civilised world', and, as though in an effort at self-conviction, he added, almost with a poetic touch, for his intonation had acquired the Texan drawl, with so many years of not speaking with the heavy Irish accent, 'I shall be ever vigilant as the Virgin's knight in combating the evils of this world', as if he had done anything else in his prior years.

He shut the diary, forgetting to add the date or day on top or bottom of his new insertion. The date of the miracle that foretold AIDS or its cure was, thus, lost forever.

That night, in the darkness of the little church, with a candle or two burning, the priest married Rosita and Jesse.

Agnes was by Rosita's side, and her husband was best man. While neither Agnes nor her husband judged the bride or groom, they looked at each other and smiled, content at the safety of their own static domesticity, and looked back again at bride and groom indulgently. After exchanging tin rings, they kissed, lingering for a moment as two visages, seated at the back of the tiny chapel, winced. The newlyweds turned and walked down the short aisle past the phantom figures, and out of the church from the nocturnal ceremony.

No wonder, when later Rosita met the red hair with her Negress, she sensed a confusing mix of curiosity, envy and, yes, even solidarity, for her two co-sisters who had been present at the church to witness her wedding vows. Had they heard from their common lover about the commandeered ceremony? Or was it that their souls were impatient and had already visited the future event in the ramshackle church on that eerie night? They could have been two spirits who went unnoticed, mistress and servant, silhouettes huddled in a back row, one with strands of coloured red hair escaping from under a flowered shawl and the other hiding her face from the five at the altar. It was as if they knew that the Powers That Be had anointed Rosita as the prime choice to clinch the partnership with their common lover. It was thus expectable that when Rosita invited them to her home, they refused her invitations either with lame excuses or with none at all. All these two women prayed for was continued attention from the gardener.

Their prayers were answered and, for many years to come, even when their sexual appetites had diminished with the passage of time, the particular pair for the night never failed to share the bed, clutching and groping each other to hearts' content, until sleep and snores replaced their childlike delights. Not so incredibly, perhaps, the four passed away within six months of one another, well into their eighties, the man first, in keeping with demographic trends and reflecting his harder outdoor life, and enabling all three of his women to partake of, and mourn, his departure. Rosita had to return from South America where she had settled; she was the one who wore the most intricately embroidered black veil for, by then, after the country's spurt of economic growth and the successful assimilation of her son in society, she could afford many of the styles and designs that were available in San Antonio, while the other two wore plainer black dresses, with red flaming strands showing from the scalp of one, and the other's gargantuan breasts barely held back in an inadequate, old black gown. Unable to cope with the departure of their third-nightly visitor, one by one, they, in their respective solitudes, breathed their last soon thereafter, each grateful and content after a full life, ready to face the next, if any.

As the three paramours completed their chapter with Jesse, the bard sang in a doleful voice:

When shall we three meet again?
In thunder, lightning, or in rain;
When the hurly burly's done;
When the battle's lost and won;
That'll be ere the set of sun.

*    *    *

Terrence was born a little more than seven months after the wedding. Following an ancient Aztec practice, which Rosita's forebears had passed down through the generations, and despite all the mixing of races, she squatted in the same manner as she had been used to as a child when she had shat outdoors in the bushes, for her family had not had indoor plumbing. Now she did it indoors. Over a large white pan half filled with water, during her third squat, as she pressed her eyes and shut out her breath, the baby slid out, pulled down by the force of gravity towards the water. She caught the baby herself, as she had seen other delivering women in her village do many a time and, as soon as it screamed, she rinsed it, then raised it and snipped the umbilical cord. In a split second, she had observed he was a boy. Already aware that has racial heritage would be of no assistance, she felt relieved that the roadmap of his life may be less hazardous than that of a girl. She straightened up, lay the baby down in an already prepared thicket of used bed-linen, and cleaned herself. She rolled up the bloodied mess in a torn piece of cloth, laid the bundle outside the door against a retaining wall, returned, and stretched out next to the baby, exhausted. She had done it all herself, without the assistance of a midwife or, for that matter, Agnes or the spirits.

Turning towards the baby, Rosita observed him closely. There was a slant in the shape of his eyes, even though they were closed, she figured, like her own indigenous ones. There was a distinct rise in the hill of his nose, she noted, revealing a strong Aztec influence. How strange, she thought, for his skin was not crinkled at all, as all babies' skins should be, and she realised that it had a translucence inherited from the father's Negro genes. The solid-textured skin glistened under the down that covered the newborn. He was going to be a very handsome man, she concluded. Smiling, she spread her right arm over him, drawing him in closer towards her. He smiled and chuckled, as yet unaware of the woes of the world, snuggled in the safety of his mother's bosom and enclosed in her arms.

She could not foresee his future but, as all mothers, she prayed that fate would smile upon him abundantly and endow him with its choicest blessings. She closed her eyelids and, on his behalf, uttered a short prayer to the Virgin of Guadalupe, whom she had never visited, but in whom she had been taught to repose her ultimate confidence. Fondly, she brought the baby closer towards herself. Involuntarily, the baby responded by moving his minuscule palm forward by just a millimetre, and grabbed her little finger. Impressed by this unexpected move, demonstrating firmness, if not telepathy, her maternal feelings for him surged. She enfolded him in her chest and, curling up, fell into a deep sleep. She did not even realise that the alert infant had groped for, and had found, her nipple and, in a moment, was content suckling his mother. From time to time, he gasped and smirked, making little noises, without in any way disturbing her deep sleep. The next day, Rosita would be up and gone to work as usual in Agnes' kitchen, tying Terrence in a piece of cloth and hanging him on her back. His spot would become a warm corner in the kitchen in her direct view, but away from the main household. When he was a bit older, Rosita stopped bringing him.

Terrence grew up protected from the outside world, in the extended backyard of the Goulds' hacienda, where Rosita had an adobe shack. She had avoided living inside the hacienda from the start in order to preserve her independence at the end of the long day and every third night she looked forward to the visit by the gardener. The location of her abode inside a thicket gave her considerable privacy and she cherished her own little world there. During the day, she could always steal a moment to run out and see Terrence. It was not as if Agnes ever rushed her, but Rosita herself took little time, her first focus being the large and growing household she was in charge of. Thus, Terrence grew up profoundly alone. Instead, Rosita's focus of attention was Patrick, making sure to respond to his every need. Though Terrence did not lack in being loved, his growth without education, a near illiterate, reflected how a menial parent could ill afford to take care of her own family even while caring for that of her employer.

Then, Patrick found Terrence and, from then on, Terrence's joy, sorrow, love, hatred, his very being, seemed increasingly to flow into Patrick's, perhaps even without the latter's full awareness, or his own, for that matter. Patrick himself responded to the extent that he could, accommodating Terrence amidst all his various activities and preoccupations, friends and Jolly, often sacrificing time that he would have preferred to spend with his little sister. It was not easy to include Terrence for, from that early day at the train station, he was aware that his relation with Terrence had better not be too pronounced for fear of society's, perhaps even his own family's to some extent at least, retribution. Thus, he could hardly take Terrence out to town in anticipation that they would be detected together by townsfolk. He was not even certain what the reaction of his classmates would be if they perceived a relation other than that of master-servant. His practical side, therefore, taught him to keep that relationship under wraps. This was fine with Terrence, since he had little interest in being with others. He was satisfied with Patrick's company and never indicated otherwise. Theirs just became an intertwined world of conviction and trust, a bond forged with few words, but rather with intuition and sensitivity. Terrence knew Patrick would appear at some point during the day, and Patrick's anxiety abated only after that meeting took place, even if for a fleeting moment.

\*　　\*　　\*

Today's particular encounter, as Patrick drove in in his father's truck, was not anticipated by Terrence, for he could not have expected Patrick to be driving. He had no reason to imagine all that had transpired, and that Patrick had made a U-turn after already driving forward for almost half an hour, assessing for a moment, and then ignoring, the loss of a crucial hour in his bolt from the grasp of the military as he finally took the risk just for Terrence. However, Patrick had sprung so many surprises on him in the past, taking him away here and there far beyond his expectations or imagination, or asking him seemingly unsolvable riddles that, when he eventually explained them, seemed so obvious yet intelligent, and his faith in Patrick was so profound that he did not flinch when

Patrick said, "Terry, I am going to Washington, the capital… You know… Perhaps for quite some time. I want you to come with me. Will you come?"

Looking up from the log of wood that he was diagnosing prior to undertaking an assigned task of chopping it, Terrence glanced at the truck. It did convey that the proposed journey was going to be long. As he rose, Patrick, who was well-aware of his own relatively diminutive figure, could not help but admire Terrence's physique though, as always, it was in passing. Like himself, Terrence, also eighteen, stood almost a head taller than Patrick and his muscles were well formed reflecting all the physical chores he was obliged to perform. He had turned into an exquisitely designed African-American Indian potpourri like those delectable racially amalgamated swimmers who can be seen on Ipanema Beach in Rio de Janeiro. Droplets of sweat hung on Terrence's forehead, which had sharp edges like the rest of his face. His jaw was pulled back somewhat, making his set of brilliant white teeth protrude just enough to reveal his African lineage. That, and his hair, which, though somewhat light, had a tell-tale curl, exposed his racial mix. He had a serious expression on his face. He nodded, murmuring, "Let me get my things." He looked around, searching. "Where is Mama?"

Patrick, with urgency in his voice, raised it somewhat. "There may be no time for that, Terry. You get your things – clothes and toilet things. That's all. I have food and money. Get me some paper. I shall explain to Rosita."

Terrence looked at Patrick blankly. Breaking the moment of silence, he went into the hut-like adobe structure behind him. He brought out a piece of blank rumpled paper and a pen with a half-broken nib with half-dried ink on it, and gave them to Patrick. He turned around and went back into the dark opening, as Patrick shook the pen for the ink to flow. He emerged before Patrick had completed writing, knowing that he should not ignore the hurry Patrick was in. Patrick was just finishing jotting down some random thoughts on paper as best he could scratch words onto it from the un-cooperating, blunt instrument.

He wrote in Spanish that he had learnt in a four-semester course in school, but using a pedestrian version that Rosita had often used with him from when he was a baby and that, without much ado, he had picked up along the way, and often used with her either in jest or when he was utterly serious.

*Querida* Rosita,

Terry *y yo vamos para* Washington, DC. *Es un secreto, nadie lo sabe excepto Mamá. Ella va a explicarte. Terry tampoco lo supo antes. Por favor no te pongas furiosa ni triste con él. No puedo ir sin él, por eso lo estoy llevando. Supongo que esto no la va a sorprender. Muéstrale esta carta y ella va a explicartelo todo. Te prometo lo cuidaré como siempre lo he hecho. Estaremos en* Washington *pronto. Ten paciencia hasta entonces.* Terry *esta escribiendo mas abajo.*
*Abrazos,*
Patrick.

Dear Rosita,

Terry and I are going to Washington DC. It is a secret. Nobody knows but Mama. She will tell you. Terry did not know either, so don't be angry or hurt. I cannot go without him, so I am taking him. Mama does not know that he is with me. So please tell her. I guess she should not be surprised. Show her this letter and she will explain everything. I promise to take care of Terry. We will get to Washington soon. Sit tight till then. Terry is writing below.
Hugs,
Patrick.

He looked at Terrence, who had a torn backpack thrown over his shoulder. He was staring back at Patrick. Whatever Terrence was thinking deep down was hidden from his face. Patrick thrust the paper to him and said, "Write."

He knew that it would take him time to form, on paper, the rounded bold letters, which he had tried to painstakingly teach him. He gave Terrence the time. Holding the pen askew to exhort the ink to continue to flow, Terrence wrote in large swaying letters, as if they had been randomly struck by a moving tornado, yet remaining on a continuous line.

> MAMA, GOODBYE FOR NOW ONLY. WE
> WILL MEET SOON. LOVE AND HUGS,
> MAMA. YOURS *EVER*, TERRENCE.

He added the '*EVER*' as an afterthought and seemed to be proud of it. Though the handwritings did not match, they left an indelible, individual mark of their bond, their trust, their dependence, on a piece of crumpled paper that would, many years later, and for some years to come, be hung in a somewhat gaudy gold frame, over a fireplace in Rosita's little living room in another continent, though who could anticipate what would transpire over time? Which human can foretell the travel of animate or inanimate objects through their lifetimes, objects that they may ephemerally possess or even create in a passing phase? The immediacy, the romance, of the moment and the force behind the blind mutual dependence would be lost; instead, the dominant weight of historical classification – that of a white master commandeering a black, presumed servant boy, on an uncertain road into the future – might prevail.

Terrence ran into the hut for one last time and left the note. When he came out, Patrick was already in the driver's seat. Terrence cranked the engine with the L-shaped starter and, with a 'hrrumphhh', the truck jerked to a start. As

Terrence climbed in next to him, Patrick looked reassured. His eyes glistened as he looked at Terrence.

"Everything will be all right, Terry, I promise."

Yet, he really did not need to say a word. Patrick's presence next to him was enough for Terrence. He did miss his mother but killed the thought and smiled. Then both looked straight ahead through the windshield with blurry eyes as their smiles vanished and, with a jolt, the truck moved forward. Terrence picked up all the packages that lay between Patrick and himself, and threw them carefully to the back. He moved a little bit closer in Patrick's direction, shook himself to ease his legs into his jeans, and settled in for the long ride.

Patrick kept his eyes fixed on the dusty road, which was dry from the lack of rain and bathed in strong sunlight. They drove into the grey-blue horizon, stopping only occasionally to fill the tank with fuel, take a bite from Agnes' carefully prepared supply of food, attend to nature's calls, and stretch their limbs by doing push-ups and freehand exercises. They were enjoying the ride and Patrick let Terrence manage the wheel only when they were in desolate areas, for he did not have a driver's license, and both knew that, until they got to Washington, there was no point in their trying to get a license for Terrence, for they would only have to answer questions and perhaps they would even be summarily separated if the slightest suspicion was aroused. They kept to themselves and, dusty and tired as they were by the time they reached Amarillo in the Texas Panhandle, Terrence had become as adept as Patrick at driving the ancient red truck that they began to call their 'Old Faithful'.

*     *     *

The boys lay side by side on the back of the truck that they had parked in the reddish rocky hills not far from Amarillo, afraid that it would be unsafe to sleep in town. Terrence had opened out the tarpaulin that was always kept in the open back to cover the produce from the country that the farmers filled the truck with whenever Patrick's father returned from the farms to the hacienda. They used their clothing bags as pillows. Still, they each needed to put the back of a hand under their heads to prop themselves up as Patrick explained the constellations to Terrence.

The sky twinkled with countless stars and they could see each other's silhouettes in their silver glow. There was no breeze, no rustle of leaves, and no movement of other earthly creatures. They smelt their sweat in the stillness of the night, but it was not unbearable, for they had long been used to each other's proximity. The heat ultimately forced them to take every vestige of clothing off except for their undershorts. Patrick was pointing to the stars. He taught Terrence to recognise Andromeda, a cluster of little stars like a diamond pendant, then Ursa Major and Ursa Minor, and all the others he recognised, saving his favorite, Orion, for last.

He whispered, pointing with the index finger of his outstretched right hand, "Look at the *Orion!* Isn't he a beauty? He is the knight in shining armour who guards the sky."

As Terrence raised his head further, as though that might help him see the constellation more easily, Patrick softly laughed.

"Can you see his broad shoulders? There... Yes, exactly. Look at his faintly shining belt and the stars that make his feet. Now, his head is *v-e-r-y* light. It is difficult to see, but it is there. If you crinkle your eyes, you'll see it. Yes? Or, no? Well, look carefully. That's it! Aaaaand, what about the dazzling sword? You cannot miss that!"

He directed Terrence's head in different directions, cupping it in his left palm and lolling it around. In the dark, Terrence shut his eyes, the soothing sensation of his head's movements overcoming him momentarily. Satisfied with himself, Patrick fell back on his pillow, smiling at the success of his enterprise. Terrence followed the trajectory of Patrick's right hand as it glided from the sky to complete the cup that his left had formed. Firmly gripping the globe of Terrence's head, he peered into it.

Terrence blurted, "Pat, *I* am your *Orion*. Will you be *mine*?" Then he stared back at the sky. It was unlike anything he had ever said before, but the words just poured out as if they were something he had felt forever, just waiting to be formed into words.

"Yes, when we are in Washington, we have to guard each other. We have to look out for each other."

"How? Sometimes I feel you are not...."

"What?"

"...Serious."

"In Washington, we can do everything. I want to go to university and I can teach you everything I learn there. I will write to Dad to help me with admission. He will understand once Mama tells him. If I can also work, and you can take up a job too, we can save some. You, too, could go to Howard University then. Maybe not right away. You have to learn a lot more before you could do that, you know. However, you *can* soon, I am sure. And, when you get out from there with a college degree, you will be my partner in making this world less bitter. Brother Rinaldi used to talk about it all. And we will meet girls with big breasts...." He mimed a pair of breasts over his chest with the backside of his palms. "And..."

"When are we going back, Pat?"

"Uff, Terry, I don't know; don't ask me *that*!" As he heard Terrence quiver a little, he added, "Aw, come closer now. You are sometimes *childish*." Then, tenderly, he said, "Come on, come closer, I told you, didn't I? I will take care of you." As though to reassure himself, he further added, "Yes, Sir, I will. Don't you worry about it."

Terrence did not reply in words. He turned over to the other side, as though pouting, curling himself into a foetal position. Perhaps his deep thoughts, his fears, were at last overcoming him. Patrick looked at him askance, made a face in the dark that nobody could see, turned in his direction and engulfed Terrence like he was a side pillow, burying his own hidden fears in this half embrace. Terrence snuggled backwards into Patrick; his acceptance was total, as always, and his being flowed into him. They fell asleep. If the stars could see, they would behold two young bodies basted in a question mark, untested lives lying on a bed of sheer anticipation.

As the boys slept, the stars danced joyfully, for how often did they witness such total sharing, such absolute oneness? In merry ecstasy, a shooting star defied the forces of gravity and broke rank to move erratically, with lightning speed, over the boys, to take a first-hand look at this idyllic view of a valiant pair on the verge of adventure. It did not care that, soon thereafter, it would itself disappear into oblivion, and it did, unbeknownst to the exhausted, softly snoring boys who had, an instant earlier, gazed at the stars in utter awe. A virtuous circle of admiration, humans for stars, stars for humans, was completed in a rare dance of nature, unique and unobserved on a little hillside in the far reaches of rural Texas.

Daybreak came, and the silence of night was broken by the chirping of birds and the sound of water from a nearby brook. The sun's accelerating force suddenly gobbled up the intimacy of darkness. Together the boys jumped up and out of the truck, and ran towards the sound of gurgling water. Hurriedly, they washed themselves, ran back for the soap, for this was the first time they had had the opportunity to have a long, full and private bath. They took off their shorts and dove into the running water of a pristine stream nestled in the depths of a hollow within the rocks, hidden in a cluster of tall tropical trees that the humidity brought on by the water had helped grow over eons. They wrestled and sank, floated up and swam, for a long time. The sun shone on them. The broad green leaves rustled, helped by a steady, cool breeze. Their dry, parched skins felt moist once again, and they lost track of time.

Eventually, they left the water. They reluctantly washed the clothes they had worn till then against the rocks on the bank. They dried themselves, putting on fresh clothes from their backpacks. They just threw back their hair without bothering to dry it fully or to comb it. Suddenly aware of the increasing heat and the possibility of encroaching humans, they rushed back to the truck, lay out the washed clothes, dug into the fast-disappearing supply of fruit, grabbed whatever emerged first, and took bites from the same. Patrick cranked the machine and jumped in, and Terrence pressed on the accelerator. They were once again heading to Washington with a resolute conviction. They drove as quickly, yet as clandestinely, as they could, heading to the north and east through the forbidden Southern states.

*　　*　　*

Patrick continued on a predictable path of personal growth during the time between Amarillo and Washington. He had already seen a bit of the world, though mainly Texas, travelling with his parents now and then, and had had the curiosity to read travelogues and the good fortune of hearing many an adventure story, albeit often exaggerated, from the friars. Terrence had had none of that. Something opened in him now. It was as though he was on a turnpike rather than a regular highway. Maturing rapidly, he seemed almost to overtake Patrick, apropos of the race that gave him superior physical height and attributes over Patrick. He quickly observed that there was a vast world beyond his adobe hut and the backyard of the hacienda. He reflectively learnt to scrutinise the world around himself, and seemed to comprehend it well. Soon, Patrick found himself seeking Terrence's advice on many matters that faced them on their way.

Terrence made it a point to drive on as much as possible during the night since, often during the day, it was not judicious for him to drive except when they hit a really desolate area. However, while he well understood the benefit of reaching Washington as quickly as possible based on Patrick's plans, he suggested to Patrick that they might drive through New Orleans, for he had heard from Patrick about the mix of cultures, the blacks playing soul music and strumming their violas in Preservation Hall, the strolling whites dressed in antique European fashions, whispering in a French accent, the seafood cuisine of the well-to-do and the equally flavourful gumbo from slave times.

Though Patrick readily agreed to take the detour, despite the fact that they would have to turn southwards to go to New Orleans, he was apprehensive about the stance of the state on matters of race. He wondered why, despite the mix of races and cultures there, Louisiana defined you to be a Negro if one of your great-grandparents was African-American, even if all other ancestors were white! This translated, according to his calculation, as having 1/132 part black blood in you. Indeed, on the one hand, he was amused at the world's finesse in distinguishing and drawing up categories and, on the other, he was intelligent enough to consider it a matter not to be taken lightly when encountering their inventors.

Many years later, Patrick remembered his New Orleans stop as mainly one in which he saw other women with flaming-red hair on the streets of the French Quarter, who would beckon to him with voluptuous, bulbous breasts protruding from under tight brassieres. His mind had floated to Jolly's mother, to her calling out, 'Jolie! Jolie!' as she glided across the bay window of that little frame house. He had wondered if she, too, came from there and from that background. Thinking about this gave him an erection though he quickly killed the thought, focussing only on Jolly. His heart pounded softly for her touch. Later, he would sometimes ponder both those bits of memory, but would never have the occasion to tell Jolly about the tussle between his attraction for her and his strange infatuation for her flaming-red-haired mother. Nevertheless, the confusion always remained within him, unspoken, unresolved, cherished and hidden.

Terrence took to New Orleans like fish to water. He ran in and out of Preservation Hall, forging an instant affinity to jazz, the blood of his paternal forefathers that flowed through him invoking ancient pain-filled tunes that merged with the sounds created by the musicians who faced him. He gulped down bowls of gumbo and platefuls of pure soul food that his Mexican mother had failed to feed him and of the existence of which he had been oblivious. At night, he dragged Patrick to the black quarter of the city on a streetcar in order to be in the company of other men and women who looked more like him and did not seem to mind or care about Patrick's unexpected presence. They tasted full bodied beers there, quite different from the aromatic wines abundant in the French Quarter, in a bar that greeted customers with a faint fluorescent light in the shape of a coconut tree that announced, 'Paree'! They feasted their eyes on their peers. Terrence looked at the men and the boys, the women and the girls. Patrick looked straight at black men for the first time. Wow! They were muscular, tall and slick, with varying African to European faces; most were exquisitely handsome and attractive. He experienced the same sensation as when he had felt compelled to look for the Catholic Brother and ogle at him, at least from a distance, before he went home at the end of every school day. Embarrassed, yet unwilling to sacrifice the delightful feeling, his eyes would turn to Terrence, looking at him with a similar appreciation, if not admiration.

Patrick sipped beer until he was a bit drunk, safe in the thought that Terrence would transport him back to their little hotel room in the French Quarter, where a branch from a magnolia tree edging in from the balcony filled the room with a strong, sweet, summer scent, causing him to fall asleep instantly. He slept shaped as an arc, with Terrence gradually enveloping him as the still, hot night progressed with the passage of the moon. The full moon danced in a fox trot with passing, nimbus clouds, delighted at their changing shapes. It seemed content, just as the shooting star had made an exuberant dive in observance of the boys' silent felicity not that long ago. They had nature's blessings.

Their break in New Orleans was short. In a few days, they started to look at each other as though in recognition of a lurking urgency. One morning, as they were getting out for the day, Patrick suggested in the little lobby of the hotel, "Terry, shall we start first thing tomorrow morning?"

Terrence replied casually in his newfound confidence, "Why not tonight, Pat? Then I could drive."

Patrick looked doubtful, but did not protest. He had learnt to value Terrence's views and ability to assess situations. He responded in mock obedience, "Yes, Sirrr. Why not? So *you* drive."

Terrence smiled at the prospect. Then he turned towards Patrick and asked, "Pat, why don't you write a letter to your dad?"

Patrick had not really thought about it, but reflected on the idea now. He could write a short one at least, to counter his dad's presumed and certain shock at the unanticipated departure of his son.

"However, what about stamps?" he asked in a reflex reaction to the proposition.

Terrence said, "Remember yesterday when we were at the river and I disappeared while you were gazing at the ships? I went into the post office at the port and got some stamps, and also stamped envelopes in case we needed some." Looking at Patrick's astonished face, he continued, "It was easy, really. I just went in and got it with the leftover change I had in my pocket from the bar last night. There were all these men, port labourers, I think, many wearing the same uniforms, who were sitting there taking a break and sipping chicory coffee.

They offered me some, too, and I took some. It was great." As Patrick's face clouded with alarm, Terrence quickly added, "No one asked questions."

Patrick questioned rhetorically, "*No one* asked *questions*? Terry, you are not supposed to disappear like that in the first place. What if someone lynched you? I would never know anything. *Don't* pull that on me ever again." Patrick looked, and was, furious.

"Well, I did not have to *say* much. A curious guy did try to start a conversation and said to me, 'Boy, do *you* have an accent', and gave a throaty laugh, and every one heartily joined in. I just said, 'Yes, Sir' and took another sip of that chicory. Then they forgot about it."

Patrick looked away to hide the colour he felt rising on his face, but Terrence went on enthusiastically, "This way, when we reach Washington, your dad's reply would be already waiting for us. See?"

Patrick looked at Terrence with incomprehension. Had all his transfer of information and training gone totally to waste, he wondered.

"Really, Terry, sometimes ..." He trailed off and, then, with energised incredulity, carried on, "We do not know Washington. We have no address there. Sometimes I get worried, Terry. Like, where do you think we are going to in Washington? A hotel suite?"

Now, frustration rising and eyes fogging up, he uttered in a low voice, "And yesterday, I was *not* staring at those ships just like that. I was not dreaming or anything. My mind was on us, on what we are doing here, what we will do, and how I will take care of us. I am your *Orion*, remember?" Then Patrick made a diabolical face, and almost screamed, "*Ain't* I?" He was somewhat taken aback at his own rage, never having experienced its intensity before, and certainly not towards Terrence.

Terrence remained calm, though shocked at Patrick's explosion, an act he had never before witnessed. Strangely, for the first time ever, he saw that Patrick was helpless and that Patrick needed him. He felt he was Patrick's equal, yet in control, on top. Yes, he could be Patrick's partner. He had never expected that the realization would come to him in this peculiar way, at that particular moment. To hide his feeling, he asked almost jocularly, "What is a hotel *sweet*?" He truly had no idea, imagining in his mind's eye that it might be a woman in a provocative dress or something. Not really expecting an answer, he instead said rather matter-of-factly, "Didn't you tell me that you would ask your dad to help you get admitted to Georgetown? I thought you could tell him to reply to you to the address of that school. Isn't there a headmaster or something, like the one in your school back home? Maybe your dad could write there?"

Then he fell silent.

Patrick was not happy to be reminded of the torturer in his past life and the fountainhead of his present fate. However, that thought lingered but a moment, for the next moment he was overcome with amazement. He could not fathom the depth of Terrence's innate intelligence, now in full bloom once it had been given the opportunity to blossom. His anger dissolved instantly. Rising and immediately falling temper would soon become a well-known hallmark of his otherwise-temperate nature, perhaps born out of the combination of his chosen life of adventure and anxiety on the one hand, and his inborn careful nature that was averse to risk and uncertainty on the other.

Patrick put his arm on Terrence's shoulder, and they walked back to their room. There, Patrick pulled Terrence towards him and gave him a bear hug. However, he did not leave him. Terrence stood still for a moment and then relaxed. He did not say anything.

Patrick whispered, "That's a great idea, Terry. I can tell Dad to write to me care of the Georgetown University president's office. He could also perhaps ask him to give me an admissions test." After a moment of silence, he said, "I am *so* sorry, Terry."

"For what? It just occurred to me, that's all. You could have thought about it too, had you not been *daydreaming* at the river!"

As a smiling Patrick raised his hand in mock attack, Terrence, too, pretended to move away, but instead they fell back into their embrace. Terrence sighed, feeling Patrick deep inside him. It was as if their contract had just been sealed. Yes, he knew now. He *could* be Patrick's Orion too. They stayed that way till Terrence slid out to get the envelope he had left on the table and to take out the rough paper and the lead pencil he had already found in the table drawer.

The letter was written. Patrick read it out loud. Terrence's suggestions to write two letters, one to his father and one by his father to the president of the university, were fully accepted. In addition, a few insertions of a practical nature – for some extra money if possible, for any guidance on where they could stay; for example, could Bishop Uncle recommend a hostel for Catholic boys or, since they were together and even Washington might not easily facilitate their living in the same hostel, perhaps a little studio somewhere – were all heeded. It was as though Terrence was in charge of Patrick's thought process.

Only at the end, Patrick added in all by himself:

> I miss Mom very much. Tell Rosita that Terrence says he misses her terribly too. All my regards to you, Dad.
>
> Your son, always,
> Patrick Gould.

Then, inexplicably, he added after Gould, 'Washington'.

Immediately, he regretted his impetuousness and wanted to erase it. However, since there was no eraser at the end of the pencil, he reluctantly had to leave in the word 'Washington'. Terrence looked at him quizzically, but said nothing further.

The letter was posted in the square, blue letter box at the corner of Prince Street as they went out for their last day in New Orleans. They went to visit the cemetery, where all the coffins were above ground and were laden with beautiful, occasionally shocking, sculptures. They spent most of their time there, sometimes shoulder to shoulder, sometimes, without even realising, fingers entwined, for such was their oneness, as they gaped at the ornate, classical, erotic works of many an unknown artist. Eventually, they hurried back to the ramshackle hotel and packed up their few belongings. That evening, as the summer sun went down and dusk brought on the expectation of another rambunctious, lusty night upon New Orleans, they were on the road out of the magnificent, swarthy city in which they had so celebrated their being together the last few nights and that would forever remain their dream locale. They dreamt of escaping there together, hidden from the rest of the world, including even their own families, for they were their own knights in shining armour and nothing else mattered.

*       *       *

As they passed through Alabama, Patrick became anxious. He was aware the state's official position decreed the separation of races, that its constitution specified that 'the legislature shall never pass any law to authorize or legalize any marriage between any white person and a Negro'. When they approached a town, Patrick would wonder out loud, "Should we go through town or skirt it? What if there is no rubble road?

Amused at having to use his father's dialect, and throwing a smile in Patrick's direction at the same time, Terrence would reply, "Go through them Negro areas. No trouble if they see us there."

met him in Parthenope, which he, too, was passing through in
his quest for antiquity, an old British pastime of the genuinely
upper classes. Exquisitely handsome, and sweating in a tight
English army uniform under the armpits, she instantly found
herself overwhelmingly attracted to him. He, too, was taken
by her beguiling Southern charm, bedecked with the excesses
of American landowners. Upon return, she made her father
sponsor him for a visit, and he responded as another war
reared its inevitable head. Characteristically, though, the
upper-class Englishman turned out to be rather asexual and,
after the initial attempts, lost interest in sex and, yet after the
medical tests, in fathering a child. In fact, at one point, he
told his wife that he had become tired of their nightly antics
and their sloppy, smelly consequences. She was so horrified
that she never approached him for sex again and, searching
elsewhere for involvement, step by step, took over the reins of
the Ladies' Society Club with single-minded determination.
This was enough to keep her involved over and above the
daily preoccupations regarding the affairs of the estate and to
ensure that it was run with probity and without scandal from
the thirty or so Negroes who still worked on, and inhabited, it.

The Englishman preferred helping out on the estate more
than performing any nocturnal duties. In fact, he had taken
to Georgia like a bull in a china shop. A true colonial civil
servant at heart and in action, he kept sturdy control over the
descendants of ex-slaves and indentured servants, keeping
them at a distance, but with a fair wage plus a small, but never
forgotten, annual bonus based on the estate's returns from
their toil in the hot, sun-soaked cotton fields. Though this
bothered the other landowners, they never had the gall to
oppose an Englishman, who, based on his distant manner and
clipped accent, they presumed to carry blue blood. Further,
they all wanted to join his 'club', which he established over a
huge plot of land, in parallel to the already existing Ladies'
Society Club, with many sports facilities, including a strange,

slow exercise called croquet, and with food served by gloved black hands, and into which membership was craved, but sparingly handed out. Membership was based on a test called 'At Home', in which aspirants came appropriately suited and booted, and had to converse over cocktails with a select group of club trustees who pretended to have just dropped by. All the while this group examined their every move and tone of voice, their words and views during conversation under a magnifying glass as it were. They then retreated to the smoking room and, by the time they emerged, they had ready a short list of new members. The list had an instant effect of elevating their stature in local society. Though wives were allowed in the ballroom and dining room, they were banned from the smoking room where the men retired to smoke cigars after dinner. After its fireplace had been lighted by the black head butler, separation marked the rest of the night between the listless men and their chattering women, who were taken home in their carriages. The bonhomie that ensued among the men needed never to be explained to their spouses the next morning or at church or to the wider reaches of society. They learnt to form themselves, under the leader's guidance, into a group called the Freemasons that he had already been familiar with during his earlier, occasional journeys through the Middle East.

Needless to overemphasise, the couple became stalwarts of the estate community, he with his implacable English manners and accent, and she with her nose in its every aspect while maintaining, with an outcome that imparted sincerity, her marked Georgian drawl that she never felt influenced to give up. Then the field hands began to leave for the North in droves because of the rapidity in the incidence of random atrocities perpetrated by the newly vengeful Ku Klux Klan as the Civil Rights movement became increasingly visible. Slowly, the pair gave up cotton production and focussed relentlessly on their respective clubs. They never felt the want of money, for he had always been a good manager and, when he died, he left her a wealthy woman, not needing to survive just on the clout of her favoured class. The superior power of wealth, and of the Southern warmth that had never left her, added to her individual stature that remained intact. This freedom allowed her to do pretty much as she pleased, including doting on a white boy and tending to his Negro companion. When the boys left, Terrence heaved a sigh of relief at his release from a white woman's villa and her attentions.

Terrence and Patrick's flight through the Carolinas went off remarkably uneventfully. They moved only at night and hid in the rushes and marshy areas during day. They never went hungry owing to Terrence's skills at hunting fish with self-made wooden harpoons or with their bare hands in the fresh backwater areas. All they had to do sometimes was to wade their hands in underwater and fish would nestle in their palms. They learnt to identify edible plants, though once Patrick ate something even more poisonous than poison ivy, since he almost went into fits, followed by stomach cramps. That was the only time Terrence had felt completely helpless, cried, and had positioned himself in a prayerful position looking towards the skies. Then he found it stupid and selfish, telling himself, even if there was a God, why would he give Terrence any special dispensation or attention to solve his personal problems? He snapped out of his self-pity and tried to solve the problem through remembering better what his father had told him.

Terrence's gardener dad had told him that, in any forest, if there is a poisonous plant, there is an antidote near it. Terrence began to pluck, paste and pour different mixtures into Patrick's mouth. The third or the fourth worked, and Patrick stopped convulsing. He came through.

He survived without any divine intervention.

Terrence raised Patrick up and held him close. "Never do that to me again," he pleaded and warned, as Patrick partially opened his eyes and gazed at Terrence in gratitude. As he shut his eyes again and seemed to collapse in a repeat performance, Terrence gave him mouth-to-mouth resuscitation in an involuntary act, knowing that he had to do whatever he could to save him. Not that he had had any training. He automatically bent to do this. It was just that he felt that Patrick needed to be revived with fresh and renewed breath that he could not muster from within himself. As Patrick revived, he was affected by an unflinching memory of Terrence close to him, trying to revive him, his breath on him, and in him. Terrence forever remembered his relief when Patrick revived the second time and he would not release him. He held him close, pressed on him hard, and forced his eyes to blink.

Once in West Virginia, they were invited in by a coalminer's family. The couple slept in one room. Their eleven children, aged seventeen to two, slept in the living room. Terrence and Patrick were given the barn. They went straight for the hay. Patrick felt no discomfort with such a large brood. Terrence could not sleep that night, unable to trust the motive of the white folk in letting them in. At first, he was a bit annoyed with Patrick's acceptance of the offer when the man found them by chance inside the entrance of an abandoned coalmine where he went regularly because he could still find enough charcoal for his own household needs. He found the two boys, felt pity for the strange combination, and asked them to come home. Terrence did not realise that material poverty sometimes bonded well with aversion to inequalities, allowing for an appreciation of others' circumstances, and the ability to annul manmade differences. By the following morning, as they shared a simple breakfast of porridge with the family, Terrence realised that he was included because of Patrick, that he could never be accepted by the family on his own. Nevertheless, the very fact that he was sitting at the same table as they made him realise that he should not homogenize the social attitudes of all white folk into one common denominator. He concluded spontaneously that they were all different, quite heterogeneous in their attitudes and views.

He was all the more incredulous when Agnes told him of the circumstances, that the headmaster was trying to send Patrick into the army, possibly suborning recruiters. He dashed to the school and confronted the headmaster. The latter's mouth fell open, though nobody could tell whether from discovery of true intent or from disbelief at such an improbable story. The mystery was never resolved since, after making the accusation, Patrick's father darted out before the headmaster could speak. Because he was convinced that the obese giant had played a trick upon the family, despite their polite and careful attention to his culinary desires, and sometimes, quietly, even his financial needs, Patrick's father vowed to avenge the family's honour through the intervention of his cousin, the Bishop.

In two months, the headmaster was transferred to a one-room school in El Paso. The school had an asbestos roof and small windows, inadequately protected with cracked or broken glass panes, and its pupils came from recently converted Negro and regular Catholic Hispanic servant families; some were illegal immigrants. Meanwhile, in San Antonio, Brother Rinaldi was made a full-fledged priest, was called Father, and named the new headmaster. With his highly honed intellectual skills, Patrick's school flourished, and wealthy, upper-class Catholic boys from as far away as Boston and Rochester, including a Gould, were soon seen studying alongside local Texan boys.

Father Rinaldi and Patrick's classmates proceeded to turn Patrick into a virtual legend, with real and imagined storytelling about his achievements and conquests. The ex-headmaster was never mentioned again in school or at the Goulds', even though it was whispered that he took soon to alcohol and went to naught, unable to bear his disgrace. Apparently, he ended up in Lubbock where he was seen to discard his black robe and take up twenty-four-hour residence in a downtown bar, until he was ultimately thrown out and into a home for the destitute when the bar owner's empathy for the perennially inebriated ex-priest ran out.

Gradually and without recognising it as such, Patrick's father felt calm. It was also that Patrick's absence finally made him more certain of his wife's somewhat rejuvenated attention. He grew closer to her than they had been in a long time. Agnes, too, made space for him, and her fixation on her firstborn was now smoothed over in equal, or almost equal, measure for her husband and daughter. At the beginning, the little girl missed her older brother terribly. Although she occasionally talked with him on the phone and he certainly wrote her interesting, albeit short, letters, he became a sweet memory for his sister.

Agnes herself could never forgive Patrick for not taking her into his confidence early enough. Being a Sagittarian and, therefore, of a cool and balanced nature, the more she pondered the matter, the more she doubted that such an exit could be precipitated at the spur of a moment. While she never stopped admiring him in a rather circumspect way, there had, indeed, been a parting of ways, a separation of their souls. Strange how time and distance possess the power to diminish even the strongest of bonds, subjecting the ordinary mortal to the ephemeral nature of feelings.

\*    \*    \*

Neither could Agnes forgive Patrick for the anguish he had caused to Terrence's parents, more so than what he had caused his own. That scene visited and revisited her time and again, day in and day out, in waking hours and in dreams. When Rosita ran into the hacienda, swaying and flapping a piece of crumpled paper in a raised hand that was swinging wildly, Agnes read it through Rosita's wails. Nevertheless, both could not help but heave a sigh of relief that the boys were together. Agnes, in an exception, poured some cognac for her Latina maid, who calmed down almost immediately and asked for just a bit more. Jesse was called in and, as he stood near a wooden pillar in the courtyard just outside the family room, Agnes brought him cognac in a taller glass. He also wanted more and his wish was willingly granted. The father remained silent, all words arrested in the depth of his belly.

Agnes, trying to muster a stern yet compassionate tone, cajoled Rosita, "You know, Rosie, I did not know about this. I mean, that Terrence was gone too. The two boys *were* always close, but I really did not think...." She trailed off.

Rosita just nodded vigorously as a cascade of tears dropped directly from her downcast eyes onto the floor.

Agnes added, "Rosie, I know my Patrick. If he took Terrence, he will look after him."

Rosita nodded vigorously again.

Jesse, holding a folded cloth hat, was wringing his hands. There was silence now.

He had been staring at the floor, with consternation written all over his face. He now came forward gingerly, put his arm on Rosita's shoulder and embarrassed her by giving her a firm, comforting hug that brought her close to him. Still silent, he tried not to move so Rosita felt the assurance of his firm chest to cry her heart out. She reclined her exhausted body against the solid rock of his six pack and they left silently. Agnes saw them turn through the outside door to her momentary relief. Rosita's gasps through spurts of sobbing could be heard as they moved outside.

Patrick's parents felt that he would be safer with a companion, even though Terrence was of mixed race. Nevertheless, they were concerned as to how their son, no, the two boys, so different from each other, would survive travelling together. Mr. and Mrs. Gould waited day and night for some news and felt optimistic that information would come sooner rather than later. As they waited, the softness in

Patrick's father took over completely and he was ready to do anything to make up for what he discovered to be precious lost time with his son, the would-be carrier of his name, the family name.

Thus, when the letter arrived and he opened it, he gave out a reverberating cry of pure joy. The families gathered around him. After receiving the happy breaking news, they departed much relieved. Even though he noted the word 'Washington' after Patrick's name, he ignored it, interpreting it as 'Patrick Gould (soon to be in) Washington', perhaps as the inadvertent exclusion of a phrase by a child in a hurry, running and in desperation. However, Agnes exulted in its significance, her anticipation of Patrick's future in a new, non-Southern world now confirmed.

Within a couple of days, he had made all arrangements that Patrick had asked for and more to cover Terrence, too. Agnes basked in the success of spot decision-making in support of her son, for she was certain that his breaking into Washington would open a destiny that none of them could possibly foresee. Even though she often missed him terribly, she made it her business to focus on the rest of the family now, for she told herself that, if she trusted fate, fate would take care of Patrick.

Rosita did not fully believe that all was well, but Jesse tried to convince her to the contrary. Having nothing else to fall back on, he said, "They, too, are missing their son."

Rosita shot back, "However, they have another baby!"

Quickly, she retracted by reassuring herself that perhaps Terrence would be better off, after all, away from San Antonio and in the national capital where, she was told by Agnes, there were many of his kind who had good jobs and responsibilities. Agnes did not elaborate on how segregated Washington was, first, because she could not alarm Rosita any further and, second, she could never have imagined its preciseness – that the White House was the centre of the quadrangles for the city's unmarked, yet indelible, dividing line for races. Thus, despite new laws forbidding racial divides, 16th Street N.W. (for north-west), the street traversing north-south from the White House north to the Maryland border, effectively divided the west for whites from the east which was for blacks, as did Pennsylvania Avenue N.W., the road that went diagonally east-west from the White House, the west and north being for whites, and the east and south for blacks. San Antonio was too far from Washington for her to fathom the precision with which the streets of Washington demarcated race. Her overall assessment was based on television coverage of the race riots after the assassination of Martin Luther King, Junior and the reported progress thereafter. She possessed little knowledge of the virulence of the separation of daily social lives of whites from blacks in the capital city that continued unaffected and untouched by the recent events.

When Patrick and Terrence reached Washington, they felt relieved for having left the southern states behind. Even though there was nobody waiting to receive them, the letter they had hoped for was awaiting their arrival. There was amicable news for Patrick as he entered the office of the president of the university. In lieu of formal high school matriculation, he would have to quickly take a series of out of school high school tests that he passed without any difficulty. From the moment he received an equivalence certificate, everything fell into place. He soon passed the university's placement test with flying colours. And once he was settled into university, Patrick told himself, he would be able to address and resolve Terrence's status, and he did.

# Book II

# Jolts in Washington

The Vietnam War had consumed the nation and had had a vicious impact also on much of the rest of the world. Opposition to the war gave rise to intense anti-American feelings amongst students in Paris. There were many student demonstrations against the US involvement in Vietnam. The students were protesting against authority, especially the Ministry of Education, the most famous graffiti perhaps being, 'I participate; he participates; she participates; they decide'. The students were joined in some part by factory workers, though the alliance between the students and the factory workers proved weak, mainly reflecting the students' arrogance and disdain for the workers. The students came from the middle and upper classes, were 'champagne communists', and looked down upon the workers from a great height of privilege and luxury. Nevertheless, this strange alliance led to the most violent demonstrations in early May 1968. The entire 'uprising' was put down by President De Gaulle and his government on May 10. There were no deaths, though there was much physical damage in the Latin Quarter. The general population sided with the government, owing to their fear of anarchy.

A rarefied American would argue among his college mates that little better could be expected from a people who had given their highest civilian honour to the American comedian, Jerry Lewis. To the typical American intellectual, it was beyond comprehension that the French could view so highly Mr. Lewis' mediocre acting and comedic pranks! If the granting of this honour was interpreted in its appropriate light, it became immediately apparent to them that the French were perennially quite adept at America bashing or using the Americans for sheer amusement.

While Patrick also could not understand the popularity of Jerry Lewis among the French, let alone his receiving the Légion d'honneur award, and distanced himself from their silliness, he nevertheless found himself sympathizing with the French in terms of their antipathy to the US involvement in Vietnam. He easily accepted and embraced the idea of insidious US tentacles in the affairs of Vietnam, rushing into the region after the French had lost their ex-colony. Certainly, Vietnam was a cause for which he was unwilling to sacrifice his own life, and his conclusions were based not just on popular mumbo jumbo, but were the outcome of in-depth research he made at the Georgetown University library on the history of the protracted rise of Leftist movements across the world.

Patrick's curiosity, after reading and researching the Sandinistas in Nicaragua, the FARC in Colombia, the Shining Path in Peru, and the more politically sophisticated, Westernized movement in Chile, ultimately directed him to an obscure peasant revolt in Naxalbari in the far northern reaches of Bengal in the cradle of the Himalayan ranges in eastern India that his father had mentioned in the context of a generally unreported famine during the Second World War. It had been caused by the policies of its ex-colonial masters, the British, led by their prime minister and popularly known war hero, Winston Churchill. Their objective had been to safeguard the grains supplied from that region for British soldiers, despite the local residents' likely, and actual, resultant deprivation of food. Millions perished. They died in hoards even on the streets of Calcutta. Yet their story had not found a mention in the annals of history, leave alone in popular folklore. Only with the passage of time, half a century later, when it had become acceptable, nay, fashionable to investigate forgotten matters bordering on genocide, would historians and Nobel laureates publish their research on this nugget of history.

Sadly, the overall economic condition of the rural poor of the region did not improve much even after India's independence, leading some tea garden *sic.* plantation labourers in the area to round up their professional manager and slaughter him. Patrick had just completed an article on the movement and, peering into the *Oxford Atlas of the World*, since he had no idea where Naxalbari was exactly located, found it to be located in a remote district near Darjeeling – an area that is universally familiar, perhaps famous, for its tea. He let his imagination fly at the depth of the plight of the indigenous workers in a tea garden that could have led them to chop up the estate manager in defiance of, and to express their frustration over, their intolerable prevailing economic condition.

The Naxalbari incident had generated a momentum among local university students and had become a 'movement'. Its leaders had taken on a Marxist-Leninist doctrine, whatever that might now represent in the aftermath of China's Cultural Revolution when the Yang Tse and Huang Ho rivers had turned red with the blood of the slaughtered population – elite and common folk alike – the aftermath of a state-sponsored and encouraged homicidal hysteria, if not insanity. Son accused parents, wife accused husband, brother accused sister, neighbour accused neighbour, and strangers accused strangers

of imagined atrocities and caused their deaths in the name of
societal cleansing encouraged by Mao Tse Tung and his yeah-
sayers that, in hindsight, never achieved any objectives other
than to create a reign of terror and rivers of human blood.
That free-for-all had to be presently replicated everywhere
else, for the good word of a fresh start that mass murder
would allegedly make possible had spread far and wide. With
China as backdrop, and United States striking Vietnam with
napalm and chemical weapons not so many years after having
used nuclear weapons on Japan, the Naxalites, like so many
other extreme Left movements, were easily gaining strength
among the people as they put forward Marxist Leninism as
the alternate, natural, better, and only, just order for society.
Patrick understood. Perhaps to some extent, despite, or in
reaction to, his bourgeois and privileged family background,
he even bought their logic.

As though Calcutta did not already have its innate problems,
it was now infested with bands of wayward brilliant young
students who, until recently, were interested in discussing
Sartre, Camus, Genet, Pirandello, Brecht and Dostoevsky
or the Theory of Limits or of Relativity over endless cups
of tea and coffee in local cafés. Now, these youngsters were
suddenly roaming the neighbourhoods and slaughtering their
peers from rival political spectra in cruel, murderous urban
guerrilla warfare. The local police had been mobilized in
full force to carry out counter-ambushes to bring back some
cohesiveness to Calcutta's dimly lit streets, home to thousands
who depended on them for a peaceful few hours at night
before their daily toil began the next morning in an endless
cycle of perfunctory, yet preciously guarded, and not-to-be-
abandoned, set of chores, eking out their precarious lives. Oh!
There were so many corners of the world where Vietnam had
aroused the basic instincts of their otherwise-docile denizens
who until now resided cosily in their abodes, oblivious to their
own governments' inane formulations or ruthless applications

of dark policies that had imperceptibly engulfed the world in all their phantom guises. Or so concluded Patrick in his youthful sincerity.

Patrick pondered the possibility of writing on the Naxals for his thesis, linking them to the fallout from Vietnam. It did not quite occur to him that his professor at the School of International Studies, which was famous for its conservative views, might not fully, or even partially, be able to appreciate this connection. Patrick was just working out the arguments in his mind, forming his deepest thoughts. He smiled at his own dexterity in designing fine links that steadily crystallized in his mind.

\*     \*     \*

However, something far from the intellectualism of global Left movements had gripped Patrick all day. That morning at the library, he had, as usual, picked up the *Washington Post*, the *New York Times*, the *Miami Herald* and the *Christian Science Monitor* one by one, scouring them for news without much success to hold his attention. Suddenly, he came across an article on so-called *snuff* movies. Apparently, these movies showed vivisection of live humans. The rumour was that they emanated from the deep interiors of Brazil, areas that were impossible for the authorities to successfully penetrate, leave alone monitor, and there was a growing demand for those movies from the more 'advanced' societies. Patrick was a bit out of breath reading the article. He could not put the matter out of his mind all day.

Upon return home from the university and dropping off his backpack, Patrick headed straight for the neighbourhood video store to check if it carried snuff movies. He felt awkward to utter the word, but had to do so. He was somewhat surprised that, without blinking an eye or batting an eyelid, the man at the counter simply reached down and brought out a video. He said that the charge was going at double the usual rate due to very high demand. Patrick quickly complied and brought it home. He felt a bit guilty that he was doing this behind Terry's back. Yet he was somewhat relieved, even relaxed, knowing that Terry would not return home for some time. While he felt uncomfortable at the very thought of what might unfold before him, he could not contain his curiosity. He slid the video into the VCR and waited.

*A voluptuous woman is picked up, without any seeming coercion, by two scruffy looking men from under a dirt-packed urban flyover. They drive their car into what could have been the Amazon Forest, or might not have been. That depended on the viewer's imagination. So far, all well. The next scene is inside a room. The woman's limbs are bound to the four posts of a bed on which she lies. She smiles nervously, appearing to believe she is in a game, sadomasochistic though it may be. Cut. One of the men with a scruffy beard climbs on over her, straddling her naked body, her bulbous breasts rolling from side to side in anticipatory excitement. Cut. The man is using surgical forceps to pull out her toenails. In astonishment and disbelief, the woman cries, shock written all over her distorted face. Cut. The man is now working on her fingernails, pulling them out one by one. The woman is shrieking, saliva meandering out from the side of her excessively shiny, moist red lips. Cut.*

There was a click of keys, a squeak of the hinges, and then the apartment door banged shut. Patrick did not hear it, transfixed to the screen.

*The man is working with a carving knife to sculpt a square at the spot where her heart should be. As he does so, blood spurts out in ripples and gushes all over her chest, her breasts now flaccid and fallen to her sides. Her eyes, bloodshot, reveal the sheer terror that has enveloped her. Her whimpers are barely audible. The man thrusts his right hand inside to grab a throbbing, pulsating heart. An animalistic hurrah of victory accompanies his raising the heart up for the world to behold, a prize for the cannibal audience that had sat through the performance. Then there is silence as the camera zooms down on the indescribably vitiated body, the face still etched in pain, all life having deserted its open, expressionless eyes staring blankly at the ceiling. The second man, who must have been filming, appears from the side of the screen and picks up the paraphernalia. He is overheard to say, "Let's get out of here." Cut.*

Patrick sat still. He realised he could not move his limbs, as though his nails had all been pulled out. He felt breathless, as if he was without a heart. What had he done, he asked himself; was this not the closest to sinning he had ever come, nothing to do with religion's dictates, but contiguous to the worst indecency, a silent reveller in murder. Lost in self-hatred and physical paralysis he sat, unable to move his mind or body.

That it was Terrence who had come into the apartment and seen the last, most shocking scene, had not been noticed by Patrick. Beads of sweat had gathered on Terrence's forehead, trickling down his sideburns that he had grown long in keeping with the prevailing style of the moment, even for blacks. Anger written all over his countenance, he shook his head forcefully. Water flew from his hair in every which direction like strings of shiny, vanishing pearls. They almost drenched Patrick, who was seated motionless on the sofa. Even as he felt the glow of warmth emanating from their physical proximity, Patrick could not help but look up at Terrence's tall stature admiringly, desirous of being resurrected from his embarrassment.

The disgust that Terrence felt was obvious. Without reciting religion, for he knew Patrick's disdain for it as Patrick never went to Church, all he said was, "Pat, don't do this kind of thing again. Don't *reduce* yourself."

Patrick realised Terrence must also have read the newspaper article and, knowing him well, Patrick assessed that Terrence, the church attendee, would never be tempted to demean himself by renting it. His admiration for Terrence shot up one notch.

That one utterance of Terrence calmed Patrick. He had been forgiven. Before Patrick could respond, Terrence had sunk into the love seat, almost burying himself under its plump cushions. As he bent forward to take off his sneakers, his body seemed to mimic that of the sofa, disappearing into the interior reaches of its broad dimensions. Patrick looked on as Terrence leant back and threw off his sweat shirt, his young muscles rippling out from under its folds, damp from a healthy jog sweat. Patrick did not remove his stare, transfixed by Terrence's immaculate form. He decided not to respond.

Terrence spoke. "Pat, there was a huge rally at the Mall. People have gone crazy. Turn the boob tube on. The police came on strong. I jogged past and was almost arrested, you know. I would have missed Wachtel's Constitutional History class tomorrow!" he bellowed.

Patrick looked at Terrence with a blank expression for a moment, still mesmerised by his physique. Then, he quickly came to himself. In Terrence's rapid drive to literacy and education, his own role had been crucial in encouraging and coaching until Terrence seemed to suddenly, almost imperceptibly, cross an undefined inflexion point. At that moment, his capabilities seemed to just take off. He received his high school diploma with aplomb and entered Howard University without the slightest difficulty. While he initially trailed three semesters behind Patrick in his studies, by the third summer, he had taken sufficient extra credits to catch up with him in the senior year. During this period, his focus had been solely on academic pursuit, and he existed in a vacuum without any interference from or interest in politics, art, music or the company of people other than Patrick, who was a constant presence in every aspect of Terrence's life. Patrick accepted Terrence's remarkable transformation in all its naturalness, without much reflection or analysis.

All these thoughts flashed through Patrick like lightning. He noticed that Terrence had just made two observations, the first reflecting how deeply he respected life and dignity without being domineering in reference to the snuff movie and, yet, the second alluding to a significant event involving the human condition, without commenting on its genesis, the Vietnam War itself. It was as though Terrence was more concerned about the dignity of self rather than being bogged down by society. Who could blame him though, for despite his never complaining about it, it was for all to see how society, his birth, had only thwarted his early growth, a condition from which he was only now unshackling himself.

Patrick felt the need for a breath of fresh air. It had been a long day emotionally. "Terry, I am going out for a bit. I feel like a jog too. Jenine will come to fix dinner for us. Just remember to tell her that she must do the laundry; otherwise, we will have no shirts to wear to school tomorrow!"

*　　*　　*

Patrick shot out of the apartment, since he already had his jogging outfit on. Terrence leant back once again on the sofa and imagined the next day's anticipated lecture on the constitutionality of the continuing practice of flying the Confederate flag on the state capitols of certain Southern states. His thought did float back for a moment to the Mall and the commotion there, but he did not focus or remember any of the myriad faces that stared at him as he sprang by. He kept in mind that he had to get home as soon as possible and be ready for tomorrow.

Patrick jogged at a steady pace down P Street. Oh yes; it is worth mentioning north-west – it was P Street, NW – since it took some doing to eventually have Terrence change from temporary visitor to regular boarder. He would have moulded more easily into P Street, SE or, for that matter, even Adams Morgan where he would certainly have attracted less attention. In NW, he did stick out like a sore thumb to the residents of his neighbourhood, despite his striking mixed race looks that were closer to a Brazilian and for which his neighbours seemed to have scant or, at best, a distant appreciation. Terrence's pleasant, friendly and polite demeanour with the landlady, Mrs. Franklin, who lived on the first floor below his small second-floor apartment, eventually won her over. She had also become accustomed to the stodgily dressed and booted black contingent that went in and out of the little church at the corner of P Street NW just before the expansive valley that cradled the P Street Bridge. She had been told that they were the descendents of slaves who had inhabited old Washington in servitude to the early high political class and who had converted their slave quarters into orderly residential ones along that part of P Street NW. It was an exceptional enclave in the heart of Georgetown, a showpiece for the prevailing ruling class, an embodiment of their openhearted embrace of politically correct, rather, convenient, race relations. At least, it was so until the blacks were gradually forced out in the mid 1970s by gentrification and its corresponding financial clout. Mrs. Franklin knew better than to opine contrarily on that.

In any event, she probably thought of Terrence as a valet of sorts, erect in physical and, hopefully, moral stature and, with the passage of time, she wished to make Patrick's life a little more comfortable by allowing Terrence to move in to live there. Little did she know that it was Patrick who had to clean up after Terrence and to focus on matters of running the household!

Domestic concerns in Terrence had not yet been kindled because, after all, he had lived most of his life in the adobe hut outside the Goulds' hacienda. Nor did he seem to be in a hurry to develop those instincts. Patrick's oneness with Terrence had simply led him to pick up that role, without complaint, without admonition, perhaps at most with a certain expectation that that aspect, too, would evolve in Terrence one day.

No one in the neighbourhood noticed as Patrick jogged along P Street, NW.

*     *     *

The cobbles on the street massaged Patrick's feet as he picked up speed through the inner lanes of Georgetown. It had drizzled and the stones glistened in the light that radiated from the gaslights along the pavements. The stones and the lights were a remnant left intact by strictures imposed by the Historical Society of Georgetown that delighted tourists, but intermittently precipitated accidents on local residents. He had learnt to be especially careful not to slip on the steel lines engraved through the cobblestones that were never taken out when the streetcars had been removed from service. As he hurtled along, his heart throbbed faster and faster, not only because of the velocity with which he cut through the hanging fog in front of him, but also in anticipation of what was in store for him at the Mall. He turned right on 23rd Street, leaving the P Street *Beach* to his right. The *Beach* was a small, hollow area of parkland that sloped upwards towards 23rd Street. It was notorious as an area where gays participated in, or merely watched, public sexual activity amongst themselves. The *Washington Post* had the annoying habit of routinely reporting such whiffs of scandal. Patrick never missed reading them and, by habit, he peered in that direction for a moment. But he only heard a whistling siren from the swaying trees in the thicket that were heavy with moisture from the rain that had just stopped. He hurried past, towards the Mall.

As he crossed 'K' Street, he reached Foggy Bottom. A stench emanating from the damp bogs that descended to the Potomac in the vicinity engulfed him. He had never been entirely at ease with the Potomac and had laboured to ignore its pitfalls. Nevertheless, it was alluring in its power, incessantly sending out sounds of distant gushing water that were soothing to his ears. It splashed the ageless rocks upriver in an endless gashing motion as though to establish its supremacy, or gobbling up without conscience, those careless skaters who fell through its icy cover in mid-winter. He breathed in and out deeply to gather renewed energy, found himself at Washington Circle, and ran around a statue of an imperious George Washington on horseback without looking up at it. He invariably suffered embarrassment whenever he passed the Circle at the fact that an army general, not known for his intellectual capabilities, had been the nation's first president and that the nation had had to increasingly magnify his contributions as president, an enterprise that Patrick figured had had great success over the years. Almost in consternation, he could never look up at the mounted Washington, staring, but neither looking anywhere nor leading anyone in particular. As usual, with almost a bent head, as though he was a bicyclist, Patrick turned sharply right into 23rd Street once again, raised his head as he ran past George Washington University Hospital. He continued southward to the Mall.

Patrick looked straight towards Lincoln Memorial sitting at the termination of 23rd Street. His heart pounded faster and faster, both because he was pushing himself really hard now and since he knew that, momentarily, he would be staring at Lincoln, his unsurpassed hero. The fact that Lincoln had contracted syphilis in his early life gallivanting in New Orleans seemed to add to his aura, not because he had the disease, but because he lived with it and managed the nation's affairs so ably despite it. After all, no cure or treatment for syphilis had been invented until the early twentieth century, so Lincoln had advanced to tertiary syphilis and developed neuro syphilis, which is usually characterised by headaches, dizziness, poor concentration, lassitude, mental confusion and blurred vision. Patrick put the thought aside, anticipating that he would soon run up the steps to view and gaze at Lincoln's expressive eyes, despite their hollowed pupils, and feel the energy that he invariably derived from the colossal marble. Jogging at the spot where Lincoln sat, Patrick, as always, would read all or parts of the extracts of Lincoln's speeches carved into the stone to the left and right. He would stare back at Lincoln, and admire his rather exaggerated, yet seemingly comfortable, posture yet again. He never quite pondered the master craftsman who must have brought Lincoln to life. His pilgrimage completed, Patrick would jog down the steps, always knowing and looking forward to the next time that he would perform the same routine, the same duty, the same adulation.

However, as he approached Constitution Avenue, he realised that unanticipated experiences might be in store for him. The closer he got to the Memorial, the more he found the street oddly littered with trash. He even saw what looked like dark, splattered blood or, he told himself, it could just be Coca Cola, that all-American symbol of the global reach of the United States. He felt some relief from his presumed reassurance. However, the amount of paper on the road surprised him. Without stopping, he picked up a paper ball as though he was a Cossack picking up a goat's head from his saddle, the primitive forebear to the modern polo. As he ran along, he un-crumpled the paper banner. It read:

"NIXON, STOP LYING ON VIETNAM –
STOP KILLING AMERICAN SONS OF
THE SOIL!"
He picked up another as he ran. It read:
"STOP FRYING LAO BUDDHISTS –
DON'T USE NAPALM!"
Then, another:
"DON'T NUKE VIETS –
GIVE THEM THEIR FREEDOM!"

And on and on. The variety was impressive, astounding really.

Instantly, he was drawn towards Constitution Avenue, crossed it and found himself moving towards the Lincoln Memorial. He realized that the activity that must have taken place had already dissipated. He was disappointed and banged his right fist into his left palm.

"Damn!"

He was irritated, but did not stop. He floated up the steps towards the seated Lincoln while oodles of sweat were overwhelming his headband. Patrick had let his hair grow long in the style of the day. His hair was drenched, and a twisted knot dangled on the side of his scalp. By now, his sweatshirt stuck to his back. The sweat had made a dark V in the front. Halfway up the steps, Patrick stopped short as he faced another being with a headband who was staring at him a few steps above the one he was on. The man's eyes were ageless and seemed to pierce through Patrick. There was a distinct hint of Oriental or East Asian features apparent in the multi-layered wrinkled skin of the man's face. Patrick instantly realised he was an indigenous American-Indian. He stepped up to his level and squatted to face the old man.

"Hi! What brings you here? Where are you from?"

"Ahh! Taos."

As if to show the direction, the man stretched his hand towards the sky beyond and swung it in a direction behind the Memorial, where the sun had set some time ago, for now the sky had taken on a deep purple hue tinged with streaks of orange and gold that were darkening by the moment.

Patrick's mind's eye peered into an opening surrounded by tall adobe buildings and a flock of Indians with feathered headdresses beating drums and dancing in endless circles around a warm and high, crackling fire, throwing up a lot of red, sparkling dust that blew in the wind like glow worms in quick motion. He was struck, bewildered by his own vision.

*Why is this ageless man here to protest the war,* he asked himself. So Patrick asked him, "Why did you come here? May I ask?"

The old man looked puzzled. "The *Ganment* has not kept one treaty with us *Injuns*. Columbus began murdering us, and then all *immigrans* forced us into camps. Now, I have come to ask for *mani* to get our *yanguns* off the bottle. They can hardly move around. They sit and drink. The womenfolk do the work. Now they, too, are taking to the bottle."

Patrick could not hide his amusement. This must have been a fun rally, he thought, a watering hole for all the disgruntled and the dishevelled, of all hues and colours, from possibly an exhaustive list of avocations and interest groups. He could not help but slip into an unexpected jocular mood. He got into a conversation with the ageless aboriginal.

"I, too, am an *Injun*," lied Patrick.

The old man looked puzzled as he asked, quite genuinely, "Which tribe?"

Patrick had to think quickly. Calcutta and the Naxalites came to his mind. They are Indian too, he thought as he blurted out, "I'm Calcuttan!"

The old man looked thoughtful, perhaps even pensive. His eyes moved towards his temple, as though in reflection. Trying hard to recall, he said ultimately with a sigh, "Ne'er heard of that tribe."

Patrick laughed aloud. He was having fun at the old man's expense. He asked, "Who told you that the government ignores you Indians? They give you subsidies, don't they?" He smiled mischievously.

Ignoring Patrick's argument, the old man replied promptly, "It was one of them white boys. Zinn or something. He said Columbus, Cortes, Pizarro, them pilgrims – all pillaged and ransacked our lands, raped our women, took our children and enslaved our men. And he from Harvard too. And those English bastards were the worst. I am told, wherever they went, they divided and conquered the local people. Their mighty empire was India, the *old* one. They divided that country before they left from there, and cursed them with a burea*crazy*. I understand it is a crazy system of governing. It makes the locals unable to decide anything. They discuss matters around and around so that they cannot conclude anything. Crazy, man." He shook his head from side to side."

Patrick was no less than flabbergasted at the extent of the old man's information, partial and fallacious though it might have been from many an angle. He could not just stop the conversation. He was getting ideas for his thesis. He prodded the amazing old man some more. "You sure?"

That was enough to make the octogenarian continue his monologue.

"Oh yes; these boys told me all. Our boys back home have forgotten history. They do not go to school for more than five or six years. That, too, all white folk come to teach their own version. Now today, some boys and one girl came to me. At first, they were hesitant to approach me. When I told them it was okay, they smiled, came to me and talked to me about my rights. Our Injun rights. We have to demand them, shout for them. We must have banners like theirs. Only then *ganment* will pay attention. The Injun boys came later to me and congratulated me, for all these other white folk come to me and give me attention. Now I am tired. I need my pipe."

His voice trailed off and he looked blankly to the front, as though for the wind god to proffer him a *hookah*. It floated down in the wind. He grabbed it and put it to his mouth. He drew on it, and it made a gargling sound as the water slithered and slurped. He blew out a string of smoke from a rounded, open mouth, and broke into a toothless smile, directed at no one in particular. Patrick seemed to have lost him totally.

Patrick looked at his watch. Gosh! Jenine would have been barking at Terrence by now for doing all the wrong things, for placing an obstacle course along her path in his wake, and he still had a half hour to jog back even at steady speed. As he looked up, he felt free. The old man's smoke enveloped him and he breathed it in. It had the scent of sweet tobacco, the type that had not been fully roasted and gave it a musk-like fragrance. He thought of giving him a hug as he pulled himself up, but could not quite make himself do so. He began picking up speed down the steps. That night, in a flight of imagination, an unidentified old Indian had temporarily surpassed Lincoln in Patrick's esteem.

*   *   *

When Patrick reached home, Mrs. Jackson was sitting immobile on her kitchen chair as if in dreadful anticipation of some terrible news. Upon hearing the bell ring, she sprang up. Her frame, more like a galleon in slow motion, sailed to the door, which she opened to find obvious relief, for she exclaimed, "Mr. Patrick, where were you? I worried. These not good times."

Shaking her head, she rolled back to the kitchen, as Terrence looked at him puzzlingly. Patrick jumped in and out of the shower, and went straight to the table that Mrs. Jackson had just laid freshly for them, and sat in front of his salad. Terrence joined him. He had been waiting patiently for Patrick's return.

"Jenine, how will you go home at this hour? The District is in turmoil."

Patrick took three dollar bills from his pocket and handed them to Mrs. Jackson, even as she seemed a bit confused with that last word. He figured that would be more than sufficient to take her back to the Anacostia clapboard house that she shared with her sister in a far-flung corner of the South East of the city. They had never left, not only because they could not afford to, but also because they had inherited it from their parents who, in turn, had inherited it from theirs. After much poking about her family circumstances over the last two years, Patrick had come to accept that there was likely to be little moving up the social ladder in her most segregated of neighbourhoods unless there was some kind of external force that could drive the transformation. He had come to accept that it was unlikely to happen to Mrs. Jackson and her family.

"Grab a cab tonight," said Patrick.

Mrs. Jackson looked at him hesitatingly, but took the money as she continued shaking her head. Then she stopped, wiped her fingers on her apron, seemed to struggle a bit in sliding the apron strings over her head, hung it on the hook behind the kitchen door, smiled at both boys and made for the door, slamming it shut behind her, loudly enough to make her feel that she had shut it strongly enough to leave the boys secure and safe. Patrick heaved a soft sigh of relief.

Patrick looked pensive as he disinterestedly munched on his salad, while Terrence stared vacantly at the television, for he was thinking of class the next day. Not even Carol Burnett's epileptic fits on the boob tube could hold his attention. They rose and moved to the sofa to relax, distracted and brooding in their own worlds. Once the 11 p.m. news came on, occasionally Patrick stole a glance at the screen, especially as the cameras scanned the Mall. He was still thinking of his Indian and realised that he had not asked the man's name. Now the encounter seemed like part of a trance, perhaps even a bit surreal, and he cherished the lingering sensation of the experience. Patrick was unable to recall the circumstances that compelled him to go to the Mall. He did not remember that he had been overly concerned about the bombs that were falling on the Vietnamese. Instead, he had returned satisfied by the intellectual meal he had had from his chance encounter with an Indian from Taos.

That night, Patrick and Terrence did not exchange their usual synopses of the day. Patrick knew that, if there was to be a discussion of Indochina, he would have to initiate it. He knew that Terrence looked at the world through a prism whose sole motto was catching up for his lost early years. Indochina could wait. He would have no time for the native peoples' cause, either. He did not have this luxury or concern. Rather, his priority was to correct his own redress by advancing his individual education, by sharpening the story of his own experience. Patrick did not need to rationalise Terrence's approach, to understand it, or to condone it. Having initiated his Terry on this path, he just wanted to cruise along with it and labor with Terrence on it, for Terrence's success or failure would be his as well. There were no words between them that night even as they retired, one reminiscing over what had transpired that evening, and the other looking to the next morning.

\*     \*     \*

Patrick awoke as usual at 6:30 a.m. to do his *Pranayam*, the morning yoga that he had learnt from Father Vincent, whose early training had been in India and who had been curious, as well as open-minded enough, to partake of that ancient country's traditional offerings rather than trying to westernise them through the usual Roman Church's time-tested means of pecuniary enticements – money for the soul, as it were, an investment he had made that repaid itself many times over in the form of money for the church. The contrary interest and enthusiasm of Father Vincent were facilitated by the fact that he had discovered quite early that such delightful Eastern practices were available to any interested Westerner for the mere asking. He only had to utter a word of interest to the seminary clerk and a yoga instructor or Ayurveda doctor would show up the next day as if they had been given some special privilege to meet with a person of pink skin who was wearing a white cassock, rather than having brown skin and being clad in a saffron cloth. Indeed, it was obvious to Patrick that Father Vincent had developed a deep sense of the country to the point that India seemed always in his mind. From all of Father Vincent's descriptions of the land and its peoples and his recounting of a plethora of unique and extraordinary experiences, India appeared, to Patrick, as increasingly exotic and enchanting.

As the priest dwelt on his favorite topic one evening when Patrick had joined him on his evening jog around the football field, Father Vincent told Patrick, "You can take Indians out of India, but you can never take India out of Indians. In the same vein, once you put India into someone, India grows like a virus for which there is no vaccine."

Patrick was very struck, even awed, by the statement, though not knowing quite what to make of it. Surely, though, it affected him. While he could not engage his energies on Indochina, reflecting his fear of his getting drafted, he felt increasingly drawn to the concept of the Subcontinent. At first, he was a bit annoyed with himself for getting concerned about a mere idea. Yet he could not control it. Patrick asked himself if it was Father Vincent's personality and the way he recounted his experiences in India that imparted to him a thirst to seek some deeper knowledge of it and, more and more, this curiosity and pre-occupation with India intensified. Whenever he was with Father Vincent, or even when he merely chanced to see him from a distance as he was walking briskly across campus, Patrick felt an inexorable pull towards the far-flung place that he had only experienced in the form of episodic accounts from this perpetually smiling priest. With time, the priest's narratives turned from mere anecdotes to intoxicating tales, generating a firm confidence and trust in the young, impressionable Patrick.

Patrick soon noted that the few Indians on campus were always together, whether they were dark or fair, vegetarian or non-vegetarian, budding physicists or economists. They seemed to possess scant, if any, interest in American football, preferring some incredibly complicated sport called cricket, which seemed more like chess, but was played on the field for five full days between two teams of eleven players each. They got so excited when they described this unfathomable game, imparting a touch of irrationality to them, that Patrick's interest in approaching them was dampened. They also seemed overconfident and rather self-possessed, isolating themselves from non-Indian students by herding together on weekends to play bridge or chess and to cook horrendously smelling curries that sent the other students running to escape the curries' pungency. Nonetheless, Patrick was eventually invited a couple of times to join them after his exhibition of interest in their concerns became obvious to some of them. He had often heard grumblings regarding curry stench from his compatriots and had secretly felt lucky that he did not suffer with his classmates who lived in the dormitories or shared apartments. Instead, he soon developed a taste for curry and began to invite himself to the hustle and bustle of the Indians' weekend cooking forays.

Patrick continued to listen to Father Vincent's stories, always with a different angle on a selected aspect of this distant country's cultures and peoples, even as his own academic familiarisation with the Naxalbari Movement became deeper. His original, somewhat tepid, interest grew into a heightened need for more information and familiarization, a keen preoccupation for India's problems once he began to comprehend them, and a steadfast determination to engage and involve himself in its affairs. In the meanwhile, he became a steady practitioner of meditation and yoga, a path that, with time, transported him to higher levels of physical stamina, muscle toning, mental equilibrium and intellectual focus.

Patrick finished his chanting of 'Om' a hundred and eight times in a slow, rounded, extended rendition. He was already in a stage to be able to feel the effect of the sound, the sound that astronauts reported when they were first in space, the sound of the eternal universe. He opened his eyes slowly. Terrence was standing straight up in front of him.

"Sorry. Last night was so hurried that I forgot to give it to you. You have a letter. Here."

Patrick's expression was a bit curious and a bit uncertain. The letter was from Jolly. Her letters always left him a bit worried until he had read them. Only then was he able to go about his business as before. Only then would his unexpressed foreboding disappear. He himself did not have a full understanding of this feeling. He never analyzed it. It was just intuition, a premonition that had never transformed into reality, at least not so far. However, with each letter, he nevertheless wondered if there was something to worry about. Until now, the foreboding always passed once he had read the letter. Having finished reading it, he would fold it and put it in a stack inside his desk. He wrote back only a few times and only a few short lines, if that.

On this day, now, that letter, the one that Patrick had vaguely feared would one day precipitate his desperation, had arrived finally. As Patrick read it, his anxiety soared.

Jolly's letter said:

> San Antonio
> July 12, 1970
> Hi Pat,
>
> How are you? Long time, no hear! I have great news. I have admission to the nursing school at Catholic University. I was worried about the tuition fees, since it is a private school, especially since I also have admission at University of Texas at Austin where tuition would be much lower.
>
> However, my mother wants me to go to the school I prefer and insisted that she would sell her stocks if necessary. At first, I felt I could not let her spend her hard-earned money (even though she has never divulged when or how she saved it). But, in the end, I realized I could never stop her. She, in her eccentric, flamboyant ways, always supported whatever I expressed a desire to do in the most spoiling way! That always gave me a kind of confidence in her. So how could I try to stop her now?

I do wonder if she would have wanted me to be a dancer or an artist, but she has never asked or told me. When I mentioned nursing, I could not detect the slightest hesitation or negativity in her face or eyes, though I myself wondered what she must think of it. How, being her daughter, could I want to be a nurse, so far from anything ethereal, and take up something so practical, so set on the ground? She only said that Washington would be far away and that I should find a good hotel for her when she visits me there.

So, I am coming! The Fall Semester begins after Labour Day. I plan to arrive end-August. Could I stay with you for a couple of weeks till I find a room to share with some other nursing student (which I am desperately hoping)? Guess what? No time for pretence. I know I *can*, of course. So you do not have to write back if you are running around during your Summer Semester. I'll see you then – soon!

Everything is fine at Agnes and her family. I went by the other day and had coffee with your mother. She does dote on her son! Everyone else is doing well. Your dad dropped in for a moment and, after hearing that I am going to Washington, looked at me with narrowed eyes (I wondered why), smiled, gave me a hug, and hurried away!

So, love and kisses until then.

Yours,
Jolly.

"Terry, come here! Jolly is coming," exclaimed Patrick.

However, Terrence did not come. He remained in the bedroom. He noticed his hands tremble a little as he was unbuttoning his just-unfolded shirt in order to put it on.

"Terry, did you hear me? Jolly is going to study at Catholic University!"

It was a double blow. *Is she coming to stay*, Terrence wondered as he steadied himself, and then sat down on the edge of the bed.

*Does how I feel not matter to Patrick at all*, Terrence asked himself. *Just how the hell are we going to do this?* Then he bit his tongue for thinking a mild expletive, even if he did not utter it. He got up, walked slowly to the connecting door to the living room, looked across at Patrick and asked, "Oh? Where will she be staying? Catholic is in the NE, quite far from here."

"She says she will stay with us for the first two weeks. She should find a place by then."

Terrence looked at Patrick quizzically.

Patrick responded, "Come on, Terry. She can have the bedroom. We can make do with the sofa and our sleeping bags for two weeks, can't we? Okay, you can have the choice of channels! Just imagine we are on one of our West Virginia camping trips, but with access to a television set!"

The matter had already been decided, as always, Terrence knew. But, this time, he pouted nonetheless. Of course, he quite ignored the many times when he had his way in matters that affected them both. He knew it was not to be in this particular case, in anything where Jolly was involved. He went back to putting on his shirt and preparing for his day at Howard. The freshness of the morning was gone. The heavy, stalled air that surrounded him made it difficult for him to breathe. He could not wait to get out of the apartment but no longer looked forward to the unfolding day.

Yes. The matter had been decided, but it had not been fully considered. Patrick looked distractedly out in the direction of P Street and the familiar elm tree standing right outside the window, its leaves shining in the early sunlight, rustling in the morning breeze, protecting the privacy of the often-noisy couple who lived in the apartment across the street. 'How fortunate are these trees. They live only for the good of others. Exposing themselves to wind and sun, to rain and snow, they protect and shade us without expecting anything in return', he recalled having read recently in one of the Hindu scriptures. Yes, he thought, it was Krishna, the Hindu god, talking to his brother, Balaram. Patrick's thoughts floated to Terry, his Orion, his crusader, all, protective and childlike. His heart steadied. The next moment, he was startled by the rattle of tyres being driven over the unused streetcar tracks, that had remained embedded in the street, the result of agitation against their removal by preservationist activists. He dwelt on Jolly's staying with Terry and himself for a fortnight. He concluded there was nothing that was to be done about this incommodious arrangement. It would be short, after all. He sat up, crossed his legs and folded his hands together in front of him, attempting to go back to his *Omkaram*. The chant could not make him tranquil. Momentarily, he stood up and bolted to the shower.

\*      \*      \*

Jolly's entrance was uncomfortable to both Terrence and Patrick. She had let herself go, becoming plump, nearly obese. The two boys avoided looking at each other in order not to reveal or share their embarrassment. They never discussed her between themselves in any serious manner, preferring, instead, as people stereotypically did about fat people, to focus on how sweet and jovial she was, pointing to her ceaseless cracking of jokes, generally full of fun and constantly provoking involvement from both the males. Patrick seemed to be taken by her every movement through the apartment. Jolly was brisk and purposeful, whether cooking up a Spanish omelette, putting the books in alphabetical order on the wall shelf, or demanding that they go for a walk through the cobblestone streets to admire the impressive architecture of Georgetown. The boys always complied.

After the first days, Terrence behaved like a pet poodle, running to the fridge to fetch her a glass of milk for what seemed to be her unquenchable thirst for liquids or to the closet to get her a hand towel with which she would wipe her lips while relating a story from San Antonio, something inconsequential, but that held the boys' interest. She had certainly not lost her old ways of attracting attention, Patrick would think bemusedly, or of behaving like her mother's spoilt little girl. He could imagine her feeding on butter croissants every evening and drinking her mother's milky chicory coffee. Suddenly, he recalled how she had once corrected his pronunciation of that French word as he had tried to say it when served a croissant at coffee time. That was so many years ago and he remembered how impressed, yet a bit irritated, he had been. Now it gave him joy to recall the event and to observe how little Jolly seemed to have changed. Yes, he accepted that he had fallen prey to her atypical, yet delectable, charms. He was not attracted to her body; rather, he was overtaken by her personality. That seemed to suffice.

Patrick also noticed how Terrence's initial foreboding had vanished. He remained focussed on his academic work, but invariably found time to join in on the fun chats with Jolly and Patrick without the slightest problem. Yet he managed to keep his own social life at Howard – for he was increasingly late in returning home – close to his chest. Patrick dared not ask Terrence for details, for he knew not what lurked under this outward behaviour. Everything seemed in equilibrium. That was enough for Patrick, though he sometimes did wonder, *Are our lives moving apart?*

Then their lives got a jolt. Being Sunday, dressed in his only suit, Terrence had left as usual for the morning service at the P Street church. He always came back gleeful, having been admired by all the coloured folk, who were generally much older than he and who had been nodding in astonishment at his piety, which was doubly enhanced by his remarkably good looks. However, today he had not yet returned. Patrick had long finished his yoga exercises, much to the bemusement, if not slight perplexity, of Jolly. She, by now, had accepted this idiosyncrasy without the slightest curiosity to know, let alone understand, these distant, alien, slow, contorting movements that were accompanied by a groan that seemed to emanate from the abdomen. He was lounging on the sofa lazily perusing the *Parade Magazine* section of the Sunday *Washington Post*, a must read that helped him maintain his fascination with the extravaganza of the show business world when, much to his surprise, Jolly came up to him and sat at the edge of the sofa. To be polite, he found himself shuffling and sinking more into it in order to enable her to settle in more comfortably but, as he did so, a disturbing consciousness, if not fear, overcame him.

"Pat, look at me," said Jolly.

Uncomfortable and shy, Patrick complied.

Jolly asked, "What do I mean to you?"

Patrick maintained a bemused silence and looked askance from her.

When there was no response, she said, "Oh, come on…. Okay; let's not talk about it."

Patrick replied, "Oh no…. I mean…. You know…. We have known each other for so long…. Remember the time when you stood behind the tree waiting for me for hours, well, at least in *baby* hours?" And, almost as an excuse, he added, "Who would think that now you have grown into an adult!" A smile broke through his lips even as a faint feeling of trauma clearly seemed to overtake him. He realised he felt absolutely no desire to bring her physically close to him.

*Oh God! However, why am I so fond of her, feel so close to her, and truthfully do not desire to be separated from her,* Patrick wondered.

Before Patrick could concoct a convincing answer, Jolly had brought her lips down on his. He did not find it distasteful, but he wondered why his gooseflesh did not stand up, though he felt his manhood stir. He not only did not want to resist, but wanted wholeheartedly for the experience to be successful. Soon, their tongues clashed, then intertwined. He was aghast when, without getting off the sofa, Jolly raised herself and, pulling her panties down, she unzipped him at the same time. Looking upwards, she held him, gliding him into her. He looked at her as woman. He felt little, but the sensation of her breasts dangling down from her loosened bra helped him stay erect, much to his relief. After she moved a few times, he ejaculated within the minute. Withdrawing, he saw a small streak of Jolly's blood on his penis.

Jolly fell on him. Moments passed in silence that neither of them broke.

"I am so sorry, Patrick. I don't know what came over me. I just could not stop myself. Oh, but why didn't you stop me?"

Patrick nodded reassuringly, even as he was struck by his own absence of euphoria, and said, "Jolly, this had to be so. I guess as the Hindus would say, this was fate. However, they also say there is a meaning in everything...."

Jolly, the nurse-to-be, the practical, budding service personnel, looked at him quizzically, doubtful for the first time about their affinity, perhaps even their similarity. She did not care if it was *fate*. All she knew was that she wanted him. She also knew from what had just transpired between them that he had never had another girl before. It reassured her that he had waited for her, for her alone. By her own logic, therefore, her wait had also been worthwhile. But did he *want* her? She was intelligent enough to remain clueless about what had just occurred.

Jolly smiled for Patrick to see and, with unmistakable love and pleading written all over her face, she said, "Pat, I have waited for this moment for so long." Then, jumping off the sofa, she continued, "Gosh! I must run to the shower. Give me a moment. Then you can take your shower while I straighten up the sofa. Terry should be returning any moment." Instantaneously, she was off to the bathroom.

Patrick lay on the sofa for what seemed to him a long time, his flaccid penis still hanging out of his pyjamas. *What happened just now?* he asked himself. *Why didn't I feel anything?* He moaned. *Was this really* written*? Why did I acquiesce? Why could I not say* no *to her?* He chastised himself, but he failed to receive an answer from within.

Patrick was angry. Jolly had not changed at all; she had remained extremely manipulative, he told himself. However, the passing thought was overtaken by a flash memory of her young, tearful face staring at him from behind the tree as he passed by with his school buddies, embarrassed and harassed as he had felt by her dexterously orchestrated theatricality. Spontaneously, a wave of empathy and caring overcame him. He stared straight up at the ceiling and remained motionless, a morass of confusion, as he pondered this conundrum and, when Jolly appeared at the door, shaking her hair dry with tightening twists of her pinkish towel, the satin bows peeking out, all he could manage to garner was a faint smile that escaped his lips and, hurriedly adjusting his pyjamas, he repeated sheepishly, "I must run. Terry could be back any minute."

By the time Patrick had showered, Terrence had yet to return, but the living room was spic and span, and Jolly was sporting a pert smile. Patrick sank back into the sofa, somewhat bewildered with the new experience, apprehensive about its less than blissful outcome, feeling under a cloud of uncertainty, even a whiff of despair. He could not explain it and tried to initiate a conversation with Jolly, but all she did was hum, take out more glasses of milk from the fridge and drink them as though they were mere water. He stared at her in disbelief, yet, her very motion to and from the fridge, with her swaying backside, caused him to smile, for he began to see once again the schoolgirl of whom he had been so fond. Soon, with these visions in his head, he fell into a mellow nap.

Jolly looked at Patrick contentedly, smiled, and went out to the balcony to wait for Terrence to return, in anticipation of having a nice Sunday chat session with him, for she knew she would have, in Terrence, a sure and appreciative audience.

*    *    *

It took Jolly longer than a fortnight to find an apartment, but, when it happened, it was quick, and came complete with an apartment mate. She found her through the Student Office. Unexpectedly, the counsellor asked if she would like to share a room on campus, at the nursing school itself. There was one placement left, and she would have to share with a Hispanic girl. Probably that was why it was still vacant, she reflected. On the other hand, perhaps the counsellor was offering the room to her because she was from San Antonio. *Oh! The ridiculous connections these Washingtonians make,* she thought. Of course, Jolly had picked up quite a bit of colloquial Spanish as a result of the various Mexican influences emanating from every corner as she was growing up. So language would not be a problem, she assured herself. However, she knew that the umbrella of Hispanic encased many possibilities. She gingerly asked if she could know more about the person. Within five sentences, she jumped to agreement. The counsellor also explained the bus route that would take her downtown if she needed to go there. She asked if it passed through Georgetown. The efficient counsellor opened out her large map of bus routes on her desk. Peering into it, she concluded in the affirmative. There seemed to be one bus that went along U Street, crossed Connecticut Avenue, and went into P Street towards Georgetown. Jolly figured it would be less than a ten-minute walk to Patrick's from the bus stop at the crossing of Wisconsin Avenue with P

Street where she might have to get off. The decision was made on the spot. She thanked the counsellor.

Leonor was from Colombia, and was far from being a *Hispanic* with its US connotations. Her father was a heart surgeon. She had wanted to be a nurse since childhood. This had been a bit of a disappointment to her upper-class parents, but they never opposed their daughter's whims and fancies, especially since the death of their son in a horrific, mysterious accident during his late childhood that had remained ever unsolved. They had doted on their daughter from that moment on. She would have preferred to go to England as they would have, as well, when they were growing up, like all upper-class Colombians wished to do. However, Oxford and Cambridge were too far from Bogota. So they struck a bargain, a compromise, for Leonor to be nearer to them, and narrowed it down to the U.S. East Coast. They were happy when Leonor got admission in Catholic University. That would allow them to meet more often, since her father visited DC regularly for conferences and consultations at the Pan American Health Organisation and the National Institutes of Health. In addition, for such short trips, her mother could accompany him relatively easily, without disrupting the enormous household that she reigned over in Bogota. They picked Catholic University since it had a nursing school as opposed to some of the other universities there, but mainly so that she would remain ring fenced in the Catholic diaspora, or so they presumed.

Leonor had jet-black hair flowing down almost to her waist, curled in a perm, and polished by brushing to a perpetual shine. Her lotus-pink face was oval, as were her eyes and tiny handfuls of breasts. She was not tall. Her waist matched her height perfectly. She was ravishing even to the female eye. She moved about with a permanent smile on her face as if she had no care in the world and, indeed, she had none. She was the perfect Latina, a chatterbox mouthing *Revolución* incessantly that, after a point, sounded delirious. Leonor was a political explorer to the extent that she indulged in the Marxism of the upper classes. She and her blue-blooded friends were certain about everything, did not, in general, have to face dissenting opinions, and never had the misfortune of experiencing a theory proved false by real life experiences. None of them had or would ever encounter the hard physical labour or endless political lectures of a FARC re-education camp to rid them of their bourgeois attitudes. Neither their own nor their families' wealth or possessions would be confiscated and redistributed to the servants who slogged for these people. They were people who were troubled over the idiosyncrasies of their pets, even as they parroted stock phrases about revolution and the proletariat at their luxury dinners and parties. Of course, Leonor would have the obligatory Che Guevara poster on her wall next to her wardrobes that were filled with designer clothing and expensive jewellery.

Nevertheless, despite their differences in social class and wealth, Jolly and Leonor seemed to get along very well. Jolly had little or no knowledge of, or interest in, global issues. Leonor had opinions, often inflexible, on everything that she voiced in impeccable grammatical English spoken with a soft, lilting accent she had picked up from the nuns who taught her to speak it back in Bogota. While she did so, Jolly would continue with her kitchen chores, occasionally glancing towards Leonor as if to indicate that she was all ears. Thus, there was no conflict between them on this count. Jolly's sole interest was to discuss Patrick. She talked to Leonor about Patrick and their childhood together, and her hopes for the future. Leonor would listen attentively, offering an occasional observation or politely making a point of query. She seemed to have perfect knowledge and instinct of when she should be the listener and when she could intervene with a comment. Also on matters of orderliness as apartment mates, there was little that bothered either of them. Both preferred to keep their belongings relatively tidy and to maintain their rooms in decent hygiene. They would alternate in bringing in a bouquet of flowers to fill the *Limoges* vase on the dresser that Leonor's mother had sent with her, as if flowers were a daily necessity. Jolly always appreciated such initiatives on Leonor's part and had little to complain about as long as she did not interfere in the kitchen, over which Jolly nurtured fixed opinions on appropriate menus for their various meals. Leonor had little interest in the kitchen and remained more than happy, indeed, relieved, for Jolly to take charge in this particular domestic corner. They found themselves sharing the apartment in perfect mutual balance.

\* \* \*

Every Sunday morning, Jolly would take the bus down to Georgetown to go to church, while Leonor would remain asleep. She was not the churchgoing type, following the practice of her parents who, despite their intrinsic Catholic culture, generally expected the clergy to visit their home for appointed occasions rather than themselves having to attend church with all and sundry. They were not exceptions. It was general practice among the upper classes of her country. It was only the lower rung of society, the masses, that the church held sway over, for the top layers were presumably well aware of the capricious role and stifling grasp of the church in that continent. Nevertheless, the upper classes and the church hierarchy were partners in maintaining a firm grip over the wealth and politics of their land, as was the pervasive practice in almost all Latin-American countries. Of course, there were those political families and a handful of orthodox lineages that felt compelled to be seen once a week in the first row of their church and, after the service, shaking hands with the priest at the church entrance. Leonor's family did not belong to that clique. Rather, her father had been a brilliant student who had gone on scholarship to Harvard Medical School and, as was common in his generation, had promptly returned to his country to practice his trade rather than being gobbled up by the United States itself, a habit that would afflict only the next generation. By then, the pernicious ramifications of US hegemony in the political and economic systems of these countries had begun to make it increasingly difficult for the middle classes to continue to live there. The young doctor and his peers had been lucky not to experience it full throttle.

The doctor soon rose in professional prominence and was always in high demand. An appointment with him meant a month's wait, at least. The best of society and their money quickly crowded out the lower classes from his waiting room. His wife encouraged this and basked in the reflected glory of her husband's induction into Bogota high society. She, her husband and Leonor often visited their mountain retreats or their country estates which were staffed by the lower classes. They remained comfortably oblivious to the perpetual poverty of the servants, who worked incessantly for a pittance. It was usual for the servants to produce opulent dinners regularly and salsa parties occasionally in addition to their daily work, while catering constantly to the sudden corporeal desires and capricious whims of their unpredictable masters. The doctor would often appear at his own lavish parties appropriately late, making a dramatic entrance, having been driven by his chauffer directly from the hospital operating room. Apologising to his waiting guests, he would rush to take a shower and return to sip on his ready Tanqueray and tonic on the rocks, a habit he had picked up from an English girlfriend at Harvard who had declined his youthful proposal to marry. She had known that her destiny was to return to Bury St. Edmunds to take care of her aging parents, ever since her elder brother, the last male in the eight-hundred-year-old Inglewood line, had bought a red double-decker bus in a London auction and had gone to live in it after planting it right on the gardens of one of their vast family acreages, and had left their parents heartbroken and alone in one of their many mansions. The brother never intended to marry, of course, a fact that he had announced through a loudspeaker making sure he would be heard through the closed French windows and velvet, drawn curtains that successfully obscured his aging parents, forever hidden in their mansion, from him. She never fully knew or was inclined to ask what had led to such a pass between her parents and sibling, possibly because she had been fed with the stories of generations of eccentric behaviour of various ancestors from her nanny as she was growing up. Buttressed by her Harvard degree, she nurtured hopes of getting a teaching job in one of the Cambridge colleges. Thus, rejected by this noble Englishwoman, the young doctor resolved to quench his urge to serve in his own country. She understood him fully. They parted, she with the memory of her many Latin nights of romance, and he with his daily aperitif of Tanqueray and tonic.

Upon return, he was picked up as a promising professional by the Betancours, whose daughter was as beautiful and elegant as only women of the best Spanish lineages could be. He was intoxicated by her ravishing looks and even came to love her in time, for she was obviously taken by him and expressed it as often as her stiff, upper-lip upbringing would permit her. Leonor was born on the tenth month after their wedding and her brother a year later. It was obvious that they practised artificial birth control after the boy's birth (for it is inconceivable that they would have had sex only during safe periods), thus demonstrating a certain disdain for church teachings early in their conjugal life.

Though her parents sent Leonor to Catholic school and she had been baptised, it was mainly for social approval, an expression of risk aversion, so to speak. She was never a regular visitor to church except for the occasional social event such as Easter or Christmas. As she grew up and her education deepened, her bemusement with and, eventually, a lack of feeling for, and a total disconnection from the church became apparent, and then it became permanent. This reflected in no small measure her studies in anthropology and sociology that laboriously investigated the dubious benefits of conversions of indigenous peoples over centuries, completely ignoring the deprivation and dehumanisation of entire races meted out in the process. The financial and political benefits to the church were obvious. What had puzzled and amazed her in particular were the piety and obeisance of the indigenous peoples to the tenets of the church and its priesthood. However, despite this lack of concern about, indifference to, and non-recognition of church affairs and issues, her solid Catholic school upbringing led her to reorient herself towards a less condemnable path for a young debutante such as herself: that of premedical studies in preparation for nursing school.

In keeping with her views, every Sunday morning, Leonor ravenously looked forward to sleeping late, rather than hurrying to church to listen to another of *Father Mackenzie's sermons that no one would hear.* In contrast, as her interest in Catholicism diminished, her interest and views on world history and international affairs took definite shape, for her steely Catholic training had planted within her an indelible discipline that enabled her to advance her intellectual interest in political affairs while pursuing studies in nursing, an almost orthogonally placed profession. She told herself that the best way she could serve the poor in her country would be to become a nurse and serve the aged and vulnerable. Even though she loved her parents, she knew she would have to steer herself away from the high and mighty, the powerful and rich, that her father had chosen to serve and her mother had selected as her peers and confidantes. She felt alienated from the attitudes and mores of that society and, over time, resisted participating in it even as she also realized that to cut herself out completely from that world would be disastrous from both emotional and financial points of view, connected as these were to her parents' largesse towards her. Thus, she had arrived at a middle path: that of moving to Washington to get her degree that would be financed by them, and subsequently return to her country with renewed vigour to pursue her beliefs in deed and action.

*    *    *

At Thanksgiving, Jolly introduced Leonor to Patrick and Terrence. The event was Jolly's idea and Patrick did not oppose it. He had become accustomed to accepting Jolly's proposals, usually after some initial, superficial reflection. Mrs. Jackson would stay late the previous night to prepare a turkey with stuffing and a pumpkin pie, return early on Thanksgiving Day to put them into the oven, and then leave to get back to her own kitchen to prepare a Thanksgiving dinner for her family, not that it was easy to figure out what that family, at the bottom of the income and social decile, had to be thankful to the Almighty for. The girls would bring in a can of cranberry sauce, a large packet of frozen beans *amandine*, and some corn on the cob, and would be responsible for taking out the baked turkey and pumpkin pie, at distinctly different points, from the oven. Patrick and Terrence would only have to make the salad for which, obfuscating their minimal required effort, they made a big fuss over purchasing the right ingredients. They did reveal their charitable nature as they resolved to compensate Mrs. Jackson additionally for her extra effort in contrast to their own minimal input. All the young men did was to open the door in the morning as the little women barged into the apartment and rushed straight to the kitchen to listen carefully, if not anxiously, to Mrs. Jackson's instructions to be carried out subsequent to her departure. The various activities had all been perfectly synchronised by Jolly, and it worked.

When Mrs. Jackson carried her portly self out of the apartment, the women ran with her to the door as if to gather

her last blessings for the success of the rest of the day. Leonor saw Terrence as she turned around to face the living room. She could not place him directly. He looked Brazilian to her, with a touch of the Amazon, an Adonis personified. She seemed immobile for a moment, but then moved forward to shake his hand as a distant voice seemed to introduce them from afar. She blushed as Terrence appeared to look at her intently as he approached her. Standing tall over her short frame, he bent forward and kissed her on both cheeks in the Latin way, then quickly turned and seated himself on a rattan chair. He first repositioned it cleverly for a continuing view of Leonor even as she moved sideways to shake Patrick's hand. Jolly flashed a tight smile, as if subjecting them to a moment's inspection, a virtual examination that they seemed to pass. Jolly's tightness seemed to pass as she loosened to a relaxed trot towards Terrence, whom she bent down to kiss on his scalp. Terrence growled fondly and hugged her.

They all lounged about, idly looking into sections of the Thursday Thanksgiving *Washington Post*, with any number of blurbs about this revered day and articles on its special significance. Jolly eventually broke the silence for Leonor's benefit.

She quizzed enthusiastically, "Leonor, you know about Thanksgiving, don't you? See, we celebrate the first harvest of the Pilgrim Fathers in New England who shared their food with the local aboriginal Indians." She then inexplicably turned rationale on its head. "That is why we have to have American-Indian food today – turkey, cranberry relish, pumpkin pie, corn on the cob…" She threw a glance towards the kitchen, the bastion of all that sumptuous food in the making, and ended it all with an all-knowing, satisfied smile meant for the boys.

Leonor was not to be beaten. She piped in without the slightest sign of embarrassment or apparent intention to hurt, "However, how many varieties of corn are we cooking?

You know the Incas harvested some two hundred and fifty varieties of corn when the Spaniard Pizarro invaded Peru." She smiled coyly. As though to add fuel to the fire, she added, "Who knows if I belong to the lineage of those first rapes that followed Pizarro. Well, perhaps not, since I am not a Pizarro, but just a Betancour." She broke into hearty laughter.

Jolly looked away embarrassed, if not shocked, at this newly opened window into Leonor's dubious ancestry, while quite ignoring her own – mainly from lack of knowledge – and Terrence gave a perplexed look, possibly at the lack of cohesion in the morning's proceedings so far. Patrick jumped up and shot across to the white bookshelf built into the wall on both sides of the chimney. He went straight to the spot he wanted and, ignoring C.P. Hill's *American History*, a volume that would always retain a role, but had by now given way to more senior, serious stuff, picked out Howard Zinn's *A People's History of the United States* instead, and ran back to the spot he was occupying. Zinn had found a place on his bookshelf since his conversation with the Taos Indian with Lincoln as their witness. Patrick sat on the floor cross-legged and reclined on the large light green cushion studded with little pieces of mirror sewn into a fraying, but still colourful, silk material and surrounded by upturned little white shells that resembled a woman's open thighs. He seemed comfortable.

He looked at his threesome audience with a swivel of his head from one corner of the room to the other. Smiling authoritatively and flipping through the pages, he read from the book, "When we read the history books given to children in the United States, it all starts with heroic adventure – there is no bloodshed – and Columbus Day is a celebration." He threw a glance towards the wall shelf that revealed exasperation, desperation perhaps. Oh yes, it was towards his childhood text. He had, by now, gained speed. "Columbus' report to the Royal Court in Madrid was extravagant. 'The Indians are so naïve and so free with their possessions that no one who has not witnessed them would believe it. When you ask for something they have, they never say no. To the contrary, they offer to share with anyone…' In the year 1495, they went on a great slave raid, rounded up fifteen hundred Arawak men, women, and children, put them in pens guarded by Spaniards and dogs, then picked the five hundred best specimens to load onto ships. Of those five hundred, two hundred died en route. The rest arrived alive in Spain and were put up for sale by the archdeacon of the town, who reported that, although the slaves were 'naked as the day they were born', they showed 'no more embarrassment than animals'. Columbus later wrote, 'let us in the name of the Holy Trinity go on sending all the slaves who can be sold'.

"He and his men… ordered all persons fourteen years or older to collect a certain quantity of gold every three months. When they brought it, they were given copper tokens to hang around their necks. Indians found without a copper token had their hands cut off and bled to death. So they fled, were hunted down like dogs, and were killed. In two years, through murder, mutilation, or suicide, half of the 250,000 Indians on Haiti were dead. When it became clear that there was no gold left, the Indians were taken as slaves on huge estates…. They were worked at a ferocious pace, and died by the thousands. By the year 1515, there were perhaps fifty thousand Indians left. By 1550, there were five hundred. In his popular book, *Christopher Columbus, Mariner,* Samuel Eliot Morison, the Harvard historian, wrote, 'the cruel policy initiated by Columbus and pursued by his successors resulted in complete genocide'."

Sounds of shuffling were not sufficient to make Patrick look up from his pages.

"When he arrived on Hispaniola in 1508, Las Casas, a young priest [who] participated in the conquest of Cuba, says, 'there were 60,000 people living on this island, including the Indians, so that, from 1494 to 1508, over three million people had perished from war, slavery, and the mines. Who in future generations will believe this?' A report of the year 1650 shows none of the original Arawaks or their descendants were left on the island.

"What Columbus did to the Arawaks of the Bahamas, Cortes did to the Aztecs of Mexico, Pizarro to the Incas of Peru, and the English settlers of Virginia and Massachusetts did to the Powhatans and the Pequot."

Patrick finished with a self-righteous, indignant flare as he dramatically snapped shut the book and dropped the heavy volume with a thud on the polished hardwood floor. Pin-drop silence followed all around. Moments passed.

Eventually breaking the silence and staring straight at Leonor, Patrick exclaimed,

"Yes, we celebrate our heritage today when we recall the sharing by those Massachusetts Pilgrims of their Indian goodies with their European neighbours." There was unhidden sarcasm in his slightly raised voice.

He had taken his revenge on Jolly for organizing the meaningless ritual of Thanksgiving supper, but immediately regretted having hurt her... the pouting girl hiding behind a tree, softly shedding tears and patiently waiting for him... especially as she now got up briskly, hiding her bloodshot eyes by shutting them for longer than a moment, and went past him, without acknowledging him, into the kitchen to attend to the turkey. Patrick knew this would not be the end of the episode, for there would be silence to follow after the dinner and he would have to apologize to her in order to untangle the tangled web he had just woven. He did not look forward to such an eventuality, but knew it would have to transpire that very night. Unsure if it would be in Leonor's presence, he felt increasingly uncomfortable at the thought and knew that he might as well come up with a nice little proposal for a fun outing during the rest of the long weekend to mollify Jolly.

Smiling in complete satisfaction, Leonor chimed in, "Colón? You mean *the* Colón after whom my *country* is named?

I simply don't believe that he did such terrible things!" Then she walked across to Patrick and bent to box his ears lightly, as if it was a massage. Turning, she walked in a leisurely fashion towards the balcony, while trying to steal a glance at Terrence as she passed him. She was quite aghast at his lack of expression throughout and, after the reading, yet totally unable to contain by now, her unabashed physical attraction towards him that seemed to have overwhelmed her and her politically correct indignation. The momentary proximity that she allowed herself to his unperturbed, reclined form, not only did not assuage the attraction, but enhanced and exacerbated it.

*I must apologise that I was not quite honest with you. Actually, Patrick might not have raised himself to get Zinn's book. He might have just shuffled himself on the cushion in reaction to Jolly's naivety. He had long learnt that the consequences of reacting would be a long pout and little understanding from Jolly, that Terrence would never express interest, for he seemed perennially ensconced in a deep first-hand knowledge of both the Hispanic and Negro experiences and, as all of them through the centuries, would fall totally silent when their matters were discussed by whites. Patrick probably just felt he might have a chat with Leonor when he found the chance. Thus, the following is what could also have transpired.*

As Leonor went to the balcony, Patrick followed and stood next to her as she bent over the sculptured black iron grille railing.

"Leonor, your quick reaction was a good one. Have you read Zinn's *A People's History of the United States*?" He smiled and added gently, "I guess not. However, you must read it, at least parts of it. I have a copy. I can lend it to you if you want to read it between semesters."

She looked at him puzzlingly. "Yes, of course. However, only if you think it important and tell me which the interesting chapters are; I will read them during the semester break." She peeped into the living room to make sure that she was out of earshot of the other two, looked at Patrick and returned his smile.

Patrick replied with a continued smile, "I will give it to you tonight." He hoped to clinch an intellectual deal with Leonor that he knew he could never have with Jolly. He was looking forward to, and was eagerly anticipating, many a *tête-à- tête* with Leonor in the months ahead.

Under Jolly's able and efficient direction, and with a helping hand from Leonor, who stooped for the evening to conquer Jolly and do whatever chores were necessary, Thanksgiving dinner turned out to be superb. Helping with heavy chores was a new and novel experience for Leonor, who had never lifted a finger at home, where there were plenty of *ayudantes*—attendants—for such things. In addition, her fashionably and firmly held feminist views were conventionally and conveniently opposed to women working in the kitchen while the men relaxed and lounged.

The main beneficiary of the women working in the kitchen was clearly Terrence, for his consumption easily surpassed that of all the others. At the end of the meal, he got up obviously satisfied, patted his tummy, and belched. The women laughed. Patrick ignored their laughter while the women cleared the table as thoughts of those early unfortunate Indians lingered in his mind. Jolly joined Patrick in the kitchen to help him stack the dishes for Mrs. Jackson to wash the next morning. Then she placed the remaining turkey, most of it the dark meat, into aluminium foil for Mrs. Jackson to take home. She had found out indirectly from Mrs. Jackson that she had not planned to bake a turkey but, rather, some Southern dishes such as pig's knuckles, chicken necks and wings, and spare ribs. As a result, during dinner, Jolly had kept an eye on how much turkey was disappearing to be certain that enough would remain for Mrs. Jackson and her family the next day. She beamed as she packed the leftover turkey. Patrick and Jolly did not exchange words, but they occasionally smiled a smile of familiarity at each other.

Leonor glanced at Terrence, finally finding herself alone with him in the living room. She said, "Hi Terrence. That was a great meal, thanks to Jolly, wasn't it?"

Terrence replied, "*¡Estupendo!*" Glancing at Leonor, he enjoyed the expression of unanticipated shock written all over Leonor's face.

"*¿Cómo sabes español? ¡Gracias a Dios!*"

"*¿Por que no? ¿Que crees? Solamente los colombianos tienen el derecho a hablar castellano?*"

"*¿Castellano?*" she enjoined, emphasising the '*ll*ano'. "*Que maravilla.*" She again emphasised the '*villa*'. Smiling, she added, "*¿Cómo, cómo, cómo?*"

"*Es una historia muy larga para ser contada en este momento.*" He smiled broadly, satisfied with his success in impressing her; not that his objective was to impress her in particular, but it had been great fun just to impress for its own sake.

Just as the obviously enchanted Leonor began to approach Terrence, Patrick and Jolly emerged from the kitchen, nipping her probable intentions in the bud.

Jolly said so all could hear, "We should be taking the bus back or we will have to spend the night here!"

The boys seemed not to hear. The girls were not invited to stay the night over. The girls nevertheless sat down. There was some small talk. To obviate that possibility, Patrick suggested a walk along the Georgetown Canal on the Saturday two days hence.

"We could walk up to Potomac Turning, if you can take it," he said and smiled at the girls in mock challenge, while trying to avoid Terrence's eyes for fear of finding an expression of irritation, if not disapproval.

Raised eyebrows were Leonor's response in the interrogative.

Patrick asked, "Have you not seen the cluster of rocks on the river from George Washington Parkway? There is a sharp turning in the river as you approach Chain Bridge from the District side. Terry and I have named it Potomac Turning." Reading non-recognition, he continued, "You know, the bridge that goes straight into Arlington, Virginia, or to Vienna if you turn right at the end of the bridge? I warn you, though…" He smiled again, shaking his forefinger at the girls. "…Getting there can be quite hazardous because you have to get off the trail and make it through some pretty stubborn and slippery rocks to get to the lookout with the most expansive, gorgeous view of the Potomac twisting and turning. It's the best view of the majestic river. In season, you can even see shad swimming upstream!" he exclaimed.

Jolly jumped up, grabbed Leonor by her shoulder and pulled her up. Leonor had been fixating on Terrence and had missed Patrick's description.

Jolly asked, "Isn't that the bridge that goes to a road that leads into Langley and the Agency on the Virginia side?" Then, mockingly in accusation, she added, "Boy, have you been snooping around there?"

Unusually for her, she suddenly felt vindicated in the world of *réparté* that Patrick seemed so much to enjoy, and which she generally treated with disinterest, if not disdain. Patrick let it pass. He already felt better, since he would sleep soundly that night after having offered Jolly an olive branch in lieu of inviting her and her friend to sleep over at the apartment with Terrence and him.

Jolly wasn't interested in Potomac Turning, however. "Why don't we go to the Smithsonian? I have been meaning to see the American History Museum for some time. Apparently, they have a great collection of evening gowns of First Ladies, and another of English and French crockery."

"You mean dishes?" Patrick's matter-of-fact reply slipped out.

"Aw! That's just in the morning, Pat. We could visit the Capitol and the Old Post Office after lunch. I guess we will not have time for the White House. I do want to see the East

Room. We have seen, on television, our presidents address the nation from there, haven't we?" She responded as if to herself. "I guess we have to do it some other weekend; early morning would be best." Then, mothering Pat and Terrence, she asked, "Tell me, when was it that you last visited our country's places of historic interest and national pride?"

Patrick almost said, 'you mean *prejudice*, don't you', but all he let escape was a lacklustre expression, a smirk, really.

Perceiving it, Jolly encouraged, "You do know that you get a great view of the city from the clock tower of the Old Post Office? I am sure you will love it."

At last, Terrence spoke. "Thanks, Jolly. I would love to do it all on Saturday." He was barely able to hide his relief that the sunsets with their brilliant ephemeral colours at the Potomac Turning that Patrick and he had enjoyed over the past years would remain theirs and theirs alone. *How could Patrick suggest going there in a bunch,* he fumed without realising that Patrick had possibly suggested it knowing full well that Jolly would never buy the idea of a long hike over rocks in order to use binoculars to see fish swimming. He had probably been well aware that she would, instead, proffer suggestions grounded on popular culture and, more importantly, based on her newest readings from the Smithsonian bookstores that she routinely frequented.

The girls squeezed their belongings into their duffle bags, Jolly's made of what looked like Belgian tapestry and Leonor's a solid royal blue with Carolina Herrera logos embroidered in white satin. Mrs Betancour, Leonor's mother, had picked it up on Fifth Avenue during one of her many quick shopping trips to New York. Hugs were exchanged, accompanied by some effusive sounds as meaningless as the language of Neanderthals such as 'see y – a – a – h', 'ch – o – u', and a few others, as the girls glided to the exit door.

Throwing open Potomac Turning to the rest of the world had been averted. Thus far, it had been Patrick and Terrence's secret spot, their hideout. The river at Potomac Turning, still this moment, gushing the next, frozen in the winter months, exuberant and chaotic as spring arrived, had waited for them in frolic and play, for their pleasure, for their eyes only. They had partaken exclusively of nature's beauty, climbing or racing across the unkempt rocks strewn about like a much-used grey steel comb, dreaming and planning together, or simply being silent, in communion with the early stars, eagerly awaiting the formation of Orion in the night sky, signalling to the stars, assuring their togetherness.

It is true that they had never discussed that spot as their own, their special, secret spot, but it had always been that way between them until now. Then why had Patrick proposed that spot for a picnic with the girls, speaking directly to them? Terrence quickly put the thought aside for fear that his hurt might magnify momentarily from a whimsical passing breeze to an uncontrollable tornado. As always, there was little in his face that revealed what he had thought or how he had killed his apprehension.

One of the boys turned off the wall switch for the ceiling light while the other turned on the standing lamp with an off-green translucent glass lamp shade. Somewhat relieved after the long day, they sank back into the sofa as the intimacy of silence and long shadows filled the room.

*    *    *

Graduation *cum laude* for Patrick had been expected. Indeed, as the school years had progressed, it was not just grades, but his analytical abilities and expansive interests in global affairs – history, politics and diplomacy – were recognised by his professors across the board, as though vindicating the early questioning spirit he had revealed in his San Antonio school. Those wits had now not only been sharpened, but chiselled exquisitely.

Patrick's success was no surprise, but no one had quite anticipated the same brilliance in Terrence. No one other than Patrick had witnessed the development of Terrence's quick wit and ability to perceive issues and solve problems. Therefore, when he declared that he was on the Dean's List, Agnes, who had decided to attend the graduation ceremony of her son at Georgetown, decided to bring Rosita along as well so that the two mothers would, together, celebrate the academic successes of their two sons.

They stayed at the Dupont Circle Hotel so that they could take the P Street bus directly to and from the apartment. When they visited, Rosita, even as she came through the door, hugged Patrick unabashedly and, for an enduring moment, their affinity, sealed with the many years of devoted caring that she had showered on this child, instantly blossomed again. Next, as Terrence stood smiling in the background, she tipped her head backward in sheer admiration and told him to bend. "Bend down, *hijo*!" she blurted.

As he did, she planted two wet kisses, happily ignoring the inconvenience of his newly hardened, manly jaws. He extended his broad, muscular arms, easily succeeding in sheltering his much smaller mother in them. Momentarily, she squeezed herself out of his grasp, intuitively looking towards the kitchen, and disappeared into it.

Agnes surveyed them both. "Look at you!"

Then, following Rosita's example, carefully and, conscious of the equality that she mistakenly imagined to be the mode in the nation's capital, never guessing how racially divided the capital was, she planted kisses on both their foreheads, beginning with Terrence and then Patrick. Patrick smiled at her with understanding, in fact admiringly, knowing very well how difficult it must have been for her not to let slip her special concerns for Patrick's welfare. Terrence disappeared into the kitchen, more comfortable for the moment to be with his mother, the housekeeper.

Patrick asked impetuously, "Ma, why didn't you bring Sis along? Her school graduation was over weeks ago. I guess Dad, as usual, would not let her leave his side!" He put on a mock expression of exasperation. Almost in the same breath, he added, "And to which college is she planning to go? Austin? That would be closest to home, I guess." While he did not want to sound contrary right from the start, he could not help but add, "You all haven't written about yourselves for some time; yet I have to keep reporting back to you every week."

The slight show of dissatisfaction was rather unusual for Patrick. He was used, from the early years when his sister's birthdays would be celebrated and his generally ignored, to Agnes' partial treatment of Sis. Agnes was prone to carrying her baby around without putting her down when shopping or visiting church while, by contrast, asking her son to run along next to her, or even run small errands for her all by himself. While quite accepting of it all, on occasion Patrick pouted about those past infractions on Agnes' part. Then, as Sis' smiling, always enthusiastic, face filled his imagination, even the slightest hint of negative feelings evaporated instantly. He looked quizzically at Agnes, hoping for a comprehensive clarification.

Agnes' prevarication was obvious from her evasive expression. As she looked away towards the balcony, Patrick saw lines on her face, bright in the morning sunlight, for the first time. He knew she had been transported through a generation. He felt pain in the hollow of his stomach. Startled back into the present, he insisted, "Yes, Mother?"

Agnes replied in a low voice, "We don't know…"

"What do you mean?"

"Well, she could not sit for her final exams…. We didn't want to tell you before your exams…"

In raised voice, he asked, "Why?"

"The sisters in her school thought it would be best for her to stay home until…" She trailed off.

Sternly, he asked, "Until what, Mother?"

Almost inaudibly, she replied, "Until she had the baby."

The momentary felicity of the arrival of the two middle-aged women had been shattered like falling glass.

"When is the baby *due*? Who is the fellow?"

"She would not go through with it…" Agnes looked pleadingly at her son.

He screamed, "What?" His words, however, did not match his feeling, which he recognised to be one of relief. He was surprised at his relief, but felt it would be out of context to express it. Then, calmly he pleaded almost in a whisper, "Why didn't you bring her? She would have liked the change of scene, I am sure."

His mother replied sternly, "Understand, Patrick, her recuperation period is not yet over."

"I am going to call her from the post office," Patrick announced impetuously as he ran out the door.

Rosita emerged from the kitchen, followed closely by Terrence.

As though to provide an excuse, Agnes explained, "You know, Rosita, all through the years, how the girl has been. Her dad and I… We gave her all our love. She loved her older brother but, from the day he left, something happened. She lost her direction in high school. She always got into trouble. However, I never expected…" She seemed to be sobbing silently.

Rosita came to her to put her hand lightly on her shoulder. It surprised Terrence, since he had never seen his mother take such liberties with her employer, but quickly realised how things changed as people grew older. Now, she and Agnes seemed more like friends, like soul mates, Rosita reaching out to console Agnes. He would never know that Agnes had failed to proffer a helping hand to Rosita when Terrence himself was conceived.

"I will get you some fresh coffee," said Rosita. Looking at Terrence, she shook her head, adding, "I will have to show a few things to this Mrs. Jackson of yours." It was a clear signal of disapproval of as yet unknown oversights in the latter's management of the kitchen.

Terrence returned the comment by a look cautioning her from doing anything of the kind. He certainly did not want any more storms in the tea cup of this apartment.

\*  \*  \*

Patrick ran down the stairs and straight through P Street, crossing Wisconsin, and turning right on 31<sup>st</sup>. His mind was running faster than he was.

*I knew it. What could come of Ma insisting on her swimming in shorts when the other girls were swimming in the swimsuits, making her a butt of their jokes, and so many such examples that come to mind? Ma must have felt like the Virgin Mary I am sure. But look what it did to Sis. God knows what other trials and tribulations poor Sis had to suffer while I am at Georgetown, content in running my own life. But at least she had never been locked in a dark pantry for jumping on the living room sofa, or left alone in the evening on the park bench for refusing to recite* Twinkle, Twinkle, Little Star *for Ma's friends. Why could Sis not endure it like I did,* he asked himself in irritation and in dismay.

Patrick was exasperated with Sis' failure. *Ouff, that fool! Why didn't she ever tell me anything about what was going on inside her? I am sure it was to save me from worry, so I would not be disturbed and be able to keep up to Ma's expectations of my grades. I am going to have a discussion with Ma when I get back. I must…. Who does she think she is? Who is she to perpetrate this on us?*

Patrick's thoughts were racing. *I must take Sis out of there. She must come stay with me. Perhaps she will come with me to India.*

There was an elderly woman next in queue at the phone box. Looking at Patrick, she smiled and gave way to him. She had loads of morning time to kill anyway. Indeed, after spending the next hour sorting through recent issuances of stamps at the post office, she had planned to walk up

Wisconsin Avenue to the Safeway supermarket and finally to get back home in time for lunch. It would now all fit very well. He thanked her without looking at her. As soon as another old woman emerged from the booth painted in royal blue and silver, Patrick entered and carefully shut the folding glass door behind him. He dialled and said, "Hello."

The sobs on the other side were almost audible to the hard-of-hearing old lady waiting patiently outside for her turn, resting on her walker, for her expression changed to curiosity and concern. Then she reflected, O*h! Young lovers.* She beamed once more as Patrick stole a glance at her, a bit anxious over his lack of privacy. He was careful to keep his vocal interventions minimal and his decibel level low.

Patrick walked back slowly. Nothing was said between mother and son when he reached the apartment. In fact, it was not discussed during the rest of the visit. Instead, when they sat down for a sumptuous lunch comprising Rosita's chicken enchiladas, rice and beans with, on the side, a Mexican tomato salad with tossed-in hot pepper and a vinegar and honey dressing, he jocularly reminisced over his childhood with Rosita and smiled towards Terrence, trying to make him envious. It had little impact on Terrence, so accustomed he was to Patrick's primacy in receiving Rosita's attention in formal situations. Scanning the dining table in a demonstrative manner, Patrick also attempted to bring Agnes into the conversation by glancing at her occasionally. But it had little effect. Sis was still on Agnes's mind.

Agnes knew there would be no point in bringing up Sis again. That suited her well. She knew how stubborn Patrick was. She knew his sixth sense had driven him to contemplate or already take some action with respect to his sister. She might not be happy with it when she eventually learnt about it, but she was conscious that she would have to accept it. Yes, her son had not changed from that afternoon in her San Antonio hacienda when he had left in a hurry with a bagful of things she had packed for him. Oh yes, he had a good head on his shoulders and would take care of his sister. Brother and sister would be fine under the former's guidance, Agnes said to herself as Patrick chatted on. *Gracias a Dios*, the lunch seemed an all-round success.

*       *       *

The visit inevitably turned tumultuous, even if it did not become catastrophic in its essential aspects. Jolly and Leonor were, of course, invited by the boys to their graduations. Right from the start, Jolly made no bones about her relationship with Patrick. Why should she? It was her right and she already had him in her grip. He had meekly said 'no' to her once, explaining that they should be friends rather than lovers, but she was convinced that it was his obsequious attentiveness to his mother that drove such statements. She had explained to him patiently that friendship was incomplete without a conjugal relationship and, that very evening, gave him a pricey cologne. He took it for no particular reason other than that he felt too exhausted to posit contrary arguments any longer. More importantly, he could not say 'no' again to that pleading young girl who, so many years ago, had waited for him alone behind the tree, forsaken and in tears. So, he just took the cologne. Jolly did not have any doubt about Patrick's intentions, treating that gesture as a sure sign of his acceptance of her. Nevertheless, she knew somewhere deep within that she would have to protect her territory and she did so like a vixen.

The graduation at Georgetown did not go well. Jolly and Leonor sat a couple of rows behind Agnes, Rosita and Terrence. Rosita turned to look back at the audience, and saw Jolly. Automatically, she blurted out, "Jolly, how nice to see you! Come sit next to us." Then she realized that those seats were not available. Terrence got halfway up in polite recognition of the girls' presence and quickly sat back down.

Agnes looked back involuntarily and smiled. "Hello, Jolly! How have you been? I *thought* I would see you today. Terrence, dear, do you mind exchanging seats with Jolly?" She did not realize that Jolly was sitting with a friend.

Terrence got up and went to sit with Leonor perhaps a bit reluctantly. A smile formed on Leonor's lips and her heartbeat galloped. Jolly seated herself next to Rosita. A pleasant conversation began, with Jolly looking backwards, pointing to Leonor. Terrence introduced Rosita and Agnes to Leonor, who looked at Rosita and then at Terrence, in instant recognition of the obvious. Rosita smiled at Leonor and Terrence, who were now sitting side by side, and she wondered, perhaps hoped. Terrence looked visibly uncomfortable as Leonor imperceptibly slipped her hand into his. Soon, their thighs touched and stayed that way, for Terrence was too shy to even slightly move his leg.

Leaning forward over Rosita, Jolly engaged Agnes in conversation throughout the convocation speech by a dignitary who extolled the graduates to serve God and country over self and family. It was unimportant that he was known to have nine children of his own with his name and was openly rumoured to have had some additional ones without and, by some miracle, none of his children, legitimate or otherwise, was known to have been drafted into the army.

Patrick's name was soon pronounced at the top of his class, along with a few other names. Agnes wished her husband was there with her to behold their son in his gown and cap, but he had had to remain behind with their daughter. She killed any straying thoughts of San Antonio. She did not wish to be troubled by them. She liked the feeling of moving forward with her son. She hung onto that thought and tried to focus on Patrick coming onto the stage to receive his certificate and a medal that would be hung around his neck with a broad red ribbon by the university president.

Agnes felt proud. The stage, the awardees and the audience all floated in front of her. She was oblivious to them all except for her son, her protégé. Now he would have to go on to higher studies, perhaps to complete a doctorate, she told herself. Oh yes, now he would also have to save himself from other distractions if he was to achieve his potential, reach his promise. She prayed to St. Patrick, her guardian saint, for that to happen.

A vision of the saint appeared momentarily to reassure her. "Agnes, have I ever failed you?"

Instantly, she was back in the real world and focussed once again on her son who, by now, had disappeared into the labyrinth of fresh graduates.

Jolly said, "Agnes, wasn't he just great? He got this special recognition for having written the best paper on some exotic group in India called the Noxious…" She trailed off. "Well, it begins with an 'n', I am sure, but can't quite recall… Sorry." She smiled without the slightest sign of embarrassment.

The obvious intimacy imparted by Jolly's account embedded like a dagger in Agnes' heart. She understood instantly. She replied, "Oh? Really?"

Jolly clearly heard the 'oh' and the tone that clothed it. She felt as though a blizzard from the Arctic Circle had passed between her and Agnes. She fell silent.

Rosita sensed it too. She looked backward and felt relieved to see Leonor chattering away like a little robin redbreast and Terrence listening to her intently. She wished she could join them, but there was no extra seat and, even if there were, she knew she could never simply get up and leave Agnes. She would have to remain sandwiched between Agnes and Jolly, even as the sharp edges of their newly forming dislike for each other were rapidly taking shape, its emergence unanticipated even a moment earlier, such can be the suddenness and intensity of human feelings. Rosita too could feel their mounting apathy towards each other and felt trapped by it. She had no possibility of removing herself from the scene as a silent drama was being played out by her immediate neighbours.

Eventually, Patrick appeared, resplendent in his flowing, formal attire and burdened with some rolled material peeping in every which direction from under his arm. Agnes got up from her seat and approached him. Jolly followed closely behind her and, in a moment, was beside her. Before Agnes could reach him, Jolly reached forward and said, "Congratulations! What a show!" She planted a kiss on his cheek.

Agnes was speechless. She stepped back. If Patrick wished, he could approach her, she told herself. She was thunderstruck as Patrick went to the others first and gave them polite, short hugs. Then he ran towards Agnes, hugged her tightly, and for a long time, and said, "*Thanks*, Ma, for everything. I love you."

Agnes hugged him lightly. He had come to her last, but it was too late. His all-embracing thanks, arching over infancy, childhood, youth and manhood, had not touched her or, if they had, they certainly were not sufficient for her. She grimaced politely and tried to look over his shoulder into the distance.

Terrence was standing towards the back, smiling patiently. Patrick approached him slowly, almost on tip toes. He gave him a bashful hug, patted him on the back and whispered into his ear, "Thanks, Orion." He added reassuringly, yet confusingly, "We still have a distance to go, don't we?" He took a step back to where no others could see his face directly and looked at Terrence intently. Narrowing his eyes, he smiled again. Then he turned back to the women.

Soon after, the four boys and girls were hugging, jumping, even shouting, as Rosita clapped her hands in unison. Even Agnes let slip a smile. For a moment, there was the appearance of true, all-enveloping joy, and everyone partook of it.

\*     \*     \*

Subsequently, Agnes became withdrawn, if not almost silent, with Patrick. It was already obvious at Terrence's graduation, and it grew worse. Patrick became increasingly impatient. On the one hand, he was afraid that his outburst against his mother was lurking in the wings, waiting for the right opportunity to explode, despite his every attempt to keep it from erupting. On the other, Agnes was never easy to appease once perturbed. Eventually, she decided to bring up the matter one afternoon when she pretended that she needed a walk and Patrick thought it would be a nice idea to walk her to the Kennedy Center through Foggy Bottom.

The townhouses looked colourful in the bright summer day with the appearance of new life all around. Cherry blossoms, roses, and azaleas were everywhere, and some magnolia as well, and not just germs and viruses that infected children in nursery schools, prompting local reporters to fill columns and air time to their hearts' content. There were the whimsically appearing jasmine and primrose clusters that were yet to bloom on creepers, clinging to the outer brick walls along the lanes and alleyways. Agnes enjoyed the walk so much that she lingered here and there, and Patrick was misled into fully relaxing, hugging her to his side as they walked on.

When they eventually emerged onto Virginia Avenue, the dream walk of mother and son had almost ended. They crossed the traffic island and headed towards the Kennedy Center. They entered from the first entrance on the right and walked down its long corridor. Agnes seemed quite impressed and, when they reached the main lobby along the Potomac side of the rectangle, she could not help but gasp with amazement at the enormous Kennedy bust in bronze. To Patrick, however, it had always looked from a distance as if it had been made of thousands of incongruous wood chips that, together, somehow had a decent enough resemblance to the man. Agnes looked up in admiration at the stark Swedish chandeliers that dangled from the five storey high ceiling. Patrick expressed a liking for the unique simplicity of their design.

To impress her even more, Patrick elaborated, "Ma, everything you see here is a gift from some other country in memory of the assassinated president."

Agnes became sombre. She did not want to be reminded of the assassination that had occurred in Texas, her state. It was a matter of deep embarrassment for many Texans. She found herself moving to open the large glass door to a suspended terrace over Rock Creek Parkway, overlooking the Potomac. The terrace was long enough to house a line of weeping willows along its length, imparting to it a definitely sombre look, yet affording visitors a relaxed walk along its edge, as cars sped by beneath it next to the flowing river. Agnes went to the edge of the terrace and stared at the river for what seemed like a long time.

Curious, Patrick walked up to her and said, "Isn't it peaceful, Ma?"

He took her to his side, hugging her closely, recalling old warm memories and banishing the bad ones that always appeared together like a schizophrenic twin. He smiled sincerely at his mother as he bent his torso backwards to see her at a slight distance. Agnes did not return the smile. She seemed thoughtful. Patrick missed a heartbeat. He knew something was brewing.

"Are you looking forward to the graduate programme, Pat?" she asked in a provocative tone while she gazed straight at the sky, which was streaked with white lines against a blue backdrop. Oblivious to humans or their earthly preoccupations, peripatetic clouds danced about madly, still in search of the fleeting sun that had just abandoned them at the meteorologist's precisely appointed moment.

Slowly, Patrick raised his gaze from the still, silver waters of the Potomac, draped in shades of deep blue and grey. He glared at Agnes. 'Yes, Mother' was all that he could manage to gurgle out.

"It will be a real challenge, Son." She smiled at him, sensing his discomfort and her own satisfaction that she derived from it. "You will have to keep away from diversions during this period, if you are to reach your goal."

Even as she phrased her words carefully, she was feeling that, if her husband would do this talking, she would have had no need to venture into such ominous paths herself, and she loathed the reality that her husband had never been at her side at such difficult junctures. No wonder the children loved him so much. She was the witch who had to perform all the unpleasant chores. She felt resentment towards her husband, the man who always smiled and laughed with the children, but who had never changed a diaper and never sat with them to teach the alphabet or math, but was always stretching into his pocket, invariably emerging with a nickel, dime or dollar to appease them whenever they asked him for handouts behind her back. However, she also felt that Patrick was naive in matters of the heart, that he was too young, that he needed guidance, and that she was there to fill the vacuum his father had left glaringly empty.

"What goal? What do you mean by diversions?"

"The goal that reflects your potential; the goal of reaching appropriate places and heights in your professional life where you will receive full recognition for what you accomplish; the goal of achieving the stature for which your *Ma* has laboured all these years, despite her own trials and tribulations, training you from childhood, despite her own lack of schooling, responding to your every whim and fancy, including sending you far, far away to Nowhere Land, miles from your home and family, and then running here to see you for herself," came the unabashed reply, in a steadily rising tone of voice, oblivious to the other visitors strolling along the length of the wide balcony. Then, after a pause, she added, "And regarding diversions, I meant those diversions that women bring, especially when it is likely that an attraction may be momentary. Pat, many women will approach you. You have a good future; it is only natural."

Silence.

"Well, you are still a child," said Agnes as an uncomfortable smile was forming on her face. Pleadingly, she added, "I am saying this as a true friend and not as a mother."

Accusingly, in a derisive tone and with a contorted face, all the while taking care to avert his eyes from hers, Patrick shot back, "Do you mean Jolly?"

"Son, it is just that you have known her since childhood. You should give yourself the chance to meet other young women… in the university… or even later in your profession, with whom you would have more common interests…" Her voice was shrill, a tinge of uncertainty and a touch of regret revealing her nervousness.

He interrupted and spat out, "Make up your mind! Are you afraid of too many women approaching me because I am a gem that you have produced, or should I go ahead and meet as many women as I like? Aren't you sounding a bit contradictory?"

She had had it. "How can you go around with someone who is so big and looks as if she could be your aunt? I have seen you obviously embarrassed by her. Do you feel proud of her? Are you in love with her? Have I not taught you to be honest with yourself?"

Patrick had wavered until this point on how far to take his relationship with Jolly. A battle had been raging inside him over making a fateful choice in favour of decency over honesty. Agnes' interference propelled him to a final decision. Truth is blind but, in his own case, Patrick became blind to it.

*How vicious could Ma be? How dare she intervene in this manner in my life?*, he thought. He proclaimed in a low, steady voice, "I gave my word to Jolly that I shall marry her. That's all there is to it."

Agnes did not read the slightest hint of conviction in that statement, but just a child's tantrum. She recognised the characteristic that he did not inherit from his father, but from her. That old, unmistakable stubbornness had taken over. Though she felt desperate, she knew she could do nothing about it, at least at that point. When she returned to San Antonio, she would have to cross the railway tracks in one of her rare clandestine trips to visit the mixed race soothsayer, a sorceress, who helped her in circumstances like this. The woman would give a talisman that she would mail to the unsuspecting Patrick, who would carry it with himself at all times seemingly for protection against the dark forces, or just to keep Agnes happy. Patrick had never suspected Agnes on such matters. It would be easy. Within a few months, his relationship with Jolly was bound to break up.

Agnes pursed her lips, trying to contain tears of anger that sought to cascade out from under her eyelids. She was hardly successful. She turned her face away from Patrick.

*"Oh, St. Patrick! What folly my son succumbs to!"*

Her implorations shifted instantaneously from witchcraft to the Omnipotent. She knew her faith would protect her; she would depend on her saint until her dying day. She stood a long time looking aimlessly at the silent, steadily flowing Potomac, finally admitting to herself that she had lost this battle with her stubborn son. However, she knew she would have to swallow his intransigence for a short span only, having no intention of accepting it in the long run.

Patrick persisted, "Why are you so controlling? Why so against my independence? You supported Uncle Sam when he married outside proper stock, importing that Korean woman from the Korean War and who then went to work at the local laundry. Even Dad maintained a scrupulous silence about the match, even a couple of years later when she bought up the laundry from the elderly couple who had run it for as long as I could remember. But you were all magnanimous right from day one, taking charge and organizing the wedding. Isn't it only with me that you have objections?"

"Pat, I will be calm without shedding tears, for I do believe that a mother's tears are not good for her son's well being. I am lucky to have been married to a good-looking man, even though we are different in so many ways, as you well know. Your dad is a tall, handsome man, and has always been. His face has sharper features than even yours. His nose is like an arrow, his eyes wide and penetrating, and his jaws exquisitely contoured. He is much more attractive than you." She was ruthless in her assessment. "I think physical attraction is more important than compatibility in the first years of marriage. After that, it is all up to fate. You would fail in this if you marry Jolly. You owe yourself better…"

"I totally agree Mother, that you may possess your own views over such matters. But I am unwilling to discuss with you my criteria for whom I find attractive. I can certainly say that beauty is in the eyes of the beholder, hackneyed though this may sound. Also, have you ever heard of or thought of *inner* beauty? Could you raise yourself to the level of admiring the higher qualities?" he concluded in disgust mingled with triumph. He continued to blurt out uncontrollably, "You are so gifted, Ma. You hold a pencil or pen and the most beautiful images unfold on paper. Your crayons, water colours and oils plead with you to be held for being shaped into magical scenes. Yet, why is your heart so closed, so narrow, so precise?"

Agnes was ashen. She was sobbing now, tears streaming down her face.

"Women have been misunderstood, mistreated and tortured through history.

"However, even you, my son? As an adolescent, I had looked forward to a serene walk through life, and certainly not the humdrum everyday life of a housewife. However, all I got were house chores. Nothing more. Your father never understood me – that is why I never painted or played the piano in the hacienda, abilities and qualities with which I entered the household of the Goulds. Instead, I spent day in and day out in the kitchen. Your father only appreciated opera, right from the days he had taken a trip to Manaus and seen some operas there that besotted him forever. He understood nothing else. Since I was not a soprano, I was reduced to a common housewife, fit only for drudgery and unwanted in every way except in bed for my body. Your castigation proves it conclusively. I had my right to move away from my God-given gifts and I don't regret it. I need only to ask God on my Judgment Day, 'why, oh why did you give me those talents when you also burdened me with a husband with little appreciation of who I am and with a child who is so unappreciative of my sacrifices for him, his education, his every need?' I really do not have to explain any of it to an ungrateful son. Indeed, I feel that you do not deserve to be called a *son*."

Though it penetrated him like a poisoned arrow, Patrick remained unconvinced with the explanations, reflecting the broader canvas on which his accusations were based. Rather, he found Agnes' lamentations to be excuses at best. Nevertheless, he did not persist, for he was affected by Agnes' sobbing, and his anger suddenly vanished. Indeed, he became a bit sheepish, having blurted out his deepest critique of his mother to her so directly. He fell totally silent.

He walked back through the glass doors to the long inside corridor, leaving Agnes behind. He looked carefully at John Kennedy's bust. How pleasant he looked from a distance, yet how rough it was from close. The sculpture seemed to replicate his life. Patrick briskly moved away from it. Soon, he lost himself, poring over works of art and delicate objects on display from all over the world in the landings of the stairs and corners of the corridors. He surprised himself at his sudden interest and his ability to appreciate fine things. He told himself, 'that bouncy little girl' with a smile, acknowledging Jolly's influence over him in the appreciation of art, of culture and her tutelage during their many visits to the various

Smithsonian buildings. His reluctance about settling for her slowly faded with each such thought.

Agnes was still standing at the same spot when Patrick returned. She was staring into the darkness that, by now, had enveloped her surroundings. As she heard Patrick approach, she turned rapidly and said, "Let's go, Patrick."

Patrick obligingly attempted to gather Agnes into his side as they walked. She shivered a little and pulled herself firmly out of his loose, formal hug, her taut figure betraying her state of mind. They walked side by side, his guilt written all over his face, engulfing his entire being.

In defeat, Patrick's irritation surged once more. He wished that he had taken revenge on his mother with greater immediacy and intensity as she made those rude comments about Jolly. How could she have commented on the beauty or lack of it in his choice of life partner in such a derogatory manner? However, the thought merely provoked him in another momentary flash of anger without enabling him sufficiently to be able to mouth it. That moment, that opportunity, had passed. Angry with himself, he regretted that harsher, more correct, words remained unspoken, his lips sealed.

In almost a jerking motion, he brought Agnes tightly to his side, refusing to accept her stiffness as he walked on. This time, Agnes did not object, assessing that the hate should pass. They moved silently on. The world saw a son caringly assisting his beloved mother in the simple motion of that meandering walk. Once again, appearance had trumped reality.

*   *   *

1972 was not the easiest year in Washington. Vietnam was over, but Watergate was devouring the nation. Patrick had decided to continue in Georgetown University; he had received a scholarship to work on a Masters degree at the

School of Strategic Studies. However, he found himself often tempted away from concentrating on his work during his first semester. In the afternoons, after sitting in all morning for the course lectures that he took care not to miss, followed by a simple lunch of a hamburger or hotdog, usually obtained in haste from the cafeteria machine, he would head across the football field for the lounge of the medical school library, where he would breathlessly watch the deliberations of the Senate Watergate Committee. The elderly Democratic Senator Sam Irwin's familiar Southern drawl enchanted him, as did his balanced and fair conduct of business as Chairman of the Committee. Young Senator Baker impressed him with his apparent neutrality in questioning witnesses, despite being a Republican. None of the senators seemed obviously stupid. Some were young and handsome, while others were older and erudite. The show of democracy in motion was thrilling to the point that the question did cross his mind whether or not it was all a show, a cynical charade, a cinema.

High officials of the executive branch, Messrs. Ehrlichman, Haldeman, Dean and Mitchell, never mind the quickly departed Vice President Agnew, seemed, to Patrick, to have arrived from another galaxy, descended upon humans with unfathomable extraterrestrial objectives that were bound to remain unachieved in primitive neighbourhoods such as Earth. Any president who had employed them must, by association, be inscrutable, unreachable. On top, Patrick found it difficult to look at Nixon on television because of his lack of physical charm. When speaking with reporters, the contours of Nixon's face appeared to be uneven and unfortunate, his nose tadpole like, almost causing Patrick to wince. He found it painful to watch Nixon during press conferences. It appeared that Nixon's facial gesticulations were a mark of his desperation, his inability to handle the media. It was easily understandable, he felt, how John F. Kennedy's charisma and good looks had overwhelmed Nixon in the Presidential elections of 1960.

By contrast, young Dean was pleasant to look at, especially when he testified at the Committee, with near-blond hair slicked with Bryl Cream and neatly parted on the side. Sometimes Patrick would lose himself watching his almond-shaped eyes set in a softly sculpted, stunningly beautiful face and miss his testimony, alerting himself back with a start, admonishing himself for losing track.

He was amused somewhat by the transparent foibles of Mr. Mitchell and felt a pang of sympathy for his petite wife, trying hard to give hints of her husband's involuntary involvement, but being scorned as an eccentric. The other two, one bald and the other with a crew-cut, were unattractive to Patrick. One had none of the manliness of a gentleman whose baldness could have revealed an exquisite head in the shape of an ostrich egg for, in life, it was peculiarly flat. The other was the antithesis of the handsome marine; rather, he appeared more like a German storm trooper taking aim with ruthless accuracy at his targets, the civilian examiners huddled across from him. These senators, in their turn, were relentless in their unyielding quest to break the unbending resolve of Nixon's men with their aim of protecting the president at all cost and, in their convoluted imagination, safeguarding the presidency and the nation from the irritating noise of mumbo jumbo democracy. While Patrick found the testimony riveting at points, he saw nothing terribly complex in them, the revelations against *All the President's Men*, trickling out over hours, days and months being so straight forward. Instead, the challenge was to maintain his unwavering attention over the drawled out narratives and often boring exchanges of the Committee.

Patrick's high point, however, was not at the Committee hearings, but when Dan Rather asked Richard Nixon at a press conference a question on Watergate and the president retorted by asking Dan Rather sarcastically if Dan was running for something. Watching live and fully engrossed,

Patrick interpreted it as 'running *for* an election' when, in a split second, Rather shot back, 'no, Sir, Mr. President, are *you*?', as in 'running *from* something', thought Patrick. At that moment, Patrick became Dan Rather's fan, taking in, like a new evangelical convert, Rather's subsequent gospels in many a documentary show, including on the United States not adhering to the more than two hundred and fifty treaties that it had entered into, over centuries, with the aboriginal American-Indians, and another one on redneck whites hunting deer for pleasure in small, enclosed spaces, all conducted in the nutshell of an hour interspersed with mindlessly inane commercials that came, thankfully, to relieve some of the tension that invariably built up as Rather's documentaries proceeded.

Patrick's favourite commercials, in an ascending order of inanity and, therefore, his enjoyment, included Bounty, the paper towel, proclaimed confidently by Nancy Walker as the 'quicker picker-upper' as one piece was shown to suffice for a table full of spilt milk; Patricia Neal's 'Fill it to the rim with Brim', the instant coffee; the family that quickly exited a French restaurant when served on plates hidden under silver domes that, when removed, revealed one carrot, one pea and the smallest conceivable piece of *chateaubriand*, and then beaming in front of burgers and *French* fries at a McDonald's fast food joint; and last, but not least, a commercial showing a six-member family, the parents all smiles and the kids rambunctious and unruly, entering a Holiday Inn room with a voiceover informing the audience that 'the best surprise is *no* surprise!' even as the camera surveyed the all-too-familiar orange bed sheets, curtains and plywood furniture, giving the viewer ample opportunity to savour the infallibility and comfort of familiarity. Even as the commercials provided welcome respite, Patrick became impatient if they took too long. By the time they ended, he felt he had had enough of them but just had to endure them for Dan's sake.

Dan remained Patrick's hero even as the former acquired, in a measure higher than the usual liberty accorded to a television anchor, a reputation for obnoxious behaviour as his success as a newscaster sky-rocketed. Patrick even voraciously read and gulped down Rather's strange musings and commentaries as a Texan in America, removing himself inexplicably and rather strangely, though only occasionally, from his primary role as the nation's top news reader.

Whenever politics or world affairs and their media coverage came up in evening conversations among classmates and friends, Patrick found himself apologising for Dan or his behaviour as mere happenstance, the result of the pressure of extreme success. When once he was challenged as to what he thought the reason had been for Connie Chung, the ravishingly attractive Chinese-American with an impeccably clear and sharp tonal rendition and a pure American diction, being dropped as Rather's co-anchor, he retorted incredulously, 'she married Maury Povich, the host of those horrific daytime talk shows', downsizing the issue as though her conjugal connection was sufficient reason for her to be removed from the arena of elite journalism, for everyone should certainly have been well aware of the low-quality television that all channels other than Public Television perhaps, readily descended to, with the sole objective of maximizing profits and cornering markets, in particular as news filtered out that multinational companies were buying up television studios.

Patrick did admit once that journalists and, in particular, journalists in the United States, as opposed to their British counterparts, mixed up their role as reporter with that of the reported. He loved citing the example of television interviewers, who would do wrenching interviews by stumping their interviewees with trivial questions such as, 'would you be a tree or its blossom' – it really did not matter what their actual or exact questions were, since there was no content or meaning in them in any event, the interviewer's only objective being to transport the viewer to a world of magic *un*realism. One evening, the unsuspecting viewer was surprised by a sudden proclamation, something to the effect of, 'dear viewer, as I do all these interviews for you, I recently had this intuition of how much you must wonder about me, how I live, and who I am', and proceeded to take the viewer through the interviewer's own, not-so-classy but unabashedly expensive, New York apartment in some presumably exclusive block, showing off her supposedly valuable heirlooms, furniture and collectibles, celebrating shamelessly, while revealing her arrested aesthetic taste and sense to the bargain. The nation had not yet become inured to the many others who would follow in that vein such as the one who shared with the audience the progress and vanquishing of her breast cancer and, subsequently, experienced soaring ratings and eventually catapulting herself to the top position in television journalism.

When someone retorted with what he thought of Dan Rather's writings or scoffed at the pomposity of his writings on issues such as patriotism or a plethora of such matters, something that was never done by Walter Cronkite except through a slip of expression or the raising of an eyebrow, Patrick would clam up, not venturing any more into diatribes against other show business stars, or simply changed the topic, or would get up to refresh his drink. At such points, if the boob tube was shut, he would just get up and turn it on just to minimize the damage already incurred from the conversation.

When by himself, he occasionally turned on *Carol Burnett*, *Maude*, *Mary Tyler Moore*, *Rhoda*, *All in the Family*, and *Sony and Cher* and, of course, *Saturday Night Live* – no one could beat Gilda Radner's cross-eyed tracking of her own bead of sweat slipping and sliding on the surface of her nose even as she read out absurd news items, completely confounding the viewer about which aspect of the skit to focus on, or John Belushi's gesticulations as he bellowed out surprisingly good music with his *Blues Brothers Band*. Patrick would laugh his guts out, instantaneously looking around in embarrassment to ensure that no one was around. He sang along with Tony Orlando and Dawn, and Helen Reddy, and danced a few steps with *Soul Train*. He became engrossed in *Upstairs Downstairs*, the stiff upper lip, period soap opera performed by English actors and, on Public Radio, he listened intently to *My Word*, a supercilious British extempore show in which the prize went to the person who used the best meaningless puns. When Terrence was around, they would turn on the *Grand Slams*, some phase of which seemed to be perennially on. This was Patrick's escape, not only from the Naxals or the exhortations of Father Vincent, but also from the unhappy memories of Agnes' visit to Washington DC.

In these ways, Patrick ignored his studies and his grades the first year of the two-year Masters program. He remained firmly rooted in following Washington politics and in the stupider bits of television to feed his escapism during the hours he should have reserved for self-study. He rooted for Nixon's resignation, making up his mind after reading that he had bearers serve him costly wine under the wrapping of a serviette while his guests would be served cheaper ones. Patrick was truly aghast. He had forgiven Nixon his physical shortcomings that were beyond his control, though Patrick had come to believe strongly, from having to watch Nixon perennially in the media, that politicians should have to pass a looks test since viewers had to see so much of them all the time. However, he could not condone the newly reported behaviour on Nixon's part. A man who could deceive his invited guests in such a degrading manner, eschewing minimal tenets of decency, could as easily deceive his society, Patrick told himself. When, at last, Nixon told the country with a droplet covering his pupils that the media would not have anyone to kick around any longer and walked out of the White House for good and onto a *heli*copter, Patrick felt triumphant. He repeated to himself whenever the thought crossed him,

*"Yes, Mr. Nixon, you and your pals do not have the nation to kick around anymore!"*

\*     \*     \*

Eventually, the graduate student advisor called Patrick in to alert, nay, admonish him, for his poor academic showing. He listened quietly, attentively, and then responded, "Father, I have been going through some serious thinking. I have been thinking of transferring to Columbia's School of Journalism. What do you think, Father?"

He took care not to divulge how much time he had been spending on a curiosity hunt for Bengal and Bengalis in an obscure corner of the world, how long he had been learning yoga in a reclusive street in the city, or the dexterity with which he had managed to get himself enrolled in Bengali classes quite some months ago. Father would certainly have disapproved for meandering away from the given curriculum.

"No," was the clear answer shot back at Patrick. "We have given you a full scholarship. We have made an investment in you, young man. We have high hopes for you. If you leave at this point in the middle of the program, your future professional career could be irrevocably jeopardized. Of course, we cannot stop you if you decide to leave. But, if something else is the matter, I would be glad to organize some special assignments for you in the next two semesters to bring your grade point average back up, my son. And, if you continue to feel strongly about journalism, you could do it after one year, with a Masters degree already in hand."

Patrick was well experienced in the devious thoughts and arguments that priests were capable of. However, this time, something told him that he was not being led astray. Nor did he have the wherewithal to oppose the priest's view without adequate financing. Where was the stubbornness that he had revealed in his early years, in his actions growing up, in high school? Now, as a maturing youth, he realized that he could not bolt somewhere else a second time, and that he had better shape up and get his act together. He would have to get his Masters degree with commensurate accolades in comfortable comparison with the decorations that adorned his Bachelors degree. He left the priest's office sheepishly, without protest, in silence, and with a new resolve to do better.

*     *     *

Leonor and Jolly arrived at the apartment early on Sunday morning. Patrick was just finishing up his *Omkaram* yoga, sitting on a wicker mat that had been rolled out on the floor. It made an incongruous scene, for he was sitting between sentinels, two upper-class, middle-aged, cross-legged neighbours, Georgetown matrons, who were clothed in loose silk attire and expensive designer head bands. Within a minute, he chanted 'Om' in a drawn out, low, almost guttural voice, opened his eyes slowly and, without looking at the seated women, stood up to greet the new arrivals. Their sudden appearance had certainly pierced his concentration successfully.

Jolly sped towards the kitchen without wishing the older women who, by now, were also raising themselves, and who were obviously not terribly impressed by the agile younger women who had barged in and were darting across without any greeting or evidence of composure in their movements.

Quickly recovering, and all smiles, one matron chimed, "Pat, thanks, as usual. It was *so* peaceful. I have all the energy for the rest of the day. I feel we are now getting into the serious bit, legs crossed and all."

The other, unabashedly seconding her mate's view, joined in, "Can't wait to get there!" Then, slipping into their well-worn, but obviously expensive and branded sneakers, they disappeared through the entrance door.

Leonor admiringly added, "Wow!"

Patrick took note of the comment and let slip out a satisfied grunt, a specialist's acknowledgement. It came from a confidence that had been soaring within himself as his familiarity with Indian mores and methods had blossomed. Referring to Jolly, he asked, "Where did *she* disappear to?"

Leonor provided the excuse. "Well, remember our visit today to the Smithsonian? She has planned a picnic on the Mall, has brought ingredients for sandwiches for an army. Now she has to make them!"

Both of them shared a short laugh. Both knew that Jolly never revealed much, if any, interest in Patrick's flirtations with the Sub-continent. Possibly, she was awed by it; probably, it was disdain. Patrick was puzzled by the disinterest, but had given himself little time to ponder the matter, and there always was Leonor to fill in for a good conversation.

Leonor feigned to look around quizzically, "And where is precious, no, pious, Terry?" She immediately responded to herself rhetorically, "In church, of course! Isn't it Sunday morning? Wearing his pinstripe suit, I presume," were her caustic remarks since she would obviously have preferred to have Terrence in or out of a pinstripe suit in her own clutches rather than in church.

They shared laughter once again, this time a little louder, confident that Jolly had no intention of deserting the kitchen at this moment. She wanted to finish making the sandwiches that she knew the rest would be clamouring for, the moment they took the first break along their long, impending walk. She would have to complete her venture well before Mrs. Jackson arrived, since the lady certainly did not like a second person in the kitchen while she brewed her soups and concocted her roasts as though to protect her craft, her alchemy, from any unwelcome intrusion.

Leonor picked up on yoga. "Pat, you seemed so serene with your eyes closed, sitting cross-legged and hands folded in front. And the chant really sounded so peaceful. Is that a particular type of yoga?" she asked, like a student wishing to learn the infinite from her mentor.

With a hint of approval, Patrick responded in a serious, yet friendly, tone, "*Om* is the sound one hears in space. It *is* the sound of the universe, of infinity. When you chant it, you are one with the universe, the cosmos, of which you are a part." Then, suddenly breaking the monotony and a mischievous smile breaking on the side of his lips, he added, "Not when you are spaced out. Then you just see stars, of course!"

Leonor stared at Patrick in sincere appreciation, and then broke into a hearty laughter. She got up, crossed over to him, dishevelled his hair and stomped back to her seat, not yet quite satisfied by Patrick's exposition.

Hence, Patrick continued, "Yoga comes from the ancient sages of India. They were in communion with the powers of the universe. Yoga incorporates every solution for man to dissipate his ailments. There would be little need for biological remedies if yoga was fully understood by us Westerners and further developed along scientific lines.

"*Asana* is a yogic posture. For example, take man, who at some point in time, stood up and walked. We tend to say that, as two limbs became free, it was possible for man to learn how to rub rock against rock to make fire, break and shape stone to make implements, and eventually to till the soil or drive a vehicle and, alas, also make armaments. We, thus, tend to say that man progressed as he acquired an erect posture. However, as man stood up, he also acquired an increased disposition to backache." A slight smile appeared on his face in response to the look of astonishment on Leonor's face at the links that were being forged as his argument progressed.

"Thus, there are many *Asanas* that help in relieving, and even curing, back pain. No need for painkillers! Believe me, my mission is also to teach some of these *Asanas* to Mrs. Jackson. Haven't you heard her 'ohs' and 'aays'? Though the few times she has come in when we were practicing, she stared at us contemptuously, as though we were merely practicing some whimsical *white* confabulations. She looks at me and my trainees, so to speak, derisively – you know that look of hers, don't you? Soon, though, I'm sure I'll win her confidence, and then we will attack her back pain with appropriate yoga exercises," he ended smugly in self-satisfied triumph.

No known force seemed to be able to stop him at this point. "The beginning is *Pranayama*, which is a breathing exercise. It cleans your lungs. It has four components, *Puraka*, or inhalation, *Kumbhaka*, or distension, *Rechaka*, or exhalation, and *Shunyaka*, or the void in air spaces that you generate as you complete exhalation." It almost sounded like rote learning, but it was coming from deep within Patrick.

Leonor remained attentive. Jolly was nowhere to be seen.

"Let's come to food. Yoga prescribes a particularly wholesome diet. It prescribes daily food intake of no more than 2800 calories for a man of 187 pounds/eighty-five kilograms who is five feet ten inches/1.78 metres tall. It goes into great detail about the types of food we should and should not eat." Suddenly smiling and, from under his breath, he divulged, "Forget about those sandwiches that Jolly is slapping together this very minute! And now to the part you must have been waiting for most anxiously! Yoga actually advocates celibacy. However, Indians have always been, and continue to be, rather practical, if not exclusively utilitarian. So they found an antidote to this prescription through the *Ayurveda* vehicle, which does not disapprove of the sublimation of the sex urge and allows for and accommodates normal urges, as long as they are carried out in moderation. Don't forget that latter-day Indians went on to write the *Kama Sutra*, the most detailed description of the art and craft of sex. Oh! Those Indians!" he exclaimed, seemingly exhausted from his erudition.

Leonor was obviously mesmerized. She did not speak for a moment, then, vigorously shaking her head in sheer wonder, asked, "How, Pat? *How*? Where did you learn all this?" She continued to shake her head rhythmically.

"The library, of course. However, my favorite is…" He ran to the bookshelf and dislodged a tattered old epic from its exact spot, bringing it back to Leonor. "…This one, by Pandit Shiv Sharma." He wondered if she would express interest in reading it. After all, she was studying to be a nurse, and a natural curiosity would not be out of order. Yet he was conscious not to burden her with too many books, having already passed on Zinn and other favorite authors of his for her spare time reading.

Seeing that she only stared at the dogs' ears of the book politely from a distance as if it was an ancient tome to be exhibited in a glass case of some library of antiquities, Patrick supplemented, "In Bethesda, there is a little townhouse that is, in reality, a little temple dedicated to an Indian saint called Ramakrishna. This saint is a rather contemporary one really, and hailed from West Bengal, a region in the east of the country that has been peculiarly predisposed to intellectual and religious contributions to India's cultural as well as political thought process. They are intellectual all right, but apparently they are not that religious compared to the rest of their compatriots. A Communist movement took its roots there entirely from an intellectual fountainhead though, of course, with an all encompassing poverty in the environment as its trigger. Anyway, it is in this little bungalow temple in Bethesda that I found a *sadhu* who teaches yoga to a handful of interested pupils. I am one of his, shall we say, more interested pupils." He let out a low, embarrassed laugh.

A passing thought grabbed Leonor and she asked, "Pat, how come you don't have Indian friends from the university when you know so much about them?"

Patrick pondered the question as though in deep reflection. Eventually, he confessed, "Perhaps I know a bit about India's ancient culture. But I find the Indians at GU a peculiar lot. I do not quite understand them, *yet*. They move in a pack, doing everything together, like an unkindness of ravens, oblivious to outsiders, shutting out all external influence, as if there is nothing to imbibe, or even consider, from elsewhere. They seem damned confident of their way of life, their competence in mathematics, their vegetarianism, red and white religious marks with which they adorn their foreheads for their morning ablutions, and are not ashamed to keep them even when they come to class. They are here only to learn our sciences and they will be off as soon as they are done. I guess they will return and have arranged marriages and settle in for the rest of their lives, producing another generation, another brood of nerds. Can you imagine spending your life with your spouse, never having seen him or her ever before until the moment of the wedding? That is what they do!"

Leonor let out an 'ooo' as a mischievous smile raced across her countenance at the sheer adventure and novelty of such a possibility. She seemed spellbound and, from her eyes, Patrick knew he could not yet stop. Nor did he intend to.

"Especially those from the south of the country. The students are mainly *Brahmins* or the top priestly caste who, in the past, had the monopoly over their sacred texts and religious rites. Apparently, they still do in much of the country. I should not be totally unfair, though. The country is so huge and her nine hundred million inhabitants – if that can be imagined – are obviously heterogeneous, like different nations under one umbrella. In the east of the country, a big chunk of the population is identified as Bengali, or Bangali in their own language Bangla. They belong to the particular region I was talking about – from where Ramakrishna came. They are a very mixed race with centuries of invasion by Muslims, including Arabs and Mongols; Europeans, beginning with the Portuguese pirates who would sail up the mighty rivers and, apart from pillaging, which was their regular job, routinely raped pretty women from upper-class Bengali families whose villas lined the Ganges and its tributaries. Then the Danes, the Dutch, the French and the English followed and, of course, eventually the English won out just as in our continent, my dear. However, the Bengalis seem to be an amusing lot. The two I know both eat beef steaks voraciously, but they insist they actually love seafood. They listen to, and know more about, jazz than I shall ever do. They read all kinds of strange European authors such as Gide, Pirandello, Sartre, Camus, Genet, Brecht, Dostoevsky and Yevtushenko, whose writings they introduced me to, and one is in graduate school in economics and the other is in statistics!

"I do chat with them sometimes, despite their being so full of themselves in a unique sort of way. At least those Tamils from the south seem quite inward looking, disinterested in others. But these Bengalis seem cocksure of their superiority after having surveyed and tasted the rest of the world. They have told me that Bengalis have surely produced the best literature, the best film director, the best humanist scientist who proved that plants breathed – and, of course, his research was stolen by the West during colonial times – and a countless other firsts in the history of the world. Oh yes, one count they do not fail to keep is how many women on campus they have laid and recount their exploits without the slightest qualms; quite gross, don't you think? Yet, I must admit, they do intrigue me, so I keep in touch with them. It is easy, too, to find them in the cafeteria having hamburgers and French fries. I engage them in historical or political debate. They can get quite lively! They are rather Leftist, eulogising the Paris demonstrations, supporting the Naxalbari movement – don't worry about details – yet are quite at ease with, and do not feel the slightest bit hypocritical about, doing graduate studies in the US. Yes, I must admit they are interesting…."

\*    \*    \*

Patrick was cut short as the door to the apartment sprang open and Terrence, with his set of shiny white teeth, all thirty-two of them showing to form an infectious smile, walked in. Patrick realised that his intellectual, globally configured exchange with Leonor was over, that he was back in the world of Terrence and Jolly, of neighbourhood hikes and picnics.

Patrick's attention floated inevitably to Terrence and fixated on the familiar beads of perspiration clinging to his forehead. They were dangling as if in protest against the tight suit he was wearing on this warm late morning. The twenty-minute brisk walk home from the P Street church had exacerbated the heat. Uncharacteristically, he seemed somewhat breathless, perhaps in anticipation of his three companions, who he knew would be anxiously waiting for him to return home and complete the foursome.

Instead of the anxiety he had anticipated, Terrence sensed a relaxed pace inside the apartment. He realized that Patrick had still not changed for the day. Leonor and he must have been chatting as usual and, of course, Jolly was putting in an effort in the kitchen, apropos of her abilities and commensurate culinary interests. He said 'hi' to the first two, and disappeared into the kitchen to meet the third, with whom he knew he could whip up some petty conversation.

In the fleeting moment between his appearance and disappearance, Leonor did not miss stealing a glance at Terrence. *How attractive he is! A confluence of a fine Indian nose, thin lips and high cheekbones, with wide African eyes and a deep brown skin tone. However, where did he get his green eyes,* she wondered. Her spell was broken by his voice echoing from the kitchen.

"Jolly, what are you cooking up? This is a feast!" Then his voice died off suddenly, exactly as it had broken the silence.

Jolly seemed perfectly at ease in the kitchen, as if she had been married into this household for ages. She exuded satisfaction with the output by which she was surrounded. "Just some tuna sandwiches and, oh yes, also some ham and cheese, apples and fruit cake. I had just enough time to bake some chocolate chip cookies, so I just shoved them into the oven – they should be ready any moment." Then, reassuringly to Terrence, and in perfect synchronization between the both of them, as though her words excused all the fat embedded in her preparations, she elaborated, "As for the sandwiches, don't worry, I have used loads of mayonnaise, but it's diet mayonnaise." She continued in a conspiratorial tone, "You know, Pat will not have regular mayonnaise. So don't blame me if those sandwiches don't taste that great." She concluded with a final thought, "I think we will also take a couple of bottles of wine. We can pick that up at the Safeway on the way out, together with some Coke, of course. What do you think, Terry, shouldn't that be enough?"

Terrence was flabbergasted at the piles of sandwiches on the kitchen table. He was convinced that it must have taken hours to make them. The apples looked fresh and waxed, though he did not see the fruit cake. He smiled and walked across the kitchen. He hugged Jolly closely and said, "Jolly, thanks for making all this. They look just great. I am awfully hungry. You know it was a long sermon this morning. May I have one?"

Jolly was smiling. "No, not one. You must have one tuna and one ham. I need a guinea pig. However, don't tell the other two. This is for you only, *special*!"

"Luv ya!"

Terrence tore into the piles of sandwiches and ate at least four or five as Jolly and he chatted away about humdrum university things until Leonor floated in and shouted, Latin-style, "What are you two hiding in the kitchen for? You missed Pat's unbelievable account of yoga, the Indian meditation exercise."

Neither expressed interest. They seemed not to hear, though both Jolly and Terrence moved towards the living room. As they appeared, Patrick sprang up and said guiltily,

"I know, I know. It will take me a minute to run in and out of the shower. Then off we go."

Momentarily, the group merrily left the apartment to face the late morning sun and breathe in the lazily lingering fresh air. They trooped towards the Smithsonian for all the treasures it had on display for them to behold free of charge, and for Jolly to draw their attention to. They readily and enthusiastically complied. At the end of the day, they returned educated, well fed, happy and exhausted. Potomac Turning remained protected and hidden, available exclusively to Patrick and Terrence and their explorations.

\*　　\*　　\*

It was not entirely unexpected for Patrick to obtain an A in his courses or an A+ on his thesis, deeply researched as it was on a matter remote if not exotic to his supervisor. On the whole, it turned out to be a year of accumulation of knowledge in its purest form. At least the teachers who were already familiar with him from his undergraduate years did not seem surprised. What was astonishing over the years, however, to every teacher, was his particular selection for specialization – international relations focussed on India – based on a fountainhead of her meditative, *evolved* religions, quite separated in texture from the powerful *revealed* religions of the Middle East, her survival, despite millennia of ransacking by barbarians from the outer reaches of her west, her variegated ethnicity emanating from centuries of strife, accommodation and assimilation, her vast geographical expanse from mountain to sea, from pasture to sand dunes but, most of all, her peculiar brand of demo*crazy*, a phrase that Patrick borrowed for his Masters thesis from the old Indian he met in a moment of serendipity at Lincoln Memorial while jogging on Independence Day. His thesis spoke eloquently of the spectrum of her political life whose complexity and chaos did not cease to confound or impress him.

The mystery that emanated regarding Patrick and needed to be explained in his advisers' minds was why a Catholic boy from faraway San Antonio would be so drawn to matters relating to India, a country that most viewed as prone to oppose US foreign policy, and to take ungrateful pride in demonstrating such opposition despite Public Law 480 handouts of wheat—albeit of fodder quality—for the throngs of the abjectly poor who inhabited her boundaries. Indeed, in most of their minds, such backwaters could only have been designed for the likes of Mother Teresa, driven by some similar inexplicable force, to serve the Almighty by muddying their hands and wetting their feet. The priests were, of course, quite oblivious of the influence of Father Jesudas, whose early stories from India had never ceased to mesmerise Patrick, or of Agnes' high expectations of Patrick that nurtured and propelled him to seek ever-newer avenues of boundless, if absurd, adventure.

Neither were they aware of the inner torture and growing conflict in his mind over the push and pull between Agnes and Jolly, and the acute stresses and strains that he suffered as a result, leading him naturally to the tempting calm of yoga in search of peace and redemption. By the time he was graduating, his classmates and some neighbourhood friends had come to recognize him as an in-depth Indophile. Some of them, progressing from Ravi Shankar's sitar music, came to sit with him in his early morning yoga exercises on a regular basis, thereby spreading his reputation as an India specialist even farther. Indeed, he did not stop there. Buttressed by a practical nature and with specific and sharpened objectives in his mind, he had even begun attending classes at the US State Department through a special placement, in two Indian languages: Hindi, the national language, a familiarity necessitated by the unavoidable objective of communication with the majority of the population, and Bangla, the sweetest sounding and alluring among India's myriad languages, and the language of Tagore, the poet novelist and Nobel laureate. Despite his inner conflicts, his balance of mind had led him not to ignore the practical while embracing the sublime, to target the unknown while consolidating the familiar. It was a rippling variegation centred on a steadiness, a confidence emerging from unfolding experiences, and buttressed by the admonition he had received from the graduate student advisor.

Terrence's focus on Patrick remained unwavering even as he grew to recognize, and then accept, Leonor's attentions. He noticed that, even during intensive political discussions that she tended to have with Patrick that could last hours, she would look askance or over her shoulder from time to time, to make sure Terrence was there without, however, expecting any verbal participation from him. Indeed, Terrence would sometimes disappear and go jogging, or for a walk with Jolly, to admire the Victorian brick row houses of Georgetown or the gardens of Dumbarton Oaks during the flower season and to chat over childhood reminiscences of growing up or about silly nothings. Their early acquaintance had flowered into a comfortably relaxed relationship between two neighbourhood pals, two siblings.

When Jolly and Terrence would return from their walks, Leonor and Patrick would still appear to be in an animated conversation over their esoteric topic of the day but, as Terrence entered, Leonor would jump up and say, in mock exasperation, "Hi, Terrence. Want to go for another walk? You know we have to leave these love birds alone for some time at least!"

Terrence never declined. As they walked, he hardly talked while she chattered away her alleged concerns for, and about, the indigenous peoples in her country. Yet, when she spoke, it appeared as if Leonor was speaking of a magical land. He always listened intently, as if to make up for any gap in his own indigenous blood mixed as it was, in his Latin upbringing or current interest and, when she slid her hand into his, he held it as if to share in their common heritage. At the beginning, he had been a little unwilling, though nonetheless unable to find any excuse to decline her soft palm. With time, he embraced it in familiarity, beginning to hold her hand more firmly, attempting to imbue his hold with resolve. At the back of his mind always lurked Patrick, what he was up to, where he was, what he was thinking. Terrence also wondered if his own growing cosiness with Leonor was truly his preference or did it emerge from that part of him that felt the compulsion merely to assimilate? Not for one moment did he wonder if he was replicating Patrick's outward behaviour, though all his moves were for the sake of Patrick, as if in solidarity, and in keeping with his Orion.

*   *   *

Colombia was, indeed, a country that gave shelter to several races. Its Cauca region was a filigree of hills and lakes that were so serene, so tranquil, that time seemed to have forgotten them. The indigenous peoples of the hill regions, with their rosy cheeks and hand-knit colourful dresses, were God-fearing, superstitious Catholic converts, deferential to the European priests and nuns, yet clever and persevering in remembering their courageous and brave past. They remained untouched by the high culture of the Bogotanos with their exclusive family names inherited from the Conquistadors. The Bogotanos preserved and spoke an impeccable Spanish, widely accepted as the most correct in all of Latin America. The hill people had no ear or tongue for it.

In the south, Colombia also embraced the Amazon and its trusting, almost childlike, darker peoples who were cousins to the tribes across the border in Brazil. Only recently did first signs of pollution arrive with gold prospectors who brought them malaria and syphilis and priests who brought them stars and stripes T-shirts to cover their nakedness, which they were taught to recognise because they had been oblivious of it earlier. Now they were shameful of their bodies, as they of course should be, according to the satisfied priests. The appearance of such external interlopers had not yet spoilt the dense, pristine foliage of the region, though the heart and soul of its inhabitants had not been left intact or undamaged.

Then, in the very north, the remnants of the old colonial life had left the indelible presence of the descendants of African slaves, lending a lively cadence to Colombian culture, imparting it with *salsa*, music and dance derived from its Caribbean heritage, from the *rumba* of Cuba and the *merengue* of the Dominican Republic. Leonor seemed in love with her country as she described it to Terrence, wide eyed, taking in every word as if to make up for lost time and in quest of a new heritage.

"Oh Terence! We have to go to Villa de Leyva. ¡*Es la vida pura*! It is my favorite place on Earth, a beautiful little colonial town where time has stood still. The town square has this old cathedral just like every other village of course, but the square itself is huge and beautiful, laid with cobblestones and surrounded by thatched cottages with handicraft shops and little cafés that serve Colombian coffee with traditional breads such as *almojabanas*, *pan de yuca*, *pan de bono* and so many others, and juices of *Feijoa*, *Lulo*, *Guanavana* and a myriad other exotic fruits that you will never find elsewhere!"

Terrence smiled and raised an eyebrow.

"I swear… Oops," Leonor said excitedly. "Try to find *Feijoa* juice anywhere else in the world, I challenge you." She squeezed Terrence's hand, dragging him on.

Terence let her, trying to imagine this distant paradise.

She continued, "The homes are all painted white. They shine brilliantly in the morning sun. The temperature is always sixteen to seventeen degrees, Celsius, of course – we don't use Fahrenheit – so the bougainvillea clusters are always blooming, and that too in so many colours, over the walls, descending from upstairs balconies almost down to the pavements of the streets below. The balconies themselves are carved in oak and mahogany. You know, I have a thought. There are some real nice getaway hotels that my cousins and I would visit when we were growing up. They were lovely old haciendas that have been converted to boutique hotels. Some day we must visit there. I *want* you to go there with me." She emphasised 'want' unabashedly.

Terrence's mind floated to the hacienda in the outskirts of San Antonio in whose exteriors he had spent so much of his childhood. Villa de Leyva touched him. Almost involuntarily, he said, "Why Leonor, what a great idea. Let's do that sometime."

Hidden by the veil of bursting colour and variety, she would also paint a sorrowful version of Colombia. This reflected her perpetually swinging moods, such a prisoner of her own culture she was. She had no difficulty in recognizing her own mood swings if not marvelling in them, expecting Terrence to understand and endorse her itinerant views. She only demanded that he be his usual, attentive self as she expounded on her speeches custom-tailored for him. He did not even have to speak.

The dream, the concept, of a *Gran Colombia*, had been summarily shredded, the country dismembered early in its history. Later, in the early part of the twentieth century, Colombia had been further dismembered by the United States, which simply took away the part that is now Panama to construct the Panama Canal. Every time the indigenous fought for human rights, the Europeans clandestinely joined hands to quash it. Even the Leftist democratic movement of mid-twentieth century that was spearheaded by the Spanish families of Colombia, who had protected their class distinction but had, over time, suffered reverses in wealth and cash flow, was crushed by American resources and espionage. Collusion of the wealthy classes with the drug lords and even the Church, those links that the powerful have exploited through the passage of time, then reared their ugly head.

The fundamental lack of land rights of the indigenous peoples, the decimation of their rights to foster the Church's version of democracy, and the prohibition of their cultural practices by the Catholic Church, had led to economic poverty and, worse, the demise of their souls. An equally malign counterweight had emerged: the drug lords. Money from the sale of illicit drugs was made available to the FARC, an emerging Leftist guerrilla movement. They subjugated village after village, extracting whatever they could from the sparse fruits of the country folks' toils. A rightist militia was not slow to form in reaction, targeting villagers with equal, if not greater, ferocity, cruelty and greed. Thus, Left and Right, together, had successfully exhausted the country's once-plentiful natural resources and minerals, including the best emeralds in the world.

\*　　\*　　\*

Leonor never had the chance to describe all this to Patrick, but she had Terrence in her grasp. Spellbound, Terrence extended his arm to move her closer to him. Leonor melted inside his tight hug and looked up at him. He lowered his face to kiss her, overcome with a feeling of tenderness, carried away by the story of a defeated people whose suffering he could only imagine, rather than by any overwhelming spontaneous urge guided by pure physicality. Their tongues were entwined for a long time. It seemed an eternity as she held on to him and probed his mouth with her tongue.

Eventually, Terrence asked, "However, could not Colombia carry out appropriate land reform? Patrick keeps talking about land reform that was carried out in this far-off state in India, where it seems land was taken away from all absentee landlords by an amendment of their Constitution, and given to the landless who had been the working tenants on the land." He said it as though that was just an ordinary feat for any society to achieve.

Leonor was somewhat startled by Terrence's moving his lips away from hers, and more so by his observation. She said, "Americans are not positioned as near to India as they are to Colombia to quash such possibilities at their will." She said this in a tone of slight irritation at Terrence's apparent innocence. Perhaps she actually believed that the wealthy Colombians who owned the land and lived without ever working, and in luxury off the toil of the peasants, would have facilitated the transfer of ownership of their own land to the landless except for the intervention of the Americans. It certainly appeared that her chic Leftist views were being severely tested by Terrence's line of questioning, but she did not respond.

Terrence realised quickly that Leonor's upper-class views on her country were to be listened to, agreed with, and never contradicted. Her views comprised exuberant joy interwoven with dark shadows. It was clear that she often exaggerated both the happy as well as the sad parts, just as one tends to do when one thinks or talks about someone one feels very strongly about, whether it is love or hate. She wanted Terrence to digest her views without question or comment. A strange compassion for this woman enveloped him despite her capriciousness, or perhaps *because* of her petulance, and he treated her indulgently and with growing warmth. She returned his warmth with a coyness that made his heart skip a beat.

Terrence observed as their relationship unfolded that Leonor often reminisced about her country, but she rarely mentioned her family. From her bits and pieces, he had gathered that she came from a privileged, economically advantaged family, that her brother's dead body had been discarded in a car parking lot by some ransom seekers even before her father could put the money together to meet their demand because it was a task he could not accomplish in a manner hidden from the attention of the authorities within the time permitted him by the kidnappers. The corpse was found in the parking lot of the National Library, which her scholastic brother often frequented for his intellectual pursuits. Whenever she accidentally ventured into speaking about her family, she would invariably conclude by suddenly announcing, "¡*Así es la vida, chico*!" Then she would abruptly change the subject.

She seemed embarrassed by the wealth of her parents and possibly more so by her dependence on it. It was apparent that her studies were being financed with ease by her father. Terrence was touched by her apparent zest for life set amidst complications and complexities that lurked in her background. She came from a society that seemed to be dysfunctional, if not toxic, and from a family that must have nevertheless suffered deep anguish despite their affluence and physical comforts in daily life in losing its male heir in a horrific manner. He compared his own less than modest background with hers and cherished the love and certainty that he had always experienced gushing from his mama, and even from his unobtrusive dad, during those moments, albeit few and far between, when he had been able to be around him. Yes, the time he spent with his father had been quality time, or so was his recollection.

During their initial period of getting acquainted, when Leonor had marvelled at Terrence's command over Spanish and they began to speak the language between themselves, he had described his own family and background with nostalgia and without the slightest remorse or embarrassment. She had listened intently and had hardly commented. He had taken that to mean total acceptance of his background and ethnicity and, once certain of his feeling, had felt fully relaxed with her.

It was not a pleasant surprise, therefore, when Leonor did not propose that he meet Mrs. Betancour during a forthcoming visit. She had inadvertently mentioned that her mother would visit Washington to see her after the annual pre-Christmas shopping spree she was planning to undertake in New York's Fifth Avenue and Madison Avenue top-of-the-line boutiques. That was an annual pilgrimage of Mrs. Betancour when she would spend unsparingly on designer dresses and jewellery in preparation for the innumerable Christmas parties that she had to attend and to organize. However, there was no indication from Leonor that she would like Terrence to meet her mother. Indeed, after mentioning it, she seemed to quickly change the subject, as with every other time that she briefly brought up her family. Terrence was perplexed and, to avoid getting hurt, further transported his thoughts to what might be transpiring at that moment in the apartment, though something prompted him not to wonder aloud about Patrick or Jolly. Perhaps it was his awe of Leonor. He did not know.

Terrence knew that they must get back quickly now; otherwise, Patrick would wonder. He sped towards home, moving Leonor along. Startled, she looked up enquiringly. Instantly, she knew that Terrence had shifted back to his regular world now, of which she was a part, but probably only a secondary part. It was the part in which his bonhomie was with Jolly and his fixation was Patrick. He had given Leonor his full attention during the long walk. Now she had better fall in line. Still clinging to him, she doubled up, occasionally skipping a step or two in order to keep up with him.

\*    \*    \*

It was ten in the evening. The girls had left quite some time back. From the television screen, Tony Orlando and Dawn wished goodnight to Terrence from their Las Vegas auditorium. As they evaporated out of sight of the couch potatoes throughout the nation, Terrence looked at Patrick. He was laid out on the sofa with his headphones on. He was reading *Autobiography of a Yogi* by Swami Yogananda. Terrence looked at Patrick admiringly. *Where does he get all these books from,* he mused.

Smiling, he approached Patrick and nudged him. The case of his cassette was lying on the coffee table. A smiling Donna Summers, in a tight, green mini skirt, a fitted shiny silver blouse and long black boots, was bent forward with spread arms and legs like a toy soldier from the *Nutcracker* ballet. His admiration quadrupled, and he wondered, *how can this man combine Donna with some Yogananda or whoever?* He could not help laughing aloud.

Patrick heard Terrence's laugh interjected into Donna's sharp, ringing tones screeching out, 'On the radio'. Removing his earphones, he raised his eyebrows, seeking the cause of Terrence's laughter. His docile self did not smile back.

Terrence did not respond directly, but nudged Patrick's tummy, and Patrick finally hollered back, ticklish and writhing in mock pain.

\* \* \*

Patrick did not hide what he was actually thinking through Yogananda and Donna. Seriousness was etched all over his face. Bringing up the topic of the girls for the first time between them, he said, "Terry, you seem to be comfortable with Leonor. Are you supposed to follow her to Bo-go-ta?" He emphasised each syllable in a theatrical caricature that did not resemble either an English or a Spanish accent. "Has she invited you?" Before Terrence could respond, Patrick continued almost breathlessly, surprising even himself, "You know, you cannot expect to live brilliantly if you select to live an ordinary life."

Terrence was flabbergasted. Calm as ever, he asked simply, "How do you mean, Pat?"

Patrick reverted to non-specificity as a tactic. "Well, consider world-class intellectuals. Think of D.H. Lawrence. He had such an ambivalent relationship with his mother and also with the women he bedded. His books exude not only this ambivalence, but also the intellectual power that comes with it. The books all finish with uncertainty without revealing if there is hope or disaster for the protagonist at the end of the road, at the end of the tunnel." He paused.

"On the other hand, you have Charles Dickens. He led such a simple family life, siring lots of offspring, living in contentment and domesticity, and his books reflect this. They tend to end in felicity at home and hearth, his heroes generally triumphant over unimaginable trials and tribulations as they traverse through life. Even those who die at the end are all beautiful in their deep and obvious suffering, as if God was particularly giving them the benefit of taking them back into His, um…. Her bosom."

He was not expecting Terrence to respond yet. "Think of André Gide, Simone de Beauvoir, Margaret Yourcenar, Jean Genet, Michel Foucault or so many of the other French intellectuals. Their intellect was of a supreme level. They all led complicated lives and that gave them the faculty one needs to be the great thinkers and philosophers that they were", he ended with resolve as he read on Terrence's face a look that asked, "Have you not done enough lecturing for one day? Has not Leonor already given you her rapt attention for hours? Now I am waiting for you to close so I can put in a word edgewise."

Nevertheless, when Patrick stopped, Terrence responded with characteristic precision, "Pat, I have not had the luxury of reading all those authors at Howard." He could not hide the touch of exasperation in his voice.

Patrick split up in laughter at Terrence's explanation, his excuse. His response, 'Terry, these authors are not taught in GU English classes, either', was not heard by Terrence, for a hot burning sensation had drowned out all sound other than a drone that was now steadily echoing inside his ears. He looked terribly serious, even angry. For the first time in all the years he had been devoted to Patrick, he chose to challenge him openly.

"Pat, why do you bring up Leonor? Wasn't it you who suggested to the girls Potomac Turning for a picnic? What if we had made it to the spot that day? Wouldn't its sanctity have vanished?" He seemed enraged.

Patrick looked at him coolly, perhaps even a bit contemptuously. *Where has all his cleverness gone,* he wondered. He simply responded, "I knew we would not make it that far with Jolly. And it would be good for her to walk a few miles, anyway. Otherwise, we would end up at Dumbarton Oaks once again. Haven't you had enough of walking through those gardens with her already? And we just went to the Smithsonian after all." Turning his face away from Terrence, he started to insert the earphones in their right place and to pick up the autobiography, which had slid to the floor.

Terrence rushed at him, turning Patrick towards himself. Glaring at Patrick, he asked himself under his breath, "Isn't this deception? Is it the result of so much reading? Is this what an intellectual is?" He had never imagined, let alone observed, Patrick in this Machiavellian light before. He released Patrick.

Patrick turned away from him and burrowed into his book once again.

\*      \*      \*

Terrence could not sleep that night. As Patrick lay still, the silence seemed overwhelming. Terrence looked out of the window. Moonlight streamed onto the bed, outlining Patrick's silhouette in full form. Terrence was motionless for what seemed a long time. Suddenly, a beautiful little canary perched on the window sill. Had it mistaken the bright moonlight for early morning? Breaking the silence of the night, it chirped a sweet song. The repetitious tone seemed melancholic as it trailed away into the folds of the night. Terrence moved slowly to get himself up from bed and tiptoed to the window sill. The chill night air fanned the bird's yellow breast feathers as it seemed to stare straight into Terrence. Then, it took flight as though suddenly realising that it was not its mate.

Terrence dwelt on the empty spot for a moment, and then walked out silently to the balcony. Once there, he leant over the edge of the black grille balustrade and looked down to an empty P Street. It was motionless except for the steady flow of late fall leaves floating lazily onto the sidewalk.

Patrick could not maintain his silence or keep still any longer. He got up. On the balcony, he found Terrence bending over, his back showing between a creased nightshirt and the loose elastic of his pyjamas. He shifted to look up towards the sky. Patrick reached out to Terrence and strung the elastic as if it belonged on a guitar. The next moment, he was standing next to Terrence, joining him in searching the heavens. Orion was not on their familiar trajectory of stars tonight. The bright moonlight had made the stars obscure, almost invisible.

Eventually both turned halfway towards indoors, but stopped as they faced each other. Terrence's eyes were glistening. Perhaps it was a teardrop. Was it the canary's melancholic song, Patrick wondered.

Terrence assessed Patrick silently. Patrick looked away. Turning around, hugging Terrence in a tight knot, Patrick brought him close for a moment, and then guided him back inside. There was no resistance from Terrence as they went in.

\*   \*   \*

The end of two years in graduate school for Patrick and Terrence coincided with graduation from nursing school for Jolly and Leonor, and brought along altogether different prospects for each of them.

Leonor had no option but to return to the family fold in Bogota, since her financing would cease immediately and she had no work permit from the US Immigration Office. Now that the moment had actually arrived, she was confused about how, and whether, to approach Terrence about visiting Bogota.

Jolly planned to join a Catholic missionary hospital attached to the convent she had attended in San Antonio. In contrast to Leonor, Jolly knew that she would have to consolidate her relationship with Patrick in a strong commitment towards matrimony before she returned to San Antonio. She needed the assurance of Patrick's promise. One afternoon, she orchestrated a walk alone with Patrick without the others, through the Mall and the Smithsonian. She asked him directly about marriage.

Patrick was not taken aback since this was not the first time she had brought up marriage, and he increasingly seemed to agree to it. He knew it would be a repeat performance. He also was well aware that Terrence had to be considered for any future path he took. Gathering his wits about him, Patrick apologetically reiterated that, as their lives progressed in different directions with different goals and objectives, a lifelong friendship would be so much more valuable and much deeper than mere matrimony. Jolly remained unconvinced, barely managing not to pout about this unanticipated, illogical statement.

To find a way out and, in a last attempt to accept Agnes' view about his marrying Jolly, Patrick elaborated, "I love you too much for me to desire you in a physical way."

Though in her guts Jolly felt that Patrick was simply a prisoner of his mother's designs, she was cautious not to openly accuse him of being a mama's boy. She simply insisted, "As soon as we are married, love will develop quite naturally into desire."

Patrick pleaded and cryptically said, "I am not what you suppose!"

Jolly did not hear Patrick, because she neither wanted nor had the ability to comprehend Patrick. Instead, she curled her lips as if she was about to burst into tears and took out the carefully selected gift she had bought for him at People's Drugs, a simple opaque, splash-on bottle of Old Spice. Reaching it out towards him with an outstretched arm, she pleaded that he should use it during the rest of the summer and think of her when he did.

Patrick glanced at her at arm's length and, in a sweeping survey, assimilated the relevance of Agnes' derogatory remark about Jolly's proportions. Though he realized that her obesity embarrassed him, he resolved to ignore it, to nullify its importance. He told himself that he had to get over it if he was to give her the dignity that a human being deserved. After all, was it not Agnes who had taught him that fear, shyness, and aversion were three characteristics men should never possess and, if they did, should take every means to overcome? He did not decline the gift. He did not run. Instead, the confluence of her chubby childlike countenance holding back tears, his conviction that he alone should care for the pouting girl waiting all these years for him, and the parting gift that she remembered to get him, all combined to weaken him to acquiesce to Jolly's insistence on marriage.

He was unable to decline Jolly, to say 'no' to her. He was aware of his error, nay, his blunder, in the pit of his stomach, but he could not leave Jolly by making the right, and inevitably cruel, decision. He took the burden on himself.

Patrick finally responded, "Jolly, you know that I love you. If you think marriage has to be the manifestation of that love, I will marry you."

That is all Jolly needed to hear, because she knew that Patrick's given word was as good as gold.

As if to confirm his promise, Patrick continued, "I should finish with my doctoral dissertation in a couple of years or so; let's plan a wedding back home then. Hopefully I will find a job immediately after I finish and you could also find a suitable job." Then, to break the monotony of the seriousness of it all, he joked weakly, "You know nurses can get a job *any*where!"

Thus, Patrick made perhaps the most important decision in his life without any respectable consultation with himself or a *tête-à-tête* with Terrence. Agnes had always taught him to be polite to women, to never talk back to his mother, to never strike his little sister, and to never order Rosita around. Now that training became instrumental in making this fateful decision that would have the strongest ramifications on the lives of all four members of the mini court over which he had reigned during the last four years.

Patrick and Terrence found themselves at a crossroads, for powerful centrifugal forces were at work to fling them apart from each other. Terrence concluded that Patrick and he were not taking the coast-to-coast trip that they had planned years earlier, since Patrick had not brought it up over the entire previous semester. Instead, Terrence began to wonder if he would receive an invitation to visit Bogota while clinging to the possibility of continuing to be physically near Patrick. He had decided that, instead of graduating with a Masters degree, he would go into the Ph.D. programme in African-American history – he had received a fellowship in any event – just to carry on near Patrick, even though he had preferred to go into the job market rather than spending at least another two years in graduate school just in the quest of a doctoral title. What did Dr. mean, anyway? It did not make you a medical doctor; rather, it led to a lot of confusion about what kind of doctor you really are!

Patrick had enjoyed his years in Washington. He realized that it was not the same as being the king of the hill of his class, as he had been at his school in San Antonio. He had not developed a close set of college friends because of the many demands he faced; his courses required unwavering attention to his studies, not to mention his intense extracurricular interest in literature pertaining to all matters Indian. Neither had he joined any fraternity, given his overall circumstances, not that it ever interested him. In his school, he had fancifully reigned over a small, but closely knit, set of comrades, who had always treated him as leader, not so much in words, but certainly in action. At university, his world had centred on the coterie of the four at home.

He wanted to go on a trip to India immediately after taking his comprehensive exams and before getting down to write his Ph.D. thesis. Indeed, he knew what his thesis topic would be and was confident he could collect supporting material – documentation and data – while in India. His thesis topic had raised eyebrows to the extent that there was a confidential investigation from the provost's office as to why Patrick would be interested in Indian communists. The university administration was illuminated with the fact that the Indian Left mainly comprised armchair Marxists, and their fear had been dissipated. Patrick's topic became acceptable. Patrick knew he wanted to travel to India and, in particular, to Calcutta. Given his lack of definite plans and the uncertainties that clung to his would-be adventures, he did not want to get bogged down with Jolly in the foreseeable future. He did not envisage returning to San Antonio. He did know that Jolly would be glad to move to any city in the country with him, perhaps even to Europe, but to India? He doubted it. He would just have to sort things out with Jolly carefully. That bridge would be crossed when they came to it.

He also wondered about Terrence, the unwavering constant in his life. Leonor's growing and successful dalliance with Terrence did nag at Patrick. However, he had decided not to put Terrence up against the wall by asking him to accompany him to India. He was well aware that Terrence and he had planned many years earlier, before the entrance of the women in their lives, to drive coast to coast, *from sea to shining sea*, over the summer once they had finished with their coursework. He had little doubt that the matter would be on Terrence's mind just as it had been on his own, but he had not raised the matter again with Terrence, since his own plans had evolved and firmed in other directions. There was one consolation, though. He knew that Terrence would be in Washington when he returned from India at the end of the summer, that both of them would write their doctoral theses during the next two years in the P Street apartment, and that the girls would not be there. He did not want to think beyond that. That was all that mattered for the moment. He would leave the rest to the long arm of time to unfold.

\* \* \*

Back in San Antonio, Jolly found a suitable, even satisfying, job in the hospital attached to the convent. Its main clients were from the Hispanic community, lower to middle class, who had a proclivity to worship the doctors as omnipotent. Most of the doctors could, however, give only partial attention to the patients there because they had their own private practices to make up for the low salaries at the hospital. What Jolly liked was that, in the doctors' absence, the nurses quite often had to fill in for them for all intents and purposes. This was a great responsibility, but it also resulted in blind admiration for many of the nurses. The meteoric rise in her popularity in the broader Hispanic community gave Jolly satisfaction and an indelible sense of honour and recognition. Yes, she felt she had come home and that she would not move from there unless, of course, Patrick wanted her to move elsewhere with him.

Her personal life was just a bit lonely without her three friends, and in particular Patrick, especially the first month or two. Her mother had descended rapidly into deeper eccentricities during Jolly's absence and had refused to visit her even once in Washington, D.C., for fear, unjustifiably so, that it would be impossible for her to find French bread for sale as good as that she baked at home and that her Jolly would probably not have the right kind of oven or bread maker to bake them, despite Jolly's reassurances to the contrary. She also suffered from the mistaken notion that acceptable French wine would be much costlier in Washington than in San Antonio, the latter being closer to New Orleans, her esteemed seat of all culture. When Jolly returned to San Antonio, she found it difficult, if not impossible, to communicate with her mother for lengthy periods, because her mother would say nothing other than mutter incessantly about Jolly's father and interspersed this with matters related to other gentlemen, or so Jolly thought when she cared to listen. Anyway, on the whole, it became rather embarrassing to listen to her nearly incoherent accounts about various men, and Jolly would have to turn her attention away from the ramblings as much as possible.

With her mother progressing inexorably towards psychosis, Jolly found refuge in casual acquaintances, delving in and out of quick friendships with Hispanics, most of whom had been her patients. However, she knew better than to get too involved with them. She was well aware that, culturally, Hispanics had a tendency to become too familiar that was only to be followed all of a sudden by a noisy fallout typically based on some miscommunication or misunderstood affair of the heart. Even Leonor, in a protective gesture, had warned Jolly of such Latin tendencies, and Jolly generally heeded those warnings. She would never decline a dinner invitation, for example, but would, without fail, take a good bottle of wine for her hosts, thinking that this would pre-empt the need to invite them to dinner in return. Of course, in any event, it would not be feasible to have guests for dinner herself given her mother's deteriorated mental state and its obvious manifestations. Despite the major thought disorder, her mother was, however, always able to make excellent recommendations for the wines that Jolly took with her to the dinners.

Jolly noticed that, after about two dinner invitations, the hosts would generally not invite her so easily, but they would continue to be in touch on the phone and, occasionally, invite her to catch a film or go have a taco or pizza together in a restaurant. She knew that they would never drop her completely because of her reputation of being good to them at the hospital and they never knew when they would again need to depend on her. Thus, after the first couple of months since her return, Jolly felt relatively happier, her limited demands for happiness having been met by the community that surrounded and admired her.

There was, however, one home to which Jolly was never invited to dinner. That was Agnes'. Even her initial forays there in pursuit of a polite hello and chat were met by correct, if cold, distant responses and little else. Sis, too, perceived the tension and eventually gave up on Jolly, seemingly taking her mother's approach. Soon thereafter, Jolly stopped going there.

Almost every night, she wrote a love letter to Patrick, not realizing that she often repeated the same words and descriptions of physical love that she may have picked up from D.H. Lawrence's *Lady Chatterley's Lover* or some such volume that failed to escape Patrick's notice. She waited impatiently for Patrick's letters, but they were not as frequent. When they did arrive, however, though they were shorter than Jolly's, they were more thoughtful and narrated interesting experiences and events from his daily life, rather than mere repetitious expressions of carnal desire. Ultimately, Jolly asked him why he did not express more fully his physical attraction for her in his letters.

Accordingly, Patrick, though slightly ill at ease, if not annoyed, began to pen words of physical love that, by his sheer literary abilities, were unmatched by hers. Jolly was convinced once again that, with a little nudging, Patrick's love for her had gushed forth and that his characteristic reticence only reflected Agnes' power and influence over him. Jolly's long days became shorter every time a letter arrived from Patrick. She would read it repeatedly and then look forward to the next week, waiting impatiently for the next letter to arrive, all the while carrying on with her nursing work with the full dedication for which she was well known. Also, the rest of her waking hours were filled up with social commitments that seemed to unfailingly crop up from nowhere.

\*     \*     \*

Patrick flew first to San Antonio to bid goodbye to his parents and to pick up Sis who was going to accompany him to India. He had pressed her subtly to do so without elaborating that he felt that it would provide her an excellent way to recover and forget. He dropped in on Jolly without notice during her duty hours to ensure that the encounter would be short. Jolly was nevertheless grateful, knowing how tough the gesture would have been for him to undertake, triumphing over and crossing Agnes in having to venture it.

A day later, Terrence bought a large backpack and some combat clothes at the army surplus outlet on M and 35th Streets, N.W. just before the entry to Key Bridge. It had been a favorite haunt of his for quite some time. There, he could invariably find army surplus at the most reasonable prices. Within another couple of days, he got a sky blue Chevy Monte Carlo, in top condition and with only twenty-five thousand miles on it at a throwaway price of $1000 from neighbours down the road. The elderly couple, who were selling their row house and moving to Miami, had taken a liking to

Terrence, seeing him walk all dressed up to and from church every Sunday. They would wait for him on the chairs in their ground-floor bay window to be able to chat with him on his way back, if they themselves were not leaving early for a slow drive to a Bethesda diner for Sunday brunch. They had, in fact, invited Terrence once to accompany them to brunch, which he had politely declined, feeling a bit nervous to venture into Bethesda given its hoity reputation.

Now they were moving and it was sweet of them to think of him. Terrence had once mentioned to them that Patrick and he planned to buy a used car to go on a cross-country trip after their exams were over. He had, of course, not known at the time that the congenial couple would move, let alone that they would sell him their car. The offer came during one of those idle chats that they seemed to look forward to every weekend and which Terrence did not mind accommodating. He had a feeling that the throwaway price they proposed was just to save him embarrassment for, otherwise, they would probably have given it to him as a parting gift. He was grateful that they were considerate of his needs and feelings and was surprised that they were not parsimonious, a trait that he generally attributed to the wealthy in direct proportion to their wealth. He told himself that he had learnt a lesson not to come to quick conclusions, and that gross generalisations could be misleading, may be even dangerous. As a final parting gesture the couple even helped him to transfer ownership and to pay the associated tax and fee for tests.

Terrence had paid for the car from the cash he had accumulated over the last two years working at the library at Howard University. He had moved from guard as an undergraduate, to filer, and subsequently to information desk clerk as a graduate student. He had been meticulous in saving part of the money after contributing to household expenses. He knew that Patrick and he might need it during their much-anticipated, yet not discussed, cross-country trip, and carefully preserved it for that rainy day. That occasion never arose. Now Terrence felt sad, indeed deeply hurt that he alone was using what he had set aside to be used and enjoyed by Patrick and him together. He accepted that he had been left with no choice in the matter.

The skies had been cloudy through the spring and summer it seemed to him. It drizzled incessantly, especially at night time. Orion had been hiding, not to be encountered, even for a fleeting moment. Terrence steeled himself for his journey across America alone. He locked the apartment and saw off his elderly friends at National Airport for their flight to Miami. Afterwards, he re-entered the District and drove across 16th Street NW. He drove further east to Mrs. Jackson's house to give her a bear hug but, more importantly, the keys to the apartment so she could dust the place once a week. Somewhat uneasily, he drove back west towards Wisconsin Avenue to head north to Interstate 270. His light blue Monte Carlo had leather bucket seats and he melted into them. The air conditioning was smooth and soundless. The radio was stereophonic, with AM and FM, and there was a tape deck for which he had brought along his favourites. He put on Ella Fitzgerald, but his box also contained Patti Labelle, Diana Ross, Aretha Franklin, Tina Turner and the two Dawn in Tony Orlando and Dawn, and even one each of Connie Francis and Dolly Parton. He liked women's voices, though he was fine with Harry Belafonte as well, perhaps influenced by a comment he overheard in childhood while playing on the roadside from a passerby that Terrence looked like Belafonte! He did not know who Belafonte was and, only many years later, did he come across his smiling face, with his name embossed on a long-playing record, and notice that Belafonte was a singer, and a good looking one at that. Since then, he found a new self- esteem about his own looks but, thankfully, refrained from breaking into song except to hum along with his favourite singers.

Terrence fastened and tightened his seat belt and, bending forward as he drove, peered through the windshield. The sky was a dull grey and a drab drizzle fell relentlessly.

# BOOK III

# TREACHERY IN CALCUTTA

Patrick already knew enough about India to realize that he would have to eventually touch Delhi simply because it was India's powerhouse and those who congregated there could provide important leads for his research and analyses. However, first, in his quest for India's universally acknowledged and admired eclecticism, he wanted to find the soul of modern India and its intellectual fountainhead, and for that he knew he would have to start in Calcutta. He decided to land there, despite thinking about the possible perverse reaction it might have on Sis. He thought it would be like throwing the baby into the deep waters to sink or swim, hoping that it should come up floating. Perhaps she did need shock treatment to enable her to cope with life once again after the debacle she had just experienced. Actually, he had already been somewhat relieved to find that she was on her way to recovery in the few days they had just spent together.

The airport in Calcutta might have been appropriately described as an army bunker because of its stark appearance, with occasional tube lights exposed and dangling from its soot-covered low ceilings, drying plants in broken pots strewn about along the narrow corridors and at dark corners, its faulty, rattling conveyor belts that miraculously managed to drag along the erratically appearing luggage, and the many unlikely, would-be helpers hovering lazily around the luggage, but refraining from touching any of them as if they were army boys contemplating the next attack, but quite sure that it was not time yet to initiate it. The siblings eventually made it to the tourist bureau's outpost nestled near the exit point. It was not difficult to find in the miniscule building. A petite, heavily made-up young woman at the counter turned out to be helpful, recommending a hotel in central Calcutta from a dog-eared brochure listing a plethora of them. She wished them luck as they gathered the information and their belongings.

Patrick was glad to emerge into the sunlight from the tomb, the outcome of egalitarianism gone awry under a rule where no labourer could be asked to do his job of keeping the surroundings clean, swept or polished, even when his wages were ensured to be inflation indexed and a productivity factor added on top, despite no semblance of work being encountered or imposed on him. As they emerged, looking sideways, Patrick was struck by Sis' obliviousness to her surroundings. Relieved, he decided not to make any disparaging comment about their immediate surroundings that might dampen her enthusiasm for her forthcoming, uncertain experiences.

\*    \*    \*

It was a nice boutique hotel in Sudder Street. The room was huge, as is typical of vintage buildings. Its fixtures, as well as the brass bed, looked a century old at least, yet the brass shone like gold. Patrick and Sis each showered and immediately afterwards fell into deep sleep as a result of the jet lag that had gripped them halfway across the globe. They awoke the next morning rested and hungry. Venturing out of their room, they headed directly downstairs for a sumptuous English breakfast in the hotel's spic and span dining room. Their hunger satisfied, they left the hotel to see the city.

Almost immediately, Patrick found himself grinding his teeth and looking away from the street urchins, who were covered in dust and grime. He tried to avoid a feeling of despair mingled with disgust, but he could not control it and sensed it lurking in his belly. He ardently hoped that these untoward and inconvenient examples of humanity, rather, of inhumanity, he told himself, would scoot off instead of encircling them whenever they stopped anywhere, whether they alighted from hand-drawn rickshaws in front of their destination in question or be it window shopping at a dilapidated bazaar which, for some odd reason, was called the New Market. He found himself engulfed in a mental prison of sorts, trying to fend off those lice-ridden little bodies that, not having ever known a childhood, seemed to have developed an expertise at busying themselves about and accosting foreigners and obese, upper-class Indian women who had protruding, exposed bellies as they went about their business, shopping and munching mouthfuls of savouries as they trudged along. These wealthy women were being followed closely by coolies with huge wicker baskets on their heads, carrying the heavy shopping loads of their flabby, short-term employers. It was the responsibility of the coolies to brush the kids off in a constant fanning motion with their free hand, while the other was placed upwards to steady the baskets they precariously balanced atop their heads.

The urchins, even as they were shooed away, darted back like wayward, but determined, flies, a monotonous, wordless, atonal sound emanating from deep in their bellies that, empty or half-filled as they were, confirmed, over and above their unkempt appearances, their identity as beggar caste. It was as if Fagin had immigrated in a time capsule to Calcutta with his brood of boys and let them out onto its streets. One could only pray that Nancy would appear momentarily to gather them in and take them back to take stock of their earnings and, hopefully, give them their meagre meals to satisfy them before they resumed their next shift for picking pockets. Of course the urchins that he was now beholding belonged to identifiable families, but for how long? When would they have to descend to the streets for their own upkeep? Was there a beautiful Oliver Twist among the urchins that were playing or crawling on the pavement unmindful of their dire futures, wronged by fate and chosen by destiny to suffer in groups or by themselves? It was all too mindboggling. Jerking back, Patrick was surprised at the impact Calcutta was having on him, since he had imagined himself to be of sturdier mettle, and he just could not help feeling that he was looking in the wrong place for the eclectic perspectives of India.

He was even more surprised to notice Sis' reaction to the city. One morning, they decided to continue down Park Street, a long street by Calcutta's standards. It was the main hub for Western-type restaurants boasting every cuisine; book shops stacking books, maps and documents from across the world and from every era; a few warehouses stocked with antique furniture, crockery and statuettes that once belonged to now impoverished, ageing aristocratic families of Bengal from whom there was a steady supply; vendors of magazines with silky, satin covers announcing breaking news and scandals, who moved around with feverish intent over their possessions laid out neatly on the pavements for all to see; and stalls that boasted imitation-French perfume, not neglecting Afghani attar. Also, there were the bars with sleazy entrances protected by ushers wearing goggles.

Patrick and Sis browsed in the Oxford and Cambridge bookstores and decided to venture down further. They walked past a U-shaped, well-appointed and freshly painted building that announced itself as St. Xavier's College. Sis had bought and devoured Fodor's and Frommer's travel guides, and had learnt about this revered institution that had functioned for over a century. They looked at the building built by Jesuit priests, many of whom had come to India as young men to devote their lives to uplift the daily life of a 'Pagan' society. Here their objective was the education of local young men in western mores rather than surreptitious intervention into the politics of royal courts or greater pecuniary acquisition for the Church, motives for which they were better known in much of the world. But neither brother nor sister was able to appreciate, leave alone admire, such laudable intentions, given their knowledge, experience and deep suffering as a result of what a similar religious setup had perpetrated on them. They walked on.

The next block was long and studded with stately bungalows that strained to exhibit themselves above long, unbroken walls and through tall pipal and banyan trees that obscured them. Once they passed the block, the scene changed abruptly. They hit upon a dilapidated cemetery. The pavement in front was populated by refugees who could not very easily be described or perceived as human, crawling in and out of waist-high shacks apparently made of jute rags, asbestos slivers, shapeless brown cardboard, irregular plywood sheets, silvery aluminium backing and rusty polythene. Dust was flying, even in the heavy air that remained still amidst the thick pollution that was beginning to choke Patrick and Sis. A disproportionate number of infants was laid out on the soiled cement in the bright sunlight, while those slightly older took a four-legged, crawling posture in an attempt to follow the even older siblings, cousins and friends, sprinting hither and yon in the cramped, dust-sprayed space.

A nonchalant stream of shiny cars of every hue and colour, ramshackle trucks, wobbly bicycles, long bamboo carts hand drawn by sweating labourers glistening in the powerful sun, rickshaws occupied by bunches of school-going children and pulled by elderly, greying men struggling to stay on the surface of the road and not be pulled up against the weight of the occupiers as if they were in a game of see-saw they were desperately trying to control and, most of all, chaotic pedestrians who seemed to have full confidence that they would not be run over as they, competing with the traffic, ran along or crossed the road without looking in any direction.

Is this the Park Street Cemetery? Patrick wondered. He looked at Sis and said definitively, "Let's go in." He moved towards the cemetery, whose grille gates were secured by a vintage lock; nevertheless, the gates were ajar that made entry and exit quite easy.

Sis replied, "Pat, do you mind if I just stay here and not go in? Look, that family there is preparing the most delicious meat curry. Can you smell it? I want to see what they do. You know, just hang around…"

Patrick was doubtful about her desire, but did not want to take on the role of older brother. "Do be careful," he said as he disappeared into the quadrangle that contained confined and forgotten dead bodies in their final, decayed skeletal stage.

Sis had read to Patrick from a guidebook that many a historical figure had been interred here during an era dating back a century to when this city had been the capital of India, the Jewel of the British Crown. How strange it felt now as he moved through a terrain that compared with the Amazon's forbidding flora and fauna, trying to get to and read the sculptured, but crumbling and precariously standing, tombstones. He managed to read one that seemed to make a grand pronouncement of a lieutenant of the East India Company: Walter Dickens, the fourth of Charles Dickens' ten children. He had died of an aortic aneurysm in 1863 at the age of twenty-two.

"Wow!" Patrick exclaimed to himself.

As he tried to close in, he must have unintentionally nudged the surrounding thicket, for a huge flock of pitch-black bats flew out from the wild vegetation, suddenly swaying the roots of an ageless banyan tree that hung from above like the chords of a giant church organ. Blinded by the strong sun, the nocturnal creatures brushed him as they dove down into the air before surging upwards, flapping their wings into the sky.

Patrick had endured all he could take. He turned to rush out from the eerie atmosphere that suddenly gave him the jitters. As he stepped out, he found Sis totally absorbed by the daily life of the families of cadaverously thin people who seemed to live on the pavement right in front of the cemetery gate, undisturbed by pedestrians who routinely, yet carefully, were making their way through the impoverished lot, in the direction of wherever they were single-mindedly headed.

"Pat," she said enthusiastically. "Look at them! There is a full meal being prepared by that family." She took care not to point openly. "They certainly are cooking an aromatic meat dish, aren't they? And look at those kids. Those four are theirs." For a moment, she thought ruefully of the foetus that had painfully dropped from her body after her recent miscarriage. It was just not to be. Now, that time and place seemed to her to be so far away. At the very least, the miscarriage had made the trip with her brother feasible. She had not discussed it with her brother any further. She banished all thought of what might have transpired otherwise. She snapped back to the present and looked closely at the strangely charming mix of humans in front of her. Meticulously, she worked out the four families that comprised the group, with an average of four children per family, all of the children ostensibly less than five or six years old. Oh, and there seemed to be a grandparent or two, who had somehow managed to outwit the ravages of their arduous lives and were now coolly resting with their backs to the sun like pelicans in repose.

"Did you see the homeless in New York on TV channels? Despite the cheap housing or shelters available to them, you find them sleeping in doorways or solitary in their seats, a fixed stare at the spot on which they are squatted cross-legged, hands outstretched perennially, seeking alms to feed their alcoholism, drug addiction, or some small, but unvanquished vice, which had robbed them in the distant past of their pride and hope forever. I couldn't help but notice that they were all by themselves, alone and lonely. I had then thought of what Mother Teresa has said – that poverty of the heart, of the soul, is much lonelier than poverty of physical want, of food, shelter and clothing. Now I see what she must have meant. These families here seem almost happy to me. They must be. No, they are happy." Romance and envy of poverty in the middle and upper classes, who would never experience it, forged forth and spilt over from Sis.

"Isn't it quite something that the government just ignores them, just letting them be?" Pat was obviously exasperated after his recent unsuccessful adventure in the graveyard.

"But that's just it! This place must have a government that does not punish you just because you are poor. The government simply ignores you. Back home, they would all probably be in a poorhouse and the children put in foster care. Pat, is it not the most fundamental form of liberal democracy? To let you be? Or should I add liberated?"

"Sis, the Communists here are very strong! In any event, they would be overwhelmed if the government tried to do anything decisive. Many of these pavement dwellers are probably refugees who came across the border from Bangladesh, which is doubly poor. Every time they have a flood there, they cross over. After all, they are cousins and have to be let in."

Sis looked quizzically at her brother. "But how come there are so many people living on the streets, Patrick?"

"In fact, they started coming across from the time India was partitioned and what are now Pakistan and Bangladesh were torn away from it. The British dismembered the consolidated India before leaving in 1947 into India and

Pakistan, and left India a dismembered carcass. In fact, if you look at the map, post-independence India looks like a limbless entity, the two wings of Pakistan extricated from its left and right! Then West Pakistan began perpetrating all manner of human rights abuses on East Pakistan as soon as Awami League, a political party based in the East, won a parliamentary majority in their national parliament that is located in the West. So India tore East from West Pakistan in 1971, ultimately unable to bear the daily flood of thousands of refugees across its borders with the East, who were escaping rape, mutilation and other atrocities of the military regime imposed from West Pakistan on the East. Of course, the refugees remained on the Calcutta streets and, even though the tide was stemmed, the influx has never stopped."

"But, why would India be interested in the people of East Pakistan?" she asked about a subject that was all foreign to her.

She knew she would never get all this from her travel books as she listened intently to her brother, who she kept on a pedestal of blind admiration as far as erudition was concerned.

Her brother, accordingly, obliged. "History has its own strange twists and turns. The Bengalis of India and the Bangladeshis are essentially the same stock, identical in race. I expect, the Indian Bengalis should be racially closer to the Bangladeshis than to any other ethnic group in India. The British divided them into East and West Bengal in 1905-06 because the Bengalis around Calcutta, then the empire's capital, were found to be too precocious for their own good, founding a political party called the Congress and implanting the idea of independence in Indian intellectual thought. Later, Mohandas Kara – am – chand Gandhi, sorry, I could be wrong with the pronunciation with that middle name. He basically seems to have usurped from the Bengalis the idea of independence, but this practical strategist changed a nascent intellectual concept into a successful mass movement, just like Picasso transformed Braque's creation of Cubism into

see. All manner of vehicles were standing absolutely still in all four directions. Would-be pedestrians waited patiently. There was total silence except for a loud, repeated rendition by a thick column of undernourished men and women who moved through the broad road like a meandering Anaconda in a slow, yet deliberate, swagger.

"Communist Party ashbe, ashchhe. Congress Party Murdabad, CPM Shorkar Zindabad." The Communist Party (Marxist) will come, is coming. Death to the Congress Party; long live the Communist government.

They were carrying bright red flags and banners, stamped with the tell-tale hammer and sickle emblem that fluttered high above them, taking in the erratic gusts of wind and, paradoxically, adding a festive air to this otherwise revolutionary scene. Neither their obvious under-nourishment nor the ruthless heat seemed to bother them in the slightest.

As if in this fairytale, one gruesome chapter would follow another, Sis whispered into Patrick's ear, "What is this?"

Patrick seemed amused at his sister's expressive comment. He had read most of what was written on the banners, of course, but decided to keep it simple for his sister. Smiling at her, he responded softly, "The Communists are about to win the state elections here. So West Bengal state will have a Communist government soon, made up of a rag-tag grouping of a dozen or so Left parties. They are basically opposed to economic, social or cultural exploitation by the West. It is a ruse, really. The likely chief minister, equivalent to our governor, maintains a pretty lavish lifestyle, it seems. The family attends the best Western academic institutions in the city. Possibly St. Xavier's, the imposing building that we passed earlier today. I would not be surprised, anyway."

He smiled again at the thought of teaching his little sister the ways of the world, and continued, "Of course, this is all well known. That is interesting in itself. It is because there is a free press here. Possibly more so than in our country, if that is believable.

And certainly not like, say, in Romania, where a ruthless Commie rules. Yet Ceausescu is our government's darling, you know, just because he does not consult the Soviet Union when repressing, oppressing and suppressing his own people!" He was greatly satisfied with himself and his global political views.

Sis was very impressed by all this, though thoroughly confused by now. Her absorptive capacity for one day had been exceeded. She looked at her brother pleadingly.

"Yes, let's turn back. This procession is going to take some time. I saw in the morning papers that, from midday, there is a hartal, a strike that will attempt to stop all activity. These processions are to start from all corners of Calcutta and meet at the Maidan."

As Sis looked at him quizzically, he explained, "The Maidan is a huge, uneven field as you approach the Hoogly River towards the west of the city. Here, look at the map." Then he decided not to open it again. "Anyway, we can go there tomorrow, to the Ochterloney Monument, a tall, lighthouse-like structure at the northern end of the Maidan."

Sis nodded as she recalled reading about the monument in Fodor and Lonely Planet.

Patrick continued, "The rest of the day will be chaotic. Communist leaders from all over India are arriving in town and apparently there will be a lot of speech giving." Then he whispered, with an air of mystery as if revealing some thus-far unshared secret to his little sister, "These Bengalis love talk, they say. But I guess before ending up at the monument we should visit the US Consul in Calcutta, Mr. Felman. One of my neighbours on P Street gave me his name and told me the consul is a young man and a good friend of his. He suggested that I drop by. I think that's a good idea, don't you? It could even be interesting." He glanced at Sis for approval, which she conveyed to him instantly with swift, repeated nods.

"So, tomorrow will be a busy day. First thing early morning, we have to take a rickshaw to Mother Teresa's. If we want to be there for morning service, we'd better be there by 5:30 sharp. Then we get back and go around 10 a.m. to the consul, and perhaps to the Maidan around coffee time."

"Great! But, aren't we going to that famous coffee house all the guidebooks mention? It is on College Street, opposite Presidency College, which is real Ivy League here and, perhaps not so paradoxically, has produced a crop of communists. Interesting, isn't it, Patrick?"

Patrick had begun to realise how quickly Sis was picking up on his explanations and making them her own. He squeezed her cheek ever so lightly, making her scream and hug him at the same time.

"We can do that this evening even, if we are up to it. However, first, back to the hotel, a cold shower and a good lunch of steak and French fries, but no salad please, thank you!"

As they turned back into Park Street, they were stunned by the still-motionless traffic. Nothing moved, as though in obeisance to a funeral procession. They walked past the immobile mishmash of vehicles and, at the next crossing, hopped on to a rickshaw and let the rickshawallah navigate his slim, hand-drawn vehicle through the traffic, pulling them rapidly towards their destination in the oppressive heat that they knew they would succumb to if they were to be exposed to it for much longer.

*   *   *

That evening, brother and sister walked from their hotel, through throngs of humans in motion, to Dharamtalla Street, from where they jumped on a tram that took them to College Street. There were two linked, yet precariously attached, cars, and they got on to the second car, immediately realising from its occupants that it was the lower class of travel, specifically cautioned by the hotel's bell captain-cum-porter and itinerant desk clerk to avoid. Having made the mistake and realising it, they nevertheless relaxed, finding themselves in the near-empty car of the tram that had barely started from its garage at the Esplanade. At the next stop, however, a mob of people trooped in and rushed to grab seats next to one another. Sis clutched onto her purse tightly and closely, and Patrick watched her carefully lest something untoward should happen.

The tram took them from Esplanade along crackling tracks and accompanied by the incessant ringing of its bell, indifferent to whether it was stopping or moving, to the College Street stop, where they alighted. They immediately noticed that College Street had an entirely different character from Park Street. There were book stalls on both sides of the street, through which ran a pair of steel-laden tracks and over which hung thick wires supplying electricity to the pantographs of the trams.

They browsed the books for some time, even though their interest, in particular keen in the case of Sis, lay in the coffee house. They did find a couple of masterpieces at throwaway prices, including an early edition of Benjamin Franklin's autobiography and, unbelievably, a volume of the original printing of Wordsworth's poems. The latter even had his own handwritten jottings in the margin of Solitary Reaper, a poem that had mesmerised Patrick when, rather uncharacteristically perhaps, he had first been taught it by Brother Aberystwyth back in his Texas high school. The storekeeper took pains to point it out in hushed tones as he glanced from side to side in apparent testimony to the treasure that he had on offer, but was keeping the secret from all other customers but them.

Patrick took the book in his hands and was instantly transported back to his San Antonio classroom. Silently, he read:

> Behold her, single in the field
> Yon solitary highland lass
> Singing and reaping by herself,

Stop here or gently pass.
Alone she cuts and binds the grain
And sings a melancholy strain
Oh, listen! For the vale profound
Is overflowing with the sound.

The sharp clanking sound of a passing tram brought him cruelly back to College Street in Calcutta from the Scottish highlands where Wordsworth had composed this poem on a stroll one sunny morning. The contrast was so acute that he was startled, though not irritated, for he was far too curious about what he guessed might be in store for them in their immediate vicinity and instant future. He returned the book politely with no one around to authenticate Wordsworth's jottings, voiding the ray of hope written over the storekeeper's face, and egged on Sis along the pavement. Sis smiled and gladly joined hands in a mild marching movement with her brother.

As they walked forward, they soon found a set of huge iron gates to their left and, inside, the buildings of the famous Presidency College, the first edifice of Western higher education established in India by the ex-colonials longer than a century earlier. However, Sis pulled Patrick back from entering the compound, dragging him instead across the tramlines to the other side of the street and into a lane whose buildings were covered with political posters of multiple colours, Party symbols and proletariat proclamations of infinite variety. They obscured the buildings to such an extent that they were devoid of any architectural identity. Sis had done her homework, as to the location of their intended destination. Like a moth to a flame, she easily entered a giant door amidst paper-covered street walls, and climbed a flight of steep, circular stairs, all the while expertly dragging her ambivalent brother along.

Lo and behold, they found themselves in the chamber of a majestic hall, with an extraordinarily high ceiling and roaring fans dangling from astoundingly long, crowbar-like giant rods that ran across two ends of the high roof. Patrick winced involuntarily as the whirling fans took on the look of trapeze artists just prior to their vault into space. As he recovered, his eyes floated down to an equally mesmerising scene, populated by animated and chattering human beings this time. The gigantic hall was crammed with small square tables draped in white tablecloths and, at first glance, it was hard to find a single chair unoccupied. Busy waiters, wearing flurried headgear and balancing trays of beverages on raised hands, flitted from table to table in a relentless motion in the service of their youngish clients.

Realising quickly enough that they should not wait to be seated, as soon as they spotted it, they dashed to a semi-empty table with a sole occupant, assessing instantaneously the possibility of sharing it. They were obviously first-time visitors, for the occupant seemed bemused that they should ask if they could sit on the empty chairs. He ushered them to two chairs with a gesture of his hand, and went instantly back to the Bertold Brecht volume in his hands, all the while emitting smoke circles from his mouth in steady regularity with a slight upward motion of his face and a sideward jerk of his mouth. He seemed completely oblivious to any discomfort he might be causing the two newcomers at the table with the tobacco smoke.

Sis spoke up. "Hi. Do you mind blowing your smoke away from me? I am suffocating." She feigned a dainty collapse on an invisible, non-existent shoulder.

Stunned, the young man looked up at her. There was fire in his eyes. 'Oh! These Americans', they seemed to emit. He was about to say, 'you Americans, you are Americans, I suppose – feel free to tell other people how you want them to behave, no matter that I was here at the table first and you saw I was smoking when you asked to sit with me'. However, he refrained at the last moment, much to his own relief. Instead, his eyes narrowed somewhat as they seemed to focus on Sis' exquisitely carved face that seemed to be chiselled from pink Carrara marble. Something softened in him. Obviously, she could have had no bad intention in her innocent remark and was oblivious of the impact it had had on breaking his thoughts and reflections on Brecht. She had to be forgiven. He smiled.

Instead, he said, "Of course, I had omitted to reflect on the fact that you Americans – you are Americans, I suppose – have been marching to make yours a smokeless environment." But, intelligently, he did not utter his last phrase, "to balance your environmental degradation I suppose," keeping it to himself.

He knew that, in 1972, people in the US smoked everywhere: in groceries, in classrooms, in shops, in hospitals, trains and planes, but, strangely, not in cinemas or on public transport! He just wanted to provoke the attractive woman he found to be accidentally in front of him.

He continued, "It is just that, to digest Brecht, a puff or two seem so much to be of assistance." He was quite aware of the rounded phrasing he had used to impress.

Patrick responded confidently, indeed, almost arrogantly, "I recall to have enjoyed Three Penny Opera thoroughly, even in the absence of crutches, be it hashish or cigar or cigarette." Content with his swift and sharp response, he smiled and asked, "By the way, what's your name? I am Patrick, and I am travelling with my sister here." Gathering her in, under his extended arm, Patrick added, "And, oh yes, we are Americans, but not Yankees, though. Nomoshkar!"

This last greeting floored Amlan, taking him completely by surprise. "I... I... I... I am Amlan," he stammered. Admiringly, he added, "Patrick, why did you not say Namaskar as even most Indians would do? Do you know Bengali?" Yet, unable to hide all his sarcasm, he blurted out, "So Brecht is popular in America!"

Having had the first punch, Patrick answered, with alacrity and unabashed honesty, "Not as much even as Sartre or Camus, whose popularity is miniscule. You see, we have our John Steinbeck, Mark Twain, Ernest Hemingway, and Harper Lee and so many others." He had a twinkle in his eye, in particular using care to use both first and last names as if Amlan was not expected to recognise them easily; so even their first names had to be included. As far as he was concerned, his rebuttal was complete, Q.E.D.

Amlan had actually read Steinbeck's East of Eden and quite a bit of Mark Twain. As an undergraduate student on scholarship at Amherst College, he had also explored unique literary quests among American scholars such as the pursuit of the unlikely Virginia Woolf. Though she had been based in Britain, Amlan had found that, at Strawberry Village in the vicinity of the University of New Hampshire, Virginia Woolf and her works were celebrated and researched by mercurial scholars and investigators. However, he could never force himself to read Woolf. Her life had not impressed him, for he could not take interest in the works of a hyper-conscious, narcissistic, neurotic individual who selfishly took her own life.

For a moment, Amlan noted Patrick's choice of rather straight-jacketed authors whom he would simply classify as social observers rather than as explorers of the human mind, and he certainly was not terribly impressed. Nevertheless, he was able to muster just enough interest to continue the conversation. He felt he could have mentioned Rabindranath Tagore, Sharat Chandra Chatterjee, Premchand and so many other Indian greats, but smiled indulgently, convinced that Patrick would have to be forgiven for probably not even having heard their names. Carefully emitting smoke from his mouth away from their table and instead towards the next, he inquired about the purpose of their visit to Calcutta, and was surprised that Calcutta was simply a segment of their trip to get to 'explore and know India a bit'. Amlan secretly admired the difficulty they had taken to come the distance to experience something different and, undoubtedly, rather dangerous.

As he chatted and reflected, Amlan became more engaged, if not engaging, increasingly unable to stop himself from stealing glances at Sis to observe her sharp features and strawberry lips. He was careful not to stare overtly or for too long so that it would not give him away. Soon, he was imagining his lips on hers and found himself sliding one leg over the other in a failed attempt to control an embarrassingly enlarging, heaving bulge.

Amlan eventually overcame his sweet enchantment by venturing into a Don Quixotic soliloquy and emitting irreverent comments and quotes even as his mind clouded over, wondering why he had never been so electrified by any girl while at Amherst. His thoughts, in fast forward mode, scattered without direction, though his countenance did not immediately reveal the mix of elation and confusion that he was experiencing. Perhaps, when he was at Amherst, he had been too focussed on coursework that had resulted in straight A's that put him on the Dean's List; perhaps he was too hell bent on returning to Calcutta to his mother's side; perhaps his unwavering objective of finding employment in a teaching college in Calcutta obviated all other interests, he wondered. Yes, it was true that he did not want to take any risk that might jeopardise his genteel existence as a North Calcuttan, reading the Indian philosopher writers and the more socially adventurous Western authors, and listening to the greatest operas, symphonies and concertos that Europe had to offer, while every material need of his was taken care of by a devoted mother and her servants.

Amlan's mother and paternal grandmother were the only other occupants of an inherited sprawling colonial mansion embellished with teak and mahogany settees and beds, six-foot-high antique mirrors encased in gold-brushed rococo cherubs and studded on the top with Italian cameos, a grand piano and an organ serviced regularly by the staff of the Calcutta School of Music and which his mother played as she sang melancholic Tagore songs at dusk, family oil portraits going back four generations that adorned its high walls, darkened, but decipherable, and meticulously cleaned every decade by an ancient-looking artist restorer and, most of all, every morning being served bed tea from a teapot under a cosy and in a cup and saucer of Royal Albert or Royal Doulton bone china by Bhagvan, the cook and bearer who had been in the family for as long as he could remember. For all this to continue, all Amlan needed to do was to hold a stable job teaching undergraduates eight to ten hours a week in a good college under Calcutta University. Indeed, that had been his goal and nothing else mattered to him then. He had achieved that goal; now, all of a sudden, a new dimension had appeared on the horizon, unanticipated and without warning.

Sis, basking in admiration at the erudite conversation between the young men, conversation that was ever informing and ever so significant to her ears, eventually spoke up. "Are we going to order something?" she asked. "The waiter has gone past a few times. He is not skirting our table anymore; he has begun to studiously ignore us!"

Somewhat startled, if not amused, Amlan responded forthwith, "It will be my pleasure to order for you our famous chicken sandwiches that go down extremely well with infusion." He looked at them inquiringly.

Patrick looked a bit doubtful, either about ordering food at such a local spot or about what infusion might be. He found himself finally caught out by Amlan's phraseology.

Amlan caught his expression and explained, "Infusion is a particular brew of coffee. No milk is added so that you enjoy its full flavour. And yes, the water is adequately boiled here, for no one is known to catch Montezuma's revenge here!"

He consciously used an expression he expected his American guests to be familiar with. Then, as if to emphasise the point, he concluded, "The chicken sandwiches have just a hint of butter, and the chicken is not fried, but roasted, though with a Bengali touch, of course. Try them. You may just like them." There was the smallest tinge of challenge in his voice.

The siblings dug in as soon as the sandwiches arrived at the table, for they were ravenously hungry by then, while Amlan watched them with some satisfaction as though he himself was the chef. He blabbered on and informed them about the Leftist parties, mainly armchair Marxists, that were rising in prominence in the state of West Bengal of which Calcutta was the capital, about their promise of land reform that would confiscate rural land from families like his own and about which he and his mother had had no regrets whatsoever since they hardly went to their lands, not even for an annual family picnic, and about the extremist Naxals who had attempted, but were failing at, a Mao Tse Tung-style armed revolution. He was impressed, indeed, amazed, at Patrick's in-depth assessment of his statements, while Patrick admired Amlan's open, collegial style, inviting them to coffee and engaging them not only in politics and literature, but also in philosophy and music, putting them at ease in otherwise unfamiliar surroundings.

It was dark outside as Patrick glanced towards the windows set into the far wall of the great hall. Upon this sudden realisation, he exclaimed, "I should be taking Sis back to the hotel. It's quite a long trek back. Nice to have met you, Amlan. Perhaps…" He trailed off as Amlan picked up.

"If it is okay with you, I could accompany you back to your hotel. It is rather late, you know. A tram will take a long time; a taxi somewhat less. And, though Calcutta taxis are quite safe, it is just as well that I go with you," he concluded.

Patrick could not quite suspect Amlan's ulterior motive intertwined with genuine concern. Indeed, he was relieved.

"If you are absolutely sure it's no trouble..." He sounded appropriately grateful.

*     *     *

The air was thin when they got out of the restaurant. The earlier heaviness had been cut through by a spate of short showers. There were puddles on the street in which were reflected parts of the floating nimbus clouds made yellow by the glow from a full moon. There was a fresh breeze that tousled Sis' hair. Amlan looked at her with an uncontrolled, all-consuming desire as the moonlight silhouetted the sharp angles of her face and her blonde hair flew in abandon.

Sis noticed Amlan's furtive glances that alternated with short, fixed stares at her. As this realisation dawned on her, she blushed. Her momentary smile was overwrought with self-deprecating thoughts. No, she could not involve herself with this dark, handsome, moustached, heavily bespectacled intellectual Bengali man when her private, personal world had been violated and corrupted by a demon priest. How could she ever explain to him what he had done to, and with, her? No, no, no.... Her lips curled. She tried to control the sobs she felt rushing in, the tsunami of consternation that would certainly betray her unless she somehow quickly nipped it. Patrick, oblivious to his sister's emotional state, walked on towards tram or taxi, whichever would appear first.

The sudden change in Sis' demeanour perplexed Amlan. Did it merely reveal a childlike pout in an obvious, unhidden manner? Or did it expose a pain deeply rooted in her past that she found difficult to conceal? Whatever it was, he found it at once exhilarating and exasperating, something beyond his grasp or control, yet something he desired to understand and to help dissipate.

When the three got off the tram and walked from Dharamtallah Street, passing Eliot Cinema and on to Sudder

Street, Amlan walked beside Sis, with Patrick rushing along ahead of them. Amlan felt gooseflesh rising and the discomfort of an erection caused by Sis' nearness.

They stopped in front of the hotel. Amlan popped the question, "Can I show you around Calcutta tomorrow morning? I can make myself free... My scheduled lecture could be postponed to the weekend!" He said the last part with an air of mock relief.

"But, we have to visit Mr. Felman, the US Consul here. Don't we, Sis?"

Well aware that they had agreed to do so, yet paralysed in her confusion, Sis mumbled, as if agreeing with both her chaperones, inaudibly and meekly, "Of course."

By now, Amlan knew what he wanted and that he would not give up until he got it. So he insisted, "But, what would she do there?"

Sis seemed to find courage from Amlan's rejoinder. "Pat, I really would love to be shown around Calcutta by Amlan," she desisted, mistakenly overemphasising the first 'A'.

Unable to hide a slight irritation, Amlan elaborated, 'Omlaan', stressing and elongating the second 'a' as if there were two, while pronouncing the first 'a' as an 'o' as in 'ostrich'.

Sis, overwhelmed and overtaken by his straightforwardness, simplicity, frankness, willingness, yet helplessness, concern and stubbornness, re-formulated the name correctly, 'Omlaan' and smiled at him quizzically, searching for his approval. Amlan gave her a quick, reassuring nod with a slight hint of a smile. He was convinced Sis would never mispronounce his name again.

Patrick had no option but to relent, though not without some lingering doubt. He murmured a reluctant agreement, thanked Amlan with a faint smile and, sensing that he might want to discuss the next day with Sis for a moment, turned away from them towards the hotel lobby and to the stairs. As he took the first steps up, he turned back and saw them approach each other. He quickly turned back and galloped up the stairs, skipping a few steps, unable to explain the sudden lightness in his being and the heartfelt relief and protective love he felt for Sis at that instant. What could be better than her successful emergence from the dark recesses in which her emotions must have been toiling since her traumatic experience, he asked himself.

Back on earth, he said to himself, gosh! Lovebirds already! The shroud of anxiety for Sis that he had carried with himself seemed to have been lifted from him and a feeling of trust, if not gratitude, towards Amlan gathered around him in its place. Yet, with a sense of foreboding, he wondered if Amlan would be able to understand, appreciate and accept Sis. Lost in thought, he thrust the ornate antique key into the keyhole, turned the doorknob, and clicked the door open, running straight to his old, long, wide bed and turning the switch on the boob tube on. His thoughts moved on as he stared at the local Bengali newsreader. He had a handsome, roundish Bengali face, pronouncing words with a lot of sh's and o's. He wondered what dose of local politics he would be enlightened with by the consul the next morning.

*    *    *

Downstairs in front of the hotel door, Amlan took Sis' face ever so softly in the cup of his palms. Even as pedestrians strolled, hand-pulled carts meandered, rickshaws plied, taxis honked, restless dogs barked and the last crow noisily flapped its wings overhead in the narrow, dingy street, he kissed her full, red lips softly, drawing on them slowly as their tongues moved and entwined, prolonging the kiss until they were both breathless. Only then did they reluctantly let their lips free.

At the beginning, Sis cringed in her guilt, her mixed feelings upfront, but then she gave in to an all-enveloping reverie, imprisoned in momentary felicity and passion. Once released from Amlan's embrace, she almost swooned, but managed to put his stained glasses back in their place, firmly like a saddle on the hollow of his sharp, straight nose. She could not help but crawl into his chest momentarily, and responded willingly as he drew her in, as if in reassurance that he would certainly be there the next morning. She felt the hardness in his manhood straining against the fabric of his trousers as he pressed against her.

Predictably, a group of urchins had gathered around them and, by now, were clapping in delight as passers-by, taken aback at the unusual, if ephemeral, public demonstration of affection, glanced rather disapprovingly as they shot past. Sis moved her face back from Amlan's ever so lightly as she admired, no, adored, the exquisitely chiselled dark face that had lighted every molecule in her body, allayed every doubt in her mind, and vanquished every sorrow in her soul. Finally pulling herself away reluctantly, she turned around and ran up the stairs in a swift motion, disappearing from his sight.

Amlan moved forward to run after her as if their first encounter had been suddenly truncated, but held himself back at the entrance steps, recalling they would meet tomorrow, and the excitement that enveloped him sent a shiver through his body. He stopped, looked up at the hazy sky where clouds had gathered once again and, for once, prayed that this feeling he had just experienced that night would stay with him forever. He breathed deeply. A slow, refreshing drizzle began, penetrating his very being. He looked up again and saw an exaltation of larks flying past, silhouetted against the full moon. Possibly, they were returning to their nests at the edge of the semi-dry ponds bordering the grasslands across the Esplanade. He paused to look at them, enchanted, and found himself humming a Tagore song:

> Oh! Please open the doors
> Don't keep me standing and waiting outdoors

Please respond; look towards me
Come to me with open arms.
My toils are over for the day
The evening star has revealed itself
The last ferry of light crossed the sky – a sea
of sunset
– and is now merely a cloud.
The cows have returned to their sheds
The birds are already nesting
The paths are all lost from view
As darkness binds them together.

He hadn't hummed this tune that his grandfather had taught him when he was a boy in a long, long time. Yet, now, he felt deeply that he could convey its full meaning to Sis. Could he do so tomorrow? He walked slowly, floating a few millimetres above ground, in exuberant anticipation, skipping a step, kicking puddles of water all around, as the urchins followed him as if he was their Pied Piper. The teeming, moving world around him had faded from his consciousness. Sis was the world, the universe. The rest was oblivion.

*     *     *

It took Amlan a long time to reach home. As he cut through Hari Ghosh Street, often abbreviated to Horigo Street in its North Calcutta neighbourhood, to enter the giant lion gates of the palatial Zamindari abode of his ancestors in which he had been born and had spent the large part of his life other than the few years in the US, the ageless Durwan, by now short of most teeth and visibly bent forward, stood up in a crooked salute, his turban half covering his forehead. Amlan smiled as he always did for, if he didn't or overlooked doing so, the next day he would hear a mouthful from the old man about how America had changed him.

Durwan had, of course, every right to do so, for he had made many a contribution to Amlan's nurturing. Just to mention a few things among all others, Durwan had carried Amlan on his shoulders and back as if he was a horse and Amlan the prince for as long as Amlan had remained interested in playing the game with him. Later, he had scolded adolescent Amlan when he had found him with a lighted cigarette tucked into his palm, yet never revealed the secret to his parents and, recently, in Amlan's adulthood, he had expressed his concern that Amlan had not yet found a bride and had gently prodded, nay, admonished, his mother for the fact that Amlan was taking too long in this venture, much to Amlan's amusement and to his mother's concern.

As Amlan strode through the gates, Durwan heaved a sigh of relief, for Dada – young sir – had come home safely at the end of his long, complicated day in the outside world, a world that could surely bring fame and fortune, but that was also fraught with risk and danger. He hurried past Amlan into the house to announce his arrival to the rest of the household – Ma and the servants – so that dinner could be readied while Amlan strolled in, showered and changed, in time for his entrance to the dining room for the most important meal of the day.

Amlan's immediate family was small. Though he had come from a long line of Zamindars or, essentially, beneficiaries of land granted by the British in recognition of their successful revenue collection activities for the British. The Zamindari families had invariably become used to opulence, mimicking British aristocracy in the wider reaches of Calcutta, oblivious of the penury they must have caused in their quest for routinely collecting tax from the poor, destitute farmer. Slowly, the line of this particular family had narrowed, as was the case of many similar lineages. Not rarely did such outcomes result from the relentless abuse of the senses by the men and the unbending strictures of widowhood for their women that combined to ensure few, and often sickly, children, effectively culling potential progeny. Despite his excessive lifestyle, during the independence movement, Amlan's grandfather had dropped the title of Choudhury as an addendum to his surname because it had been given by the British to one of his ancestors as a successful revenue collector. He had also taken to wearing dhotis made of khadi, a handspun rough cotton as suggested by Mahatma Gandhi in order to boycott British goods, particularly the fine mill-spun cotton that came from the Manchester mills. Nevertheless, among some of the family stories that his grandmother would tell Amlan as she sat in front of him during meals as a child, it was confided in hushed tones, yet with a degree of jocularity, that his grandfather had reverted back to mill-spun cotton after the khadi cut into his skin. The British had strangled manufacturing in India through various tariff commissions that levied heavy tariffs on Indian products while placing low tariffs on goods produced in Britain and exported to India, using cotton, wool and other raw materials imported from India at artificially low prices. However, this fact that enraged the Indian Congress Party could ultimately make little difference to Amlan's grandfather in light of the sensitivity of his skin.

The reason for Amlan's father – Baba – passing away at a relatively early age was also from the long-term ramifications of opulence and indulgence, though of a more limited nature. His worsening obesity, unattended to and uncontrolled over his adult life, had led to the inevitable heart attack. Amlan was an undergraduate at Amherst at the time. A daily diet of Hilsa with mustard oil, mutton rogan josh or lobster malai curry, deep fried luchi, a flaky, deep-fried bread, or rice pilaf stirred in ghee, a refined butter and, for dessert, payesh, a rice pudding made with stirred, thickened milk and crusted with sliced almonds and raisins, and complemented by a variegated selection of Bengali sweets made of chhana – cottage cheese made from heavy milk – steeped in sugar, or natun gur, a molasses from the palm tree sap and reminiscent of maple syrup, completed satisfactorily with an apology for a digestive called paan, a leaf from the Betel tree, folded over sweet condiments and zarda or tobacco wafers, eventually caught up with Baba. Otherwise, he was not known to have had any other cardinal vice. He was soft-natured and studiously caring of his spouse and son. No amount of admonition by his wife or pleadings from his widowed mother, who spent most of her days and evenings in the marble-laid Puja room conducting her ablutions of her numerous gods and goddesses, and would emerge from there only to witness her son or grandson relish their meals, had any perceptible effect on him, other than to protractedly sulk in silence.

Baba died a contented man. His last word while he took his wife's right hand was a faint, yet well formed, 'Amlan', as though uttering an unfulfilled last wish to see his son, or perhaps it was a last blessing. It had been impossible for Amlan to fly home in time to be at his Baba's side. However, he did light Baba's funeral pyre, after first breaking down over his father's corpse, so that his cousins had to pull him back and direct him to his duty. Subsequently, he maintained the strictest Hindu rituals of himself boiling prescribed vegetables and lentils for a soup without any oil or spice, sleeping on a thin coir mat on the floor, and not shaving or combing his hair during the thirteen-day mourning period. At its expiry, he went with a priest to the banks of the Ganges to utter Sanskrit verses and, as prescribed, to shave his head and underarms, to not only remove bodily impurities, but also to extricate his soul from the deep pain caused by the vacuum left by his father.

Amlan completed Shraddho, a long priestly ceremony stipulated for the peace and the release of the departed's soul from earthly connections, yet well prepared for the next, for an exhaustive supply of household requirements, including bed, mattress, pillows, linen, provisions including enormous

quantities of rice, lentils, fruit and vegetables, and brass
utensils to prepare them in, were displayed for all to see in
sombre orderliness in a courtyard adjacent to where the rites
were performed. Of course, after the rites were completed,
those items would head out with the priest, as a part of his
non-pecuniary remuneration package, as was usual custom.

The ceremony was conducted by a Brahmin priest in
Sanskrit, an event that took much longer than usual since
Amlan had especially selected a young priest with a Masters
degree who could explain to him, in Bengali, the meaning
of every recited verse, punctuating the proceedings and
doubling their length, much to the discomfort of the majority
of several attendees, who were quite used to hearing Sanskrit
slokas without ever having to, or wanting to, be attentive to
their meaning. The day after Niyam Bhanga, a festive non-
vegetarian lunch of many courses to celebrate the end of the
strict temporary rules of mourning and the continuity of life
in which all and sundry relatives and friends participated and
eighteen Brahmins were fed colossal meals as per a millennia
old diktat, Amlan flew back and resumed his interrupted
semester. Indeed, he had taken a huge risk by coming home
before completing his degree, since there was a high chance
that his student visa would not be renewed by the US Consul
in Calcutta. This had become common occurrence those days.

The then US Consul, an emaciated-looking woman – a
heavily dyed brunette with a thin, creased, unsmiling face –
had the reputation for uncharacteristically not mingling at
all in Calcutta society and for revoking student visas on the
slightest pretext. Perhaps she found issuing visas irksome and
avoidable, extra work or she might have been following orders
to contain the possibility of Asian immigration to the US, so
why not ease the pain and nip the problem in the bud at the
point of issuing visas? All of Calcutta seemed to be terrified of
this intractable woman who, it became common lore, seemed
to find sadistic pleasure in decisively ruining the nascent

and starry eyed dreams of sizeable numbers of students who wished to study in the US. Possibly because he had only one year left to graduate, or perhaps since he was fortunate enough that the interviews were being conducted by the vice consul on that particular day, Amlan's re-entry was approved. It certainly allayed his own foreboding though, earlier, there had been no question in his mind that he would have to reach Calcutta in time to light his father's funeral pyre and perform the last rites, even if his student visa was cancelled and he could not return to graduate from Amherst College.

*     *     *

Upon his return to Massachusetts, different episodes continued to annoy Amlan, and one in particular. When he visited the Long Island, New York, home of his close school friend, Robert, for Thanksgiving, Robert's mother had expressed doubt, and almost ridiculed that such a thing as refusal to grant a US visa could be possible, and took issue with it. She was totally naïve concerning the gratuitous nastiness and capriciousness of the US State Department and Immigration Service employees. The ice-cold officialdom had long practised turning away people who did not look right though, perhaps not so curiously, surreptitiously admitting sundry war criminals into the US. After all, even though they had committed crimes against humanity, they were staunch anti-communists and they were not Jews, Catholics or people of colour. The woman's own father had come to the US through Ellis Island from a Warsaw ghetto before World War II and, somehow, the decades that had passed in between, seemed not to have illuminated her. Even this upper-class denizen of Long Island did not seem sufficiently informed about such issues having become quite oblivious of her own precarious background, except as a ruse to proudly narrate it as a success story of the family. Amlan had never become used to the inexplicable opacity of Americans on many such matters, though he had learnt to remain bemused and silent when some of his classmates would ask, after a few beers at the student union bar, 'why does the world hate us so much when we have sacrificed and done so much for them', and this at Amherst College, a bastion of the US Left, if one can imagine at all a real Left in the US.

So he had felt good when, during one of his trips to Robert's parents, his mother barged indoors from basking in the sun in the back garden, exasperated and grumbling, "Do you know, Amlan…" She always mispronounced his name, dragging the 'a's as in 'apple', but he was quite used to it from college, anyway. "…what my neighbour on the other side of the backyard said to me just now on Yom Kippur, the Day of Atonement?" She looked quite shocked.

He could barely ask and had just looked at her inquiringly when she said, "She wishes me Happy Yom Kippur! She thinks it is a happy occasion, can you believe that? And this Italian family has lived there as our neighbour for nearly twenty-five years!"

Amlan pondered the matter. A person who knew little of the rest of the world or America's role in it, except from her own immediate perspective, expected the rest of the world to be abreast of her own narrow world. Second, the extent of American neighbourly interest or curiosity reached not even across suburban backyards. Now, there were pros and cons to these characteristics of course, but, before he could gather his thoughts cohesively, Robert floated in, smiling at his mother and wondering aloud if lunch would be ready soon. Amlan felt better, remembering that Robert was, among the few of his classmates, somewhat more aware of the US's global reach and role, and of the many shortcomings of his compatriots, despite never having gone abroad, and, after all, the Long Island school system had produced him too. Though, Amlan recalled with some amusement, whenever Amlan said his schooldays were the best period in his life, Robert retorted that his were the worst and that Carrie was his best film, especially the last scene where Sissy Spacek sends electric darts through her classmates graduating from high school at their prom dance, and they always ended up laughing, Robert gleeful just at the very thought of that scene, and Amlan puzzled by its absurdity.

However, it had become difficult for Amlan to forget the daily thoughtless remarks that he would have to hear and then try to ignore. While he was admired for his brilliance, he also read the derision and disdain among his classmates about Asians or Indians doing well scholastically. It was not surprising that Robert had already felt the pinch of looking different from the majority in his Long Island school. Amlan realised he had mixed thoughts, mixed feelings all the way and, before he let himself get bogged down in them, he had decided that Robert was his friend.

Accordingly, Amlan accepted Robert's invitation many a time to go along with Robert to his parents who turned out, after all, to be affable and caring, if a bit curious and interfering. Their contribution to his life included visits to the Metropolitan Museum, the Museum of Modern Art and other attractive spots in New York, dining in good restaurants, becoming familiar with many Ashkanazi Jewish delectables such as ragalakh, matzoh brai and gafilta fish, and long drives through the hidden beautiful interiors and beaches of Long Island. So Amlan smiled and declared that he was much looking forward to supper, and was promptly informed that the salmon was just emerging from the oven and was ready to be served!

Back at college, Amlan's heart cried out for what he imagined to be his mother's predicament. How would she manage by herself, he wondered often. Around whom would she organise those big dinners? Though she had promised not to give up non-vegetarian food – fish, at least – was she really keeping that promise or had she turned vegetarian for fear of criticism from relatives for breaking the age-old custom requiring widows to give up foods purported to give rise to their animal spirits, which meant all non-vegetarian food, eggs, garlic, onions, ginger and certain types of lentils that were considered too tasteful? His heart ached, thinking Baba was not there now and Ma no longer had a reason to spend an hour every evening plaiting her hair in a braid and then fixing it in a bun with silver hairpins, the centrepiece adorned with a mini, jingling cluster. Would she continue to dab her face with Nivea cream followed by Pond's face powder and apply eyebrow pencil? Continue using the Crimson Lake lipstick? Baba would no longer smile at her slyly upon return from high court, where he practiced, or at least visited, to touch base with professional colleagues and friends. Neither would she be able to smile back, shyly, as she was habituated to doing even after all their years together. He could not extricate himself from these thoughts while running to complete his thesis, which he needed to be of top quality if he was to be on the Dean's List. Yet what had seemed so important yesterday now caused little anxiety or even interest in him. How he managed to be included, nonetheless, on the List, he never understood. Rather, he felt embarrassed about it. He made up his mind to return to Ma at the moment he was presented with a choice: accept an assistantship for doing a Ph.D. or return home to Calcutta.

In Calcutta, Amlan breezed through a Masters degree in Calcutta University, whose standards had fallen unmistakably over years of student politics under Communist influence that had also ensured filling of professorial ranks based on Party sympathy rather than merit. Perhaps due to the touch of Amherst, Amlan was taken into Presidency College, still the bastion of prestige in academic circles. This was much earlier than its reduction to an institution in which students even failed university exams, and well before its own conversion to a deemed university with powers to grant its own degrees, thereby ensuring poor-quality instruction and degrees, laced by the poison of Party politics and dogma. When Amlan joined, however, reflecting the prevalent state of higher education in the entire state, a job in Presidency still represented pride of place within the limited education sphere of undergraduate education in the state. Amlan did not proceed to doctoral studies, since he felt increasingly strongly that his quest for knowledge would be better served through reading and self-teaching rather than through a dilapidated, emaciated education system.

Amlan dove into books, splurging his resources when buying them. He also borrowed heavily from the British Council Library. Topped by his love for music, his income was half spent on purchases of books and tapes on the first weekend of every month after receiving his salary. He had not anticipated falling in love, of all things, with this unlikely American girl. How could he have fallen in love with someone he had just met? Was this love at first sight? Could the phenomenon really occur? He found himself deeply attracted to her and felt no ambivalence other than wondering if he would have to follow her to America and leave Ma behind. He somehow felt confident that he would have to abandon neither; that he would resolve the issue when it arose, that the basis of love must have some rationale and innate universal approval. With these thoughts in his head, Amlan entered the square courtyard of the mansion.

\*     \*     \*

Amlan stood in front of his sprawling, two-storey abode. The stained glass windows reflected prism like colours in the light from the gas lamps within the grounds, that emanated flickering, incandescent rays of light from ornately gilded lampposts, now somewhat faded. The untraditional designs on the stained glass looked more galactic than floral, perhaps the creation of a gifted wife many generations ago who might have expressed herself only through such domestic endeavours of music or art, rather representative of early epochs. He walked under the portico supported by large pillars that were adorned with leafy mouldings giving them a palm tree-like look. Light cobwebs hung on the top. A tall stick with a short broom on top of it stood against one of the pillars, in testimony of the relentless attacks of dust from outside and the inevitable failure to keep up with the dusting by a household of elderly servants, honest and reliable, who were more family than employees by now and would never be driven to work other than the pattern that they themselves had developed over decades.

An old Bentley stood under the terrace, taken out on rare occasions when the driver returned from time to time from his village in Bihar, where he now preferred to live with his family and community after many years of service to Amlan's family to which he had arrived as a boy during Amlan's grandfather's time. Recently, he had been given a small pension that was sufficient for his upkeep and that of his wife and their meagre needs of village life. Amlan had little desire to navigate Calcutta streets in the walrus-like Bentley, preferring to hop in and out of taxis and on and off trams. The car, when not used, stood covered in a huge rucksack cloth that gave it the appearance of a barge sheltered on land, its hull and freight covered in a shapeless heap.

Scaling the few wide stairs from the portico, the giant crystal chandelier threw down a vibgyor, a rainbow of colours on Amlan as he entered the expansive hall. He ignored the gallery of life-sized marble statues that lined either side. He had remained unaware of their vintage, though he had heard since childhood that some of them were the works of reputed Italian sculptors and were deemed to be priceless. As the family's wealth had accumulated, its obvious symbols had grown too. The sculptures were dominated by women with exposed, attractively endowed breasts though, of course, the women of the household lived constricted lives that were confined within the inner halls. They rarely ventured out into the main hall. That was reserved for their men, or for British visitors, both male and female. Those practices had disappeared from society by now, even as the statues had taken on a facade of sexless objects, almost as if they did not exist at all, except when they were dusted once a week or fortnight.

Every night, they stared at Amlan with their varied fixed expressions – smiling, doubtful, beautiful, wondering, despondent, forgotten or simply expressionless – but Amlan, too, had become habituated to ignoring them, except on a Sunday afternoon when, after a heavy lunch, and if he remained at home, he might choose to survey his realm, looking at these statues more closely as he passed through the hallways or at the priceless Flemish still life, and oil portraits of ancestors authored by Italian painters and some by Sunil Bose, the Indian portrait artist often employed in his day by British royalty. Amlan would, on those occasions, take time to scrutinise them all but, in particular, the inscrutable eyes of his great-grandfather hanging imposingly from two storeys high over the central landing on the two flights of stairs that crossed like an X at the landing. He was the one who had broadened the family's business interests from the earlier urban and rural land ownership. He had ventured into mercantile and banking operations after initial forays into manufacturing, for he had quickly encountered the forbidding constraints posed by the prevailing trade and tariffs regime of the colonial masters. Ironically, eventually, many of his clients were British and European shipping lines and emerging and well-established manufacturing and fashion houses, and he often found himself in situations of having to sanction, extend, or write off the loans he had made to them. No wonder he found it appropriate to be immortalised bedecked in jewels from head to toe and dressed in a mix of Indian and Colonial brocaded regalia, looking down over future generations from a colossally high spot near the ceiling.

As a child, Amlan had wondered whether his great-grandfather had earned or rented his regalia for posing for the portrait. He had once asked Baba about it, who had seemed amused, so he asked Didu, grandmother, who informed him that her father-in-law had been a very brave Zamindar in his early years who stood up to the British for unreasonable infractions committed by them on his subjects, which made his daily life unbearable. So he decided to expand his professional interests and became extremely successful in the commercial and financial sectors. He even began to loan them money so that, in the end, they had to win him over by anointing him with a knighthood and the title of Sir. From that day on, they were among the most highly respected of Calcutta families, one among a handful with such recognition from the British monarch. While admiring his ancestry, and even being somewhat proud of it and aware of the privileges that it had brought him, Amlan did not allow himself to bask in its glory, for he was too intelligent not to know that that era had passed and that he now belonged squarely in the middle economic class. However, he remained ever so protective of the stature his family still enjoyed in Calcutta society and, cognisant of the stylised behaviour expected of him in their social circle, he complied congenially with those expectations.

Amlan's favourite painting was a giant-sized Titian of a lactating Madonna and Child. It was hanging there, quite unbeknownst to the covetous Western world, on the side wall, almost under the stairway as if to hide it and to protect it from too much light. Amlan had witnessed a dark veil cover it over the years and had got into the practice of seeing it with a flashlight and, once, when he had suggested to his mother that they should have it cleaned and restored, she had immediately declined. Asked why, she gave two reasons: first, no one could be trusted to do an adequate job and that the work was likely to leave home and never return, and second, if the matter came to the tax department's notice, a heavy wealth tax would be put on it, something that they could hardly afford.

When Amlan jokingly wondered aloud that his mother had thought so much about the matter, she surprised him by indicating that, over the years before his death, Baba had educated her about all inheritance matters and valuable objects and how to protect them in his absence. She also said on that occasion that when the need arose, Amlan would have, ready in his lap, all associated papers. Furthermore, the papers would be comprehensive and correct, because Baba had methodically updated them despite all the complications of getting them through the High Court. Of course his being a high court advocate – lawyer – helped but, in any event, he had never wanted himself or Amlan to suffer the terrible consequences that lack of organisation or documentation had caused the financial decline of many a Zaminari Calcutta family since independence.

Amlan's appreciation of his parents went up one notch that day for, behind their low-key, lazy living style, they had obviously thought not only of the present but of the future, that had gone way beyond focussing on past glory alone. Consequently, the Madonna and Child continued to languish, protected in their dark spot, and adored occasionally by this Calcutta boy. At the top of the flight of the central stairs and to the side hung a countryside by Constable and, on most nights, as he passed it to enter his bedroom, Amlan took a moment to look at it. He knew every brush stroke on it and, when he later saw a few more in the Boston Museum, he felt that the one at home was more appealing and alluring, tranquil and soothing.

Tonight, Amlan entered Ma's bedroom. She was focussed attentively on a piece of embroidery. A bouquet of red roses in satin stitch was slowly, yet surely, emerging in exquisite shapes for the impending baby shower of an expecting niece.

She looked a bit distant, for her full concentration was on the roses, but nonetheless managed a smile. Before she could put her feet down from the finely carved, high mahogany bed, Amlan stopped her. She looked at him inquiringly.

"Ma, stay put. I am sure Bhagwanda is already bringing a tray full of food, half of which I will not be able to touch. You know him. As he grows older, you cannot make him see your point. He goes about doing his own thing, in his own way."

From childhood, Amlan had been taught to use the diminutive da – from dada, elder brother – at the end of the male servants' names as a mark of recognition and regard. He never changed the mode when he entered adulthood as sometimes people did. In return, he had received their goodwill and sincere concern, respect and unwavering loyalty.

Mother and son smiled in agreement.

He continued, "And now, please, don't you too insist on my consuming more food! I already had some chicken sandwiches in Coffee House."

Knowing that he usually had only coffee there from his own admission since he generally reserved his appetite for dinner at home, she looked at him with an expression of mock disapproval. "Anyway, just now I want to talk to you," he concluded.

The way he uttered this last sentence, son to mother, she hoped this would be the moment for which she had been waiting these past two years. Whenever she had asked him if she should start looking for eligible brides for him, he had invariably objected, asking in mock alarm, "Do you really believe that I can settle down with a woman of your choice? You will probably bring me one with long hair that you can plait every evening, with a pink face that you can powder and with almond eyes ready for applying mascara, and make her ready for your son's return home, right?"

Ma would protest instantly, "Stop joking about such an important matter. It is my terrible misfortune that your father isn't here today. Otherwise, he would take on the whole responsibility and you would not be able to fool around like this."

This was said much to his astonishment, because he knew that Baba would be totally out of his depth on the issue, never having dealt with women's affairs his entire life except for his adoration for his deeply religious mother and his acceptance of a bride who was gifted to him and to whom he gave sole and undivided attention for the rest of his life.

She would continue to complain, "I cannot enter a wedding pandal without the women asking me whether I have found a bride for you and offering suggestions and possibilities, and even gossiping behind my back that I do not want to get you married. I cannot bear this suffering and shame any longer…" Then she would feign to sob softly, and ask, in a thinner voice, "Is it too much to ask my son in your father's absence? After your Baba's passing on, can you even imagine how my days pass, how the nights linger? Is it not every Bengali mother's wish to hold and nurture a grandson, to bring him up with love and affection? If only I had just a couple of grandchildren!"

The use of masculine gender used adroitly, would not escape Amlan, as if he was committing double jeopardy in his mother's eyes. He would respond, with as much seriousness as he could muster, trying, at the same time, to control his rising irritation, "Ma, give me some more time. I will bring you a beautiful bride, a fairy, an angel. And I promise, why two? I will give you ten grandchildren. That should consolidate our lineage once and for all, won't it?

She would, nevertheless, continue, her tone rising almost to a hysterical pitch. "Thakur! God, will my son refuse to understand the simple needs of a widowed mother who has never asked him for anything but, at the end of her life, is pleading for a simple wish?" She would end in a wail, directing her glances at Baba's large photograph on the wall at the head of the bed, for it could never hang disrespectfully towards her feet. It remained garlanded, always with a thick strand of Rajanigandha, the sweetly aromatic, white flower of Bengal used in joyous occasions and for funerary decorations alike. This time, however, Ma knew there was something different in Amlan's voice. She gave him her full attention, betraying her heightened angst.

At that moment, Bhagwan entered the room with a big tray covered in lace and heaped with silver utensils that held a variety of dishes, and with a maid and a minor servant in tow, who were carrying a large silver dish and spoons with the family monogram, a large marble glass, a copper jug of fresh lime water and large napkins with intricately embroidered scenes of village Bengal, very likely sewn by long-dead women of the family. Such tokens, maintained with great care and devotion, comprised family pride and announced its continuance. As Bhagwan uncovered the dish cloth, Amlan saw a variety of vegetarian and non-vegetarian dishes with the dessert having been alternated as was the custom for every night.

He walked across the room to the marble table with a sculptured teak base that was placed beneath a mini chandelier that hung from the high ceiling. Amlan sat down and began his meal. Didu appeared through the door and asked why he had not sat in the dining room, complaining that she had been waiting there and that no one had taken care to inform her of the change of venue. Ma got down from the bed, carrying her weight efficiently and, almost running to her mother-in-law and holding her by the hand, ushered her to the marble table to sit with her grandson. Didu seemed satisfied enough as she sat down to admire him as he ate his meal. For once, Ma failed to look on appreciatively at her son devouring his meal, because of her every wish to hear him reveal what he had intended to divulge to her. She could hardly hide her curiosity, her expectation.

Amlan tried about half of every dish as Ma continued with her embroidery, which she felt would keep her nerves more under control. Didu chattered about the trials and tribulations of her day in the Puja room and that she had been late in putting several deities to sleep just before sunset, as prescribed, mainly due to the deliberate and purposeful neglect of the servants in appearing to assist her and, when they did arrive, how horrified she was, as always, about their continuing errors in following the correct rules and procedures set forth in the scriptures. These were the very servants who now encircled the table in observance of the progress of their young master's opulent and exquisitely arranged meal.

Ma lamented that times had not only changed; they had deteriorated. Amlan nodded forcefully in pretended solidarity with Didu. Mother and son both knew that, otherwise, hell might break loose. Ma looked up from her embroidery, and then looked back at it, counting every minute for the meal to end.

To complete his routine, Amlan indicated, loudly enough for everyone to hear, where Bhagwan could have added a bit of salt or a bit of sugar or where a dish could have been slightly less spicy or hot. This he had to do every night to assure the servants in general, and Bhagwan in particular, that he had given recognition to their efforts. The final moment of domesticity in this household of grandmother, mother and son, and a brood of devoted servants, thus ended for the day.

The ritual completed to everyone's satisfaction, Amlan was the first to rise from the table. Didu followed and went straight out, declaring she had to get up at sunrise the next day to prepare special condiments in preparation for a big Puja for the god, Narayan, and his consort, Lakshmi, at sunset. As she left, she admonished the maid to remember not to make any noise when the priest would chant the prayers for Lakshmi, the goddess of wealth, since Lakshmi was shy and had a tendency to escape with all the wealth and, therefore, that of the family would vanish also, if there were too much noise or disproportionate attention to her. The maid had heard this a million times, yet looked demure and guilty, as if she had already committed the infraction of making noise tomorrow. Bhagwan cleared the table and one of his assistants wiped it with a clean, damp cloth. He asked Ma and Amlan at what time they should be served bed tea the next morning and, after receiving instructions, left the room.

Ma dropped her embroidery from her lap onto the bed and looked up. Amlan came up to her and, looking her in the eyes, said, "Ma, I found the girl I want to marry, the girl you are waiting for, to come into our family, to join our household."

She gasped in delight, but could barely ask in a trembling voice, "Who is she? Is she from North Calcutta? Do you have a picture of her?" North Calcutta was where most of the bonedi or old, as opposed to nouveau riche, Bengali families resided in their crumbling bungalows.

Barely audible, Amlan said, "Ma, I do not know if she feels the same way as I. Give me a few more days…" Then he added jocularly, "And pray hard!"

Ma immediately found herself floating in a sea of uncertainly. Oh! What could a mother do with such a heartless, thoughtless son, she asked herself, even as she stared at him with innate love, confident that he would not disappoint her in any way, this son who had sacrificed all pecuniary attractions of settling in America just to return to his widowed Bengali mother. Quickly, she smiled at him in reassurance that she trusted him. He smiled back, raised himself from her bed, and moved out to the terrace under the full moon to reflect and to have his last cigarette of the day.

Alone in the moonlight, he lighted a Charminar cigarette, drew in and blew out. The foul smell was neutralised by the surrounding aroma of Rajanigandha. An eyrar of terracotta swans stood tall surrounding giant pots of flowering plants emanating the most confounding mix of smells. He pondered Omar Khayyam's Rubbayat and Thomas Hardy's Jude the Obscure, wondering what fate awaited him. Should he celebrate the moment as Khayyam suggested or should he ensure certainty by avoiding the risky path that he was about to take? He stood still for a long time. Eventually, he turned from the ornately grilled boundary of the terrace and walked back into the house. Moving through the corridors, he entered his suite diagonally across from his mother's.

Amlan's suite contained a study lined with a library of books handed down through generations that had been enlivened with his own contemporary acquisitions, a bedroom and a separate living area furnished with inherited workmanlike furniture and protected by faded brocade curtains that were quite unfit for Calcutta's generally hot climate. Undressing, he stood under a cool, soothing shower of water flowing serenely on him directly from a large copper showerhead. He applied Maharani sandalwood soap from Mysore, his favourite and one he used round the year, except for the two winter months when he used Pears, the more oily soap better suited to counter the winter dryness. The lather gone, after having repeated the round twice, he emerged from the shower, dried himself with a large Bombay Dyeing, all-cotton, striped brown and white towel, and looked at himself appreciatively in the mirror. His manhood stirred. He smiled. Yes, he was ready to risk, to love, to settle, to take the next step in life.

He approached his four-post teakwood bed sculpted with an elaborate floral design at its head and foot, an heirloom from his great grandfather, reached for the lily white pair of cotton Panjabi Pyjama set, slid them on, went to the easy chair, opened out its long arms, laid back in it, sinking into the supporting pillows, and extended his legs on the stretched limbs. His mind floated once again to a vision that soon enveloped him. Sis was everywhere, a glow of light. He entered the illumination as it surrounded him. He shut his eyes. He did not want to come out of the feeling he was experiencing, out of his reverie. He allowed himself to doze, but not to get up or retire to his bed lest he should fall asleep and lose the lingering remnants of his enchantments. Nevertheless, soon, at the end of this long, inexplicably eventful day, he fell into an undisturbed slumber on the easy chair, only to awake next morning to a tray of fresh Darjeeling tea and two light Marie tea biscuits, brought in by Bhagwan unfailingly at the appointed hour, and without knocking.

As Bhagwan moved about to open the curtains, Amlan smiled and volunteered, "Bhagwanda, the tea this morning is excellent." He overemphasised the first syllable.

From Amlan's tone, and finding him asleep in his arm chair, Bhagwan knew something was different, something had made Dada happy and relaxed and, though he did not know the genesis of this special mood, he felt that some good news was to be awaited. Though he felt a cautious joy, he decided it would be best not to respond to Amlan and, offering a polite smile in response, glided out of the room.

*     *     *

The morning could not pass more slowly even as Amlan moved about his suite restlessly, just managing to comply with his morning routine of Pranayam Yoga. Having decided to skip his lectures for the day, he had little to prepare. He attempted to pore over little details in the English language dailies, the Statesman and the Amrita Bazar Patrika. As usual, he left the Bengali dailies, Ananda Bazar Patrika, Jugantar, Bartoman, and Pratidin for Ma. Though she perused them only occasionally, there had never been any consideration of reducing the number of newspapers that were delivered to the household every morning. That was simply an index of Bengali intellectual involvement, if not readership. No piece of news held Amlan's attention this morning, however. His mind strayed, floating in and out of reality, away from his immediate surroundings to his unlimited expectations from the day that was yet to unfurl.

The grandfather clock in the dining room clicked ceaselessly – tick tock, tick tock – but seemed unable to reach the appointed hour at which he was to leave. Eventually, it struck 9:45, with one thunderous, echoing gong. Amlan headed out, almost running, holding himself together. Momentarily, he fell into an even strut, since too much of a speed would surely arouse questions through the open windows in the neighbourhood. He reached Cornwallis Street and hopped on to a slowly passing tram. When it entered College Street, he looked left as he passed Presidency College on the right, hoping that none of his students – some barely a few years his junior – would see him bunking class and playing hooky. As it was, he was sometimes unable to control his class that was clearly more suitable to strict Dickensian treatment from professors and to a show of superficial subservience from students rather than to his liberal approach towards them. Often, the outcome was complete chaos in class, or absenteeism or, at best, proxyism, where, reflecting mutual give and take, a different student would answer when someone's name was called, since the latter had escaped from class. Amlan would never be able to figure this out in a class of a hundred students and, he, having just emerged from the American student-teacher relationship in which professors even allowed students to smoke in front of them and drink Coca Cola in class, could not stop expecting that one day his students too would start behaving in a similarly mature fashion. He felt that, if his students wrote carefully thought out and composed essays and produced good academic results, he also would ignore their occasional childish waywardness. However, for now, he made sure to look away from the direction of the college so that none of his shishyas or students, would notice their guru playing truant himself.

Before long, the tram swerved right into Dharamtallah Street. After a few more stops, he jumped off the tram, ran across the street while avoiding passing vehicles that squeezed past, entered a narrow lane that took him past the Elliot Cinema, left New Market behind, and walked on briskly until, finally, he reached Sudder Street. It was a fifteen-minute walk at most, but it felt like eternity.

At 10:30 sharp, he was at the hotel desk pestering the busy receptionist to ring for Patrick and Sis. As she was dialling the room, the two emerged from the ante-room, a small area populated with the usual ornate teak period furniture upholstered in a faded crimson brocade. Sis profusely, and Patrick more formally, smiled as they entered the lobby. They had obviously been waiting, browsing the morning papers after a full English breakfast in the much larger, contiguous dining hall.

\*     \*     \*

Quickly, Patrick bade them goodbye for the day, somehow feeling quite relaxed to leave Sis in the Calcuttan's care, sanguine that nothing could have comprised a better, more fulfilling day for her. His appointment with Mr. Felman had been set for 11 a.m. He just needed to walk or take a taxicab to Ho Chi Minh Sarani, where the US Consulate was situated behind two-floor-tall, extended security walls. He arrived just in time, got out of the cab, and pressed the brass buzzer on the side of the elaborately grilled giant gates, ignoring the commissionaire protecting the entrance to the compound.

Patrick was in a relaxed mood and was looking forward to chit-chatting with the consul on West Bengal politics. As the mammoth gates slid open sideways with a low whirring sound, he stood in front of an imposing white-washed building inside, a bit uncertain of the rather forbidding, faceless structure. He entered its hallway with a sense of awe and with his self-assurance suddenly waning.

A man of unidentifiable ethnic composition, who was wearing a black tunic covered halfway by a white apron and donning what could be passed off as a chef's cap, greeted him with a 'come een', revealing immediately that he must have a French connection. He preceded Patrick up the wide staircase that was covered in a spotless white taffeta carpet That seemed hardly practical for a staircase. But then it was the US Consulate where a display of wealth's effect was to be expected. Patrick followed gingerly.

Once upstairs, Patrick was led through a wide balcony that had been enclosed with unblemished, off-white stained glass panes with no significant design, converting the space into a comfortably air conditioned, large study-cum-library. The strong sun outside entered ever so lightly through the glass. Patrick could have a full view of the surrounding green outside, past the windows that had been left ajar to let in the air. He sat in a sofa chair that was pointed out to him by his expressionless guide, who simply said, 'Seet' and then left without a further word. Patrick realised that the chair looked toward the outside so that the interior details of the apartment would be out of his view. Feeling a bit uncomfortable in the formal surroundings, Patrick did not turn to look at the books lined in several rows on an adjoining shelf that ran along a long wall behind him. Rather, he looked straight ahead at the garden and waited, in what he found to be a forbidding atmosphere, created and perpetuated by the Frenchman who seemed to be lurking somewhere in the background.

Within a couple of minutes, a youthful-looking Mr. Felman arrived, tennis racquet in his hand and impeccably uniformed for the game. Having possibly crossed forty recently, he was decidedly handsome and well preserved, the outcome of nature and the nurture of an American diplomat's life. It was obvious that he had exerted himself in his game, for his brows were still ornamented with lingering, shiny beads of perspiration. As he tossed his racquet on an adjacent straight-backed, wooden chair, Patrick found himself standing up affectedly.

"Hi, I am James Felman. You are, of course, Patrick Gould. I have been waiting for some days for this moment, you know," he volunteered, somewhat to Patrick's wonderment.

"I know I am a bit late, but would you allow me five more minutes? I'll jump in and out of the shower. The result should be more comfortable for both of us." He winked, looking over his shoulder as he walked away indoors before Patrick could respond. As if as an afterthought, he added as he vanished, "Laurent will bring in freshly brewed coffee and croissants. I collected them this morning from Flury's on Park Street; the best there is, you know. My usual diet after tennis! Please don't wait for me if they are served. I'll join you in a minute."

Patrick at last looked at the bookshelves, his eyes slowly caressing the titles. He gathered that a good number were on South Asian politics, its internecine convulsions and its global implications. He relaxed, for he felt confident that he should be able to keep a steady conversation going with his host. He warmed to the thought of a debate as he noticed a middle shelf lined with treatises on West Bengal's Marxist politics and politicians, and on the Marxist-Leninist Naxalbari movement, named after the North Bengal tea garden and about which he had written his research paper not that long ago. He took out one, then another, and then one more. Time flew.

Laurent had silently floated in at some point without Patrick being aware of it, carrying a tray with the promised croissants and steaming aromatic coffee. Putting the tray down and delaying a moment, he propounded in a low voice, "You may have them both. I will bring in more when Monsieur comes in." Then he disappeared.

Patrick found them better than those from Washington's P Street Café. He took no time to gobble them up, sipping delicious coffee in between. Certainly Colombian, he thought, and slurped additional sips, his mind floating for a moment to Leonor. He began to feel quite comfortable in his new surroundings.

He did not realise that Mr. Felman had entered until he heard him say, "Call me James, if you will let me call you Patrick, of course." He again winked and smiled.

Patrick noticed that James' hair was neatly brushed back with a flawless side parting and glistening over a wide, spotless forehead at the top of an exquisitely chiselled face. Patrick observed his whip-like body and his absolutely hunch-free gait and realised, in his turn, that James had also sized him up when his eyes had moved over Patrick in a split second. Patrick felt warm behind his neck, almost blushing. Gathering himself up, all he could manage was to mumble, "Of course, James, thanks. Please feel free to call me Patrick. It would be a pleasure."

James beckoned him to the sofa-chair. Patrick sat down obediently as James eased into a full sofa at right angles to him. They looked at each other intently for a moment; then, looked away, slightly embarrassed perhaps before looking back.

James was the first to speak. He sounded serious. His voice was low. There was no trace of the supercilious irreverence in it a moment ago. "Patrick, you drew out so many of the books on West Bengal politics…" He ended with a query in his voice. As Patrick wondered how he could have known, James proffered an explanation. "I know simply from the way the books are placed now. The order is quite changed," he said mildly and with a reassuring smile as Patrick so obviously betrayed his own embarrassment at having disturbed the original order.

He had become involved, perhaps even excited, in coming across so many interesting, relevant volumes, shifting and shuffling them all over the shelf as he went along his short-lived research.

Yet, Patrick seemed to read in James' smile a certain confidence that could only be based on prior information that he might have gathered on Patrick. Then he dismissed the thought wryly, for he was too small a fry for James to have gone to that much trouble. Instead, he smiled back and simply responded, "Sorry. I got carried away. You have quite an interesting collection." He presumed, and eagerly anticipated, that they would soon be discussing various aspects of local politics.

Sensing Patrick's thoughts, James informed him, with some directness, "Patrick, I know you have done a dissertation on Bengal politics and that you have learnt to speak Bangla. The language courses that you took at the State Department program in Rosslyn are managed by a colleague of mine. In a cable to me, my colleague mentioned you by name and what an unusually enthusiastic student – no, unusually young and enthusiastic student, he said, as I recall – you had been and, since you were only a student at Georgetown, you had to get special permission from the State Department to enroll. Obviously, your name immediately rang a bell when you asked to meet. When you asked for an appointment and the usual background information landed on my desk, I knew. So I have also been eager to meet you."

Absentmindedly, James picked up a croissant from the second batch that Laurent had silently brought into the room. He took small bites of it while sipping coffee. It suddenly occurred to him to offer the tray to Patrick. Dutifully, Patrick put another scrumptious piece of bread into his mouth and reached for the coffee pot.

"Some years ago, I, too, had taken Bangla when I was expecting to be transferred to Calcutta. I am happy to meet someone whose interests and curiosity are so similar. I am very glad, indeed," he concluded abruptly, conveying the spirit of a pre-ordained meeting, as if afraid of giving away a deep secret, or perhaps suddenly conscious that he had hardly given Patrick any chance to speak so far.

Even as he felt a bit awkward and squeamish about a heretofore unfamiliar individual knowing so much about him, and a bit worried how much more he might know, Patrick was impressed by the way James had come across, reassured yet inclusive, with considerable depth and involvement in assessing him, however distant the source of that information might have been. Or, somewhere at the back of his mind, bringing back the passing thought that he had set aside, he wondered once again, is it all serendipity?

"It is strange. Even as we have attempted to nip Pink Movements all across the world, with no small amount of success in our Latin backyard, here lies a microcosm of a region, safely nestled in a corner of democratic India, where Marxism is flourishing," James revealed his intrinsic view.

Patrick listened on intently.

"Here, they continue with virulent workers' strikes and entrench their land redistribution in blatant contraposition of inalienable property rights. This has resulted in next to zero productivity of physical capital, as well as the flight of capital from the state to other market oriented locations. Except for the Marwaris from the remote bastion of Marwar and Shekhawat in the Western state of Rajasthan, who have immigrated here over a couple of centuries as small businessmen, but now control most productive sectors, including jute and other manufacturing and even the tea gardens. They have learnt to make peace with the local Marxists who look the other way while the Marwaris extract a highly exploitative rate of return on their capital that can neutralise the high risk of investment here."

Patrick murmured, "Yes, the role of Marwaris has indeed been controversial in North-East India and, why, even in Bangladesh."

James was quick to apologise. "Of course, I should have known better than to presume any less from this straight-A student."

This again raised Patrick's eyebrows as to the source of all this information about him though, after these ephemera, he became engrossed once again in James' continuing elaborations.

"You know that, in recent years, the Naxals have been causing mayhem, killing in Calcutta streets, spreading the movement to Bihar, Orissa and all the way to Telangana in northern Andhra Pradesh, and even as far north as Nepal. It has become a long Eastern corridor stretching north to south. I agree that the distribution of income and wealth has not been the best in some of these regions. That does not, however, justify Marxism, does it? Yes, even American missionaries are up there criticising the abominable leakages from the government's spending programs, though the missionaries have some successful programs with adequate resources, opening schools, feeding children, teaching them English and technical professions. Of course, the quid pro quo is that they bring Jesus to these populations, they convert them, vitiating the process somewhere along the way…" James trailed off, giving away his own Jewish background that had propelled him to be generally suspicious of Christian missionaries. As it was, he always found the US State Department to be a bastion of WASPs who, in his view, were anti-Catholic, anti-Jewish, anti-Black, Right wing and religious (at least outwardly, like Republicans).Thus, he had already unwittingly revealed to Patrick another variation of the multiple views over ethnicity in the United States.

James could not stop himself, having found a willing listener, fully conversant with the subject under consideration. He did not usually get the rapt attention that he was now receiving. So he continued, "These Bengalis need close surveillance. They have to be watched. They are poetic, musical, intellectual, social, friendly and seemingly open. However, they are unpredictable, capricious, overtly intellectual and unproductive. Indians used to say, 'what Bengal thinks today, India thinks tomorrow'. By and large, it is the same today. Yet, these Bengalis are devoid of any interest in work, incapable of generating material product or monetary income. No wonder, with all the free time they have, they produce only, and so much, culture, but where does it lead them – to commotion, chaos and confusion. They debate every issue and scoop out the last spoonful of marrow from its guts, leaving an uncertain, if not unfathomable, outcome in their wake.

"Patrick, do you know that, in the 1950s, Calcutta had the second busiest airport in the world after Chicago? People from not only all over India, but also from the entire East Asia region came here for higher education, for medical treatment, to attend classical music soirées, to learn, to participate, to settle and to take back. Today, Bengal is becoming a backwaters for Indians themselves, a pariah within the nation." He ended in a crescendo, almost regretfully, as if, somewhere hidden in the expression of all of his wrath, there was not only pain and concern, but also wishful thinking for the situation to turn around.

As James talked, Patrick sensed a familiarity. He felt as if he was with someone who would understand his thesis – or perhaps this bureaucrat was already aware of it – someone with whom he would like to spend a long, quiet weekend debating and learning, somewhere in the luscious southern Bengal jungles with shy Royal Bengal tigers, or in the luxurious northern Bengal tea gardens with rampaging elephants and rhinos, in full view of the snow clad Himalayan ranges. It would be thrilling to go on daytime jaunts, swim before lunch in pristine swimming pools and, after lunch served by tea garden chefs, famous for their culinary excellence in "continental" dishes, to explore and debate James' various hypotheses, Patrick fantasised.

Patrick could not but notice James' long artist's fingers as he moved his arms about expressively. They reached over the back of Patrick's sofa and lay there and, as they moved, they involuntarily touched Patrick's neck from behind in swift motions, caressing and soothing the back of his neck.

Patrick found himself sinking into, and immersed in, a reverie, wondering if James' sleight of hand was accidental or intentional. It did not matter. As James spoke on, time and again, his arm reached across, as if inadvertently, to Patrick's sofa chair, touching his fingers, then his arm, then his neck, connecting with a touch, then disconnecting, then connecting again, each time sending a soft electric shock through Patrick's body. Patrick became increasingly aware of the physical proximity, and the currents that ran through his body with every touch. He moved slightly away as if in fear of what might come next, and immediately realised that, as if in reaction, the contacts became lighter, softer, though they were still very much there. He focussed – trying hard not to get lost in straying thoughts – intently on what James was saying, yet all the while hoping that the contacts would not cease.

"I really need support in this project. I will be frank with you. I have the resources already sanctioned from HQ – you know, the State Department's sister agency – provided I get the right person for the job. I am sure, with your background, your reading skills and familiarity with the issues, you could ask for a visiting position at the Institute of Development Studies here. What do you think? You could research on an array of issues per their interest or desire. The only limitation, of course, is that you will have to lead a pretty Calcuttan, I mean really local, lifestyle, mingling with those Leftist researchers there, and eventually with the politicos, using a research agenda for cover. The Bengalis would eat out of any intellectual's hands, I am sure. You can come here any time, needless to say, whenever you want to listen to music, have a home meal, whatever. However, you have to balance out those forays lest they should suspect something." There was a pause as James looked at Patrick intently. Patrick did not speak.

"I am sure you can do it. You would just need to report what their thinking is, where it is heading, how it is changing, if they know of any impending street action or strikes, and so on. You will see; it will all fall into place. And, of course, you would become the top Bengal specialist in the U S of America!" He sounded celebratory.

There was protracted silence once again.

"What do you think? Willing to chip in for Uncle Sam? For Apple Pie and Motherhood?", he half joked nervously, not knowing what Patrick's decision would be. "By the way, your bank account back home will be credited every month at the scale of the Young Professionals Program of the Agency, untouched and tucked away," he embellished.

After more continued silence, Patrick replied at last, "Surely you must recognise that this Socialist evolution has had some beneficial ramifications. Look, the caste system has more or less disappeared from West Bengal even compared to economically more progressive Tamil Nadu. There is, I understand, a true sense of equality and fair distribution of incomes, something that could hardly be claimed by our own country...."

James cut Patrick short, "Yes, maybe among the Bengalis, from their shrinking pie. However, go into a Marwari or Gujarati home and see where the money has gone. The Marwaris have basically taken over the industrial sector. Even cash crops such as tea and jute are entirely in their hands today. Is this the just distribution of income that you cite? And the Gujaratis have taken over real estate and construction, the other money churner. This manifests the nexus between the Bengali Marxist politician and the non-Bengali commercial class. In this division, all that the Bengali working class has churned is a ravaged manufacturing sector, thanks to militant trade unionism. The Marwaris put the factories under lock-out. They flee with their capital at the first opportunity they find elsewhere. And the Left politicians rest, assured that the disgruntled worker will continue to vote for them, for only they could unlock their predicament, their vicissitudes in conducting daily life. The more the quality of life worsens, the more the blue collar workers get locked into their hole. It is a vicious circle."

Patrick agreed in silent acquiescence. "True, it is interesting that the West Indians had such enterprise that they even went as indentured servants for the promise of a better future with the British to the West Indies, Fiji, East Africa and South Africa – you name it – while the Bengali stayed put. Their love of the soil of Bengal seemed so deep that they were also willing to suffer famine and destitution. The Bengal famine during the Second World War killed some two million Bengalis, as the British needed provisions during the War and the local Zamindars collaborated with their colonial masters in hoarding and then diverting stocks to the warfront, depleting local market supply to almost non-existent levels. Come to think of it, the British, indeed, Winston Churchill, could have been charged with genocide; just that they were on the winning side at the end of the War," he jested. He could not but add, "And who knows about that today, or who would care?"

Patrick as yet had failed to respond to James' offer, but it was not as though he was not already considering the offer seriously, for it had great potential in providing him valuable information for his continuing research while assuring him financial comfort; and, most important, it would induct him in closed diplomatic circles while promising high adventure and challenge.

James' fire had not yet burnt out. "The Parsees are producing steel and locomotives here, the Sikhs control motoring, auto parts and miscellaneous repair services, the Sindhis are big in textile retailing, all again from the western regions. The southern Tamils are everywhere in executive and clerical positions. The Bengalis are in the process of giving up even English, vitiating their ability to communicate with their own compatriots. They run public sector behemoths like Durgapur Steel and Bengal Pottery. Bengal Pottery closed.

They took over Shaw Wallace, another fledgling company. Then that too closed. Who cares about labour's daily life? Don't tell me it is these politicians. All they are interested in is that the unemployed lumpen proletariat join their Party cadres. That is why they keep the border with Bangladesh open. Refugees are given food ration cards as long as they become card-holding members of the Party, again sure voters. Of course, their coffers remain well stocked from high and low sources, but also by bullying neighbourhoods into contributing to the Party. Only a few cookie factories remain in Bengali hands in the form of cottage industries." His laugh, in an undertone, was derisive.

Patrick found another contrarian argument for the sake of continuing the discussion. "However, the Leftists have emphasised primary education and health, haven't they?"

"What? Are you talking about West Bengal or Kerala? Look, Kerala has been quasi-Marxist since their electorate has always been anti-incumbent. They vote against the ruling cabinet, once Marxist, next Congress, next Marxist, now Congress, and so on. So Kerala's quality health-education combine is an achievement that has little link with the communists as such. In fact, researchers have connected it to a queen of Malabar, the princely state where Kerala is configured in present times, who sent a brilliant doctor from her realm to the US a century ago to learn and bring back modern medicine and methods, which she then methodically implemented. And, as far as West Bengal is concerned, the health and education indices are declining disastrously on a comparative scale with the rest of India, as the Left takes over. Now it ranks somewhere in the middle, a steep fall from being among the top states at the time of India's independence. There is no mistake about this," James finally ended. "Tell me something about yourself," James prompted Patrick, donning a shy smile as he put a stop to his own soliloquy.

What went on in Patrick's mind at that moment is uncertain. Was he carried away by a mistaken sense of patriotism? Had he to succumb on the basis of any other encroaching feeling? Was it an orchestrated seduction on James' part and Patrick's involuntary response to it? It is hard to dissect, and it will remain unknown.

James rose from his extended posture on the sofa. Approaching Patrick, he said, "Just to make sure that you do partake of my home and hearth whenever you like, come, get up, let me show you around my apartment." Extending his hand, he pulled Patrick up from his seat.

Their hands mingled. It was as if the decision had already been made for Patrick to join force with James to trace and track the communists in a forgotten corner of the world. That would certainly help ensure that America remained the land of the free.

As Patrick rose and walked hand in hand with James, he noticed that he stood just an inch taller than James, though James had maintained a tighter physique. Because of so much emphasis on university coursework and research in the library, Patrick had neglected his swimming and jogging over the last year and had suffered a slight slackening of his muscles. He felt self-conscious about what he, somewhat exaggeratedly, judged to be his flabbiness relative to James, even though, to the layman's eye, no such difference was discernible. He felt almost grateful as James put his right arm around his shoulder, even though it was just a simple protective gesture of ushering Patrick away from the brightness of the glass-panelled study and into the darker hallway, for James had observed that, as the sun became stronger on the outside, the glare was obscuring Patrick's view of the interior of the apartment.

They meandered past an odd series of rooms, large and small, but all invariably immaculately organised. James explained their explicitly different purposes and uses. However, the comments failed to make a mark on Patrick.

Rather, his focus was on James' physical proximity as they
moved from room to room. He found himself somewhat ill
at ease but, despite himself, could do nothing to stop it. He
tried his best not to think of Terrence. He was in motion,
side by side with James. Remnant feelings receded from his
consciousness until all thoughts of Terrence were effectively
banished from his mind.

The final spot on the tour was James' bedroom. As James
explained some of the antique decorations that adorned the
ceiling, Patrick wondered why he had been brought to this
particular part of the gargantuan apartment until he saw the
visage of Laurent appear in the passageway and his hands
silently closed the curtains at the exit door of the sprawling
bedroom. Patrick heard the door close from outside as if with
a trick of hand. Patrick turned around to look at James. James
had moved his arm from Patrick's shoulder, had positioned
himself in front of Patrick, and was looking him directly in
the eye.

*     *     *

Amlan and Sis headed straight to the National Museum
on Chowringhee Road just around the corner from the
hotel. The collection was impressive, but the thing that Sis
could not avoid observing was the presence and smell of
dust everywhere, including on the exhibits. The cleaners were
sitting in corners in strategic locations, two to a chair, to take
maximum benefit of the breeze from a whirring fan rotating
some distance away. Even so, they had to wipe away the
stubborn sweat gathering on their foreheads from the stifling
heat. The visitors were obviously mainly rural folk who were
staring at the exhibits, quite unable to understand the posted
descriptions in English and Hindi, the national languages of
India, since their education, if they had any, did not go beyond
Bangla, the regional language. From time to time, they bent

forward closely towards a painting and extended a cautious finger to rub its corner, as if to check whether the colours used were fast and reliable or cheap and easily erased by touch. All the while, the guards sat oblivious of this breathing into and touching of the paintings.

Sis found this at once atrocious and hilarious, but she was also cautious not to reveal any contrary expression or opinion, lest Amlan's feelings should be hurt or ire aroused for stating the obvious. She knew better than to be the stupid American. Amlan looked irritated one moment and terrified the next by the gawking visitors. When he saw an elderly woman stick a bindi – auspicious red dot – on the forehead of a black granite Lakshmi from the Gupta period, followed by a devout pranam – ablution by bringing her palms together in front of the deity – he had had his last straw and led Sis out of the room and through the museum gates. Sis gave in politely as he heaved a sigh of relief, both making sure not to look into each other's eyes.

The walk to Victoria Memorial was short and could be accomplished swiftly; however, the late morning sun, the pungent air and the humidity would have converted it into an uphill task. So he hopped into a yellow and black taxi with Sis. The inside of the taxi was full of dirt and grime, but the elderly Sikh driver was jovial, making friendly comments to Amlan about his phoren – foreign – girlfriend. Amlan took it lightly and smiled back as Sis looked quizzically at him. Momentarily, they arrived at the edifice, which had been financed by the Maharajas and Zamindars of a long-past subservient British India. The giant statue of the empress was not there at the spot where it had always been, on the roundabout in front of the central gates. She had been replaced by a diminutive statue of Sri Aurobindo, a revered anglophile Bengali revolutionary during his youth, turned ascetic in his prime. It came as a surprise to Amlan how poorly sculpted the replacement was as a piece of art. It looked miniscule on the huge dais on which Victoria had been seated and where now Aurobindo had been made to stand. It looked more suited for a corner of a local park, maybe the Triangular Park in South Calcutta or the square Deshbandhu Park in the North, but certainly not as a replacement for Victoria at her memorial. Here, in front of the colossal marble memorial for Victoria, Amlan thought the statue of Aurobindo looked puny and ridiculous. No wonder he had not even been able to recognise whose the statue was until he had walked to the pedestal and examined the roughly slapped-on piece of alloy on which Aurobindo's name had been inscribed in hardly ornamental letters. He wondered which confounded government department might have commissioned the statue, how much money might have changed hands, and what artist with Party membership might have created this absurdity, this abomination.

The morning was not turning out the way Amlan had hoped it would. Yet, there was no alternative but to continue. He searched for Victoria's statue, unable to believe that it would be removed altogether, and thanked the stars that it had not disappeared, but was sitting imperiously as ever just inside the memorial gates. The matronly figure looked precariously balanced on a rather narrow pedestal, for her girth was huge and accentuated by the rounded imperial gown flowing down around it.

At last, he smiled at Sis and said, "There is Rani Victoria, who called India the Jewel in her Crown. She had a most interesting life. She herself was half German and only chance put her on the throne above other claimants. Albert, her very handsome husband, was fully German, so all of their many offspring were three quarters German. Yet, she and her progeny became Britain's rulers. Of course, several of her children were married off to various European royal houses and, a couple of generations later, one German great nephew, the kaiser, fought the First World War with his cousin, the British King. This family brought unprecedented death and destruction to the world! At its worst, it was merely to feed their own vanities and idiosyncrasies and, through the war's ripple effects on colonies and ex-colonies, reduced all of humanity to the utter misery of warfare. World history is telling, isn't it?" Amlan asked rhetorically.

"Quite a massive structure, though hardly as enchanting or exquisite as the Taj Mahal according to the tour books," Sis tried to break into the monotony of Amlan's lecture.

Sis enjoyed them when Patrick was present to participate in a tête-à-tête but, in his absence, she found Amlan's speech a bit too overarching. Amlan noted it and let it pass. What Sis found more interesting were the changes in Amlan's facial expressions as he spoke and the shifts in the modulation of his voice and, behind his thick, dark-rimmed glasses, the black, well-shaped eyebrows and the expressive eyes that mesmerised her.

"That's true. The architects were not as varied as those who descended from all over the world for the construction of the Taj Mahal. Also, the Maharajas who chipped in to put up the memorial must have had conflicting opinions, culminating in this rather strange structure in flight that represents various classical architectural designs." He smiled at her, raising his hands and moving them towards her head, donning on her an imaginary crown.

"Queen Victoria was supposed to have been heartbroken after her prince husband's sudden demise in his early forties, but…" His voice changed to a mock whisper. "…She was also supposed to have had an affair with her Scottish horse master, Mr. Brown, and…" He continued in a tone of ultimate alarm, "After Brown's death, she even had to close a relationship with her Indian butler-in-waiting. She must have had quite a personality." He ended with an artificially clipped OxBridge—a pejorative combining Oxford and Cambridge—accent, as he had been taught to pronounce in his English medium school where all instruction was in English and students were punished if they broke into vernacular.

By now, Amlan and Sis were standing in front of the entrance to the memorial building. Finding almost no one at that interior point of the complex, Amlan extended his arm around Sis' waist and gingerly gathered her in towards himself. Slowly and silently, they spent over an hour, beginning at the central hall and progressing through the large adjacent chambers, looking at life-sized portraits of the Powers That Be of British India, their arms and armaments, and several pencil, pen and water colour sketches of the army life of the period. Not that they held any particular interest for either of them but, as they lingered, their awareness of each other sharpened, and remained heightened and intense. The cool marble edifice that the external world seemed to have forgotten, offered them all the privacy they craved, and they delayed their departure from there as long as they could.

Suddenly, telepathically, both felt hungry and blurted out almost at the same moment if they should not think of lunch. They fell laughing, clinging to each other. Their faces came close, but they did not kiss. Instead, they came out of the building and proceeded, hand in hand, to take the back exit of the grounds through the surrounding lawns. Their palms were warm and became sweaty as Amlan squeezed hers and she responded without reserve. As they walked, a small wooden kiosk, painted green and covered in ivy, appeared to the left of them. A narrow pebbled path led to it. With a firm, loving pull, Amlan led Sis onto the path.

Sis' heart was pounding. She could not, and did not, stop him. She seemed to slow down, pulling Amlan back a bit, but so lightly that he did not feel it. The kiosk had creaky old wooden windows with opaque, cracked glass panes that had been stained with grime that had collected over many years. There was no door, however. Amlan, by now oblivious of his surroundings, dragged Sis within its confines.

"I love you." He felt sick with longing as the words popped uncontrollably out of his mouth.

"I, too, I think… But, Omlaan, we just met yesterday. We don't know each other. You hardly know me or my background and my experiences. I… I was…" She could not finish. Instead, she looked away.

Amlan did not hear a word Sis was saying. He brought her face close to his. His lips touched hers. His tongue reached her mouth and slid deep inside until it intertwined with hers. Their bodies writhed together. They continued until neither could breathe. Sis eventually forced his tongue out and clipped her mouth shut, almost swooning. With all his might, Amlan held her waist from below and, bending forward, kissed her again, slowly raising her, their tongues hungrily sliding back and forth once again, as if it was never to end.

As Amlan proceeded carefully to touch her breasts, Sis shut her eyes, experiencing heavenly delight. The very next moment, she drew herself back. "Not here, please. God! Look at my hair. No, let's go." Extricating herself from his grip, she moved towards the exit.

Suddenly conscious of the liberties he had taken, Amlan quickly retreated from his advances. "I am sorry. I did not quite realise what I was doing. How daft of me!"

"It's all right, Omlaan. It's just that this does not seem like the right place. Also, well, I wanted to tell you something." She paused as Amlan looked at her enquiringly. "This trip with my brother… He has brought me along because, well, I had not been feeling too well, you know, and, um… he said I would feel better if I came along."

"Oh! I am very sorry. We have a grand old, but truly great, family doctor. We have been in his care for three generations now!" he joked. "We could ask him to drop by later this evening, after his office hours perhaps. He will set you right in no time, I am sure," he half joked, though obviously concerned.

"It's not that…" She trailed off. "Well, can we go now?"

Somehow, their hunger, which had transformed itself into physical desire for each other, had abated. As she barged out of the dilapidated kiosk, Amlan followed closely. He looked up to see the steeple of St. Paul's Cathedral just beyond the side walls of the memorial and, to deflect what had just transpired between them, suggested that they go take a look at it.

Sis looked nervous and agitated. Suddenly turning pale, she blurted out, "I don't like cathedrals or churches, Omlaan. Can we go someplace else?" She looked a bit sick; her face, which had been flushed well beyond its normal pink inside the kiosk moments ago, was now as pale as milk.

Why is she on the verge of tears, Amlan wondered, "Have I said something? No, I have not." He realised that Sis' reaction was not normal, but he did not press the point. It called for deeper attention, perhaps a discussion later, but this was not the right moment. What he felt was needed now was a Scotch and soda at Calcutta Club situated just across the road.

Softly, he asked, "Do you think you can walk a couple of minutes to the Club for a drink? Would you like that or should I take you back to the hotel?" Reacting to her silence, he continued, "We could meet tomorrow. I already have made some plans for what we could do."

His eyes glowed with expectation and excitement. At this moment in his life, he had realised that there was nothing more important than spending time with Sis, and he must do all he could to make it happen. He could not be bothered if he missed classes another day. All such matters seemed of little consequence. He did not want the life choice he had made to be turned into a missed opportunity.

Sis was alarmed. She wanted to cling onto Amlan desperately, not to let him go. "No, no. I would not mind a drink. Frankly, I would like one." She did not know, however, what Amlan had meant by 'the Club'. It hardly mattered as long as she got to spend more time with him.

They walked past St. Paul's, Amlan noticing that Sis was almost at pains to avoid looking even at its façade. He grew more curious, but kept the curiosity well within himself.

Moments later, when they walked up to the wide steps of the entrance of Calcutta Club, several bearers turned to salute him a salaam, their fingers touching their foreheads with a tight, silent slap. Amlan returned a slight nod in recognition, clearly obviating any possibility of familiarity, maintaining, with tact, the reality of rarefied layers of Calcutta society. He led Sis towards the left from the middle of the central hall, into a well-appointed bar. He complained about the furniture though, apologising for the new vinyl sofas that had recently replaced the original, classy leather furniture. He lamented that taste was a thing of the past in the emerging social realities. He explained that the floodgates of membership had been opened recently to Marwaris in light of the Club's falling into financial constraints as more of its Bengali members were reneging on their membership and other dues to the Club.

Amlan conveniently ignored that, not so long ago, the British, who had established all the clubs in Calcutta, their first capital city in India, took great pains not to allow any Indians into their clubs, Bengalis included. When they left, it was as if it was natural for Bengalis to take the clubs over and, in turn, for them to complain about those whom they perceived to be of lesser ethnic backgrounds, woefully entering into their preserve and polluting it. Amlan seemed not to be totally devoid of the remnants of such views and feelings, so ingrained were the attitudes of superiority among Bengalis, even as their power and influence sank all around them. Sis looked around. "How can you tell who they are?" she asked innocently.

"Oh, that's easy. Generally, by what they wear and how the women carry their saris. Bengalis prefer cotton; Marwaris prefer synthetic fibre. Also, by how they speak English, since it is only the newest generation that speaks it fluently. Then, of course, there are differences in facial features and physique. And they order vegetarian food when in their own company. So there are lots of indicators," he half joked.

Amlan stopped for a moment, apparently a bit reflective, but could not help continuing. "Perhaps one should not say this for fear of being branded a racist. Nevertheless, since they are generally vegetarian and their women being home bound and sedentary, the women tend to get flabby as they continue bearing an endless series of babies. Come to think of it, both the men and women gain weight from excessive consumption of saturated fat and sugar. Ironically, their avowed vegetarianism, derived from their rural background and religious fixation, is obviously essential to counter their ill-begotten wealth that they amass in such scale only through heartless commerce, adulteration, and impurities in whatever they supply."

Amlan could not stop now. "Marwaris are usually flat faced in sharp contrast to the Rajputs, who come from the same north-western state of Rajasthan." He laughed. "The Rajputs are Kshatriyas, a warrior caste whose lineage is said to go back to the original Aryan immigrants from the Ukrainian plains, whereas the Marwaris, subordinate in the rung of castes, come from a mix of villages in that area that took up commerce and trade."

Sis was visibly confused. She ventured, "This morning, while Patrick and I were waiting for you, I was reading the Statesman. On the front page, there was a collection of pictures of ten students who had received top ranks in the general high school board exams. I remember seeing two names, a boy and a girl, who were identified as Marwari, and a couple of others who were Tamils, and I meant to ask you who these groups were. However, I recall the Marwaris as having quite sharp, angular features, quite handsome, really. Was that an aberration or am I confused, I wonder."

Amlan was defensive. "I am glad you found some of them beautiful. On their recent scholastic achievements, you see, as I just told you, their newest generation enjoys many privileges. They have the benefit of private tutors, the best schools and the best sports trainers. So their newly experienced achievements are not surprising. In fact, now they establish their own schools, colleges, universities even, though mainly as tax shelters rather than for reasons of philanthropy that drove the early Bengali. The Marwaris even have the nerve to say that they are bringing culture back to Bengal, that they themselves are the New Bengalis. In fact, they are bringing out a new, slick magazine to establish that. The impudence!" Then, with profound grief, he added, "And you know what? The Bengalis can do damn all!" Amlan knew instantly that he might have spoken too much, so he confessed, "There you are. Now you know everything about my biases, my likes and dislikes." He looked at Sis. "Judge me, pretty lady," he pleaded, his brows curled in question.

Sis was obviously somewhat doubtful about Amlan's strong ethnic views. Perhaps he says more than he actually believes, she mused. However, her thoughts were, in reality, elsewhere. She started, "Omlaan, I want to say something. It is important…"

A middle-aged, somewhat sloppy bearer approached them. "Aajke ki debo, Sir?" He smiled, daring, also, to look at Sis. "What can I serve you tonight, Madam?"

"These people have the greatest sense of time," thought Amlan in sarcasm. Nevertheless, without the slightest hint of this comment, Amlan smiled at the man while he explained to Sis, "Rafiqda has known me for as long as I can remember. Ma would bring me here to the swimming pool since I was five, I think. After a swim, I would have a chicken patty and ice cream soda. That was the routine. And it was Rafiqda who would invariably serve us. Now, of course, he serves me Scotch and soda, though he has never hidden his disapproval about it." Then he responded to the waiter, without waiting for Sis' answer, "Rafiqda, bring me the usual." He ignored the elderly man's grimace. "And, for Didi …?" he looked at Sis inquiringly.

Sis replied, if a bit shyly, "A cream soda, please." She tried to obviate further disapproval from the man. Also, she wanted to get on with the matter that she desperately desired to discuss with Amlan.

However, Rafiq would not disappear so quickly. "Sir, abaar oi beesh gulo keno khachho?",

In exasperation, Amlan looked impatiently away from him, commenting to Sis in an undertone that now the man had commented on why Amlan chose to drink poison repeatedly. Sensing that some of the man's insistence was mere acting to attract attention from the attractive foreigner, Amlan added, "Ki, didi ke pochhondo? Aashchhe baar boudi bole daakte hobe!" However, he desisted from translating for Sis what he had just said: Do you like her? Next time, you will have to address her not as sister, but as sister-in-law.

Rafiq's expression remained inscrutable. "Anything is possible these days," he seemed to indicate with his brows steadfastly in place. "Dada, how long were you in America?" he asked, implying, "So this is what you were doing there, huh?"

Momentarily astounded by Sis' spellbinding beauty, he piped in, stammering shyly, "Didi khoob sundar dekhte, tobe gaye ektu shaarle aro bhalo hoto."

Amlan smiled and translated for Sis, "The fellow says that you are beautiful, but that you should put on some weight."

Both broke into laughter.

Then, Amlan looked at the man and commanded, "Scotch ta aanbe ki?"

"Dada, ekhhuni." Forthwith. He ran off.

Sis attempted once again to resume. "Omlaan, I don't know…" She sounded thoughtful, distant perhaps. "I realise that we like each other very much. It is a miracle in some ways, isn't it? It is so strange, really. We cannot explain it, I suppose," she abruptly concluded, hoping for some sort of rejoinder from Amlan.

There was none. Instead, Amlan looked at her intently, anticipating that Sis may have something to say that was connected to her outburst about churches. Still somewhat distracted, he wondered aloud as to when they would get their drinks, though Rafiq had just promised that he would bring them immediately.

Sis became pensive. "Omlaan, certain things happen in my country, back home that you possibly cannot quite imagine here.... Well, I grew up in a Catholic background and sometimes these priests, sort of... take advantage of us kids. Sometimes it goes too far. This father – how strange, isn't it, that we call them father or brother – forced me to do it regularly with him for some time. He got this fear into me that, if I ever told anyone about it, the Virgin Mary would be angry with me, since he represented Jesus, her son.

"It was always inside the church, after school and before I could get back home. In the confession box, behind the altar, between the pews, wherever he fancied. I had no feeling for him. It seemed to get almost into a habit since I knew there was no escape from it. For some time, I told my mom that I did not want to go to Sunday school, that I did not like confession, or mass, or retreats, whatever excuse I could give to avoid him at normal times. To me, the encounters had to be hidden as if I had bargained with the Devil himself. I felt I could not deliver myself from my sins. My mother is a devout, rigid Catholic. I suppose it would have been beyond her to grasp or even imagine and believe what I was trying so desperately to convey to her...." Sis trailed off.

Sis hadn't looked at Amlan through her entire description of her diabolical experience, or that of her conviction that her mother would never comprehend her consternation, let alone intervene on her behalf to put an end to it.

Amlan had been speechless once he had realised the monumental nature of what Sis had been saying. He suddenly felt a sharp wedge pierce his heart. Yet, all he could spurt out was something indirect. "Darling, who told you that we don't have these problems here? But, I thought those priests always preyed on boys!" He failed miserably in his attempt at a joke at this crucial moment.

However, soon, grief overcame him like a shadow over his soul, dark clouds permeating his entire being, as Sis now looked at him helplessly. Then, a resolve that can only nest in the scion of a long lineage of deep individual pride and compassion, replaced the grief. "I am so... sorry," he slowly uttered as he moved closer to her. As he took her hands in his, he said, "I love you and that is all that matters. If you love me too, what else could matter?"

"Omlaan, just before this trip, I became pregnant." She was looking down at the floor, her voice barely above a whisper. Her words, hardly audible, emerged in spurts as large teardrops unabashedly fell from her eyes onto the floor. "I miscarried after three months. I visited a midwife across the train tracks south of the city to make arrangements to drop it, but ultimately I did not have to go through with it. It was as if the baby had realised that it was not welcome, that it would only be a burden on me," she said in a distant tone, her thoughts drifting, floating to the Negro area in south San Antonio, a strange, rundown neighbourhood far, far away from her own. Whites liked to ignore and to forget this area. It was only to be utilised when they needed some place else to store their shame or to have secret pleasures.

"I suppose I became so hysterical, my parents thought they would have to put me in a nuthouse for a while until I could be assimilated back into society. Then Patrick called from Washington to say that he was planning a trip to India. I could not bear the thought of his being away since I had been waiting for him to return home to San Antonio so that I could be with him. When he called me from Washington after Ma told him, when she visited him for his graduation, I managed to tell him that he must come home before leaving for India. He flew down immediately after his semester was over and asked me if I would like to join him on the trip. I jumped at the opportunity to travel with him – he is my hero and has always been, you know." Sis looked at Amlan with resolve. "Omlaan, I still am suffering inside. I don't think I am ready for a relationship with anyone. I don't know if I will ever be…" She trailed off.

Tears were streaming down Amlan's face. All he wanted to do was to hug her, even as a strain of deep anger at the priest began flowing within him. His anger was an unfocussed and confused mix of wrath against the priest, the Church, the circumstances of parochial Texas, and Sis' unprotective or, at best, naïve, mother. His vituperation against society, the West, the world, rose to new heights. He found himself shaking and, holding onto her, nested his head against her chest like a baby, and she found herself cradling him as if he was a child.

The sudden appearance of Rafiq quickly brought them back to the present. He was standing with a tray containing two semi-thick glasses filled with the requested drinks. There was also a small bowl of potato chips and one of spiced peanuts. Amlan gathered himself quickly and reached out for his glass containing two shots of whisky. He added several cubes of ice from the ice bucket, and gulped down half the glass in one go. Rafiq turned and left as if he could not bear to see the young man drink like an alcoholic. Amlan waited a moment, warmth slowly invading his body, his eyes red from weeping and exacerbated by the hard drink. He looked at the glass, and downed the remaining liquor in another uninterrupted swallow.

He stared at her with bloodshot eyes and took her palms in his, pressing them hard, almost hurting her. She cringed.

"Will you marry me?" he asked her tearfully.

Sis stared blankly at Amlan. At the same time, she was drowning in a sea of gratitude and bottomless admiration. Disbelief transfixed her to the spot on which she was sitting.

She was unable to move. She remained silent for a long time. A long time.

Finally, Sis managed to reply, "Yes, Omlaan, even though I do not deserve you." It was a response that also protected her from embarrassment if he withdrew the offer once he was sober again. Even if such an eventuality transpired, it would not matter. For a man to propose to her, even in a drunken stupor, was more than she dared ever to expect. Somehow, at the very least, the enormous burden of the unspeakable past that had been bearing down on her had been swept away as if a devastating hurricane had just blown past. She breathed more easily. She felt an incredible lightness in her being. She glanced at her glass of ice cream soda and, curious to taste Amlan's favourite childhood drink, picked it up and took a sip of it.

Amlan replied, after the intense atmosphere that had been generated from their conversation had lightened somewhat, "So, I declare us married. From now on until death do us part, you are mine alone and I am humbly yours. Ceremonies that will follow will be mere social encumbrances and formalities." He gave an enormous smile and hugged Sis in the darkness of the bar. Pointing his forefinger towards a passing Rafiq, he hollered, "Rafiqda, aar ekta Scotch ano." And he waited eagerly for another round of drinks.

*   *   *

That night, Calcutta came to a standstill. Someone had informed the Marxist home minister—in a Congress-Left coalition government—by telephone that there would be a bomb attack by Naxals – Marxist Leninists – on the upscale Metro Cinema. Who could have made the call remained a matter of speculation in all the newspapers the following morning. However, what was certain was that the police commissioner had made sure that the cinema was sufficiently manned by a group of plainclothesmen. When no explosion occurred, they just picked up young, unshaven, unkempt men who looked incongruous among the posh audience and led them away to nip any possibility in the bud. In the wee hours of the morning, those who failed to confess to the planning of the crime that had not occurred were hung upside down from the ceiling of their cells and given intermittent electric shocks to their genitalia. The next day, they were dropped off in various residential blocks of Calcutta.

The Naxal Movement picked up in the subsequent period. More street fights among the Left groups themselves started and the police intervened at their own pleasure. A few policemen died and others were hurt; but scores of Naxals were dead, more were wounded and scores disappeared forever. A number of dead bodies were found on the streets of North Calcutta, the outcome of the establishment's cold ferocity and its impunity. Unsurprisingly, a few misdirected college students, who were from rich, wealthy, well-connected families and who had joined the movement more out of boredom or rebellion against their parents or parental authority than any true convictions, were quietly shipped off to Oxford or Cambridge. Parental influence had saved them from genital torture or worse. There were no consequences for their actions other than temporary or permanent exile to England.

Three months later, an analysis of the phone call revealed that the insurgent who had made the call to the home minister had imitated an American accent, a mix of a Texan twang and an Eastern twirl, an unexpected conclusion by a team of Bengali speech specialists appointed by government. Eventually, the matter came to naught, since the individual was never identified. In between, however, there were many a hartal—strikes—and michhil—processions—against the Yankee, many office days lost, many a school closed and college gate barred, traffic blocked and ambulance sirens turned on, and lanes of windows and doors bolted, until these occurrences became routine. The populace was cowed down to accepting the Left's encroachment and impending installation in a majority government.

Bengal was going through a metamorphosis. The productivity of its economy was diving into deep sea, students were forgetting English because there were few who remained to teach it to them, and infrastructure was a word that could have been removed from the dictionary. Nothing could stop the Left from zooming in and taking over. To the Left, they would transform Bengal, for Bengalis were no longer the lackeys of the British; they spoke their own tongue, they cared about poetry and literature, about equality and justice, and eschewed commerce and industry while emphasising agriculture – thus, humane, venerated objectives would be achieved. That the Left political bosses were to become the recipients of state-provided land, homes and other beneficence, that they would protect their habits of the daily Scotch whisky they had acquired when they themselves had lived abroad, or that their progeny were being shipped off to the West for higher studies, did not seem to bother them as long as outward stringency was strictly maintained by Party cadres.

The rest of Bengal outside Calcutta was, indeed, perceived to emerge as a new breed, confident of their indigenous origin, their native culture, proud of their autarky, oblivious of their lack of integration with economically progressive India, and decidedly comfortable in the narrow north-south slit of land that they called Paschim Banga or West Bengal – pronounced Poshchim Bongo in their sweet, non-phonetic language – a chosen people tilling green, fertile fields justly distributed through successive and successful land reform efforts, unlike in most of the rest of India, into minute parcels among all its denizens, protected from hegemony driven encroachments, however defined, from big industry and its exclusively pecuniary interests. The bigger eastern part of Bengal – two-thirds of Bongodesh, or the land of Bengal – had been ruthlessly torn apart by the British colonial masters more than half a century ago and nothing could be done about it for the moment. At least a new nation, Bangladesh, had been formed of that portion, solely at India's behest, daring the threat of Nixon's Sixth Fleet, politely ignored by Europe from any cooperation in containing Pakistan's pogrom there, and supported only by the Soviet Union with a thirteen-year treaty that guaranteed India's boundaries from Western intervention while it took such an audacious step as to help create a new country in its sphere of influence. For the Bengali Leftist in Poshchim Bongo, what could be better than to help create this new nation state that had Bangla as its national language and a song by Tagore as its national anthem? Now, both sides could safely continue to dream together of a shonar Bangla, a Golden Bengal that had been immortalised for centuries in the verses of so many home-grown, illustrious poets, Muslim and Hindu alike. That dream would be impossible to strike out from the Bengali soul or consciousness, where language was supreme, culture omnipotent, equality a fundamental right, efficiency and productivity a concept of barbarians, an embarrassment reserved for the economically advanced.

\* \* \*

That night, Patrick returned to the hotel exhausted, having performed his initial task, under strict guidance and without a single technical error. He had been appropriately tutored and had learnt that very morning on the pillow that it did not matter which shade of red is got rid of, since it tended to progress inexorably from the slightest shade of pink. It was important to simply light the right fire as a facilitator, an enabler, a conduit. He reflected on the day, with little feeling for its impact, or on his success and singular perfection. He felt hardened inside, steeling himself for the activities he anticipated on a day to day future trajectory, trying to ignore for the moment, his family, his many connections and his other interests.

However, he could not forget. Before going to bed, he tried to call Terrence in Bogota from the hotel reception. He desperately wanted to hear his voice. He seemed so far away, as if he did not exist anymore. He had little luck in getting a connection. He went out to an STD-ISD booth on the sidewalk and tried again. The phone rang on the other side of the world, and he felt unmistakable palpitations in his heart.

Patrick heard Terrence's voice saying, "¡Hola! ¡Hola!"

Praying that he would get an answer of recognition, he shouted back, "Terrence? Terrence?" However, there was only a long silence.

Then he heard Leonor ask, "¿Dígame?"

Just as Patrick began to answer, the line went dead. At that moment, Patrick knew that not only had he lost Terrence, but also that he had lost him to Leonor… forever. He placed the heavy archaic black phone back on the receiver, paid the bill spat out by the small machine by the side of the phone and, suddenly feeling infinitely tired, re-entered the hotel and trudged up the stairs towards his room.

\*   \*   \*

Sis was waiting in the hotel room for her brother to return, for she had got back quite early. It was just after dusk when Amlan had dropped her off. As Patrick entered, she felt a blind admiration for this brother of hers, for his sheer abilities. For herself, she felt ashamed, an unfathomable remorse, believing that only Patrick could explain or resolve her mixed feelings, her deep confusion, her inability, her unwillingness to say 'no' to Amlan's proposal, for the position between a rock and a hard place where she now found herself.

When Sis related her day to the exhausted Patrick, he had no choice but to perk up and listen intently. He had never expected she would receive a proposal to marry in such a faraway place and, knowing the local politics and problems, he became ostensibly concerned. How will Ma and Dad react? Patrick wondered.

However, soon, Patrick's thoughts reversed course. Sis' stay-over in Calcutta would fit in well enough in the evolving scheme of events. He himself would be staying on, so why not Sis? She would be living elsewhere, which should also be convenient. He could visit her regularly. Hopefully, she was marrying into a decent Bengal family. He knew already from what little Amlan had revealed about his own background, from his English accent, from the book he was reading, from his conversation and from his world view that he was not ordinary. It reflected solid nurture and a strong nature, if too opinionated a personality. Yes, he should suffice very well for Patrick's immediate needs.

Further, it would be ideal for Sis to settle down; what would she go back to in San Antonio anyway? What had Ma in store for her? No, it seemed much better for Sis to continue in Calcutta, at least while he was here. By the time he completed his assignment, Sis would possibly have come out of her trance, and Amlan his. They would probably break off their engagement. She would then most likely return with Patrick to the US and stay with him at his regular posting which, if all went well for him in Calcutta, was certainly likely to be at the Langley headquarters.

Accordingly, Patrick raised his eyebrows in theatrical fashion and, smiling mischievously, gave his sister a bear hug, whispering a sweet congratulation in her ear, thus clinching her resolution in favour of an engagement. To hear Patrick was sheer celebration and joy to Sis, though she was a bit surprised at her usually discerning brother's immediate and warm reception of the idea. She hugged him back with quintessential tears of joy that adroitly hid her confusion.

Patrick got up and turned towards the shower as he documented in his mind four major events that had comprised this single day that was now concluding. The recession of

Terrence from his daily life, the entrance of James into it, obtaining his first full-time salaried job, however serendipitous, and Sis' engagement to an unlikely man in an even more unlikely spot on a corner of the globe, left him overwhelmed. He turned back, smiled affectionately at Sis, and entered the shower that was already pouring forth a welcome torrent of cool water from its large overhead spout, just right to take out the heat of the day from his tired body.

As Patrick stood under the shower, soothing water streamed pleasantly over his fatigued body. His mind, nevertheless, could not help but be visited by disturbing thoughts from back home. He could not help but think of the emotional distancing from Agnes, his mother, which he had experienced in the whole matter regarding Jolly, as well as Sis, and over what had been building up over Agnes' non-recognition of her son's inner self. Patrick had remained unable and fearful about openly discussing these issues with her, let alone confronting her. The opacity or deliberate unwillingness on Agnes' part negated any theoretical claims that 'a mother always knows', and Patrick found the phrase ridiculous. In fact, it made him angry.

To calm himself and evict such stray thoughts at the end of the eventful day, Patrick decided to prolong his shower into a bath. He now wanted the water to be slightly warm so it would allow the bath salts, which he had observed on the shelf, but had not had the time or inclination to use earlier, to mix well with the water. He let warm water flow into the large old-fashioned tub and melt the soap crystals into it. When the tub was almost spilling, he turned off the antique brass taps. Then he carefully slid into the inviting bubbles. He closed his eyes and heaved a deep sigh. He disappeared completely in the depths, his mind blank and his soul unmoved. He felt nothing other than the equilibrium of some dark universal force.

*    *    *

After leaving Sis at her hotel, Amlan walked into the still, but dangerous, night. He decided to take the longest way – an hour-long walk – home since he could not bear to enter the confines of the house or to face his mother so soon after the harrowing, yet deeply affecting, life event he had experienced. He had not kissed Sis as they said goodbye; the preceding emotions had been too intense, too painful. As he walked, he told himself that he had done the right thing, that he still felt close to the object of his affection, that he was going to take her into the home of his ancestors, that she would experience that there is love and honour in the world and that, with him, she would carry that honour further into posterity. However, first, he would not only have to convince Ma about a foreigner entering their home and hearth, but he would resolve never to mention the unmentionables to his mother, since they had nothing to do with her.

When he eventually entered home, he quickly crossed the front hall, climbed the stairs and went into his wing unobtrusively, not even having acknowledged Durwan at the main gate. It was convenient, since he was snoozing in the dilapidated guards' room. Amlan showered, and then waited impatiently for his mother to complete her evening ablutions. As he heard the conch shell sound thrice to initiate the sleep of the daylight gods and welcome the evening gods for protection at the passing of dusk into night, he knew that the proceedings were completed. He crossed over to her wing.

"Ma, I told you I needed one more day. I met an American girl from Texas yesterday. I think I like her a lot; very much, in fact, and I would like to marry her. How do you feel about that, Ma? Would it be okay with you? Would you bless my decision?" he ended, without elaborating, and with his voice trembling, despite his every wish to steady it, as he wrestled with his mixed feelings of love and compassion that were still battling to fight his disdain over the facts he had learnt from

Sis. He was seeking his mother's approval as if that would help him overcome his lingering, last doubts.

The large bedroom was already dark except for the Tiffany table lamp, lighted in readiness for Ma to carry on with her embroidery whenever she desired. Its glow lightened the room just so much as to defer to the calm of the receding dusk, yet to answer to the call of the fast-approaching nightfall. Indeed, she had just sat in her chair and reached for her sewing. Her face was partly in a shadow. She looked up at him. Amlan could not tell the expression on her face. However, he knew she was trying to find words to express herself.

Here was this boy who made me wait two years before I could even inquire after possible brides among relatives, friends and well-wishers in general, she was telling herself. Now, he decides to marry a foreign girl in just one day! Could I have borne a more impetuous child? And, of course, as always, his father abandons me at my most trying moments with our son!

Amlan could now see her as she moved her head involuntarily into the ray of light emanating from the table lamp. Her face was bathed in honest confusion. Amlan was anxious as to how she would react.

Yet, she herself knew that, if she failed to manage the moment with utmost dexterity, she could lose her son forever. Nevertheless, she could not muster too much enthusiasm in her voice either. What emerged was, "Excellent, my Gopal. She must be still in Calcutta? Why don't you introduce her to me tomorrow? I hope she will not mind our traditional, rather modest, manner of hospitality." There was more than a slight irony that lined the tone of her voice.

"Ma, if you wish, I could go and bring her now."

"Yes, do." Her voice shook from the anxiety and uncertainty that her immediate future foretold.

"But, I would like your Bou to enter home for the first time in Dadu's Bentley."

"Of course. Ask Bhagwanda to call Rahim to drive you to the hotel. Where is she staying?"

"I will drive myself."

"Be careful. You are not used to it anymore since you returned from there. College Street is in a terrible state of disrepair, not even fit for a professional driver to cope, what with the road having been dug out all along the tram tracks."

"I will be fine."

"All right then." She did not realise that poor condition of the roads was not the issue but, rather, the amount her son had had to drink earlier that evening.

*    *    *

Predictably, the black Bentley managed to find itself in Sudder Street with great speed. Distances in Calcutta are short, especially when the streets are devoid of vehicles and pedestrians as, indeed, they were this night. Amlan parked the car in an ample space in front of the hotel. He got out and sauntered through the hotel lobby without stopping at the reception but, when he realised that he did not know the room number, he went back, found out the room number, and took the rickety elevator up. He knocked on the door and stood waiting breathlessly for it to open.

Patrick had been reflecting on the events of his day, when there was a knock on the door. Curious who could be knocking at this late hour, he turned the knob and opened the door just a bit. Seeing Amlan, he smiled quizzically. "Come in," he said, his smile and his curiosity frozen on his face.

Sis, by now seeing Amlan, ran to the door. "Is everything all right?" she asked anxiously in reflection of the events of the day they had shared, yet without any idea what Amlan's sudden appearance might signify.

"Could you come home with me now?" Amlan straightforwardly asked her. "Ma would like to meet you." He smelt slightly sweaty, his underarms were wet, his expression perturbed, and concern was written all over his face. His eyes were still a bit bloodshot. It was obvious that he had had a complicated day, compulsive yet deliberative, that had yet to end.

Sis sensed that not all had gone well at Amlan's home. She was not shocked. She wondered what Amlan might have shared with his mother. Still, she had to be at his side at this crucial moment. Softly, she responded, "Of course, Omlaan. It will take me only a minute to change." She went to grab some clothes and disappeared into the bathroom.

Patrick looked at them, turning from one to the other. He butted in, "I suppose I will have to go along, looking at the late hour. You understand; I can't just let Sis go out alone at this point."

"She will not be alone. She will be with me. I am sure we will have a better opportunity for you to visit my home. But, if you feel you must, you could, of course, chaperone your sister now," he ended, with very little welcoming or encouragement in his voice.

Patrick ignored the half-heartedness of the invitation, and ran back in to change as Sis reappeared. He emerged almost instantaneously, as if he feared they would have left had he not. He exited the room behind them, locked the door, and ran down the stairs after them.

No words were exchanged during the fifteen-minute drive. This heightened the mystery of the moment. The siblings recognised College Street and Presidency College, and noted that they were being transported further away from the centre of town. Soon, they passed a massive public swimming pool on the right.

Amlan broke the heavy silence. "This is Hedua. I could have swum here when I was a child, since this is so near home. However, I was taken to Calcutta Club for swimming lessons and that is where I continue to this day. I suppose that the club was considered more exclusive, not public, so to speak. These differences continue to this day, you know." He spoke in typical sentiment of those who are empathetic in their verbal expressions about achieving equality in society, yet seem content to live with inequality all around them and benefit from their exclusivity as well.

He continued, "They used to have great water polo games and water ballets at Hedua. Now, both have fallen out of grace. The municipal corporation has run out of funds to finance such activities or celebrate sports events. One cannot help but lament the pilferage of public funds that put an end to such joyous social events."

This sudden interjection by himself seemed to calm Amlan. Sis admired his social conscience and concern, even in an extremely tough moment. However, she remained silent, essentially with her heart in her mouth, regarding whatever charged atmosphere might await her. Patrick looked carefully around himself, wondering if and when he might have to venture into these northerly neighbourhoods on any forthcoming assignments.

*    *    *

Against the moonlight there was a dark silhouette that was looking over the terrace's railing. As the Bentley zoomed into the driveway, the figure disappeared, engulfed in the surrounding shadows. The car stopped under the portico just in front of the steps into the mammoth house. Amlan got out and came around to help Sis out. Patrick helped himself out from the rear seat. The servants had not been alerted; only Durwan had seen Amlan drive ferociously in and intuitively knew not to raise a hue and cry, so no one ran out to greet them. The courtyard was dark, since the lights had been turned off, except for two flickering gas lamps. The scent of magnolia and gardenia mingled to produce an almost surreal atmosphere.

The visitors followed the host, Sis anxiously, while Patrick a bit sullenly, up the stairs that seemed lugubrious in the all-enveloping darkness. They were led directly to Amlan's mother's quarters. Before they could enter, she floated out ever so imperceptibly and stood erect in front of them. She was wearing a sari in the fashion of a Bengali housewife, its side covering the back of her head as a sign of feminine modesty that was expected by society on all formal occasions. A bunch of numerous keys, large and small, knotted to a corner of the sari, was slung over her shoulders, leaving a tell-tale sign of who the doyen of the household was. The sari itself was simple, white in the body, but bordered with an intricate black and deep green whalebone design. It was not red since she was a widow. It was difficult to know if she had taken any pains to change for their visit.

She held a steady gaze as she faced Sis. The moon shone directly on Sis' face through the tall, open French windows in the hallway. Sis looked back simply, innocently. She seemed shy, a bit demure. Perfect lines defined her face. The straight, yet not over-emphasised, contours of her nose, her rose complexion turned a platinum under the soft lunar rays, exquisitely natural, bud-shaped lips, a perfectly matching set of eyes under faultlessly paired eyebrows, combined to draw Ma's attention and relief. For a moment, forgetting societal uncertainties and personal doubts, Sis's verisimilitude made Ma realise what must have attracted her son so much to this foreigner.

Softness overcame Ma. She gathered herself and, in a tone intended to convey as much warmth as she could muster, asked Sis gently, "What is your name?" Before Sis could respond, she interrupted, "That's all right. I will call you Lokkhima. I have been waiting a long time for you." Then, as if as a second thought, she quickly added, "Wait here before you enter the rooms. I'll be back in a minute." She disappeared in another direction of the hallway, away from the suites.

She unlocked a room on the corridor whose doors had been shut. She turned on the low-wattage light inside. Nevertheless, two high altars – marble shelves, really – adorned with statues and paintings of myriad gods and goddesses came into view. Some appeared dark; others glowed. Though their forms or faces could not be fully deciphered in the low light of the room, strings of white Rajanigandha with which they were all garlanded lent them definition. The sweet aroma of the flowers floated into the dark hallway where the three of them stood and waited. Ma could be seen hazily, busying herself with what appeared to be miniature objects. Before she realised, Sis looked away, as if to obviate any inauspicious impact of her straying glances. Patrick looked on, a bit amused and supercilious, but also curious as to what was to occur next.

Instantly, Ma reappeared in front of them. In her palms, she held a small plate that glistened like real gold and a miniature terracotta lamp with a beautifully shaped, stable flame rising from a wick, ensconced firmly on it. Patrick observed that the plate was occupied by other little things as well. He could figure out husk of rice or perhaps wheat, some green grass, and a small silver bowl filled with a beige liquid from which emanated an exquisite aroma. His curiosity was aroused.

Ma stood still for a moment in front of Sis. She picked up the lamp and rotated it several times in front of her face, illuminating it as it passed in front. Amlan stared at them both, quite stunned at his mother's love for him, at her adroitness, at her unflinching willingness to adjust to him. However, would she be able to love Sis as a daughter as much as he did as his lover? He hoped that his mother would be able to love her Lokkhima truly one day. For now, by merely calling her by that name, she had obliterated Sis' past, revealed her lack of interest in it and her sole interest in drawing Sis in as her son's wife. That was more than good enough for the moment, he reassured himself.

Patrick was taking it all in with cool neutrality, as if the short, silent ceremony was more important than the antecedents behind it. He saw Ma dip her middle finger into the small silver bowl, wet it, draw it out and dot the middle of Sis's forehead, accompanied by a short, silent prayer that appeared to be recited rather than being spontaneous. She repeated the action twice. Then she sprinkled some of the husk and bright green grass on Sis's head and beckoned Amlan towards the plate.

Amlan nervously approached it and looked into it. He dipped his forefinger into another small bowl that Patrick must have missed earlier for, when he retrieved his finger, it appeared to be bloody. He brought up his palm to Sis's head, and painted it with a long line with the sindur or vermillion powder along the side parting in Sis's hair. Ma took Amlan's finger and made it touch the centre of Sis's forehead just at the hairline, leaving the imprint of a bold red dot there. There was no mistaking that the bonds of marriage had been firmly tied between the nuptial couple according to Hindu shastra directive.

Ma squeezed Sis' cheeks with a smile, signalling the end of the procedure. Amlan stepped forward, bent to touch Ma's feet, and raised himself back. Sis, taking the cue, followed Amlan exactly. As she rose, Ma hugged her, all smiles, declaring confidently, "O amader shonge mishe jaabe." She will assimilate perfectly with us.

Amlan's mother was quite unconcerned that the foreigners, including the object of the statement, could not comprehend the wider dimensions of her remark as easily as she had made it. Actually, the statement had been made for Amlan, not only as a conviction, but also as a hope, an expectation, a caution, and a warning.

Patrick understood Ma, since he spoke Bengali. The circumstances of the day had been mesmerising. How would he explain all that happened to Ma and Dad? He was thinking

of them intensely. He felt concerned for his parents, a feeling
that he rarely experienced these days. He would have to call
them first thing in the morning. He would have to concoct an
account for his staying on, as well as give a credible explanation
about Sis' action – or inaction – and why he did not intervene
to stop this madness. He was thinking about how she could
live the rest of her life in this forgotten corner of the world.

Patrick dared not ponder how he would convince his
parents that he thought this was a good option for Sis in
her current circumstance. Moreover, that, by all accounts, he
thought that Amlan loved Sis or, at the least, he was attracted
to her, and vice versa, and what else was there in life other
than relationships based first on physical attraction? He would
have to keep his chat with his parents well contained and
reassuring. He would convince them by promising that he
would drop in as often as possible to see Sis while he remained
here. However, after he left, what then? Also, would they
come to the wedding? Surely there would be a wedding? He
had heard that Bengali weddings were fantastic affairs. How
big would this one be? Surely Amlan's mother would broach
the issue of Sis' parents attending the wedding? Patrick could
not think anymore. His mind was confused and cluttered
with too many contrary thoughts swimming without direction
or resolution. He suddenly wanted to return to the hotel as
quickly as possible.

Sis had partaken of the entire procedure, not just as
a passive participant. She had tried her best to hear Ma's
verses, inaudible as they were. As Amlan had covered her in
vermilion, she had felt infused by him in heart, soul and body,
her gooseflesh rising and her inner voice telling her that she
was now his. She vowed to herself that she would never leave
this gentle man, his abode, that his mother, who so welcomed
her, would be like her own, that their household would be
hers, that the servants would be in her care. No thought
passed her mind that son or mother could ever change their

position towards her in the future. That was Sis. Finally, as the procedure ceased, she turned around to look at Patrick as if for emotional, no, substantive, support for what had occurred, as if the thought of Mom and Dad had invaded her thoughts too. Patrick smiled back at her lovingly, though a bit unconvincingly. Sis looked away from him and towards Amlan.

Awkwardly, Patrick stood a bit apart. Propelled by the real world at last, Amlan approached him, ushering him towards his mother. He introduced them to each other.

Having ignored him thus far as if he was no part of the proceedings just terminated, Ma now looked towards Patrick most naturally. "Patreek, you are also a member of this family from now on. You know, you and I have a lot of work to do to get these naughty children presented to my society, my relatives and friends, and you to yours." She used simple, broken English. She added thoughtfully, "We have to have the wedding function, you know. Priests, guests, dinner with a grand menu; everything. And I must call your mother and father." She looked up directly at him, in query of whether they were dead or alive. "They must come. They have to come; no?" Instantly, she resumed, "You don't have to go back to your hotel; it is very late, and there may be curfew also." Then she had second thoughts. What would the servants think? That we have no qualms? That I acted out of impulse? That I had lost all sense? That this is what class difference is all about? Oh! That would be shameful. She immediately contradicted her just-proposed invitation. "I suppose that you have all your things at the hotel and it may be more comfortable there. No? Amlan could drop you off if you preferred to go back, of course. Amlan?"

Amlan nodded obligingly. Sis heaved a silent sigh of relief, since she certainly preferred to return to breathe a little, and to get into her night dress. Patrick read Ma's change of mind perfectly, and agreed politely that going back would be more efficient for the next morning, while thanking Ma for the invitation to stay.

As they turned towards the stairs, Ma touched Amlan's shoulder lightly, holding him back. "Drive carefully tonight. Focus on the roads. It has been a trying day for you. There must be a lot on your mind. The streets may also be under curfew. You will be able to manage, won't you?"

Amlan nodded with a serious look on his face, more concerned about the safety of his guests than for himself. He followed them closely down the stairs.

Ma called back, "You can fix a time when they might come over tomorrow to have dinner and discuss the arrangements."

Amlan did not look back.

In the car, Sis carefully considered Amlan as Patrick wondered once more if Agnes would comprehend at all, let alone appreciate, her daughter's precipitous decision and her son's passive, yet approving, reaction to it. Far from agreeing to come to the wedding in Calcutta, this hell of a city, what would happen if she proceeded to attempt to reverse the whole matter through the US Consulate? In that case, he would have to seek James' assistance to counter his mother's actions. However, perhaps he could persuade her to acquiesce to the marriage and come to Calcutta, after all. There was no predicting his mother's actions or reactions – he knew that well. However, would Sis care at all if Mom came or not? No, Patrick concluded, Mom's absence would be of little consequence to Sis, though it would matter to her if Dad did not show up. But Dad would never venture out without Mom; consequently, it was imperative to convince Ma first. Then, she would ask Dad to come along with her. He raised his hopes for a moment.

Yet, if they did not come, he would invite James and elicit his support to invite some local Americans, perhaps even other Westerners. Surely James would have friends he could fall back on.

A single day... A single night... So much... We are reaching the hotel... It is over for now. Oh! Terrence, let's see what tomorrow brings.....

\*　　\*　　\*

The Naxals, Marxist-Leninists, were dropping off like flies under police firing during the following week. They were organised to fight the police through the wee hours of the mornings. The long, heavy nights produced hills of cadavers. It was generally believed that the minister for internal security belonging to the Marxist party, as opposed to the more doctrinaire Marxist-Leninists, was aware of, if not signatory to, all this. But Calcutta families remained quiet for sheer fear that their young members might be picked up at any time and sent off for questioning, given electric shock treatment, hung upside down for hours under high wattage lighting, or worse.

As Calcutta's political situation worsened, Patrick was given living quarters within the consulate compound. It was a sunny, furnished flat. The food came from the consul's kitchen, usually carried by Laurent on a tray. There was domestic help in the form of a cheerful woman who was immaculately dressed in a starched white sari. Patrick's comfortable Bangla was well utilised, to her utter glee. Outside the compound, Patrick was easily accepted at corner tea stalls and in the lower-cost front benches of the cinema halls that showed old Hollywood movies. While he blended in pretty well and the locals soon became familiar with the eccentric young foreigner who spoke Bangla and began to treat him as the commonplace Westerner who might have come to learn yoga or smoke hashish, Patrick refrained from discussing his unusual background, carefully protecting his identity and interests.

Patrick used the information he gathered from the locals to generate disinformation in the most unobtrusive, ingenuous manner. While friendships with local youths blossomed and his low-paid research at the Institute proceeded flawlessly, his clandestine salary was stacking up at his bank account in Washington. At the end of each work day, he took a taxi to visit Sis, religiously avoiding being seen in any consulate car with diplomatic plates. At night, he became accustomed to alighting from the taxi some distance away and at different points, always taking care to slip into the consulate compound surreptitiously after checking in every direction around him. He led a perfect double life. In a sense, he had done so, and perhaps had become attuned to it, from childhood. It did not bother him now in any intrinsic sense.

\*     \*     \*

Amlan had asked Sis if he, too, could address her as Lokkhi. Sis asked politely what it meant and why Ma had added the suffix ma to it, and what would it signify to Amlan to use that name for her. At first, Amlan had felt a bit at a loss for words but, taking a deep breath, he had explained to her its significance. First, Lokkhi was the Bangla pronunciation of Laxmi, the goddess of wealth, home and hearth. Laxmi was also happily married to the deity, Narayan or Vishnu, one of the trinity, Brahma, Vishnu and Shiva – creator, maintainer and destroyer – respectively. A diligent, pious daughter-in-law was often referred to as Griholokkhi, or Laxmi of home and hearth. Further, a beautiful bride might even qualify to be called Swarnalaxmi—Shornolokkhi in Bangla—the regal, golden Laxmi signifying wealth and opulence. Hence, it was natural for Ma to re-name her Lokkhi, reflecting the practice in many traditional homes of renaming a bride entering a new household, indicating that she was being received as a daughter rather than as a daughter-in-law. The suffix ma – mother, when transliterated – was to denote affection to the next generation, to the daughter, used in Bengali culture in reverse order, to express fondness. So, just as Sis herself would address Amlan's mother as Ma, so could the latter use the suffix ma to address Sis.

Thus, Amlan cleverly discussed with Sis her feelings about such a modification in the manner in which people addressed her, almost asking for her permission to do so. Sis, of course, agreed for she knew that she was opting for a new persona. But the practice – construction of a relationship in reverse – with such specific cultural connotations and practices, seemed overly complex to her, matters that she could not fully comprehend. She would soon realize that the domestic support staff would all address her as Bouma, again with the same suffix. In their case, Amlan would explain that it was because they almost looked up to her as the mistress, or a mother figure though, of course, as a lesser one than Ma herself. Amlan would joke that Sis would have to earn that spot with the passage of time in the estimation of the servants. It did not matter that they were all far older than her or were far more experienced in their respective responsibilities or jobs than she was in any particular line of work. Amlan also explained that Bou, in her instance, simply meant daughter-in-law of the house and that she should not be surprised if, on occasion, Ma referred to her as Bou or Bouma when referring to her in third person or even when addressing her directly.

Sis found all these permutations in cultural practices merely in addressing members of a household – in this instance, herself – fascinating. However, she was scared too, for she could hardly convince herself that she would master the nuances or even the broader aspects successfully in any finite period of time. She might be able to understand or correctly use many of them over time, but all of them, perhaps never. Nonetheless, she vowed that she would certainly keep on trying and would be content as long as Amlan saw that she was doing so. She felt that, with his support, she might be able to make the transition.

\*      \*      \*

Lokkhi was given a bedroom next to Ma's. She moved there when Patrick shifted to the consulate. Ma kept vigil that the newlyweds did not stray in any form until a proper socio-religious wedding ceremony was completed so that there would be no question later on as to at what point their first baby was conceived. She even frowned upon too much proximity between Amlan and Lokkhi, lest a fatal mistake should occur. Amlan indulged his mother, impatient, yet almost enjoying, the build-up to the soon-to-be-held grand event.

The would-be bride's parents had already informed the couple, Ma, and Patrick that their health would not permit such a long trip from Texas to Calcutta. In their ignorance, they really had been quite unsure if part of the journey had to be covered by foot or on an elephant. Their mutual discussion touched upon various fearsome possibilities until they had both agreed that such a journey could be suitable only for the young and the able. Despite the fact that they would not attend, their blessings and best wishes were with their daughter and her prospective husband. Furthermore, the presence of their son, responsible and educated as he was, should surely be taken as their signal of confidence and trust. Underneath it all, Agnes' perplexity knew no bounds at this, to her, ludicrous turn of events. She saw no option but to conclude, to her deepest regret, and even as her heart was breaking, that she was at a point at which she could stoop no further in the direction in which her son had ventured or had misdirected his sister. There was, there should be, a limit to acts of forgiveness that could be expected of a mother and, in her gut, she knew she had reached it.

The final polite exchange about the decision of the parents not to fly across for the wedding took place well after several phone calls had transpired between Patrick and Agnes, the latter castigating the former for his overt indulgence of, and final succumbing to, the wayward desires of his undisciplined sister. During this period, before Agnes gave up trying to dissuade Sis from marrying Amlan, Agnes had phoned and talked to her daughter to ask her if she had been kidnapped. When informed that that was certainly not the case, Agnes asked Sis if she was certain she would be happy, and an answer had shot back that, though the future could not be guaranteed, she was, indeed, happy at this particular point of time. Also, Sis emphasised to Agnes that happiness was a condition that she expected to continue into the foreseeable future. Defeated in her attempt to derail the marriage, Agnes gave up finally and handed the phone over to her husband.

Dad cried into the phone, confessing to his daughter that he felt that he would lose his little girl forever to those injuns. Sis was softer towards him and assured him that this would never happen and that there was ample space in the house whenever he desired to come visit her. She very carefully avoided mentioning the possibility of her ever visiting San Antonio. She explained that these people were cultured, with long roots like those of the Goulds, that they had a hacienda four times as large as the one in San Antonio, and that they lived in a much larger city. Dad eventually blessed her, sobbing softly, as if he had already lost her forever.

Putting the phone down, Dad went back to the TV to continue to watch the Sunday football in progress between the Dallas Cowboys and the Washington Redskins. The Super Bowl was next week and he did not want to miss the important games just before that. Agnes returned to the kitchen to continue to discuss dinner. Rosita looked at her inquiringly, but to no avail. Agnes said nothing to her about the phone call from Calcutta. Instead, she instructed Rosita to make a simple dinner tonight, because she and her husband did not have much appetite. She departed quickly from the kitchen for her bedroom and, upon entering it, sat down alone on her side of the king-sized bed and wept openly as her grief deepened

by the minute at the unbearable thought of having lost both
son and daughter in one go.

*    *    *

The wedding was a decent affair, simultaneously
interesting, unique, tedious and senseless. The ceremony itself
took over two hours, Lokkhi decked in a bright, red Benarasi
sari bordered with a swan and elephant gold embroidery,
her face covered in a light red veil, and Amlan in dhoti and
Punjabi – though he had had to remove the shirt and cover
his exposed upper body with a simple, silk chador. Amlan
and Lokkhi sat cross-legged facing each other in front of a
profusely rising fire made of logs and enlivened by occasional
spoons of ghee, clarified butter, being poured into it. Amlan
repeated the Sanskrit slokas after the purohit who had taken
pains the previous night to translate the quintessential stanzas
for Lokkhi also to understand and, therefore, did not hesitate
to recite his hard work in English for her benefit. Lokkhi
followed his utterances intently, not relaxing from making
sincere attempts to comprehend what role and responsibility
were being bestowed on her as a Bengali housewife. Typical
of her, she harboured no foreboding of any of her roles being
a burden. She also noted with some relief that her husband
would have a plethora of responsibilities to bear.

When the mantras had been read, her veil was lifted to
expose her face to Amlan by a female cousin of his, who
had patiently been sitting behind Sis, having been charged
with this small, but important and much envied, task among
competing cousins. The pair looked at each other, timed
exactly for the astrologically correct moment meant for them
to set their eyes on each other for shubho drishti, or auspicious
glance. They looked, smiled and, shyly, looked away, as if they
had never seen each other before which, indeed, would have
been the case in earlier generations, including that of Amlan's

parents. However, the emotion of the moment made them react the same way and they experienced the same exaltation as that felt by couples in bygone eras.

Bride and bridegroom were made to stand up. Immediately, without the loss of a second and demonstrably rapidly, the corners of the sari and chador were tied in a firm knot by the purohit. Joined, they walked seven times around the rising, crackling, burning fire, with fire as witness to their eternal promise to each other. It was over! Their hearts sang, and the invitees sitting around rejoiced with much laughter and loud exchanges of opinions as to how handsome the couple looked, while others hurried away to the dining area that was lined with row upon row of placements for dinner, comprising a dozen dishes and served by a fleet of uniformed servers as was usual custom.

Amlan smiled at all around while Lokkhi matched him with her own resplendent smile. A throng of American, British, and European guests came forward, 'oohing' and 'aahing' over the dazzling jewellery she was bedecked with. It was beyond their wildest imagination that so much ornate decoration could adorn one human body at a single instance for, indeed, Lokkhi had been made to wear a large sample of the family jewellery that had come down through four generations, and she loved every moment of it. The Indian family members and friends moved busily about in every direction in the courtyard, which had been covered with a huge, chastely decorated pandal, converting it into a ballroom with chandeliers, pillars and floral decorations. This was the moment to exchange notes regarding prospective matches: which young man was in a remunerative, firm position, which young woman had completed university graduation, and if they were pleasant and attractive or, in other words, deciphering if they had the right attributes to enter the marriage market. At the same time, the unlikely presence of so many foreigners infused the environment with an unmistakable charm, a special excitement. It made a merry mix of chattering faces, in various colours, looks, dresses and languages.

Amlan and Lokkhi were led to throne-like chairs under a canopy at the head of the enclosed area, and the guests lined up to congratulate them individually. Each group took great care not to miss the opportunity of being photographed in the act of delivering their gifts. It took the form of a method exercise, a proof of their presence, of the delivery of mementos to the newlyweds, and a crosscheck for posterior ticking off the list of gifts. As they passed, the elders blessed the bride and groom with a soft touch of the hands on their heads, while the more youthful guests hugged them tenderly. When the crowd thinned and most had gone in to the dinner area, Patrick took a few steps forward to greet his sister and brother-in-law. He hugged Sis for a long moment, extending it for as long as he could, not bothered about her ornate attire. Sis wept silently. Amlan was touched by the unhesitant demonstration of feeling between the two American siblings. Finally, Patrick turned to Amlan and gave him a warm handshake, and followed it up with a light hug.

Ma had stayed completely out of sight, away from the wedding venue. This was ritualistically required of her as mother, lest her longing for her son while he was being joined in matrimony should cast an evil spell on the formation of a crucial bond between husband and wife. She had remained in the dining area supervising the professional caterers. Now that the wedding was over and any evil spell dispersed, she ventured into the temporary ballroom, gingerly approached the thrones set on the raised dais, climbed the double steps and, trembling slightly, looked adoringly at son and daughter-in-law with wet eyes, hugged them one at a time, and then together. The profusion might have made her a bit self-conscious – or was it, in fact, carried out as a bit of a show? It is difficult to say – she looked around surreptitiously as if to minimise the impact of such an open exhibition of affection, or might have been checking if her actions were being appropriately appreciated.

As boy and girl bent forward to touch her feet, she raised them, tightly hugging them again, tears running down her cheeks shamelessly. As one mother far, far away was losing her daughter, another mother was gaining one. She felt compassion for the absent, deprived mother. Far, far away, Agnes was preparing breakfast for Dad at that moment. Briefly, a thought flashed through Agnes' mind that her daughter was getting married that day. The next moment, she re-focussed on the eggs she was trying to fry sunny side up, concerned that they should not get too dry.

Ma hugged Lokkhi again, as if it was Agnes who was doing so. Amlan basked, and Patrick stood back, looking impressed. James emerged from amidst other foreign guests and whispered something to Patrick, who introduced him to the hostess who, in turn, greeted him politely, and then the two men disappeared to have dinner.

That night, Amlan and Lokkhi lay on the bridal bed decorated with strands of Rajanigandha with an occasional red rose in between, hanging from the bedposts enclosing the bed like a curtain surrounding it. She lay still, trying her best not to think of her past, wanting terribly for Amlan to embrace her. When he did, she shivered. Amlan did not withdraw. He whispered into her ears and tickled her in soft, straight strokes, not missing the right spots as he moved down. She hugged him involuntarily and held him close for a long time. She did not cringe or grow rigid with fear. He gently laid her down, raised her sari, parted her legs ever so slowly and, sure of his hardness, was inside her instantly. What he had been ready for, for some time, had just occurred. She was transported from Hell by a dark angel to heavenly fulfilment. She had arrived home in body and soul.

\*     \*     \*

The Naxal Movement was progressing relentlessly in the extreme north and south of the city. Newspapers, radio and television were full of commentary, generally deriding the infiltration by extremist Leftist elements embellished with various conspiracy theories about their ascendance. Among them, a not insignificant one was that of the Central Intelligence Agency being the culprit in infusing extremist propaganda into the young, urban intelligentsia. Its Machiavellian objective was presumably to facilitate the Naxals to challenge and thwart the advances being made by the socially more acceptable and less radical Communist parties that had increasing mass appeal.

Patrick had been given the charge of dealing directly with the Naxals, the hardcore Marxist-Leninists. He had, needless to say, to be particularly careful in making contacts and in carrying out his tasks. He performed masterfully, returning to his apartment in the wee hours of the morning. Before going to sleep, he would chronicle how gun battles were taking place among various factions, how the police were colluding with the Marxist parties in many of these battles and assisting in the decimation of the very same extremists who were also Patrick's contacts and targets.

In his secret memoranda, Patrick attempted to impress upon James that the extremist Marxist-Leninists were not the problem; rather, the problem was with the lesser Marxists, that the former were brilliant students often from Presidency College, who had thought deeply about society and its lack of justice from a solid intellectual premise, while the latter were mediocre opportunists, exactly the sort that had emerged with the progress of the Russian Revolution. He tried to convince James that it was the Marxist-Leninists or Maoists that pursued the path of Mao's Cultural Revolution. They were taking action, however misguided, to empower the powerless in India. By contrast, the opportunistic Marxists, who also assumed a pro-China policy seemingly more as a stance, were hell-bent only on usurping power. It was the Marxist-Leninists who stood for what Abraham Lincoln stood for; that is, to emancipate the downtrodden from their slavery.

However, Patrick increasingly found James unable or unwilling to understand his analysis, visibly distancing himself from Patrick's views. Instead, Patrick noticed that James would occasionally let slip a patronising smile as though Patrick was a mere amateur, unaware of and untutored in the ways of modern complexities. Patrick found his observations from field experiences in the danger-fraught lanes and by-lanes of Calcutta, even those based on insider information, being summarily ignored. It made no difference how cogent Patrick thought his insights were. His frustration grew by the day, but there seemed to be little he could do about James' soft indifference and polite dismissal of his analyses and conclusions.

James' attention seemed more focussed on Patrick himself rather than on Patrick's opinions about Leftist activities in Calcutta. Likewise, Patrick was becoming more distracted by James' attentions. Even as he found himself responding, Patrick loathed it at the same time, as if it was an affliction from which he would like to be cured. His frustration in his work grew with James' continued lack of attention or seriousness towards his efforts. Yet, he found himself inextricably entwined in a world of physical supplication that fulfilled a craving that, hitherto, Patrick had neither addressed nor acted upon.

Life moved on, seemingly in slow motion. A night's adventure on the streets was buttressed by an innate and natural camaraderie Patrick developed with local youth. His easy facility with Bangla enabled him to chit chat in corner teashops and street corners. These advantages were complemented by the ready excuse that his research at the Institute needed him to stay on in Calcutta. His sister's insistence that he linger in Calcutta for a bit longer until she settled down fully in her new – old – Bengali family also came in handy when he found himself having to explain to the expatriate crowd.

At the end of each day, Patrick would sit religiously at his desk and furiously jot down the new information he had obtained, carefully analysing it and drawing conclusions, knowing full well that there was a very high likelihood that his data would be politely questioned and effectively rejected the next day by his boss and redoubtable partner, often discarded by the time the office was to close, if not before then. At best, James would appear to think about the data that was presented and, then, with a smile, propose another type of adventure to Patrick. Patrick was never able to refuse.

The one hour of the day that Patrick most looked forward to was just about twilight, when he would reach Horigo Street. Durwan would salute him as he entered the oval driveway. He could not wait to run up the stairs, and then diagonally across the long verandas to the thakur ghar, or abode of the gods, the small room where Ma had organised the small gold tray to welcome Sis that first night. Lokkhi was likely to be standing inside with her back to Patrick, in front of the shelves full of deities, male and female, families with children, fierce and compassionate, in majestic regalia or in ascetic garb. She held an ornate brass lamp with multiple points for wicks firmly in her right hand and a flowing, yak-hair brush in her left. She would let her right hand move in a rhythm, the small flames in a continuous flickering ballet, their light moving from corner to corner of the room, passing before every god, every goddess, lesser or great, while her left arm moved in slow motion as if to cool them after the warmth of the synchronised flames.

Bhagwan would stand behind her, towards the left corner of the room, careful that he was not in her way, and ringing a small bell whose incessant shrill sound filled the small room. Towards the right corner would stand ayah with a conch shell that she clutched with both hands. Ma would stand near the entrance of the room just behind Lokkhi, though slightly to the right so that her view of the deities was not obstructed.

Didu would be sitting cross-legged on a simple cloth mat right in front, making sure that she had the best seat for the show, counting beads on a wooden rosary, and muttering an inaudible mantra. Patrick would join the group, standing silently just outside the room. At the end of the process that would last ten to fifteen minutes, ayah would sound the conch shell thrice, each time with a long, echoing boom, blowing into it with all her might until she had lost her breath. Once she put the conch shell down on the shelf after carefully washing it with Ganges water, the routine was over, for dusk had passed and the night had silently set in. With a satisfied look on her face at her novice's brilliant performance, Ma would be the first to emerge from the puja room.

As Sis stepped out, Patrick was invariably bewildered and entranced. She would be wearing an off-white flowing silk sari with a bright red border, preserved for this particular purpose. It was worn in the typical Bengali manner, like her mother-in-law, a bunch of relatively minor keys thrown over her shoulder. Her head of hair would be partially covered by a slightly stretched-out part of the sari, and it slipped occasionally to reveal her hair done up in a tight bun and held in place with intricately designed silver pins and miniature jingling bells. If the sari receded, she would recover it immediately in an attempt to place it back on the bun, in its rightful place, stealing a quick glance at Ma to see if she had been annoyed with her carelessness in letting the sari slip from her head. Ma would merely smile at her reassuringly, on occasion moving towards her to help her Lokkhi place it back herself.

In her hands, Lokkhi would have the familiar large gold plate, which was filled with special home-made condiments that had been placed in front of and, thus, blessed by, the panoply of deities. The proshad, or nectar, was now ready for distribution. She would come, beaming, straight to Patrick. As Patrick pointed to his favourite delicacies for the evening, she would pick them up one by one and pop them into his mouth. Patrick would not fail to bring his hands together in an expected display of respect to the celestial powers. Ma would look on indulgently at this display of affection between the siblings, wondering how much longer it would be before Amlan got back from work to complete the trio.

Lokkhi would then distribute the condiments, making the selection herself, to Bhagwan and Ayah, then down the stairs, to Durwan and Driver, Muslim though the latter was. Being Muslim did not stop Rahim from gratefully accepting. The rest of the support system would also receive bits, as would the neighbourhood children, who came mainly from the adjacent slums and who would invariably swarm in like bees to pollen. Sandesh – a variety of delicious sweets based in cheese – would be retained for Amlan to await his return home, and only a small piece of banana or tangerine would remain for Ma and herself. Of course, Lokkhi had learnt this pattern of distribution from Ma, who nodded approvingly from a distance as Lokkhi proceeded with her march among the expectant denizens in and around the household.

Patrick would usually have only a short span of time to chat with Sis after she completed her distribution before he had to bolt from there. What would he talk about, anyway, after seeing the felicity she had already achieved? Just the visual admiration of her ways was enough for him; no further words were needed. As Sis would give him a deep, warm smile merely by squinting and pursing her lips, he would run down the stairs and slip out of the mansion even before Durwan could slap himself a salute, and hop into a taxi.

*    *    *

Tonight, after leaving Lokkhi, Patrick went out into the dark and, rather than into a taxi, he jumped onto a passing tram that was on its way farther north towards the Shyambazar five-street crossing. Almost there, he slid off the slowly moving tram and entered, on his left, westwards into a narrow alleyway that usually bustled with customers crowding at a line of shops selling tea, cauliflower samosa and mutton cutlets and other savouries for vegetarians and non-vegetarians alike. He always cut through to Upper Circular Road and Baghbazar, a sure bet for extracting clandestine information on street politics and probable occurrences from one of his trusted contacts, a disconnected list of confidantes that he had steadily and successfully built up.

However, as he entered the alley, he immediately noticed its phantom appearance. It was shorn of any sign of life. There were no lights anywhere. Initially, he figured that there was a power cut in progress. However, there would have been at least a few passers-by, even if there was no electricity, but there was not a soul in sight. His curiosity propelled him to enter the alley, despite a premonition that something could be very wrong. As he ventured in, he heard soft, yet steady, footsteps behind him. He quickly realised that the sound did not belong to one person, but two; no, three perhaps, or maybe more. His heart beat faster. He must have blown his cover somehow, he told himself. The Naxals must have figured out his nocturnal routine through some local snitch. Someone had betrayed him. He sped up his pace. On left or right, not a single house light was on. People in the neighbourhood must have been warned. Behind him, he heard steps falling lightly, now running through the still, soundless, stolid air. Patrick, too, fell into a steady run just ahead of the rapidly approaching sounds.

He slipped his right hand into his trouser pocket and suddenly turned around. He could see three silhouetted figures rushing towards him. Something glistened momentarily in the hands of one of them. Must be a knife, Patrick warned himself.

Clasping his pistol firmly in the recesses of his pocket, he warned the three musketeers in clear Bangla as they stopped short at a safe distance, "You are making a mistake. I am not the one you want. I am your friend. I am only doing research on the Naxal Movement, focussing on its political rise, objectives, the social dilemma and outcomes achieved. You can check at the Institute of Development Studies. I am an anthropologist and so is my research. It is field based. That is why I spend so much time on the streets." He gasped.

"You American bachcha—urchin—even as a researcher, with so much knowledge about Bengal and Bengalis, you have become a turncoat! Why?"

The neighbours could certainly hear the dangerous conversation that was going on.

There was disbelief in the eyes of the bearded fellow, hair unkempt, clothes ruffled and a knife protruding from the hold of his right hand, with his comrades by his side. Patrick recognised him from the Coffee House, where he had seen him several times, in particular during late afternoons, at times by himself poring over a book, pouring himself a cup of infusion, or in animated conversation with mates or colleagues. Patrick had observed others like him, but had never paid much attention to them, passing them off as ineffectual Bengali intellectuals, habituated to skipping college lectures to find the truth elsewhere. He had learnt not to overemphasise their importance. In this case, he had obviously made a mistake, a huge mistake.

As the Naxal raised his hand, rushing towards Patrick, Patrick whipped out his gun and shot once, straight at his heart. Because of the built-in silencer, there was just a thudding sound. The youth fell instantly. Patrick held his gun and looked at the other two, who looked completely stunned. They had been used to daggers, cudgels, hammers and sickles, but not guns. Guns were used by the weak, by the police, or by the duplicitous Marxists in the coalition government. Their expressions could not hide their shock. Their unpreparedness reflected itself in their lethargy in responding. By the time they seemed to be dragging out their weapons, Patrick had already reloaded, refitted the silencer, and was raising the gun to face them directly.

In desperation, both turned around, but could not go far. With a sure aim, Patrick shot them individually in their backs. The rage that he had felt as three of them had attempted to accost a single man slowly melted, giving way to the onset of alarm. Trotting fast, but careful not to run, he found himself at the end of the tunnel, entering the thoroughfare of Upper Circular Road. He turned left in the direction that would take him back to central Calcutta and to the safety of his temporary home behind the forbidding walls of his country's consulate. Wet to his bones from the sweat that was running in streaming rivulets and had instantaneously covered his body, he calmly hailed a passing taxi, of which Calcutta never seemed to be deprived. Inside, as the talkative driver complained of the lack of passengers because of Communist street wars and infighting, sweat comingled with the tears that were finally cascading down Patrick's face, momentarily blinding him. The driver looked at him through the rear-view mirror and asked if all was well with the family. Patrick ignored him. Respecting Patrick's distress and whatever it comprised, the driver did not press further. He drove on silently.

The murders were duly reported in the papers the next day as the probable outcome of another internecine fight between Marxist-Leninists and Marxists, the two most virulent groups. A few days later, after the post mortems had been completed, the papers reported that a foreign pistol had been used and that probably they were either coming across the border from China or that it was the final proof that the CIA was involved depending, of course, on the particular political stance of the respective papers that were reporting the incident. A few processions were held to protest foreign intervention, and a day of commerce and economic activity was lost through a day long hartal.

The strike was quite successful. Many people simply stayed home, played bridge or carom, or discussed politics tempestuously in their immediate neighbourhoods. Others returned home to late lunches of musoor dal with fried fish, mixed vegetable sauté with five-spices, and shrimps or Rohu head, mutton curry, mango chutney, laal doi and roshogolla – a typical Sunday lunch pre-poned (a widely used Indian coinage) to the middle of the week. Those who had been served poppy seed paste in mustard oil and chopped green chillies mixed in steaming Basmati rice enjoyed a thus-induced post-lunch afternoon siesta. Those who had slept were woken up to aromatic Darjeeling tea, accompanied by Britannia sugar-coated Nice and chocolate layered Bourbon biscuits that were always available in corner shops that stayed open to provide the quintessential Bengali his condiments even on a holiday precipitated by a strike.

By dusk, tempers from the strike had abated. Also, the party mood was over. Tomorrow would be a different day. Perhaps, after all, one could get to work.

*    *    *

Despite James' many attempts to cajole and comfort Patrick, the onset of self-revulsion of being a murderer seemed to overpower every facet of his very being. James made many an effort and used all possible means to make him realise the risks of war. They were made in vain. Patrick stayed inside his flat, reclusive and unwilling to communicate with the external world, oblivious to Sis or Amlan, let alone his parents back in Texas.

There was no way James could give up his urgent attempts to placate Patrick. There was too much at stake. Patrick was in his pyjamas as James walked into his flat. "Patrick, sometimes in this line of work one has no option but to act decisively in self-defence, as I had clearly explained to you. Believe me, you did the right thing; there was nothing wrong about it. Otherwise, you would not be here today," he made his point decisively.

Patrick seemed inconsolable and did not respond. He continued to stare at the floor as he sat at the edge of his bed. All my work, my devotion in learning Bangla, the history of the region, the culture, my entire journey, have come to nothing... zero, he said to himself again and again.

James sat down next to him, trying to gather him in his arms. "Patrick, think about it rationally. Could you have done anything else under the circumstances? You were literally surrounded. There must have been a lot of hatred in there. There would have been no escape..."

Patrick remained silent as James spoke on. He was thinking, I should have opted for an alternative path. I should not have fallen prey to greed, to your fat financial package. I did not have to succumb to your advances. I could have carried out my research with a local salary as I had meant to. Don't you see? I could have done it all differently. His inner decibel level had risen steadily, now having reached a crescendo bursting through his brain. He stormed out of the bedroom.

James looked around cautiously, as if to see if Laurent were anywhere nearby or within earshot. He slowly walked out after Patrick, who was standing at the French windows of the balcony library, peering blankly at the night sky. Patrick's mind was floating... He was in the P Street apartment... It was the middle of the night under a starlit sky... Terrence, look, there is a bird sitting on the sill... Terrence, where are you; where did you go? Come back... I have so much to discuss... James is talking, but what does he want to say now? It is of no consequence. The bastard!

Patrick turned around. James was in his satin-silk pyjamas. As always, he looked handsome. A beam of moonlight lit his eyes and the bridge of his nose. His full lips were glistening. Despite what he had just been thinking, Patrick found James irresistible as he scrutinised his face from a distance. Then Patrick was overcome by loathing. He tried to walk past James to return to his room, but James extended his arm to hold Patrick back. Patrick drew himself away, using whatever force he could muster. James did not make any further move and retreated to his own bedroom. When Patrick was, at last, back in his own room, he plopped himself on his bed and fell into a fitful sleep.

Laurent tiptoed in, removed Patrick's shoes and, ever so carefully, his clothes, and covered his naked body with the designer black cotton bed sheet that had lain crumpled at the foot of the bed. Laurent stared at the sleeping Patrick for a long time as he sat in his night shorts on the settee that he had previously positioned near the large window so that Patrick could read in natural light while reclining on it. Did he get to see others like Patrick during his oh so many years of service with James? The night fell absolutely silent except for the occasional wail of a pack of street dogs or the infrequent cawing of a flock of crows. One sleepless human sat half naked on the front seat observing the frightened, sleeping body of another who was laid out on the bed in front of him. Darkness and silence were the only witnesses. Who knows what thoughts, what desires, empathy, pity, envy, what passing clouds floated through Laurent's mind, or when he finally tiptoed out of Patrick's room that night?

*     *     *

By the time two local policemen dropped in at the consulate in the late morning, James had spoken to his contact in the Party, since he knew well that a connection between the deaths and their source, in particular given the use of foreign firearms, would eventually be made. Several phone calls later, the matter was on its way to being efficiently hushed up and, hopefully, forgotten. Perhaps James had used his own network to pre-alert the Marxists to Patrick's nocturnal activities and they had given him the go-ahead as long as it was the Marxist-Leninists who were to be struck down. Now James had to face up to the eventuality that had just unfurled.

What had occurred was that three of the elite brigade of the Marxist-Leninists were there that night to silence the exposed American. It was meant to be a warning, but it got out of hand as the leader lost his temper and would not stop from meting out the ultimate punishment. Instead, as the Marxists had hoped, all three of them got eliminated. Naturally, Patrick had to be shipped out as quickly as possible from the scene. The move had everyone's approval. Even Patrick acquiesced as he languished inconsolably in self-pity. He himself could not bear to remain in Calcutta any longer. He realized that Sis would have to look after herself and that he could not prolong his stay on her account alone.

James' feelings will never be known. It is true that he could not have anticipated the intensity or the vehemence of Patrick's reaction. He had expected Patrick to be more mature, something that Patrick had utterly failed to demonstrate. Perhaps he should get back to DC for a training period at the Langley HQ, an opportunity that he had not had so far. Yes, that would do him good. James moved like lightning in order to arrange the matter. He reached for the hotline that would connect him directly to the Deputy Director in charge of Reconnaissance in the sub-continental region. A conference call with the State Department might have been surer, but he could not be certain that their phones would not be tapped. No, perhaps it would be safer just to speak to the DD at Langley. At least that would keep the matter simple and self-contained for the moment, provided that it did not implode at State at a later point.

At a few uncertain, foggy crossroads in one's life, risks must be taken to cut through its density. This was one such point in his, James told himself. His fingers softly glided over the keys of the touchtone phone. Yes, a need for action, a thrust to remove, or perhaps protect, Patrick overtook him. Otherwise, the matter might just break open with egregious ramifications for Indo-US relations, for which James would then be blamed back at HQ for botching up or, even worse. Possibly it would be noticed even by the White House. Would James miss Patrick? Did he really care for Patrick? Wasn't James inured to relationships of convenience in his profession, where appearance was all important, where outcome was a product of sharpness and speed intertwined with deceit and ruthlessness? Where, if at all, did love or compassion fit into such a world?

Expediency was of the essence. By five the next morning, Patrick was travelling business class on Pan Am from Calcutta to New York, to connect there to Washington, DC. The faces of three dead young men obscured his vision, their haunting, all-encompassing shock written on their faces. He accepted an offer of a Mimosa from the stewardess, and then another. He swallowed four or five Kali Phosphoricum, a homeopathic tablet popular in Calcutta to help sleep that Laurent had given him over the last week. As he fell into a fitful slumber, Patrick beseeched Father Vincent, Oh! Father, I did not understand… I have made a terrible mistake… The stewardess was passing by. She lingered, looked at him caringly, bent and pulled a grey blanket, as yet folded near his feet, over him and tucked his blue pillow under his head. Rising, she resumed her vigil through the aisles.

When he landed at John F. Kennedy Airport, there was an official waiting for Patrick at the airplane door, from where he was whisked away to a secret Long Island retreat. Once there, he showered, stretched out and was promptly served a steak and potato dinner in the privacy of his room. He was hungry, but had little interest in the dish, though he did eat most of it. He had no idea where he was, nor did he care, for his mind was a blank. In the bathroom, he found a full set of toiletries. He brushed his teeth and cleaned them with floss. He returned to bed and fell asleep, jet lagged and fatigued, despite having little physical activity, having been cooped up in the plane for many long hours.

Eventually, he got up or was woken up. He found a suited young man in his room. He looked attractive; he obviously used the gym regularly. Patrick gave him his attention. He heard the man say, "Do you feel well rested now?"

"Yes, thanks," Patrick responded distantly, anticipating that a session of cross-questioning would be initiated.

"Good." There seemed to be a smile that flashed across the man's face. "We will fly to DC together a bit later. You will go through some de-briefing there. No big deal, really. Just routine stuff."

"Of course," Patrick replied, well realising there was no way out of his present situation, his predicament.

*　　*　　*

The only thing that Patrick wanted to do at the airport while connecting to DC was to phone Sis. His chaperone readily agreed. The call was matter-of-fact. Sis sounded far, far away. Patrick mentioned he had been suddenly called to Washington, asked whether she was alright by herself, reminded her to call Mom and Dad at least once a month and to try to write them letters occasionally in order to remain in touch with them. He asked her to tell them that, given the nature of his work, it was difficult for him to call them regularly.

Sis listened on, hardly getting an opportunity to speak, but she was glad to be listening to her brother's voice. She kept to herself her confusion, her hurt, if not despair at not having heard from him for several days. The line was bad in any event, so it was fine that he alone spoke. Her voice faded away in the transmission each time she responded, Patrick immediately jumping in to fill the vacuum. He raised his voice and repeated his words for Sis to understand, but, as he paused between sentences and words, he could hear Sis sobbing very, very softly across the oceans. He tried not to be affected, but his voice choked… The line went dead.

From the expression on the man's face, Patrick realised that he had overheard everything, perhaps not intentionally, what with the loudness with which he had to speak. Patrick found that it did not embarrass him since, after all, his job, his assignment, had taken everything away from him. So why should he not declare to the world that he still had family whom he loved, cherished and cared for? Yet, he knew at the back of his mind that he had passed on the responsibility, the burden, of speaking to their parents to his sister, not being too sure of what to tell them himself, or where he stood with them.

The one-hour flight to District of Columbia precipitated a further dramatic deterioration in Patrick's mood. He seemed to be degenerating into a catatonic stupor. He was aware that he was sinking into a mental paralysis, feeling as if there was nothing he could hold onto that would save him from drowning in it. He wanted to call Agnes – perhaps it would help, though he was not sure. However, after he got off the plane, he was immediately whisked into a cab, and knew that any phone calls would have to wait. He looked out the window and realised that he was being taken straight to the Langley HQ.

When they arrived and got out of the taxi, Patrick took his chance and asked if he could call home before the debriefing began. Much to his surprise, he was led to a furnished office with a few files lying around and a red phone sitting on a grey steel desk. He sat on the swivel chair and eagerly dialled Texas, oblivious to the man who stood watching him without making any move to exit the room.

Agnes expressed little surprise at Patrick's announcement of his sudden return; rather, she felt somewhat vindicated.

That feeling was soon overtaken by a foreboding as Patrick insisted that she should call Sis regularly and that, given the demands of his job, it was unlikely that he would be able to do so. What could Patrick have implied? Was he safe? What was the reason behind his sudden return? Her mind clouded, numbed by the worst fears a mother might anticipate of an impetuous, disobedient son. The man stood listening silently to Patrick's instructions and statements as if he knew what was going on in Patrick's mind and what was to come. Agnes' coolness, that had become increasingly apparent over time since the episode at the Kennedy Center between mother and son, and had worsened since Sis' wedding, the responsibility for which Agnes had passed squarely on to Patrick's shoulders, vanished for a moment. Yet, the distancing prevailed and came across over the phone line; it was almost audible to Patrick. He knew he had no choice but to ignore the vacuum at this critical moment and clearly indicate to his mother what he needed to convey. After inquiring about Dad, Jolly and Rosita, and a further perfunctory, polite exchange of words, he fell silent.

Agnes spoke little about herself and restrained herself from asking details from Patrick, though she did pass on the information that Jolly had not been keeping well. Since her mother's death, Jolly had been living alone in an apartment that she perhaps could not maintain too well, possibly because of her progressing obesity. The doctor had given her a warning about the high probability of an onset of high blood pressure and diabetes. However, apparently, she would not, or could not, do much about it. Agnes could not understand how a trained nurse could find herself in that situation, not once wondering if that might be because of a certain loneliness, the possibility that Jolly missed Patrick terribly.

Patrick noticed that most of their conversation centred on Jolly. Was Mom really concerned about her at all? Was it that, finally, she realised that news of Jolly would be of interest to him? Did she think, belatedly, that Jolly and Patrick should

have got together after all, for that would have been the only
sure way the Gould line might continue? If so, was there fear
or desperation on his mother's part of avenues being closed,
a helplessness perhaps, in being unable to do anything about
it, a resignation in having to accept the prevailing situation?
The call left many questions unaddressed or unanswered, the
void unfilled, any love unexpressed. When they put down their
phones, the mother's derision had been clearly conveyed, and
the son's consternation was left fully intact.

Patrick had remained calm throughout the call, though
he realised that the call had not helped or comforted him
in any way. He had been unable to share any of his anguish
with Agnes who, as short-sighted human beings without
knowledge of the future and having forgotten the past can be,
had become stuck in the present. That exchange of words at
the Kennedy Center and the single episode of Sis' marriage to
Amlan, stubbornly and wrongly interpreted as Sis' separation
from the family with the overt support of Patrick, had made
Agnes refractory, rejecting the inalienable links to her son and
to their countless mutual experiences, breaking her inimitable
bond with, and love for, him. In his current state, Patrick could
not convert Agnes's opacity to empathy for his desperation.

After ringing off, Patrick thought, for a moment, of
ringing Jolly, but he did not. Even as the thought of Jolly
returned and invaded his mind, in spurts and with some
concern, he forced himself to obliterate every image of her,
her soft details that could easily populate his mind and distract
him from the task at hand.

Instead, Patrick touched the phone and dialled Terrence.
The number swept easily into his memory. Terrence answered
and said '¡Hola!' in his deep voice.

Patrick was genuinely happy to hear Terrence. He could
feel Terrence's elation from the loud exclamation when he
realised who it was that was calling.

"Terry, how are you? It was so difficult to talk to you from India. Here I am back in DC." He made light of it with a slight laugh, somewhat bitter, perhaps even ironic. "So I thought I would call you from the U S of A; your voice really sounds as if it is floating in from the far reaches of Latin America," he joked wryly.

"I am fine, Pat. Good to hear you. Leonor and I have been wondering, worried, really…"

Patrick cut him short. He did not want to hear about Leonor. He wanted to talk to, and about, his Terry exclusively for a moment. He did not want competition at this point. Didn't Terry have any sensitivity? Any sense or sensibility? He was angry. However, he could not talk about themselves; not with his minder standing on top of Patrick, anyway.

"Sis got married to an Indian in Calcutta. The wedding was quite an event. She seems very happy as a housewife in another corner of the world. Quite strange, really, you there in Colombia, Ma and Dad in Texas with Rosita and Jesse, and Sis in Calcutta!" He was blabbering.

Without realising, Terrence insisted, "Pat, you must come to Bogota in October. You still have another month. Leonor and I are getting married on October 12. Agnes and Mom are already planning to come. Their flight will be quite short, you know, so it was easy to convince them. Mom is preparing a huge trousseau, if she really puts together everything that she bragged she was doing; you know Mom, don't you?" He laughed proudly. "And, oh yes! Agnes is taking charge of the wedding dress, what with her sewing and all. She insisted on bringing it all the way from Texas. Can you believe it?" Then, as if lamenting the defeat of his family by his bride's, he added, "Leonor's family is laughing all the way! Of course, they are organising the dinner, the ceremony and all that, but it is being catered or outsourced to others. Come to think of it, it is working out quite well. No complaints on either side." In a low voice, he continued as if he feared being overheard,

"Really, from what I see, I do not think they know much about these things. I mean, they have pots of money and all, but no talent or taste, so to speak." There was again some derisive, low laughter.

Patrick reminded himself that he had lost Terrence at some point in the past. He was no longer listening to his family related chatter. Yet, he found himself agreeing aloud, "Yes, yes, of course… Great… Nice… Yeah."

The line was fading. Terrence was continuing in a low voice, "Pat, here in the southern hemisphere, I search for the Orion every night. I see the same Orion as you do in the north. Only it seems a bit upside down! Don't you forget to look at the night sky. We will look at our Orion at the same time, continents apart though we may be." Then, after a pause, "I am still your Orion, ain't I?"

Patrick was straining his ears. There was a heavy guttural sound that had invaded the line. Terrence's voice was coming through in fits and starts. Patrick put the phone down, as he heard unmistakable shuffling of the feet of the minder-cum-guard next to him that was repeated twice. He dragged himself to follow the man, out of the room and along a long corridor, in the direction that he was being led.

\*     \*     \*

What occurred in the debriefing session behind closed doors is difficult to speculate. By the time Patrick emerged from the building and got into a limousine that had been provided to drop him off in Georgetown, the sun was setting and leaving the sky in deep purples and blues, with the faintest hint of orange still lingering, sandwiched within the deeper colours. Towards the east, dark rain clouds had gathered. Slowly, these clouds were moving north, south and west, an unfolding canopy. The limousine was about to cross Chain Bridge into the District and turn east into Canal Road. It would have had to continue along briefly until stopping at the traffic lights at Arizona Avenue, and then continue further eastwards towards Georgetown University, with the Potomac flowing on the right.

Patrick asked the driver to stop on the right side of Canal Road for a second, after crossing the bridge and passing the lights on the Virginia side. He said that he would like to get out and walk. He murmured that the weather was mild. He looked towards the sky and commented to himself that it was still colourful. It was rapidly darkening though, as the river gnashed the rocks as it rushed along spurred by the evening winds. The driver seemed to demur but, finding a narrow emergency parking on the right, swerved and stopped as he let out a slight grumble.

Patrick was out of the car as if he had just been let out of prison. He walked back a bit and climbed over the short retaining wall that obscured the old familiar path that led to the forbidding rocks where the Potomac so majestically seemed to turn its course. There, at that spot, Patrick had spent many an hour with Terrence, gazing at the massive rocks, the gushing water below, and the ever-changing hues of the sky above, until it was dark and they could gaze at their Orion. No one else had trespassed or ever reached there. It had been just their own. It seemed distant now, so vague, lost in the mists of time.

Patrick walked slowly under the umbrella of trees, through the rough bushes and shrubbery until he stood facing the vast opening of the wide river. He deftly climbed onto the rocks that had provided Terrence and him with the space and the solace of being with each other. As he had always done when he was there, he looked down from the overhang.

This is Potomac Turning, he reassured himself. The river arrives and, facing obstacles, turns abruptly to make way for itself in another direction creating, in its wake, a spellbinding spectacle of ferocious beauty that I have so enjoyed.

The next moment, he was observing water and rock colliding, one moment gushing; the next pristine, beaten back from the steady rock. He assessed this unending, eternal battle, without hope, without meaning, without solution.

This is where I belong, where I have always belonged. In nature, because only nature understands me and appreciates me. Nature will accept me.

Potomac Turning is my home, the Potomac my receptacle. I am one with it. The river runs deep below. It is genderless, yet so beautiful. It wants me. It is opening its arms to welcome me. It is my partner in nature. It awaits me. How can I deny its warm embrace? It is singing. It is silent. It is moving. It is still. I feel its every drop in my every vein.

I am one with the river. I am it...

*     *     *

> Beheld him! Single in the field
> Yon solitary highland lad
> Reaping and singing by himself
> I stopped there and gently passed.
> Alone, he cut and bound the grain
> And sang a melancholy strain
> Did you listen? For the vale profound
> Was overflowing with his sound.
> No tenor did ever chant
> More welcome notes to weary bands
> Of travellers in some shady haunt
> Among Arabian sands.
>
> A voice so thrilling ne'er was heard
> In springtime from an alto bard
> Breaking the silence of the seas
> Among the farthest Hebrides.

Will no one tell me what he sang?
Perhaps the plaintive numbers flowed
For old, unhappy far-off things
And battles long ago?

Or was it some more humble lay
Familiar matter of yesterday?
Some natural sorrow, loss or pain
That had been and may be again?

Whate'er the theme the young man sang
As if his song could have no ending
I saw him singing at his work
And o'er the sickle bending.

Printed in the United States
By Bookmasters